THE CORN MAIDEN

And Other Nightmares

Also by Joyce Carol Oates

THE CORN MAIDEN

And Other Nightmares

JOYCE CAROL OATES

A Mysterious Press Book
for Head of Zeus

First published in 2011 by Mysterious Press, an imprint of Grove/Atlantic, New York.

This edition first published in the UK in 2012 by Head of Zeus Ltd.

The following stories were first published in the following publications:
"Nobody Knows My Name," *Twists of the Tale*, edited by Ellen Datlow, Dell, 1996
"Death-Cup," *Ellery Queen's Mystery Magazine*, August 1997
"The Corn Maiden," *Transgressions*, edited by Ed McBain, Forge, 2005
"Fossil-Figures," *Stories*, edited by Neil Gaiman and Al Sarrantonio,
William Morrow, 2010.
"A Hole in the Head," *Kenyon Review*, Fall 2010
"Beersheba," *Ellery Queen's Mystery Magazine*, October 2010
"Helping Hands," *Boulevard*, 2011

9 7 5 3 1 2 4 6 8

A CIP catalogue record for this book is available from the British Library.

ISBN (HB): 9781908800220
ISBN (TPB): 9781908800237
ISBN (E): 9781781850510

Printed in Germany.

Head of Zeus Ltd,
Clerkenwell House
45-47 Clerkenwell Green,
London EC1R 0HT

www.headofzeus.com

to Jonathan Santlofer

Contents

THE CORN MAIDEN
And Other Nightmares

THE CORN MAIDEN*
A Love Story

APRIL

You Assholes!

Whywhy you're asking here's why her hair.

I mean *her hair*! I mean like I saw it in the sun it's pale silky gold like corn tassels and in the sun sparks might catch. And her eyes that smiled at me sort of nervous and hopeful like she could not know (but who could know?) what is Jude's wish. For I am Jude the Obscure, I am the Master of Eyes. I am not to be judged by crude eyes like yours, assholes.

There was her mother. I saw them together. I saw the mother stoop to kiss *her*. That arrow entered my heart. I thought *I will make you see me*. I would not forgive.

*Note The Sacrifice of the Corn Maiden is a composite drawn from traditional sacrificial rituals of the Iroquois, Pawnee, and Blackfoot Indian tribes.

Okay then. More specific. Some kind of report you assholes will type. Maybe there's a space for the medical examiner's verdict *cause of death.*

Assholes don't have a clue do you. If you did you'd know it is futile to type up reports as if such will grant you truth or even "facts."

Whywhy in the night at my computer clickclickclicking through galaxies and there was revealed on my birthday (March 11) the Master of Eyes granting me my wish that is why. *All that you wish will be made manifest in Time. If you are Master.*

Jude the Obscure he named me. In cyberspace we were twinned.

Here's why in sixth grade a field trip to the museum of natural history and Jude wandered off from the silly giggling children to stare at the Onigara exhibit of the Sacrifice of the Corn Maiden. *This exhibit is graphic in nature and not recommended for children younger than sixteen unless with parental guidance* you stepped through an archway into a fluorescent-lit interior of dusty display cases to stare at the Corn Maiden with braided black bristles for hair and flat face and blind eyes and mouth widened in an expression of permanent wonder beyond even terror and it was that vision that entered Jude's heart powerful as any arrow shot into the Corn Maiden's heart that is why.

Because it was an experiment to see if God would allow it that is why.

Because there was no one to stop me that is why.

We never thought Jude was serious!

We never thought it would turn out like it did.

We never thought . . .

. . . just *didn't*!

Never meant . . .

. . . *never*!

Nobody had anything against . . .

. . . . .

(Jude said it's Taboo to utter that name.)

Jude was the Master of Eyes. She was our leader all through school. Jude was just so cool.

Fifth grade, Jude instructed us how to get HIGH sniffing S. Where Jude got S., we didn't know.

Seventh grade, Jude gave us X. Like the older kids take. From her secret contact at the high school Jude got X.

When you're HIGH you love everybody but the secret is basically you don't give a damn.

That is what's so nice! HIGH floating above Skatskill like you could drop a bomb on Skatskill Day or your own house and there's your own family rushing out their clothes and hair on fire and screaming for help and you would smile because it would not touch you. That is HIGH.

Secrets no one else knew.

XXX videos at Jude's house.

Jude's grandmother Mrs. Trahern the widow of somebody famous.

Feral cats we fed. Cool!

Ritalin and Xanax Jude's doctors prescribed. Jude only just pretended to take that shit. In her bathroom, a supply of years.

Häagen-Dazs French Vanilla ice cream we fed the Corn Maiden.

The Corn Maiden was sleepy almost at once, yawning. Ice cream tastes so good! Just one pill ground up, a half teaspoon. It was magic. We could not believe it.

Jude said you can't believe the magic you possess until somebody instructs how to unleash it.

The Corn Maiden had never been to Jude's house before. But Jude was friendly to her beginning back in March. Told us the Master of Eyes had granted her a wish on her birthday. And we were counted in that wish.

The plan was to *establish trust.*

The plan was to prepare for the Corn Maiden in the knowledge that one day there would be the magic hour when (Jude predicted) like a lightning flash lighting up the dark all would become clear.

This was so. We were in readiness, and the magic hour was so.

There is a rear entrance to the Trahern house. We came that way.

The Corn Maiden walked! On her own two feet the Corn Maiden walked, she was not forced, or carried.

Of her own volition Jude said.

4

It was not so in the Onigara Indian ceremony. There, the Corn Maiden did not come of her own volition but was kidnapped.

An enemy tribe would kidnap her. She would never return to her people.

The Corn Maiden would be buried, she would be laid among the corn seed in the sun and the earth covered over her. Jude told us of this like an old fairy tale to make you smile, but not to ask *Why*.

Jude did not like us to ask *Why*.

The Corn Maiden was never threatened. The Corn Maiden was treated with reverence, respect, and kindness.

(Except we had to scare her, a little. There was no other way Jude said.)

On Tuesdays and Thursdays she would come by the 7-Eleven store on the way home from school. Why this was, Jude knew. Mostly high school kids hang out there. Older kids, smoking. Crummy mini-mall on the state highway. Rug remnant store, hair and nails salon, Chinese takeout & the 7-Eleven. Behind are Dumpsters and a stink like something rotten.

Feral cats hide in the scrub brush behind the Dumpsters. Where it's like a jungle, nobody ever goes.

(Except Jude. To feed the feral cats she says are her Totem.)

At the 7-Eleven Jude had us walk separate so we would not be seen walking together.

Four girls together, somebody might notice.

A girl by herself, or two girls, nobody would notice.

Not that anybody was watching. We came by the back way.

5

Some old long-ago time when servants lived down the hill. When they climbed the hill to the big houses on Highgate Avenue.

Historic old Skatskill estate. That was where Jude lived with just her grandmother. On TV it would be shown. In the newspapers. In *The New York Times* it would be shown on the front page. The house would be called *an eighteenth-century Dutch-American manor house.* We never knew about that. We never saw the house from the front. We only just went into Jude's room and a few other rooms. And there was the cellar.

From Highgate Avenue you can't see the Trahern house very well, there is a ten-foot stone wall surrounding it. This wall is old and crumbling but still you can't see over it. But through the gate that's wrought iron you can see if you look fast, while you're driving by.

Lots of people drive by now I guess.

NO PARKING   NO PARKING   NO PARKING on Highgate. Skatskill does not welcome strangers except to shop.

The Trahern estate it would be called. The property is eleven acres. But there is a shortcut from the rear. When we brought the Corn Maiden to the house, we came from the rear. Mostly the property is woods. Mostly it is wild, like a jungle. But there are old stone steps you can climb if you are careful. An old service road that's grown over with brambles and blocked off at the bottom of the hill by a concrete slab but you can walk around the slab.

This back way, nobody would guess. Three minutes' walk from the mini-mall.

6

Nobody would guess! The big old houses on Highgate, way up the hill, how the rear of their property slopes down to the state highway.

Jude warned *The Corn Maiden must be treated with reverence, respect, kindness, and firmness. The Corn Maiden must never guess the fate that will be hers.*

"Marissa."

The first signal something was wrong, no lights in the apartment.

The second, too quiet.

"Marissa, honey . . . ?"

Already there was an edge to her voice. Already her chest felt as if an iron band was tightening around it.

Stepped inside the darkened apartment. She would swear, no later than 8 P.M.

In a dreamlike suspension of emotion shutting the door behind her, switching on a light. Aware of herself as one might see oneself on a video monitor behaving with conspicuous normality though the circumstances have shifted, and are not normal.

A mother learns not to panic, not to betray weakness. Should a child be observing.

"Marissa? Aren't you . . . are you *home*?"

If she'd been home, Marissa would have the lights on. Marissa would be doing her homework in the living room with the TV on, loud. Or the CD player on, loud. When she was home alone Marissa was made uneasy by quiet.

Made her nervous she said. Made her think scary thoughts like about dying she said. Hear her own heartbeat she said.

But the apartment was quiet. In the kitchen, quiet.

Leah switched on more lights. She was still observing herself,

8

she was still behaving calmly. Seeing, from the living room, down the hall to Marissa's room that the door to that room was open, darkness inside.

It was possible—it was! if only for a blurred desperate moment —to think that Marissa had fallen asleep on her bed, that was why . . . But Leah checked, there was no slender figure lying on the bed.

No one in the bathroom. Door ajar, darkness inside.

The apartment did not seem familiar somehow. As if furniture had been moved. (It had not, she would determine later.) It was chilly, drafty as if a window had been left open. (No window had been left open.)

"Marissa? Ma*rissa*?"

There was a tone of surprise and almost-exasperation in the mother's voice. As if, if Marissa heard, she would know herself just mildly scolded.

In the kitchen that was empty. Leah set the groceries down. On a counter. Wasn't watching, the bag slumped slowly over. Scarcely saw, a container of yogurt fell out.

Marissa's favorite, strawberry.

So quiet! The mother, beginning to shiver, understood why the daughter hated quiet.

She was walking through the rooms, and would walk through the few rooms of the small first-floor apartment calling *Marissa? Honey?* in a thin rising voice like a wire pulled tight. She would lose track of time. She was the mother, she was responsible. For eleven years she had not lost her child, every mother's terror of losing her child, an abrupt physical loss, a theft, a stealing-away, a *forcible abduction*.

"No. She's here. Somewhere . . ."

Retracing her steps through the apartment. There were so few rooms for Marissa to be in! Again opening the bathroom door, wider. Opening a closet door. Closet doors. Stumbling against . . . Struck her shoulder on . . . Collided with Marissa's desk chair, stinging her thigh. "Marissa? Are you *hiding*?"

As if Marissa would be hiding. At such a time.

Marissa was eleven years old. Marissa had not hidden from her mother to make Mommy seek her out giggling and squealing with excitement in a very long time.

She would protest she was not a negligent mother.

She was a working mother. A single mother. Her daughter's father had disappeared from their lives, he paid neither alimony nor child support. How was it her fault, she had to work to support her daughter and herself, and her daughter required special education instruction and so she'd taken her out of public school and enrolled her at Skatskill Day . . .

They would accuse her. In the tabloids they would crucify her.

Dial 911 and your life is public fodder. Dial 911 and your life is not yours. Dial 911 and your life is forever changed.

Suburban Single Mom. Latchkey Daughter.

Eleven-Year-Old Missing, South Skatskill.

She would protest it was not that way at all! It was not.

Five days out of seven *it was not.*

Only Tuesdays and Thursdays she worked late at the clinic.

Only since Christmas had Marissa been coming home to an empty apartment.

No. It was not ideal. And maybe she should have hired a sitter except . . .

She would protest she had no choice but to work late, her shift had been changed. On Tuesdays/Thursdays she began at 10:30 A.M. and ended at 6:30 P.M. Those nights, she was home by 7:15 P.M., by 7:30 P.M. at the latest she was home. She would swear, she was! Most nights.

How was it her fault, slow-moving traffic on the Tappan Zee Bridge from Nyack then north on route 9 through Tarrytown, Sleepy Hollow, to the Skatskill town limits, and route 9 under repair. Traffic in pelting rain! Out of nowhere a cloudburst, rain! She had wanted to sob in frustration, in fury at what her life had become, blinding headlights in her eyes like laser rays piercing her brain.

But usually she was home by 8 P.M. At the latest.

Before dialing 911 she was trying to think: to calculate.

Marissa would ordinarily be home by about 4 P.M. Her last class ended at 3:15 P.M. Marissa would walk home, five and a half suburban blocks, approximately a half mile, through (mostly) a residential neighborhood. (True, Fifteenth Street was a busy street. But Marissa didn't need to cross it.) And she would walk with school friends. (Would she?) Marissa didn't take a school bus, there was no bus for private school children, and in any case Marissa lived near the school because Leah Bantry had moved to the Briarcliff Apts. in order to be near Skatskill Day.

She would explain! In the interstices of emotion over her *missing child* she would explain.

Possibly there had been something special after school that day, a sports event, choir practice, Marissa had forgotten to mention to Leah . . . Possibly Marissa had been invited home by a friend.

In the apartment, standing beside the phone, as if waiting for the phone to ring, trying to think what it was she'd just been thinking. Like trying to grasp water with her fingers, trying to think . . .

A friend! That was it.

What were the names of girls in Marissa's class . . . ?

Of course, Leah would telephone! She was shaky, and she was upset, but she would make these crucial calls before involving the police, she wasn't a hysterical mother. She might call Marissa's teacher whose name she knew, and from her she would learn the names of other girls, she would call these numbers, she would soon locate Marissa, it would be all right. And the mother of Marissa's friend would say apologetically, *But I'd thought Marissa had asked you, could she stay for supper. I'm so very sorry!* And Leah would say quickly laughing in relief, *You know how children are, sometimes. Even the nice ones.*

Except: Marissa didn't have many friends at the school.

That had been a problem in the new, private school. In public school she'd had friends, but it wasn't so easy at Skatskill Day where most students were privileged, well-to-do. Very privileged, and very well-to-do. And poor Marissa was so sweet, trusting and hopeful and easy to hurt if other girls chose to hurt her.

Already in fifth grade it had begun, a perplexing girl-meanness. In sixth grade, it had become worse.

"Why don't they like me, Mommy?"

"Why do they make fun of me, Mommy?"

For in Skatskill if you lived down the hill from Highgate Avenue and/or east of Summit Street you were known to be *working class.* Marissa had asked what it meant? Didn't everybody work? And what was a *class* was it like . . . a class in school? A class*room*?

But Leah had to concede: even if Marissa had been invited home by an unknown school friend, she wouldn't have stayed away so long.

Not past 5 P.M. Not past dark.

Not without calling Leah.

"She isn't the type of child to . . ."

Leah checked the kitchen again. The sink was empty. No package of chicken cutlets defrosting.

Tuesdays/Thursdays were Marissa's evenings to start supper. Marissa loved to cook, Mommy and Marissa loved to cook together. Tonight they were having chicken jambalaya which was their favorite fun meal to prepare together. "Tomatoes, onions, peppers, cajun powder. Rice . . ."

Leah spoke aloud. The silence was unnerving.

If I'd come home directly. Tonight.

The 7-Eleven out on the highway. That's where she had stopped on the way home.

Behind the counter, the middle-aged Indian gentleman with

the wise sorrowful eyes would vouch for her. Leah was a frequent customer, he didn't know her name but he seemed to like her.

Dairy products, a box of tissue. Canned tomatoes. Two six-packs of beer, cold. For all he knew, Leah had a husband. *He* was the beer drinker, the husband.

Leah saw that her hands were trembling. She needed a drink, to steady her hands,

"Ma*ri*ssa!"

She was thirty-four years old. Her daughter was eleven. So far as anyone in Leah's family knew, including her parents, she had been "amicably divorced" for seven years. Her former husband, a medical school dropout, had disappeared somewhere in northern California; they had lived together in Berkeley, having met at the university in the early 1990s.

Impossible to locate the former husband/father whose name was not Bantry.

She would be asked about him, she knew. She would be asked about numerous things.

She would explain: eleven is too old for day care. Eleven is fully capable of coming home alone . . . Eleven can be responsible for . . .

At the refrigerator she fumbled for a can of beer. She opened it and drank thirstily. The liquid was freezing cold, her head began to ache immediately: an icy spot like a coin between her eyes. *How can you! At a time like this!* She didn't want to panic and call 911 before she'd thought this through. Something was staring her in the face, some explanation, maybe?

Distraught Single Mom. Modest Apartment.

Missing Eleven-Year-Old. "Learning Disabilities."

Clumsily Leah retraced her steps through the apartment another time. She was looking for . . . Throwing more widely open those doors she'd already opened. Kneeling beside Marissa's bed to peer beneath in a burst of desperate energy.

And finding—what? A lone sock.

As if Marissa would be hiding beneath a bed!

Marissa who loved her mother, would never never wish to worry or upset or hurt her mother. Marissa who was young for her age, never rebellious, sulky. Marissa whose idea of badness was forgetting to make her bed in the morning. Leaving the bathroom mirror above the sink splattered with water.

Marissa who'd asked Mommy, "Do I have a daddy somewhere like other girls, and he knows about me?"

Marissa who'd asked, blinking back tears, "Why do they make fun of me, Mommy? Am I *slow*?"

In public school classes had been too large, her teacher hadn't had time or patience for Marissa. So Leah had enrolled her at Skatskill Day where classes were limited to fifteen students and Marissa would have special attention from her teacher and yet: still she was having trouble with arithmetic, she was teased, called "slow" . . . Laughed at even by girls she'd thought were her friends.

"Maybe she's run away."

Out of nowhere this thought struck Leah.

Marissa had run away from Skatskill. From the life Mommy had worked so hard to provide for her.

"That can't be! Never."

Leah swallowed another mouthful of beer. Self-medicating, it was. Still her heart was beating in rapid thumps, then missing a beat. Hoped to God she would not faint . . .

"Where? Where would Marissa go? *Never.*"

Ridiculous to think that Marissa would run away!

She was far too shy, passive. Far too uncertain of herself. Other children, particularly older children, intimidated her. Because Marissa was unusually attractive, a beautiful child with silky blond hair to her shoulders, brushed by her proud mother until it shone, sometimes braided by her mother into elaborate plaits, Marissa often drew unwanted attention; but Marissa had very little sense of herself and of how others regarded her.

She had never ridden a bus alone. Never gone to a movie alone. Rarely entered any store alone, without Leah close by.

Yet it was the first thing police would suspect, probably: Marissa had run away.

"Maybe she's next door. Visiting the neighbors."

Leah knew this was not likely. She and Marissa were on friendly terms with their neighbors but they never visited one another. It wasn't that kind of apartment complex, there were few other children.

Still, Leah would have to see. It was expected of a mother looking for her daughter, to check with neighbors.

She spent some time then, ten or fifteen minutes, knocking on doors in the Briarcliff Apts. Smiling anxiously into strangers' startled faces. Trying not to sound desperate, hysterical.

"Excuse me . . ."

A nightmare memory came to her, of a distraught young mother knocking on their door, years ago in Berkeley when she'd first moved in with her lover who would become Marissa's father. They'd been interrupted at a meal, and Leah's lover had answered the door, an edge of annoyance in his voice; and Leah had come up behind him, very young at the time, very blond and privileged, and she'd stared at a young Filipino woman blinking back tears as she'd asked them *Have you seen my daughter . . .* Leah could not remember anything more.

Now it was Leah Bantry who was knocking on doors. Interrupting strangers at mealtime. Apologizing for disturbing them, asking in a tremulous voice *Have you seen my daughter . . .*

In the barracks-like apartment complex into which Leah had moved for economy's sake two years before, each apartment opened directly out onto the rear of the building, into the parking area. This was a brightly lit paved area, purely functional, ugly. In the apartment complex there were no hallways. There were no interior stairs, no foyers. There were no meeting places for even casual exchanges. This was not an attractive condominium village overlooking the Hudson River but Briarcliff Apts., South Skatskill.

Leah's immediate neighbors were sympathetic and concerned, but could offer no help. They had not seen Marissa, and of course she hadn't come to visit them. They promised Leah they would "keep an eye out" and suggested she call 911.

Leah continued to knock on doors. A mechanism had been triggered in her brain, she could not stop until she had knocked on every door in the apartment complex. As she moved farther from her own first-floor apartment, she was met with less sympathy. One tenant shouted through the door to ask what she wanted. Another, a middle-aged man with a drinker's flushed indignant face, interrupted her faltering query to say he hadn't seen any children, he didn't know any children, and he didn't have time for any children.

Leah returned to her apartment staggering, dazed. Saw with a thrill of alarm she'd left the door ajar. Every light in the apartment appeared to be on. Almost, she thought Marissa must be home now, in the kitchen.

She hurried inside. "Marissa . . . ?"

Her voice was eager, piteous.

The kitchen was empty of course. The apartment was empty.

A new, wild idea: Leah returned outside, to the parking lot, to check her car which was parked a short distance away. She peered inside, though knowing it was locked and empty. Peered into the backseat.

Am I going mad? What is happening to me . . .

Still, she'd had to look. She had a powerful urge, too, to get into the car and drive along Fifteenth Street to Skatskill Day School, and check out the building. Of course, it would be locked. The parking lot to the rear . . .

She would drive on Van Buren. She would drive on Summit. She would drive along Skatskill's small downtown of boutiques, novelty restaurants, high-priced antique and clothing stores. Out to the highway past gas stations, fast-food restaurants, mini-malls.

Expecting to see—what? Her daughter walking in the rain?

Leah returned to the apartment, thinking she'd heard the phone ring but the phone was not ringing. Another time, unable to stop herself she checked the rooms. This time looking more carefully through Marissa's small closet, pushing aside Marissa's neatly hung clothes. (Marissa had always been obsessively neat. Leah had not wished to wonder why.) Stared at Marissa's shoes. Such small shoes! Trying to remember what Marissa had worn that morning . . . So many hours ago.

Had she plaited Marissa's hair that morning? She didn't think she'd had time. Instead she had brushed it, lovingly. Maybe she was a little too vain of her beautiful daughter and now she was being punished . . . No, that was absurd. You are not punished for loving your child. She had brushed Marissa's hair until it shone and she had fastened it with barrettes, mother-of-pearl butterflies.

"Aren't you pretty! Mommy's little angel."

"Oh, Mommy. I am not."

Leah's heart caught. She could not understand how the child's father had abandoned them both. She was sick with guilt, it had to be her fault as a woman and a mother.

She'd resisted an impulse to hug Marissa, though. At eleven, the girl was getting too old for spontaneous unexplained hugs from Mommy.

Displays of emotion upset children, Leah had been warned. Of course, Leah hadn't needed to be warned.

Leah returned to the kitchen for another beer. Before dialing 911. Just a few swallows, she wouldn't finish the entire can.

She kept nothing stronger than beer in the apartment. That was a rule of her mature life.

No hard liquor. No men overnight. No exposure to her daughter, the emotions Mommy sometimes felt.

She knew: she would be blamed. For she was blamable.

Latchkey child. Working mom.

She'd have had to pay a sitter nearly as much as she made at the clinic as a medical assistant, after taxes. It was unfair, and it was impossible. She could not.

Marissa was not so quick-witted as other children her age but she was not *slow*! She was in sixth grade, she had not fallen behind. Her tutor said she was "improving." And her attitude was so hopeful. *Your daughter tries so hard, Mrs. Bantry! Such a sweet, patient child.*

Unlike her mother, Leah thought. Who wasn't sweet, and who had given up patience long ago.

"I want to report a child missing . . ."

She rehearsed the words, struck by their finality. She hoped her voice would not sound slurred.

Where was Marissa? It was impossible to think she wasn't somehow in the apartment. If Leah looked again . . .

Marissa knew: to lock the front door behind her, and to bolt the safety latch when she was home alone. (Mommy and Marissa had practiced this maneuver many times.) Marissa knew: not to answer the door if anyone knocked, if Mommy was not home. Not to answer the telephone immediately but to let the answering machine click on, to hear if it was Mommy calling.

Marissa knew: never let strangers approach her. No conversations with strangers. Never climb into vehicles with strangers or even with people she knew unless they were women, people Mommy knew or the mothers of classmates for instance.

Above all Marissa knew: come home directly from school.

Never enter any building, any house, except possibly the house of a classmate, a school friend . . . Even so, Mommy must be told about this beforehand.

(Would Marissa remember? Could an eleven-year-old be trusted to remember so much?)

Leah had totally forgotten; she'd intended to call Marissa's teacher. From Miss Fletcher, Leah would learn the names of Marissa's friends. This, the police would expect her to know. Yet she stood by the phone indecisively, wondering if she dared call the woman; for if she did, Miss Fletcher would know that something was wrong.

The ache between Leah's eyes had spread, her head was wracked with pain.

Four-year-old Marissa would climb up onto the sofa beside Leah, and stroke her forehead to smooth out the "worry lines." Wet kisses on Mommy's forehead. "Kiss to make go away!"

Mommy's vanity had been somewhat wounded, that her child saw worry lines in her face. But she'd laughed, and invited more kisses. "All right, sweetie. Kiss-to-make-go-away."

It had become their ritual. A frown, a grimace, a mournful look—either Mommy or Marissa might demand, "Kiss-to-make-go-away."

Leah was paging through the telephone directory. *Fletcher.* There were more than a dozen *Fletcher*s. None of the initials seemed quite right. Marissa's teacher's first name was—Eve? Eva?

Leah dialed one of the numbers. A recording clicked on, a man's voice.

Another number, a man answered. Politely telling Leah no: there was no one named "Eve" or "Eva" at that number.

This is hopeless, Leah thought.

She should be calling ERs, medical centers, where a child might have been brought, struck by a vehicle for instance crossing a busy street . . .

She fumbled for the can of beer. She would drink hurriedly now. Before the police arrived.

Self-medicating a therapist had called it. Back in high school she'd begun. It was her secret from her family, they'd never known. Though her sister Avril had guessed. At first Leak had drunk with her friends, then she hadn't needed her friends. It wasn't for the elevated sensation, the buzz, it was to calm her nerves. To make her less anxious. Less disgusted with herself.

I need to be beautiful. More beautiful.

He'd said she was beautiful, many times. The man who was to be Marissa's father. Leah was beautiful, he adored her.

They were going to live in a seaside town somewhere in northern California, Oregon. It had been their fantasy. In the meantime he'd been a medical student, resentful of the pressure. She had taken the easier route, nursing school. But she'd dropped out when she became pregnant.

Later he would say sure she was beautiful, but he did not love her.

Love wears out. People move on.

Still, there was Marissa. Out of their coupling, Marissa.

Gladly would Leah give up the man, any man, so long as she had her daughter back.

If she had not stopped on the way home from the clinic! If she had come directly home.

She knew this: she would have to tell the police where she had been, before returning home. Why she'd been unusually late. She would have to confess that, that she had been late. Her life would be turned inside out like the pockets of an old pair of pants. All that was private, precious, rudely exposed.

The single evening in weeks, months . . . She'd behaved out of character.

But she'd stopped at the 7-Eleven, too. It was a busy place in the early evening. This wasn't out of character, Leah frequently stopped at the convenience store which was two blocks from Briarcliff Apts. The Indian gentleman at the cash register would speak kindly of her to police officers. He would learn that her name was Leah Bantry and that her daughter was missing. He would learn that she lived close by, on Fifteenth Street. He would learn that she was a single mother, she was not married. The numerous six-packs of Coors she bought had not been for a husband but for her.

He'd seen her with Marissa, certainly. And so he would remember Marissa. Shy blond child whose hair was sometimes in plaits. He would pity Leah as he'd never had reason to pity her in the past, only just to admire her in his guarded way, the blond shining hair, the American-healthy good looks.

Leah finished the beer, and disposed of the can in the waste basket beneath the sink. She thought of going outside and dumping all the cans into a trash can, for police would possibly search the house, but there was no time, she had delayed long enough waiting for Marissa to return and everything to be again as it had been. Thinking *Why didn't I get a cell phone for Marissa, why did I think the expense wasn't worth it?* She picked up the receiver, and dialed 911.

Her voice was breathless as if she'd been running.

"I want—I want—to report a child missing."

Lone Wolves

I am meant for a special destiny. I am!

He lived vividly inside his head. She lived vividly inside her head.

He was a former idealist. She was an unblinking realist.

He was thirty-one years old. She was thirteen.

He was tall/lanky/ropey-muscled five feet ten inches (on his New York State driver's license he'd indicated 5'11"), weighing one hundred fifty-five pounds. She was four feet eleven, eighty-three pounds.

He thought well of himself, secretly. She thought very well of herself, not so secretly.

He was a substitute math teacher/"computer consultant" at

Skatskill Day School. She was an eighth grader at Skatskill Day School.

His official status at the school was *part-time employee.*

Her official status at the school was *full-tuition pupil, no exceptions.*

Part-time employee meant no medical/dental insurance coverage, less pay per hour than full-time employees, and no possibility of tenure. *Full-tuition, no exceptions* meant no scholarship aid or tuition deferral.

He was a relatively new resident of Skatskill-on-Hudson, eight miles north of New York City. She was a longtime resident who'd come to live with her widowed grandmother when she was two years old, in 1992.

To her, to his face, he was *Mr. Zallman;* otherwise, *Mr. Z.*

To him, she had no clear identity. One of those Skatskill Day girls of varying ages (elementary grades through high school) to whom he gave computer instructions and provided personal assistance as requested.

Even sixth grader Marissa Bantry with the long straight corntassel hair he would not recall, immediately.

The kids he called them. In a voice that dragged with reluctant affection; or in a voice heavy with sarcasm. *Those kids!*

Depending on the day, the week. Depending on his mood.

Those others she called them in a voice quavering with scorn.

They were an alien race. Even her small band of disciples she had to concede were losers.

In his confidential file in the office of the principal of Skatskill Day it was noted *Impressive credentials/recommendations, interacts well with brighter students. Inclined to impatience. Not a team player. Unusual sense of humor. (Abrasive?)*

In her confidential file (1998–present) in the principal's office it was noted in reports by numerous parties *Impressive background (maternal grandmother/legal guardian Mrs. A. Trahern, alumna/donor/trustee (emeritus), impressive I.Q. (measured 149, 161, 113, 159 ages 6, 9, 10, 12), flashes of brilliance, erratic academic performance, lonely child, gregarious child, interacts poorly with classmates, natural leader, antisocial tendencies, lively presence in class, disruptive presence in class, hyperactive, apathetic, talent for "fantasy," poor communication skills, immature tendencies, verbal fluency, imagination stimulated by new projects, easily bored, sullen, mature for age, poor motor coordination skills, diagnosed Attention Deficit Syndrome age 5/prescribed Ritalin with good results/mixed results, diagnosed borderline dyslexic age 7, prescribed special tutoring with good results/mixed results, honor roll fifth grade, low grades/failed English seventh grade, suspended for one week Oct. 2002 "threatening" girl classmate, reinstated after three days/legal action brought against school by guardian/mandated psychological counseling with good/mixed results.* (On the outside of the folder, in the principal's handwriting *A challenge!*)

He was swarthy skinned, with an olive complexion. She had pale sallow skin.

He was at the school Monday/Tuesday/Thursday unless he was subbing for another teacher which he did, on the average,

26

perhaps once every five weeks. She was at the school five days a week, Skatskill Day was her turf!

Hate/love she felt for Skatskill Day. *Love/hate.*

(Often, as her teachers noted, she "disappeared" from classes and later "reappeared." Sulky/arrogant with no explanation.)

He was a lone wolf and yet: the great-grandson of immigrant German Jews who had come to the United States in the early 1900s. The grandson and son of partners at Cleary, McCorkle, Mace & Zallman, Wall Street brokers. She was the lone grandchild of New York State Supreme Court Justice Elias Trahern who had died before she was born and was of no more interest to her than the jut-jawed and bewigged General George Washington whose idealized image hung in the school rotunda.

His skin was dotted with moles. Not disfiguring exactly but he'd see people staring at these moles as if waiting for them to move.

Her skin was susceptible to angry-looking rashes. Nerve-rashes they'd been diagnosed, also caused by picking with her nails.

He was beginning to lose his thick-rippled dark hair he had not realized he'd been vain about. Receding at the temples so he wore it straggling over his collar. Her hair exploded in faded-rust fuzz like dandelion seed around her pointy pinched face.

He was Mikal. She was Jude.

He'd been born Michael but there were so many damn Michaels!

She'd been born Judith but—*Judith! Enough to make you want to puke.*

Lone wolves who scorned the crowd. Natural aristocrats who had no use for money, or for family connections.

He was estranged from the Zallmans. Mostly.

She was estranged from the Traherns. Mostly.

He had a quick engaging ironic laugh. She had a high-pitched nasal-sniggering laugh that surprised her suddenly, like a sneeze.

His favored muttered epithet was *What next?* Her favored muttered epithet was *Bor-ing!*

He knew: prepubescent/adolescent girls often have crushes on their male teachers. Yet somehow it never seemed very real to him, or very crucial. Mikal Zallman living in his own head.

She detested boys her own age. And most men, any age.

Making her disciples giggle and blush, at lunchtime flashing a paring knife in a swooping circular motion to indicate *castra-tion: know what that is?* as certain eighth grade boys passed noisily by carrying cafeteria trays.

Boys rarely saw her. She'd learned to go invisible like a playing card turned sideways.

He lived—smugly, it seemed to some observers—inside an armor of irony. (Except when alone. Staring at images of famine, war, devastation he felt himself blinking hot tears from his eyes. He'd shocked himself and others crying uncontrollably at his father's funeral in an Upper East Side synagogue the previous year.)

She had not cried in approximately four years. Since she'd fallen from a bicycle and cut a gash in her right knee requiring nine stitches.

He lived alone, in three sparely furnished rooms, in Riverview Heights, a condominium village on the Hudson River in North Tarrytown. She lived alone, except for the peripheral presence of her aging grandmother, in a few comfortably furnished rooms in the main wing of the Trahern estate at 83 Highgate Avenue; the rest of the thirty-room mansion had long been closed off for economy's sake.

He had no idea where she lived, as he had but the vaguest idea of who she was. She knew where he lived, it was three miles from 83 Highgate Avenue. She'd bicycled past Riverview Heights more than once.

He drove a not-new metallic blue Honda CR-V, New York license TZ 6063. She knew he drove a not-new metallic blue Honda CR-V, New York license TZ 6063.

Actually he didn't always think so well of himself. Actually she didn't always think so well of herself.

He wished to think well of himself. He wished to think well of all of humanity. He did not want to think *Homo sapiens is hopeless, let's pull the plug.* He wanted to think *I can make a difference in others' lives.*

He'd been an idealist who had *burnt out, crashed* in his late twenties. These were worthy clichés. These were clichés he had earned. He had taught in Manhattan, Bronx, and Yonkers public schools through his mid- and late twenties and after an interim of recovery he had returned to Columbia University to upgrade his credentials with a master's degree in computer science and he had returned to teaching for his old idealism yet clung to him like lint on one of his worn-at-the-elbow sweaters, one thing he knew he would never emulate his father in the pursuit of money, here in Skatskill-on-Hudson where he knew no one he could work part-time mostly helping kids with computers and he would be respected here or in any case his privacy would be respected, he wasn't an ambitious private school teacher, wasn't angling for a permanent job, in a few years he'd move on but for the present time he was contentedly employed, he had freedom to *feed my rat* as he called it.

Much of the time she did not think so well of herself. Secretly.

Suicide fantasies are common to adolescents. Not a sign of mental illness so long as they remain fantasies.

He'd had such fantasies, too. Well into his twenties, in fact. He'd outgrown them now That was what *feeding my rat* had done for Mikal Zallman.

Her suicide fantasies were cartoons, you could say. A plunge from the Tappan Zee Bridge/George Washington Bridge, footage on the 6 P.M. news. A blazing fireball on a rooftop. (Skatskill Day? It was the only roof she had access to.) If you swallowed like five, six Ecstasy pills your heart would explode (maybe). If you swallowed a dozen barbiturates you would fall asleep and then into a coma and never wake up (maybe). With drugs there was always the possibility of vomiting, waking up in an ER your stomach being pumped or waking up brain damaged. There were knives, razor blades. Bleeding into a bathtub, the warm water gushing.

Eve of her thirteenth birthday and she'd been feeling shitty and her new friend/mentor the Master of Eyes (in Alaska, unless it was Antarctica) advised her why hate yourself Jude it's bor-ing. Better to hate *those others* who surround.

She never cried, though. Really really never cried.

Like Jude O's fear ducts are dried out. Cool!

Ducts reminded her of *pubes* she had first encountered as a word in a chat room, she'd looked up in the dictionary seeing *pubes* was a nasty word for those nasty crinkly/kinky hairs that had started to sprout in a certain place, between her legs. And in her armpits where she refused to apply *deodorant* until Grandmother nagnagged.

Grandmother Trahern was half blind but her sense of smell was acute. Grandmother Trahern was skilled at nagnagnagging, you might say it was the old woman's predominant skill in the eighth decade of her life.

Mr. Z.! Maybe he'd smelled her underarms. She hoped he had not smelled her crotch.

Mr. Z. in computer lab making his way along the aisle answering kids' questions most of them pretty elementary/dumb ass she'd have liked to catch his eye and exchange a knowing smirk but Mr. Z. never seemed to be looking toward her and then she was stricken with shyness, blood rushing into her face as he paused above her to examine the confusion on her screen and she heard herself mutter with childish bravado *Guess I fucked up, Mr. Zallman, huh?* wiping her nose on the edge of her hand beginning to giggle and there was sexy/cool Mr. Z. six inches from her not breaking into a smile even of playful reproach giving not the slightest hint he'd heard the forbidden F-word from an eighth grade girl's innocent mouth.

In fact Mr. Z. had heard. Sure.

Never laugh, never encourage them. If they swear or use obscene or suggestive language.

And never touch them.

Or allow them to touch you.

The (subterranean) connection between them.

He had leaned over her, typed on her keyboard. Repaired the damage. Told her she was doing very well. Not to be discouraged! He didn't seem to know her name but maybe that was just pretense, his sense of humor. Moving on to the next raised hand.

Still, she'd known there was the (subterranean) connection.

As she'd known, first glimpsing the Corn Maiden in the seventh grade corridor. Silky blond corn-tassel hair. Shy, frightened. A new girl. Perfect.

One morning she came early to observe the Corn Maiden's mother dropping her off at the curb. Good-looking woman with the same pale blond hair, smiling at the girl and hastily leaning over to kisskiss.

Some connections go through you like a laser ray.

Some connections, you just know.

Mr. Z. she'd sent an e-message *you are a master mister z.* Which was not like Jude O to do because any message in cyberspace can never be erased. But Mr. Z. had not replied.

So easy to reply to a fucking e-message! But Mr. *Z.* had not.

Mr. Z. did not exchange a knowing smile/wink with her as you'd expect.

Ignored her!

Like he didn't know which one of them she was.

Like he could confuse her with *those others* her inferiors.

And so something turned in her heart like a rusty key and she thought calmly, *You will pay for this mister asshole Z. and all your progeny.*

Thought of calling the FBI reporting a suspected terrorist, Mr. Z. was dark like an Arab, and shifty-eyed. Though probably he was a Jew.

Afterward vaguely he would recall *you are a master mister z* but of course he'd deleted it. So easy to delete an e-message.

Afterward vaguely he would recall the squirmy girl at the computer with the frizz hair and glassy staring eyes, a startling smell as of unwashed flesh wafting from her (unusual at Skatskill Day as it was unusual in the affluent suburban village of Skatskill) he had not known at the time, this was January/February, was Jude Trahern. He had no homeroom students, he met with more than one hundred students sometimes within days, couldn't keep track of them and had no interest in keeping track. Though a few days later he would come upon the girl in the company of a fattish friend, the two of them rummaging in a waste basket in the computer lab but he'd taken no special note of them as they'd hurried away embarrassed and giggling together as if he'd opened a door and seen them naked.

But he would remember: the same frizz-haired girl boldly

seated at his computer after school one day frowning at the screen and click-clicking keys with as much authority as if the computer were her own and this time he'd spoken sharply to her, "Excuse me?" and she'd looked up at him cringing and blind-seeming as if she thought he might hit her. And so he joked, "Here's the famous hacker, eh?"—he knew it was the kindest as it was the wisest strategy to make a joke of the audacious/inexplicable behavior of adolescents, it wasn't a good idea to confront or embarrass. Especially not a girl. And this stunted-seeming girl hunched over like she was trying to make herself smaller. Papery-thin skin, short upper lip exposing her front teeth, a guarded rodent look, furtive, anxious, somehow appealing. Her eyes were of the no-color of grit, moist and widened. Eyebrows and lashes scanty, near-invisible. She was so fiercely plain and her unbeautiful eyes stared at him so *rawly* . . . He felt sorry for her, poor kid. Bold, nervy, but in another year or so she'd be left behind entirely by her classmates, no boy would glance at her twice. He could not have guessed that the tremulous girl was the lone descendent of a family of reputation and privilege though possibly he might have guessed that her parents were long divorced from one another and perhaps from her as well. She was stammering some feeble explanation *Just needed to look something up, Mr. Zallman.* He laughed and dismissed her with a wave of his hand. Had an impulse, out of character for him, to reach out and tousle that frizzed floating hair as you'd rub a dog's head partly in affection and partly to chastise.

Didn't touch her, though. Mikal Zallman wasn't crazy.

Is she breathing, d'you think?

She is! Sure she is.

Oh God what if . . .

. . . she *is*. See?

The Corn Maiden slept by candlelight. The heavy open-mouthed sleep of the sedated.

We observed her in wonder. The Corn Maiden, in our power!

Jude removed the barrettes from her hair so we could brush it. Long straight pale blond hair. We were not jealous of the Corn Maiden's hair because *It is our hair now.*

The Corn Maiden's hair was spread out around her head like she was falling.

She was breathing, yes you could see. If you held a candle close to her face and throat you could see.

We had made a bed for the Corn Maiden, that Jude called a *bier*. Out of beautiful silk shawls and a brocaded bedspread, cashmere blanket from Scotland, goose-feather pillows. From the closed-off guest wing of the house Jude brought these, her face shining.

We fumbled to remove the Corn Maiden's clothes.

You pull off your own clothes without hardly thinking but another person, even a small girl who is lying flat on her back, arms and legs limp but heavy, that's different.

When the Corn Maiden was bare it was hard not to giggle. Hard not to snort with laughter . . .

More like a little girl than she was like us.

We were shy of her suddenly. Her breasts were flat against her rib cage, her nipples were tiny as seeds. There were no hairs growing between her legs that we could see.

She was very cold, shivering in her sleep. Her lips were putty-colored. Her teeth were chattering. Her eyes were closed but you could see a thin crescent of white. So (almost!) you worried the Corn Maiden was watching us paralyzed in sleep.

It was Xanax Jude had prepared for the Corn Maiden. Also she had codeine and Oxycodone already ground to powder, in reserve.

We were meant to "bathe" the Corn Maiden, Jude said. But maybe not tonight.

We rubbed the Corn Maiden's icy fingers, her icy toes, and her icy cheeks. We were not shy of touching her suddenly, we wanted to touch her and touch and *touch*.

Inside here, Jude said, touching the Corn Maiden's narrow chest, there is a heart beating. An actual *heart*.

Jude spoke in a whisper. In the quiet you could hear the heart beat.

We covered the Corn Maiden then with silks, brocades, cashmere wool. We placed a goose-feather pillow beneath the Corn Maiden's head. Jude sprinkled perfume on the Corn Maiden with her fingertips. It was a blessing Jude said. The Corn Maiden would sleep and sleep for a long time and when she woke, she would know only our faces. The faces of her friends.

• • •

It was a storage room in the cellar beneath the guest wing we brought the Corn Maiden. This was a remote corner of the big old house. This was a closed-off corner of the house and the cellar was yet more remote, nobody would ever ever come here Jude said.

And you could scream your head off, nobody would ever hear.

Jude laughed, cupping her hands to her mouth like she was going to scream. But all that came out was a strangled choked noise.

There was no heat in the closed-off rooms of the Trahern house. In the cellar it was a damp cold like winter. Except this was meant to be a time of nuclear holocaust and no electricity we would have brought a space heater to plug in. Instead we had candles.

These were fragrant hand-dipped candles old Mrs. Trahern had been saving in a drawer since 1994, according to the gift shop receipt.

Jude said, Grandma won't miss 'em.

Jude was funny about her grandmother. Sometimes she liked her okay, other times she called her the old bat, said fuck her she didn't give a damn about Jude she was only worried Jude would embarrass her somehow.

Mrs. Trahern had called up the stairs, when we were in Jude's room watching a video. The stairs were too much for her, rarely she came upstairs to check on Jude. There was an actual elevator in the house (we had seen it) but Jude said she'd fucked it up, fooling with it so much when she was a little kid. Just some friends from school, Denise and Anita, Jude called back. You've met them.

Those times Mrs. Trahern saw us downstairs with Jude she would ask politely how we were and her snail-mouth would stretch in a grudging little smile but already she wasn't listening to anything we said, and she would never remember our names.

101 Dalmatians Jude played, one of her old videos she'd long outgrown. (Jude had a thousand videos she'd outgrown!) It was a young-kids' movie we had all seen but the Corn Maiden had never seen. Sitting cross-legged on the floor in front of the TV eating ice cream from a bowl in her lap and we finished ours and waited for her and Jude asked would she like a little more and the Corn Maiden hesitated just a moment then said *Yes thank you.*

We all had more Häagen-Dazs French Vanilla ice cream. But it was not the same ice cream the Corn Maiden had not exactly!

Her eyes shining, so happy. Because we were her friends.

A sixth grader, friends with eighth graders. A guest in Jude Trahern's house.

Jude had been nice to her at school for a long time. Smiling, saying hello. Jude had a way of fixing you with her eyes like a cobra or something you could not look away. You were scared but sort of thrilled, too,

In the 7-Eleven she'd come inside to get a Coke and a package of nachos. She was on her way home from school and had no idea that two of us had followed her and one had run ahead, to wait. She was smiling to see Jude who was so friendly. Jude asked where was her mom and she said her mom was a nurse's aide across the river in Nyack and would not be home till after dark.

She laughed saying her mom didn't like her eating junk food but her mom didn't know.

Jude said what our moms don't know don't hurt them.

The Sacrifice of the Corn Maiden was a ritual of the Onigara Indians, Jude told us. In school we had studied Native Americans as they are called but we had not studied the Onigara Indians Jude said had been extinct for two hundred years. The Iroquois had wiped out the Onigaras, it was survival of the fittest.

The Corn Maiden would be our secret. Beforehand we seemed to know it would be the most precious of our secrets.

Jude and the Corn Maiden walked ahead alone. Denise and Anita behind. Back of the stores, past the Dumpsters, we ran to catch up.

Jude asked would the Corn Maiden like to visit her house and the Corn Maiden said yes but she could not stay long. Jude said it was just a short walk. Jude pretended not to know where the Corn Maiden lived (but she knew: crummy apartments at Fifteenth Street and Van Buren) and this was a ten-minute walk, approximately.

We climbed the back way. Nobody saw. Old Mrs. Trahern would be watching TV in her room, and would not see.

If she saw she would not seriously *see*. For at a distance her eyes were too weak.

The guest wing was a newer part of the house. It overlooked a swimming pool. But the pool was covered with a tarpaulin,

Jude said nobody had swum in it for years. She could remember wading in the shallow end but it was long ago like the memory belonged to someone else.

The guest wing was never used either, Jude said. Most of the house was never used. She and her grandmother lived in just a few rooms and that was fine with them. Sometimes Mrs. Trahern would not leave the house for weeks. She was angry about something that had happened at church. Or maybe the minister had said something she found offensive. She had had to dismiss the black man who'd driven her "limo-zene." She had dismissed the black woman who'd been her cook and house cleaner for twenty years. Groceries were delivered to the house. Meals were mostly heated up in the microwave. Mrs. Trahern saw a few of her old friends in town, at the Village Woman's Club, the Hudson Valley Friends of History, and the Skatskill Garden Club. Her friends were not invited to the house to see her.

Do you love your mom? Jude asked the Corn Maiden.

The Corn Maiden nodded yes. Sort of embarrassed.

Your mom is real pretty. She's a nurse, I guess?

The Corn Maiden nodded yes. You could see she was proud of her mom but shy to speak of her.

Where is your dad? Jude asked.

The Corn Maiden frowned. She did not know.

Is your dad living?

Did not know.

When did you see your dad last?

Was not sure. She'd been so little . . .

Did he live around here, or where?

California, the Corn Maiden said. Berkeley.

My mom is in California, Jude said. Los Angeles.

The Corn Maiden smiled, uncertainly.

Maybe your dad is with my dad now, Jude said.

The Corn Maiden looked at Jude in wonderment.

In Hell, Jude said.

Jude laughed. That way she had, her teeth glistening.

Denise and Anita laughed. The Corn Maiden smiled not knowing whether to laugh. Slower and slower the spoon was being lifted to her mouth, her eyelids were drooping.

We would carry the Corn Maiden from Jude's room. Along a corridor and through a door into what Jude called the guest wing, where the air was colder, and stale. And down a stairway in the guest wing and into a cellar to the storage room.

The Corn Maiden did not weigh much. Three of us, we weighed so much more.

On the outside of the storage room door, a padlock.

Anita and Denise had to leave by 6 P.M., to return to their houses for supper. So boring!

Jude would remain with the Corn Maiden for much of the night. To *watch over*. A *vigil*. She was excited by the candle flames, the incense-smell. The pupils of her eyes were dilated, she was highhigh on Ecstasy. She would not bind the Corn Maiden's wrists and ankles, she said, until it was necessary.

Jude had a Polaroid camera, she would take pictures of the Corn Maiden sleeping on her bier.

As the Corn Maiden was being missed the next morning we would all be at school as usual. For nobody had seen us, and nobody would think of *us*.

Some pre-vert they'll think of, Jude said. We can help them with that.

Remember, the Corn Maiden has come as our guest, Jude said. It is not *kidnapping*.

The Corn Maiden came to Jude on the Thursday before Palm Sunday, in April of the year.

Dial 911 your life is no longer your own.
Dial 911 you become a beggar.
Dial 911 you are stripped naked.

She met them at the curb. Distraught mother awaiting police officers in the rain outside Briarcliff Apts., Fifteenth St., South Skatskill, 8:20 P.M. Approaching officers as they emerged from the patrol car pleading, anxious, trying to remain calm but her voice rising, Help me please help my daughter is missing! I came home from work, my daughter isn't here, Marissa is eleven years old, I have no idea where she is, nothing like this has ever happened, please help me find her, I'm afraid that someone has taken my daughter!—Caucasian female, early thirties, blond, bare-headed, strong smell of beer on her breath.

They would question her. They would repeat their questions, and she would repeat her answers. She was calm. She tried to be calm. She began to cry. She began to be angry. She knew her words were being recorded, each word she uttered was a matter of public record. She would face TV cameras, interviewers with microphones out-thrust like scepters. She would see herself performing clumsily and stumbling over her lines in the genre *missing child/pleading mother.* She would see how skillfully the TV screen leapt from her anxious drawn face and bloodshot eyes to the smiling innocent wide-eyed Marissa, sweet-faced Marissa with gleaming blond hair, eleven years old, sixth grader, the camera lingering upon each of three photos of Marissa provided by her mother; then, as the distraught mother continued to speak, you saw the bland sandstone facade of the "private"— "exclusive"—Skatskill Day School and next you were looking at the sinister nighttime traffic of Fifteenth Street, South Skatskill, along which, as a neutral-sounding woman's voice explained, eleven-year-old Marissa Bantry normally walked home to let herself into an empty apartment and begin to prepare supper for her mother (who worked at a Nyack medical clinic, would not be home until 8 P.M.) and herself; then you were looking at the exterior rear of Briarcliff Apts., squat and ugly as an army barracks in the rain, where a few hardy residents stood curious staring at police officers and camera crews; then you saw again the mother of the missing girl Leah Bantry, thirty-four, obviously a negligent mother, a sick-with-guilt mother publicly pleading *If anyone has seen my daughter, if anyone has any idea what might have happened to Marissa . . .*

Next news item, tractor-trailer overturned on the New Jersey Turnpike, pileup involving eleven vehicles, two drivers killed, eight taken by ambulance to Newark hospital.

So ashamed! But I only want Marissa back.

It was BREAKING NEWS! which means exciting news and by 10 P.M. of that Thursday in April each of four local TV stations was carrying the *missing Marissa* story, and would carry it at regular intervals for as long as there were developments and as long as local interest remained high. But really it was not "new" news, everyone had seen it before. All that could be "new" were the specific players and certain details to be revealed in time, with the teasing punctuality of a suspense film.

It was a good thing, the distraught mother gathered, that cases of missing/abducted children were relatively rare in the affluent Hudson Valley suburbs north of New York City, as crimes of violence in these communities were rare. This meant dramatically focused police attention, cooperation with neighboring police departments in Tarrytown, Sleepy Hollow, Irvington. This meant dramatically focused media coverage, replication of Marissa Bantry's likeness, public concern and participation in the search. *Outpouring of sympathy*, it would be called. *Community involvement.* You would not find such a response in a high-crime area, Leah was told.

"Something to be grateful for. Thank you!"

She wasn't speaking ironically. Tears shone in her bloodshot eyes, she wanted only to be believed.

It was in the distraught mother's favor, too, that, if her daughter had been abducted and hadn't simply run away of her own volition, hers would be the first such case in Skatskill's history.

That was remarkable. That was truly a novelty.

"But she didn't run away. Marissa did not run away. I've tried to explain . . ."

Another novelty in the affluent Hudson Valley suburbs was the mysterious/suspicious circumstance of the "considerable" time lapse between the child's probable disappearance after school and the recorded time the mother reported her missing at 8:14 P.M. The most vigilant of the local TV stations was alert to the dramatic possibilities here. *Skatskill police will neither confirm nor deny that the department is said to be considering charging Bantry, who has no previous police record, with child endangerment.*

And how it would be leaked to this same TV station, the distraught mother had evidenced signs of "inebriation" when police arrived at her home, no one at the station was in a position to say.

So ashamed! I want to die.
   If I could exchange my life for Marissa's.

Hours, days. Though each hour was singular, raw as a stone forced down the throat. And what were days but unchartable and unfathomable durations of time too painful to be borne except as singular hours or even minutes. She was aware of a great wheel turning, and of herself caught in this wheel, helpless, in a state of suspended panic and yet eager to cooperate with the very turning of the wheel, if it might bring Marissa back to her. For she was coming to feel, possibly yes there was a God, a God of mercy and not just justice, and she might barter her life for Marissa's.

Through most of it she remained calm. On the surface, calm. She believed she was calm, she had not become hysterical. She had called her parents in Spokane, Washington, for it could not be avoided. She had called her older sister in Washington, D.C. She had not seemed to hear in their shocked and incredulous voices any evidence of reproach, accusation, disgust; but she understood that that was to come, in time.

I am to blame. I know.

It doesn't matter about me.

She believed she was being damned calm! Answering their impudent questions and reanswering them and again repeating as in a deranged tape loop the answer that were all she had in the face of their suspicion, their doubt. She answered the officers' questions with the desperation of a drowning woman clutching a rope already fraying to haul herself into a lifeboat already leaking water. She had no idea, she had told them immediately she had no idea where Marissa's father was, for the past seven years there had been no contact between them, she had last seen him in Berkeley, California, thousands of miles away and he had had no interest in Marissa, he had sought no interest in his own daughter, and so truly she did not believe she could not believe that there was any likelihood of that man having abducted Marissa, truly she did not want to involve him, did not wish to seem in the most elliptical way to be accusing him . . . Yet they continued to question her. It was an interrogation, they sensed that she had something to hide, had she? And what was that, and why? Until finally she heard herself say in a broken defeated voice all right, yes I will give you his name and his last-known address and telephone number that was surely inoperative after so long, all right I will tell you: we were never

47

married, his name is not my child's name, he'd pretended even to doubt that Marissa was his child, we had only lived together, he had no interest in marriage, are you satisfied now?

Her shame, she'd never told her parents. Never told her sister.

Now they would know Leah's pathetic secret. It would be another shock, a small one set beside the other. It would cause them to think less of her, and to know that she was a liar. And now she must telephone to tell them before they discovered it in the media. *I lied to you, I was never married to Andrew. There was no marriage, and there was no divorce.*

Next, they needed to know exactly where she'd been after she had left the Nyack clinic at 6:30 P.M. of the day her daughter had disappeared. Now they knew she was a liar, and a desperate woman, now they had scented blood. They would track the wounded creature to its lair.

At first Leah had been vague about time. In the shock of her daughter missing, it had been natural for the mother to be vague, confused, uncertain about time.

She'd told them that she had been stuck in traffic returning home from Nyack. The Tappan Zee Bridge, route 9 and road repair and rain but yes, she had stopped at the 7-Eleven store near her apartment to buy a few things as she often did . . .

And was that all, had that been her only stop?

Yes. Her only stop. The 7-Eleven. The clerk at the cash register would recognize her.

This was a question, a probing, that had to do with Leah

Bantry's male friends. If she had any, who would have known Marissa. Who would have met Marissa. Who might simply have glimpsed Marissa.

Any male friend of the missing girl's mother who might have been attracted to the girl. Might have "abducted" her.

For Marissa might have willingly climbed into a vehicle, if it was driven by someone she knew. Yes?

Calmly Leah insisted no, no one.

She had no male friends at the present time. No serious involvements.

No one she was "seeing"?

Leah flared up, angry. In the sense of—what? What did "see-ing" mean?

She was being adamant, and she was speaking forcibly. Yet her interrogators seemed to know. Especially the female detec-tive seemed to know. An evasiveness in Leah's bloodshot eyes that were the eyes of a sick, guilty mother. A quavering in Leah's voice even as she spoke impatiently, defiantly. I told you! God damn I have told you.

There was a pause. The air in the room was highly charged.

There was a pause. Her interrogators waited.

It was explained to Leah then that she must answer the officers' questions fully and truthfully. This was a police investigation, she would be vulnerable to charges of obstruction of justice if she lied.

If she lied.

A known liar.

An exposed, humiliated liar.

And so, another time, Leah heard her voice break. She heard herself say all right, yes. She had not gone directly to the 7-Eleven store from Nyack, she had stopped first to see a friend and, yes he was a close male friend, separated from his wife and uncertain of his future and he was an intensely private man whose identity she could not reveal for he and Leah were not exactly lovers though, yes they had made love . . .

Just once, they had made love. One time.

On Sunday evening, the previous Sunday evening they had made love.

For the first time they had made love. And it wasn't certain that . . . Leah had no way of knowing whether . . .

She was almost pleading now. Blood seemed to be hemorrhaging into her swollen face.

The police officers waited. She was wiping at her eyes with a wadded tissue. There was no way out of this was there! Somehow she had known, with the sickening sensation of a doomed cow entering a slaughter chute, she had known that a part of her life would be over, when she'd dialed 911.

Your punishment, for losing your daughter

Of course, Leah had to provide the police officers with the man's name. She had no choice.

She was sobbing, crushed. Davitt would be furious with her.

Davitt Stoop, M.D. Director of the medical clinic. He was Dr. Stoop, her superior. Her employer. He was a kindly man, yet a short-tempered man. He was not in love with Leah Bantry, she knew; nor was Leah in love with him, exactly; and yet, they were relaxed together, they got along so very well together, both were parents of single children of about the same age, both had been hurt and deceived in love, and were wary of new involvements.

Davitt was forty-two, he had been married for eighteen years. He was a responsible husband and father as he had a reputation at the clinic for being an exacting physician and it had been his concern that he and Leah might be seen together prematurely. He did not want his wife to know about Leah, not yet. Still less did he want Leah's coworkers at the clinic to know. He dreaded gossip, innuendo. He dreaded any exposure of his private life.

It was the end, Leah knew.

Before it had begun between them, it would end.

They would humiliate him, these police officers. They would ask him about Leah Bantry and Leah's missing daughter, did he know the child, how well did he know the child, had he ever seen the child without the mother present, had he ever been alone with the child, had he ever given the child a ride in his car for instance this past Thursday?

Possibly they would want to examine the car. Would he allow a search, or would he insist upon a warrant?

Davitt had moved out of his family home in February and lived in an apartment in Nyack, the very apartment Leah Bantry had visited on Thursday evening after her shift. Impulsively she had dropped by. Davitt might have expected her, it hadn't been certain. They were in the early stages of a romance, excited in each other's presence but uncertain.

This apartment. Had Marissa ever been there?

No! Certainly not.

In a faltering voice telling the officers that Davitt scarcely knew Marissa. Possibly he'd met her, once. But they had spent no time together, certainly not.

Leah had stayed in Davitt's apartment approximately a half hour. Possibly, forty minutes.

No. They had not had sex.

Not exactly.

They had each had a drink. They had been affectionate, they had talked.

Earnestly, seriously they had talked! About the clinic, and about their children. About Davitt's marriage, and Leah's own.

(It would be revealed, Leah had led Davitt Stoop to believe she had been married, and divorced. It had seemed such a trivial and inconsequential lie at the time.)

Leah was saying, stammering, Davitt would never do such a thing! Not to Marissa, not to any child. He was the father of a ten-year-old boy, himself. He was not the type . . .

The female detective asked bluntly what did Leah mean, "type"? Was this a "type" she believed she could recognize?

Davitt forgive me! I had no choice.

I could not lie to police. I had to tell them about you. I am so very sorry, Davitt, you can understand can't you I must help them find Marissa I had no choice.

Still, Marissa remained missing.

"People who do things like this, take children, they're not rational. What they do, they do for their own purposes. We can only track them. We can try to stop them. We can't understand them."

And, "When something like this happens, it's natural for people to want to cast blame. You'd be better off not watching TV or reading the papers right now, Miss Bantry."

One of the Skatskill detectives spoke so frankly to her, she could not believe he too might be judging her harshly.

There were myriad calls, e-mail messages. Blond-haired Marissa Bantry had been sighted in a car exiting the New York Thruway at Albany. She had been sighted in the company of "hippie-type males" on West Houston Street, New York City. A Skatskill resident would recall, days after the fact, having seen "that pretty little pig-tailed blond girl" getting into a battered-looking van driven by a Hispanic male in the parking lot of the 7-Eleven store a few blocks from her home.

Still, Marissa remained missing.

. . . hours in rapid succession jarring and discontinuous as a broken film projected upon a flimsy screen she would not sleep for more than two or three hours even with sedatives and she slept without dreaming like one who has been struck on the head with a mallet and she woke hollow-headed and parch-mouthed and her heart beating in her chest like something with a broken wing.

Always as she woke in that split-second before awareness rushed upon her like a mouthful of filthy water *My daughter is gone, Marissa is lost* there was a sense of grace, a confusion in time like a prayer *It has not happened yet has it? Whatever it will be.*

Like a sudden bloom of daffodils there appeared overnight, everywhere in Skatskill, the smiling likeness of MARISSA BANTRY 11.

In store windows. On public bulletin boards, telephone poles. Prominent in the foyers of the Skatskill Post Office, the Skatskill Food Mart, the Skatskill Public Library. Prominent though already dampening in April rain, on the fences of construction sites.

MISSING SINCE APRIL 10. SKATSKILL DAY SCHOOL/15TH ST. AREA.

Hurriedly established by the Skatskill police department was a MARISSA Web site posting more photos of the missing blond girl, a detailed description of her, background information. ANYONE KNOWING ANYTHING ABOUT MARISSA BANTRY PLEASE CONTACT SKATSKILL POLICE AT THIS NUMBER.

Initially, no reward was posted. By Friday evening, an anonymous donor (prominent Skatskill philanthropist, retired) had come forward to offer fifteen thousand dollars.

It was reported by the media that Skatskill police were working *round the clock.* They were *under intense pressure,* they were investigating *all possible leads.* It was reported that *known pedophiles, sex offenders, child molesters* in the area were being questioned. (Information about such individuals was confidential of course. Still, the most vigilant of area tabloids learned from an anonymous source that a sixty-year-old Skatskill resident, a retired music teacher with a sexual misdemeanor record dating back to 1987, had been visited by detectives. Since this individual refused to speak with a reporter, or consent to be photographed, the tabloid published a photograph of his front door at 12 Amwell Circle on its cover, beneath the strident headline LOCAL SEX OFFENDER QUERIED BY COPS: WHERE IS MARISSA?)

Each resident of Briarcliff Apts. was questioned, some more than once. Though no search warrants had been issued, several residents cooperated with police allowing both their apartments and their motor vehicles to be searched.

Storekeepers in the area of the Skatskill Day School and along Marissa Bantry's route home were questioned. At the 7-Eleven store in the mini-mall on the highway, so often frequented by young people, several clerks examined photographs of the missing girl, solemnly shook their heads and told police officers no, they did not believe that Marissa Bantry had been in the store recently, or ever. "There are so many children . . ." Questioned about Leah Bantry, whose photograph they were also shown, the eldest clerk said, carefully, that yes, he recognized this woman, she was a friendly woman; friendlier than most of his customers; but he could not say with certainty if she had been in his store on Thursday, with or without her daughter. "There are so many customers. And so many of them, they look like one another especially if they are blond."

Detectives queried teenagers, most of them from Skatskill High, and some no longer in school, who hung out at the mini-mall. Most of them stiffened at the approach of police officers and hurriedly shook their heads no, they had not seen the little blond girl who was missing, or anyway could not remember seeing her. A striking girl with electric blue hair and a glittering pin in her left eyebrow frowned at the photo and said finally yeah she'd maybe seen Marissa "like with her mother? But when, like maybe it wasn't yesterday because I don't think I was here yesterday, might've been last week? I don't know."

Skatskill Day School was in a stage of siege. TV crews on the front walk, reporters and press photographers at all the entrances. Crisis counselors met with children in small groups through the day following Marissa's disappearance and there was an air in all the classrooms of shock, as if in the wake of a single violent tremor of the earth. A number of parents had kept their children home from school, but this was not advised by school authorities: "There is no risk at Skatskill Day. Whatever happened to Marissa did not happen on school grounds, and would never have happened on school grounds." It was announced that school security had been immediately strengthened, and new security measures would begin on Monday. In Marissa Bantry's sixth grade class children were subdued, uneasy. After the counselor spoke, and asked if anyone had a question, the class sat silent until a boy raised his hand to ask if there would be a search party "like on TV, people going through woods and fields until they find the body?"

Not after a counselor spoke with eighth graders, but later in the day, an eighth grade girl named Anita Helder came forward hesitantly to speak with her teacher. Anita was a heavyset girl with a low C average who rarely spoke in class, and often asked to be excused for mysterious health reasons. She was a suspected drug-taker, but had never been caught. In class, she exuded a sulky, defiant manner if called upon by her teacher. Yet now she was saying, in an anxious, faltering voice, that maybe she had seen Marissa Bantry the previous day, on Fifteenth Street and Trinity, climbing into a minivan after school.

". . . I didn't know it was her then for sure, I don't know Marissa Bantry at all but I guess now it must've been her. Oh God I feel so bad I didn't try to stop her! I was like close enough to call out to her, 'Don't get in!' What I could see, the driver was leaning over and sort of pulling Marissa inside. It was a man, he had real dark hair kind of long on the sides but I couldn't see his face. The minivan was like silver-blue, the license plate was something like TZ 6 . . . Beyond that, I can't remember."

Anita's eyes welled with tears. She was visibly trembling, the memory so upset her.

By this time Skatskill detectives had questioned everyone on the school staff except for Mikal Zallman, thirty-one years old, computer consultant and part-time employee, who wasn't at the Skatskill Day School on Fridays.

It was an ugly expression. It was macho-ugly, the worst kind of ugly. It made him smile.

Feeding my rat. Alone.

Alone he'd driven out of Skatskill on Thursday afternoon immediately following his final class of the week. Alone driving north
in his trim Honda minivan along the Hudson River where the
river landscape so mesmerizes the eye, you wonder why you'd
ever given a damn for all that's petty, inconsequential. Wondering why you'd ever given a damn for the power of others to hurt
you. Or to accuse you with tearful eyes of hurting them.

He'd tossed a valise, his backpack, a few books, hiking boots
and a supply of trail food into the back of the van. Always he
traveled light. As soon as he left Skatskill he ceased to think of
his life there. It was of little consequence really, a professional
life arranged to provide him with this freedom. *Feeding my rat.*

There was a woman in Skatskill, a married woman. He knew
the signs. She was lonely in her marriage amid yearning to be
saved from her loneliness. Often she invited him as if impulsively, without premeditation. *Come to dinner, Mikal? Tonight?*
He had been vague about accepting, this time. He had not
wanted to see the disappointment in her eyes. He felt a tug of
affection for her, he recognized her hurt, her resentment, her
confusion, she was a colleague of his at the Skatskill School
whom he saw often in the company of others, there was a rapport between them, Zallman acknowledged, but he did not
want to be involved with her or with any woman, not now.
He was thirty-one, and no longer naive. More and more he
lived for *feeding my rat.*

It was arrogant, was it, this attitude? Selfish. He'd been told so, more than once. Living so much in his own head, and for himself.

He hadn't married, he doubted he would ever marry. The prospect of children made his heart sink: bringing new lives into the uncertainty and misery of this world, in the early twenty-first century!

He much preferred his secret life. It was an innocent life. Running each morning, along the river. Hiking, mountain climbing. He did not hunt or fish, he had no need to destroy life to enhance his own. Mostly it was exulting in his body. He was only a moderately capable hiker. He hadn't the endurance or the will to run a marathon. He wasn't so fanatic, he wanted merely to be alone where he could exert his body pleasurably. Or maybe to the edge of pain.

One summer in his mid-twenties he'd gone backpacking alone in Portugal, Spain, northern Morocco. In Tangier he'd experimented with the hallucinatory *kif* which was the most extreme form of aloneness and the experience had shaken and exhilarated him and brought him back home to reinvent himself. Michael, now Mikal.

Feeding my rat meant this freedom. Meant he'd failed to drop by her house as she had halfway expected he would. And he had not telephoned, either. It was a way of allowing the woman to know he didn't want to be involved, he would not be involved.

In turn, she and her husband would not provide Mikal Zallman with an alibi for those crucial hours.

When, at 5:18 P.M. of Friday, April 11, returning to his car along a steep hiking trail, he happened to see what appeared to be a New York State troopers' vehicle in the parking lot ahead, he had no reason to think *They've come for me.* Even when he saw that two uniformed officers were looking into the rear windows of his minivan, the lone vehicle in the lot parked near the foot of the trail, because it had been the first vehicle of the day parked in the lot, the sight did not alarm or alert him. So confident in himself he felt, and so guiltless.

"Hey. What d'you want?"

Naively, almost conversationally he called to the troopers, who were now staring at him, and moving toward him.

Afterward he would recall how swiftly and unerringly the men moved. One called out, "Are you Mikal Zallman" and the other called, sharply, before Zallman could reply, "Keep your hands where we can see them, sir."

Hands? What about his hands? What were they saying about his hands?

He'd been sweating inside his T-shirt and khaki shorts and his hair was sticking against the nape of his neck. He'd slipped and fallen on the trail once, his left knee was scraped, throbbing. He was not so exuberant as he'd been in the fresh clear air of morning. He held his hands before him, palms uplifted in a gesture of annoyed supplication.

What did these men want with *him*? It had to be a mistake.

. . . *staring into the back of the minivan. He'd consented to a quick search. Trunk, interior. Glove compartment. What the hell, he had nothing to hide. Were they looking for drugs? A concealed weapon? He saw the way in which they were staring at two paperback books he'd tossed onto the rear window ledge weeks ago, Roth's* The Dying Animal *and Ovid's* The Art of Love. *On the cover of the first was a sensuously reclining Modligliani nude in rich flesh tones, with prominent pink-nippled breasts. On the cover of the other was a classical nude, marmoreal white female with a full, shapely body and blank, blind eyes.*

It was Taboo to utter aloud the Corn Maiden's name.

It was Taboo to touch the Corn Maiden except as Jude guided.

For Jude was the Priest of the Sacrifice. No one else.

What does Taboo mean, it means death. If you disobey.

Jude took Polaroid pictures of the Corn Maiden sleeping on her bier. Arms crossed on her flat narrow chest, cornsilk hair spread like pale flames around her head. Some pictures, Jude was beside the Corn Maiden. We took pictures of her smiling, and her eyes shiny and dilated.

For posterity, Jude said. For the record.

It was Taboo to utter the Corn Maiden's actual name aloud and yet: everywhere in Skatskill that name was being spoken! And everywhere in Skatskill her face was posted!

Missing Girl. Abduction Feared. State of Emergency.

It is so easy, Jude said. To make the truth your own.

But Jude was surprised too, we thought. That it was so real, what had only been for so long Jude O's *idea.*

Ju*dith!*

Mrs. Trahern called in her whiny old-woman voice, we had to troop into her smelly bedroom where she was propped up in some big old antique brass bed like a nutty queen watching TV where footage of the *missing Skatskill Day girl* was being shown.

Chiding, You girls! Look what has happened to one of your little classmates! Did you know this poor child?

Jude mumbled no Grandma.

Well. You would not be in a class with a retarded child, I suppose.

Jude mumbled no Grandma.

Well. See that you never speak with strangers, Judith! Report anyone who behaves strangely with you, or is seen lurking around the neighborhood. Promise me!

Jude mumbled okay Grandma, I promise.

Denise and Anita mumbled Me, too, Mrs. Trahern. For it seemed to be expected.

Next, Mrs. Trahern made Jude come to her bed, to take Jude's hands in her clawy old-woman hands. I have not always been a good grandma, I know. As the judge's widow there are so many demands on my time. But I am your grandma, Judith. I am your only blood kin who cares for you, dear. You know that, I hope?

Jude mumbled Yes Grandma, I know.

Has vanished.

We are among the few known survivors.

. . . terrorist attack. Nuclear war. Fires.

New York City is a gaping hole. The George Washington Bridge is crashed into the river. Washington, D.C., is gone.

So the Corn Maiden was told. So the Corn Maiden believed in her Rapture.

Many times we said these words Jude had made us memorize. The world as we have known it has vanished. There is no TV now. No newspapers. No electricity. We are among the few known survivors. We must be brave, everyone else is gone. All the adults are gone. All our mothers.

The Corn Maiden opened her mouth to shriek but she had not the strength. Her eyes welled with tears, lapsing out of focus.

All our mothers. So exciting!

Only candles to be lighted, solemnly. To keep away the night.

The Corn Maiden was informed that we had to ration our food supplies. For there were no stores now, all of Skatskill was gone. The Food Mart was gone. Main Street was gone. The Mall.

Jude knew, to maintain the Rapture the Corn Maiden must be fed very little. For Jude did not wish to bind her wrists and ankles, that were so fragile-seeming. Jude did not wish to gag her, to terrify her. For then the Corn Maiden would fear us and not trust and adore us as her protectors.

The Corn Maiden must be treated with reverence, respect, kindness, and firmness. She must never guess the fate that will be hers.

The Corn Maiden's diet was mostly liquids. Water, transparent fruit juices like apple, grapefruit. And milk.

It was Taboo Jude said for the Corn Maiden to ingest any foods except white foods. And any foods containing bones or skins.

These foods were soft, crumbly or melted foods. Cottage cheese, plain yogurt, ice cream. The Corn Maiden was not a retarded child as some of the TV stations were saying but she was not shrewd-witted, Jude said. For these foods we fed her were refrigerated, and she did not seem to know.

Of course, finely ground in these foods were powdery-white tranquilizers, to maintain the Rapture.

The Corn Maiden of the Onigara Sacrifice was to pass into the next world in a Rapture. Not in fear.

We took turns spooning small portions of food into the Corn Maiden's mouth that sucked like an infant's to be fed. So hungry, the Corn Maiden whimpered for more. No, no! There is no more she was told.

(How hungry we were, after these feedings! Denise and Anita went home to stuffstuff their faces.)

Jude did not want the Corn Maiden to excrete solid waste she said. Her bowels must be clean and pure for the Sacrifice.

Also we had to take her outside the storage room for this, half-carrying her to a bathroom in a corner of the cobwebby cellar that was a "recreation room" of some bygone time Jude said the 1970s that is ancient history now.

Only two times did we have to take the Corn Maiden to this bathroom, half-carried out, groggy and stumbling and her head lolling on her shoulders. All other times the Corn Maiden used the pot Jude had brought in from one of the abandoned greenhouses. A fancy Mexican ceramic pot, for the Corn Maiden to squat over, as we held her like a clumsy infant.

The Corn Maiden's pee! It was hot, bubbly. It had a sharp smell different from our own.

Like a big infant the Corn Maiden was becoming, weak and trusting in all her bones. Even her crying when she cried saying she wanted to go home, she wanted her mommy, where was her mommy she wanted her mommy was an infant's crying, with no strength or anger behind it.

Jude said all our mommies are gone, we must be brave without them. She would be safe with us Jude said stroking her hair. See, we would protect her better than her mommy had protected her.

Jude took cell-phone pictures of the Corn Maiden sitting up on her bier her face streaked with tears. The Corn Maiden was chalky white and the colors of the bier were so rich and silky. The Corn Maiden was so thin, you could see her collarbone jutting inside the white muslin nightgown Jude had clothed her in.

We did not doubt Jude. What Jude meant to do with the Corn Maiden we would not resist.

In the Onigara ceremony Jude said the Corn Maiden was slowly starved and her bowels cleaned out and purified and she was tied on an altar still living and a priest shot an arrow that had been blessed into her heart. And the heart was scooped out with a knife that had been blessed and touched to the lips of the priest and others of the tribe to bless them. And the heart and the Corn Maiden's body were then carried out into a field and buried in the earth to honor the Morning Star which is the sun and the Evening Star which is the moon and beg of them their blessing for the corn harvest.

Will the Corn Maiden be killed we wished to know but we could not ask Jude for Jude would be angered.

To ourselves we said Jude will kill the Corn Maiden, maybe! We shivered to think so. Denise smiled, and bit at her thumbnail, for she was jealous of the Corn Maiden. Not because the Corn Maiden had such beautiful silky hair but because Jude fussed over the Corn Maiden so, as Jude would not have fussed over Denise.

The Corn Maiden wept when we left her. When we blew out the candles and left her in darkness. We had to patrol the house we said. We had to look for fires and "gas leakage" we said. For the world as we have known it has come to an end, there were no adults now. We were the adults now.

We were our own mommies.

Jude shut the door, and padlocked it. The Corn Maiden's muffled sobs from inside. *Mommy! Mommy!* the Corn Maiden wept but there was no one to hear and even on the steps to the first floor you could no longer hear.

HATEHATEHATE you assholes Out There. The Corn Maiden was Jude O's perfect revenge.

At Skatskill Day we saw our hatred like scalding-hot lava rushing through the corridors and into the classrooms and cafeteria to burn our enemies alive. Even girls who were okay to us mostly would perish for they would rank us below the rest, wayway below the Hot Shit Cliques that ran the school and also the boys—all the boys. And the teachers, some of them had pissed us off and deserved death. Jude said Mr. Z. had "dissed" her and was the "target enemy" now.

Sometimes the vision was so fierce it was a rush better than E!

Out There it was believed that the *missing Skatskill girl* might have been kidnapped. A ransom note was awaited.

Or, it was believed the *missing girl* was the victim of a "sexual predator."

On TV came Leah Bantry, the mother, to appeal to whoever had taken her daughter saying, Please don't hurt Marissa, please release my daughter I love her so, begging please in a hoarse voice that sounded like she'd been crying a lot and her eyes haggard with begging so Jude stared at the woman with scorn.

Not so hot-shit now, are you Mrs. Brat-tee! Not so pretty-pretty.

It was surprising to Denise and Anita, that Jude hated Leah Bantry so. We felt sorry for the woman, kind of. Made us think

71

how our mothers would be, if we were gone, though we hated our mothers we were thinking they'd probably miss us, and be crying, too. It was a new way of seeing our moms. But Jude did not have a mom even to hate. Never spoke of her except to say she was Out West in L.A. We wanted to think that Jude's mom was a movie star under some different name, that was why she'd left Jude with Mrs. Trahern to pursue a film career. But we would never say this to Jude, for sure.

Sometimes Jude scared us. Like she'd maybe hurt *us*.

Wild! On Friday 7 P.M. news came BULLETIN—BREAKING NEWS—SKATSKILL SUSPECT IN CUSTODY. It was Mr. Zallman!

We shrieked with laughter. Had to press our hands over our mouths so old Mrs. Trahern would not hear.

Jude is flicking through the channels and there suddenly is Mr. Z. on TV! And some broadcaster saying in an excited voice that this man had been apprehended in Bear Mountain State Park and brought back to Skatskill to be questioned in the disappearance of Marissa Bantry and the shocker is: Mikal Zallman, thirty-one, is on the faculty of the Skatskill Day School.

Mr. Zallman's jaws were scruffy like he had not shaved in a while. His eyes were scared and guilty-seeming. He was wearing a T-shirt and khaki shorts like we would never see him at school and this was funny, too. Between two plainclothes detectives being led up the steps into police headquarters and at the top they must've jerked him under the arms, he almost turned his ankle.

We were laughing like hyenas. Jude crouched in front of the TV rocking back and forth, staring.

"Zallman claims to know nothing of Marissa Bantry. Police and rescue workers are searching the Bear Mountain area and will search through the night if necessary."

There was a cut to our school again, and Fifteenth Street traffic at night. ". . . unidentified witness, believed to be a classmate of Marissa Bantry, has told authorities that she witnessed Marissa being pulled into a Honda CR-V at this corner, Thursday after school. This vehicle has been tentatively identified as . . ."

Unidentified witness. That's me! Anita cried.

And a second "student witness" had come forward to tell the school principal that she had seen "the suspect Zallman" fondling Marissa Bantry, stroking her hair and whispering to her in the computer lab when he thought no one was around, only last week.

That's *me*! Denise cried.

And police had found a mother-of-pearl butterfly barrette on the ground near Zallman's parking space, behind his condominium residence. This barrette had been "absolutely identified" by Marissa Bantry's mother as a barrette Marissa had been wearing on Thursday.

We turned to Jude who was grinning.

We had not known that Jude had planned *this*. On her bicycle she must've gone to drop the barrette where it would be found.

We laughed so, we almost wet ourselves. Jude was just so *cool*.

But even Jude seemed surprised, kind of. That you could tell the wildest lie your own and every asshole would rush to believe.

Now she knew his name: *Mikal Zallman.*

The man who'd taken Marissa. One of Marissa's teachers at the Skatskill Day School.

It was a nightmare. All that Leah Bantry had done, what exertion of heart and soul, to enroll her daughter in a private school in which a pedophile was allowed to instruct elementary school children.

She had met Zallman, she believed. At one of the parents' evenings. Something seemed wrong, though: Zallman was young. You don't expect a young man to be a pedophile. An attractive man though with a hawkish profile, and not very warm. Not with Leah. Not that she could remember.

The detectives had shown her Zallman's photograph. They had not allowed her to speak with Zallman. Vaguely yes she did remember. But not what he'd said to her, if he had said anything. Very likely Leah has asked him about Marissa but what he'd said she could not recall.

And then, hadn't Zallman slipped away from the reception, early? By chance she'd seen him, the only male faculty member not wearing a necktie, hair straggling over his collar, disappearing from the noisy brightly lighted room.

He'd taken a polygraph, at his own request. The results were "inconclusive."

If I could speak with him. Please.

They were telling her no, Mrs. Bantry. Not a good idea.

This man who took Marissa if I could speak with him *please*.

In her waking state she pleaded. She would beg the detectives, she would throw herself on their mercy. Her entire conscious life was now begging, pleading, and bartering. And waiting.

Zallman is the one, isn't he? You have him, don't you? An eyewitness said she saw him. Saw him pull Marissa into a van with him. In broad daylight! And you found Marissa's barrette by his parking space *isn't that proof*!

To her, the desperate mother, it was certainly proof. The man had taken Marissa, he knew where Marissa was. The truth had to be wrung from him before it was too late.

On her knees she would beg to see Zallman promising not to become emotional and they told her no, for she would only become emotional in the man's presence. And Zallman, who had a lawyer now, would only become more adamant in his denial.

Denial! How could he . . . deny! He had taken Marissa, he knew where Marissa was.

She would beg *him*. She would show Zallman pictures of Marissa as a baby. She would plead with this man for her daughter's life if only if only if only for God's sake they would allow her.

Of course, it was impossible. The suspect was being questioned following a procedure, a strategy, to which Leah Bantry had no access. The detectives were professionals, Leah Bantry was an amateur. She was only the mother, an amateur.

The wheel, turning.

It was a very long Friday. The longest Friday of Leah's life.

Then abruptly it was Friday night, and then it was Saturday morning. And Marissa was still gone.

Zallman had been captured, yet Marissa was still gone.

He might have been tortured, in another time. To make him confess. The vicious pedophile, whose "legal rights" had to be honored.

Leah's heart beat in fury. Yet she was powerless, she could not intervene.

Saturday afternoon: approaching the time when Marissa would be missing for forty-eight hours.

Forty-eight hours! It did not seem possible.

She has drowned by now, Leah thought. She has suffocated for lack of oxygen.

She is starving. She has bled to death. Wild creatures on Bear Mountain have mutilated her small body.

She calculated: it would soon be fifty hours since Leah had last seen Marissa. Kissed her hurriedly good-bye in the car, in front of the school Thursday morning at eight. And (she forced herself to remember, she would not escape remembering) Leah hadn't troubled to watch her daughter run up the walk, and into the school. Pale gold hair shimmering behind her and just possibly (possibly!) at the door, Marissa had turned to wave good-bye to Mommy but Leah was already driving away.

And so, she'd had her opportunity. She would confess to her sister Avril *I let Marissa slip away.*

The great wheel, turning. And the wheel was Time itself, without pity.

She saw that now. In her state of heightened awareness bred of terror she saw. She had ceased to give a damn about "Leah Bantry" in the public eye. The distraught/negligent mother. Working mom, single mom, mom-with-a-drinking-problem. She'd been exposed as a liar. She'd been exposed as a female avid to sleep with another woman's husband and that husband her boss. She knew, the very police who were searching for Marissa's abductor were investigating her, too. Crude tabloids, TV journalism. Under a guise of sympathy, pity for her "plight."

None of this mattered, now. What the jackals said of her, and would say. She was bartering her life for Marissa's. Appealing to God in whom she was trying in desperation to believe. *If You would. Let Marissa be alive. Return Marissa to me. If You would hear my plea.* So there was no room to give a damn about herself, she had no scruples now, no shame. Yes she would consent to be interviewed on the cruelest and crudest of the New York City TV stations if that might help Marissa, somehow. Blinking into the blinding TV lights, baring her teeth in a ghastly nervous smile.

Never would she care again for the pieties of ordinary life. When on the phone her own mother began crying, asking why, why on earth had Leah left Marissa alone for so many hours,

Leah had interrupted the older woman coldly, "That doesn't matter now, Mother. Good-bye."

Neither of the elder Bantrys was in good health, they would not fly east to share their daughter's vigil. But Leah's older sister Avril flew up immediately from Washington to stay with her.

For years the sisters had not been close. There was a subtle rivalry between them, in which Leah had always felt belittled.

Avril, an investment attorney, was brisk and efficient answering the telephone, screening all e-mail. Avril checked the *Marissa* Web site constantly. Avril was on frank terms with the senior Skatskill detective working the case, who spoke circumspectly and with great awkwardness to Leah.

Avril called Leah to come listen to a voice-mail message that had come in while they'd been at police headquarters. Leah had told Avril about Davitt Stoop, to a degree.

It was Davitt, finally calling Leah. In a slow stilted voice that was not the warm intimate voice Leah knew he was saying *A terrible thing . . . This is a . . . terrible thing, Leah. We can only pray this madman is caught and that . . .* A long pause. You would have thought that Dr. Stoop had hung up but then he continued, more forcibly *I'm sorry for this terrible thing but Leah please don't try to contact me again. Giving my name to the police! The past twenty-four hours have been devastating for me. Our relationship was a mistake and it can't be continued, I am sure you understand. As for your position at the clinic I am sure you understand the awkwardness among all the staff if . . .*

78

Leah's heart beat in fury, she punched *erase* to extinguish the man's voice. Grateful that Avril, who'd tactfully left the room, could be relied upon not to ask about Davitt Stoop, nor even to offer sisterly solicitude.

Take everything from me. If You will leave me Marissa, the way we were.

"Mommy!"

It was Marissa's voice, but muffled, at a distance.

Marissa was trapped on the far side of a barrier of thick glass, Leah heard her desperate cries only faintly. Marissa was pounding the glass with her fists, smearing her damp face against it. But the glass was too thick to be broken. "Mommy! Help me, Mommy . . ." And Leah could not move to help the child, Leah was paralyzed. Something gripped her legs, quicksand, tangled ropes. If she could break free . . .

Avril woke her, abruptly. There was someone to see her, friends of Marissa's they said they were.

"H-Hello, Mrs. Branty . . . Bant*ry*. My name is . . ."

Three girls. Three girls from Skatskill Day. One of them, with faded-rust-red hair and glistening stone-colored eyes, was holding out to Leah an astonishing large bouquet of dazzling white flowers: long-stemmed roses, carnations, paperwhites, mums. The sharp astringent fragrance of the paperwhites prevailed.

The bouquet must have been expensive, Leah thought. She took it from the girl and tried to smile. "Why, thank you."

It was Sunday, midday. She'd sunk into a stupor after twenty hours of wakefulness. Seeing it was a warm, incongruously brightly sunny April day beyond the partly-drawn blinds on the apartment windows.

She would have to focus on these girls. She'd been expecting, from what Avril had said, younger children, Marissa's age. But these were adolescents. Thirteen, fourteen. In eighth grade, they'd said. Friends of Marissa's?

The visit would not last long. Avril, disapproving, hovered near.

Possibly Leah had invited them, the girls were seated in her living room. They were clearly excited, edgy. They glanced about like nervous birds. Leah supposed she should offer them Cokes but something in her resisted. Hurriedly she'd washed her face, dragged a comb through her snarled hair that no longer looked blond, but dust-colored. How were these girls Marissa's friends? Leah had never seen them before in her life.

Nor did their names mean anything to her. "Jude Trahern," "Denise . . ." The third name she'd failed to catch.

The girls were moist-eyed with emotion. So many neighbors had dropped by to express their concern, Leah supposed she had to endure it. The girl who'd given Leah the bouquet, Jude, was saying in a faltering nasal voice how sorry they were for what had happened to Marissa and how much they liked Marissa who was just about the nicest girl at Skatskill Day. If something like this had to happen too bad it couldn't happen to—well, somebody else.

The other girls giggled, startled at their friend's vehemence.

"But Marissa is so nice, and so sweet. Ma'am, we are praying for her safe return, every minute."

Leah stared at the girl. She had no idea how to reply.

Confused, she lifted the bouquet to her face. Inhaled the almost too rich paperwhite smell. As if the purpose of this visit was to bring Leah . . . What?

The girls were staring at her almost rudely. Of course, they were young, they knew no better. Their leader, Jude, seemed to be a girl with some confidence, though she wasn't the eldest or the tallest or the most attractive of the three.

Not attractive at all. Her face was fiercely plain as if she'd scrubbed it with steel wool. Her skin was chalky, mottled. You could sense the energy thrumming through her like an electric current, she was wound up so tightly.

The other girls were more ordinary. One was softly plump with a fattish pug face, almost pretty except for something smirky, insolent in her manner. The other girl had a sallow blemished skin, limp grease-colored hair, and oddly quivering, parted lips. All three girls wore grubby blue jeans, boys' shirts, and ugly square-toed boots.

". . . so we were wondering, Mrs. Bran—Bantry, if you would like us to, like, pray with you? Like, now? It's Palm Sunday. Next Sunday is Easter."

"What? Pray? Thank you but . . ."

"Because Denise and Anita and me, we have a feeling, we have a really strong feeling, Mrs. Bantry, that Marissa is alive. And Marissa is depending on us. So, if—"

Avril came forward quickly, saying the visit was ended.

"My sister has been under a strain, girls. I'll see you to the door."

The flowers slipped through Leah's fingers. She caught at some of them, clumsily. The others fell to the floor at her feet.

Two of the girls hurried to the door, held open by Avril, with frightened expressions. Jude, pausing, continued to smile in her earnest, pinched way. She'd taken a small black object out of her pocket. "May I take a picture, Mrs. Bantry?"

Before Leah could protest, she raised the cell phone and clicked. Leah's hand had flown up to shield her face, instinctively.

Avril said sharply, "Please. The visit is over, girls."

Jude murmured, on her way out, "We will pray for you anyway, Mrs. Bantry. Bye!"

The other girls chimed in *Bye! bye!* Avril shut the door behind them.

Leah threw the flowers away in the trash. White flowers!

At least, they hadn't brought her calla lilies.

. . . in motion. Tracing and retracing The Route. Sometimes on foot, sometimes in her car. Sometimes with Avril but more often alone. "I need to get out! I can't breathe in here! I need to see what Marissa saw."

These days were very long days. And yet, in all of the hours of these days, nothing happened.

Marissa was still gone, still gone.

Like a clock's ticking: still, still gone. Each time you checked, still gone.

She had her cell phone of course. If there was news.

She walked to the Skatskill Day School and positioned herself at the front door of the elementary grades wing, which was the door Marissa would have used, would have left by on Thursday afternoon. From this position she began The Route.

To the front sidewalk and east along Pinewood. Across Pinewood to Mahopac Avenue and continue east past Twelfth Street, Thirteenth Street, Fourteenth Street, Fifteenth Street. At Fifteenth and Trinity, the witness had claimed to see Mikal Zallman pull Marissa Bantry into his Honda CR-V van, and drive away.

Either it had happened that way, or it had not.

There was only the single witness, a Skatskill Day student whom police would not identify.

Leah believed that Zallman was the man and yet: there was something missing. Like a jigsaw puzzle piece. A very small piece, yet crucial.

Since thc girls' visit. Since the bouquet of dazzling white flowers. That small twitchy smile Leah did not wish to interpret as taunting, of the girl named Jude.

We will pray for you anyway, Mrs. Bantry. Bye!

Important for Leah to walk briskly. To keep in motion.

There is a deep-sea creature, perhaps a shark, that must keep in motion constantly, otherwise it will die. Leah was becoming this creature, on land. She believed that news of Marissa's death would come to her only if she, the mother, were still; there was a kind of deadness in being still; but if she was in motion, tracing and retracting Marissa's route . . . "It's like Marissa is with me. Is *me*."

She knew that people along The Route were watching her. Everyone in Skatskill knew her face, her name. Everyone knew why she was out on the street, tracing and retracing The Route. A slender woman in shirt, slacks, dark glasses. A woman who had made a merely perfunctory attempt to disguise herself, dusty-blond hair partly hidden beneath a cap.

She knew the observers were pitying her. And blaming her.

Still, when individuals spoke to her, as a few did each time she traced The Route, they were invariably warm, sympathetic. Some of them, both men and women, appeared to be deeply sympathetic. Tears welled in their eyes. *That bastard* they spoke of Zallman. *Has he confessed yet?*

In Skatskill the name *Zallman* was known now, notorious. That the man was—had been—a member of the faculty at the Skatskill Day School had become a local scandal.

The rumor was, Zallman had a record of prior arrests and convictions as a sexual predator. He'd been fired from previous teaching positions but had somehow managed to be hired at the prestigious Skatskill School. The school's beleaguered principal had given newspaper and TV interviews vigorously denying this rumor, yet it prevailed.

Bantry, Zallman. The names now luridly linked. In the tabloids photos of the missing girl and "suspect" were printed side by side. Several times, Leah's photograph was included as well.

In her distraught state yet Leah was able to perceive the irony of such a grouping: a mock family.

Leah had given up hoping to speak with Zallman. She supposed it was a ridiculous request. If he'd taken Marissa he was a psychopath and you don't expect a psychopath to tell the truth. If he had not taken Marissa . . .

"If it's someone else. They will never find him."

The Skatskill police had not yet arrested Zallman. Temporarily, Zallman had been released. His lawyer had made a terse public statement that he was "fully cooperating" with the police investigation. But what he had told them, what could possibly be of worth that he had told them, Leah didn't know.

Along The Route, Leah saw with Marissa's eyes. The facades of houses. On Fifteenth Street, storefronts. No one had corroborated the eyewitness's testimony about seeing Marissa pulled into a van in full daylight on busy Fifteenth Street. Wouldn't anyone else have seen? And who had the eyewitness been? Since the three girls had dropped by to see her, Leah was left with a new sensation of unease.

Not Marissa's friends. Not those girls.

She crossed Trinity and continued. This was a slight extension of Marissa's route home from school. It was possible, Marissa dropped by the 7-Eleven to buy a snack on Tuesdays/Thursdays when Leah returned home late.

Taped to the front plate-glass door of the 7-Eleven was

HAVE YOU SEEN ME?

MARISSA BANTRY, 11

MISSING SINCE APRIL 10

Marissa's smiling eyes met hers as Leah pushed the door open.

Inside, trembling, Leah removed her dark glasses. She was feeling dazed. Wasn't certain if this was full wakefulness or a fugue state. She was trying to orient herself. Staring at a stack of thick Sunday *New York Times*. The front-page headlines were of U.S.-Iraq issues and for a confused moment Leah thought *Maybe none of it has happened yet.*

Maybe Marissa was outside, waiting in the car.

The gentlemanly Indian clerk stood behind the counter in his usual reserved, yet attentive posture. He was staring at her strangely, Leah saw, as he would never have done in the past.

Of course, he recognized her now. Knew her name. All about her. She would never be an anonymous customer again. Leah saw, with difficulty, for her eyes were watering, a second HAVE YOU SEEN ME? taped conspicuously to the front of the cash register.

Wanting to embrace the man, wordless. Wanted to press herself into his arms and burst into tears.

Instead she wandered in one of the aisles. How like an overexposed photograph the store was. So much to see, yet you saw nothing.

Thank God, there were no other customers at the moment.

Saw her hand reach out for—what? A box of Kleenex.

Pink, the color Marissa preferred.

She went to the counter to pay. Smiled at the clerk who was smiling very nervously at her, clearly agitated by the sight of her. His always-so-friendly blond customer! Leah was going to thank him for having posted the notices, and she was going to ask him if he'd ever seen Marissa in his store alone, without her, when suddenly the man said, to her astonishment, "Mrs. Bantry, I know of your daughter and what has happened, that is so terrible. I watch all the time, to see what will come of it." Behind the counter was a small portable TV, volume turned down. "Mrs. Bantry, I want to say, when the police came here, I was nervous and not able to remember so well, but now I do remember, I am more certain, yes I did see your daughter that day, I believe. She did come into the store. She was alone, and then there was another girl. They went out together."

The Indian clerk spoke in a flood of words. His eyes were repentant, pleading.

"When? When was—"

"That day, Mrs. Bantry. That the police have asked about. Last week."

"Thursday? You saw Marissa on Thursday?"

But now he was hesitating. Leah spoke too excitedly.

"I think so, yes. I cannot be certain. That is why I did not want to tell the police, I did not want to get into trouble with them. They are impatient with me, I don't know English so well. The questions they ask are not so easy to answer while they wait staring at you."

Leah didn't doubt that the Indian clerk was uneasy with the Caucasian Skatskill police, she was uneasy with them herself.

She said, "Marissa was with a girl, you say? What did this girl look like?"

The Indian clerk frowned. Leah saw that he was trying to be as accurate as possible. He had probably not looked at the girls very closely, very likely he could not distinguish among most of them. He said, "She was older than your daughter, I am sure. She was not too tall, but older. Not so blond-haired."

"You don't know her, do you? Her name?"

"No. I do not know their names any of them." He paused, frowning. His jaws tightened. "Some of them, the older ones, I think this girl is one of them, with their friends they come in here after school and take things. They steal, they break. They rip open bags, to eat. Like pigs they are. They think I can't see them but I know what they do. Five days a week they come in here, many of them. They are daring me to shout at them, and if I would touch them—"

His voice trailed off, tremulous.

"This girl. What did she look like?"

". . . a white skin. A strange color of hair like . . . a color of something red, faded."

He spoke with some repugnance. Clearly, the mysterious girl was not attractive in his eyes.

Red-haired. Pale-red-haired. Who?

Jude Trahern. The girl who'd brought the flowers. The girl who spoke of praying for Marissa's safe return.

Were they friends, then? Marissa had had a friend?

Leah was feeling light-headed. The fluorescent lighting began to tilt and spin. There was something here she could not grasp. *Pray with you. Next Sunday is Easter.* She had more to ask of this kindly man but her mind had gone blank.

"Thank you. I . . . have to leave now."

"Don't tell them, Mrs. Bantry? The police? Please?"

Blindly Leah pushed through the door.

"Mrs. Bantry?" The clerk hurried after her, a bag in his hand. "You are forgetting."

The box of pink Kleenex.

Flying Dutchman. Dutchwoman. She was becoming. Always in motion, terrified of stopping, Returning home to her sister.

Any news?

None.

Behind the drab little mini-mall she was drifting, dazed. She would tell the Skatskill detectives what the Indian clerk had told

90

her—she must tell them. If Marissa had been in the store on Thursday afternoon, then Marissa could not have been pulled into a minivan on Fifteenth Street and Trinity, two blocks back toward school. Not by Mikal Zallman, or by anyone. Marissa must have continued past Trinity. After the 7-Eleven she would have circled back to Fifteenth Street again, and walked another half block to home.

Unless she'd been pulled into the minivan on Fifteenth Street and Van Buren. The eyewitness had gotten the streets wrong. She'd been closer to home.

Unless the Indian clerk was confused about days, times. Or, for what purpose Leah could not bear to consider, lying to her.

"Not him! Not him, too."

She refused to think that was a possibility. Her mind simply shut blank, in refusal.

She was walking now slowly, hardly conscious of her surroundings. A smell of rancid food assailed her nostrils. Only a few employees' cars were parked behind the mini-mall. The pavement was stained and littered, a single Dumpster overflowing trash. At the back of the Chinese takeout several scrawny cats were rummaging in food scraps and froze at Leah's approach before running away in panic.

"Kitties! I'm not going to hurt you."

The feral cats' terror mocked her own. Their panic was hers, misplaced, to no purpose.

Leah wondered: what were the things Marissa did, when Leah wasn't with her? For years they had been inseparable: mother, daughter. When Marissa had been a very small child, even before she could walk, she'd tried to follow her mother everywhere, from room to room. *Mom-my! Where Mom-my going!* Now, Marissa did many things by herself. Marissa was growing up. Dropping by the 7-Eleven, with other children after school. Buying a soft drink, a bag of something crunchy, salty. It was innocent enough. No child should be punished for it. Leah gave Marissa pocket change, as she called it, for just such impromptu purchases, though she disapproved of junk food.

Leah felt a tightening in her chest, envisioning her daughter in the 7-Eleven store the previous Thursday, buying something from the Indian clerk. Then, he had not known her name. A day or two later, everyone in Skatskill knew Marissa Bantry's name.

Of course it probably meant nothing. That Marissa had walked out of the store with a classmate from school. Nothing unusual about that. She could imagine with what polite stiff expressions the police would respond to such a "tip."

In any case, Marissa would still have returned to Fifteenth Street on her way home. So busy, dangerous at that hour of day.

It was there on Fifteenth Street that the "unidentified" classmate had seen Marissa being pulled into the Honda. Leah wondered if the witness was the red-haired Jude.

Exactly what the girl had told police officers, Leah didn't know. The detectives exuded an air, both assuring and frustrating, of knowing more than they were releasing at the present time.

Leah found herself at the edge of the paved area. Staring at a steep hill of uncultivated and seemingly worthless land.

Strange how in the midst of an affluent suburb there yet remain these stretches of vacant land, uninhabitable. The hill rose to Highgate Avenue a half mile away, invisible from this perspective. You would not guess that "historical" old homes and mansions were located on the crest of this hill, property worth millions of dollars. The hill was profuse with crawling vines, briars, and stunted trees. The accumulation of years of windblown litter and debris made it look like an informal dump. There was a scurrying sound somewhere just inside the tangle of briars, a furry shape that appeared and disappeared so swiftly Leah scarcely saw it.

Behind the Dumpster, hidden from her view, the colony of wild cats lived, foraged for food, fiercely interbred, and died the premature deaths of feral creatures. They would not wish to be "pets"—they had no capacity to receive the affection of humans. They were, in clinical terms, undomesticable.

Leah was returning to her car when she heard a nasal voice in her wake:

"Mrs. Bran-ty! H'lo."

Leah turned uneasily to see the frizz-haired girl who'd given her the flowers.

Jude. Jude Trahern.

Now it came to Leah: there was a Trahern Square in downtown Skatskill, named for a Chief Justice Trahern decades ago. One of the old Skatskill names. On Highgate, there was a Trahern estate, one of the larger houses, nearly hidden from the road.

This strange glistening-eyed girl. There was something of the sleek white rat about her. Yet she smiled uncertainly at Leah, clumsily straddling her bicycle.

"Are you following me?"

"Ma'am, no. I . . . just saw you."

Wide-eyed the girl appeared sincere, uneasy. Yet Leah's nerves were on edge, she spoke sharply: "What do you want?"

The girl stared at Leah as if something very bright glared from Leah's face that was both blinding and irresistible. She wiped nervously at her nose. "I . . . I want to say I'm sorry, for saying dumb things before. I guess I made things worse."

Made things worse! Leah smiled angrily, this was so absurd.

"I mean, Denise and Anita and me, we wanted to help. We did the wrong thing, I guess. Coming to see you."

"Were you the 'unidentified witness' who saw my daughter being pulled into a minivan?"

The girl blinked at Leah, blank-faced. For a long moment Leah would have sworn that she was about to speak, to say something urgent. Then she ducked her head, wiped again at her nose, shrugged self-consciously and muttered what sounded like, "I guess not."

"All right. Good-bye. I'm leaving now."

Leah frowned and turned away, her heart beating hard. How badly she wanted to be alone! But the rat-girl was too obtuse to comprehend. With the dogged persistence of an overgrown child she followed Leah at an uncomfortably close distance of about three feet, pedaling her bicycle awkwardly. The bicycle was an expensive Italian make of the kind a serious adult cyclist might own.

At last Leah paused, to turn back. "*Do* you have something to tell me, Jude?"

The girl looked astonished.

"'Jude'! You remember my name?"

Leah would recall afterward this strange moment. The exultant look in Jude Trahern's face. Her chalky skin mottled with pleasure.

Leah said, "Your name is unusual, I remember unusual names. If you have something to tell me about Marissa, I wish you would."

"Me? What would I know?"

"You aren't the witness from school?"

"What witness?"

"A classmate of Marissa's says she saw a male driver pull Marissa into his minivan on Fifteenth Street. But you aren't that girl?"

Jude shook her head vehemently. "You can't always believe 'eyewitnesses,' Mrs. Bantry."

"What do you mean?"

"It's well known. It's on TV all the time, police shows. An eyewitness swears she sees somebody, and she's wrong. Like, with Mr. Zallman, people are all saying it's him but, like, it might be somebody else."

The girl spoke rapidly, fixing Leah with her widened shining eyes.

"Jude, what do you mean, somebody else? Who?"

Excited by Leah's attention, Jude lost her balance on the bicycle, and nearly stumbled. Clumsily she began walking it again. Gripping the handlebars so tightly her bony knuckles gleamed white.

She was breathing quickly, lips parted. She spoke in a lowered conspiratorial voice.

"See, Mrs. Bantry, Mr. Zallman is like notorious. He comes on to girls if they're pretty-pretty like Marissa. Like some of the kids were saying on TV, he's got these laser eyes." Jude shivered, thrilled.

Leah was shocked. "If everybody knows about Zallman, why didn't anybody tell? Before this happened? How could a man like that be allowed to teach?" She paused, anxious. Thinking *Did Marissa know? Why didn't she tell me?*

Jude giggled. "You got to wonder why any of them *teach*. I mean, why'd anybody want to hang out with *kids*! Not just some weird guy, but females, too." She smiled, seeming not to see how Leah stared at her. "Mr. Z. is kind of fun. He's this 'master'—he calls himself. On line, you can click onto him he's 'Master of Eyes.' Little kids, girls, he'd come on to after school, and tell them be sure not to tell anybody, see. Or they'd be 'real sorry.'" Jude made a twisting motion with her hands as if wringing an invisible neck. "He likes girls with nice long hair he can brush."

"Brush?"

"Sure. Mr. Zallman has this wire brush, like. Calls it a little-doggy-brush. He runs it through your hair for fun. I mean, it used to be fun. I hope the cops took the brush when they arrested him, like for evidence. Hell, he never came on to me, I'm not pretty-pretty."

Jude spoke haughtily, with satisfaction. Fixing Leah with her curious stone-colored eyes.

Leah knew that she was expected to say, with maternal solicitude, *Oh, but you are pretty, Jude! One day, you will be.*

In different circumstances she was meant to frame the rat-girl's hot little face in her cool hands, comfort her. *One day you will be loved, Jude. Don't feel bad.*

"You were saying there might be—somebody else? Not Zallman but another person?"

Jude said, sniffing, "I wanted to tell you before, at your house, but you seemed, like, not to want to hear. And that other lady was kind of glaring at us. She didn't want us to stay."

"Jude, please. Who is this person you're talking about?"

"Mrs. Branly, Bant-ry, like I said Marissa is a good friend of mine. She is! Some kids make fun of her, she's a little slow they say but I don't think Marissa is slow, not really. She tells me all kinds of secrets, see?" Jude paused, drawing a deep breath. "She said, she missed her dad."

It was as if Jude had reached out to pinch her. Leah was speechless.

"Marissa was always saying she hates it here in Skatskill. She wanted to be with her dad, she said. Some place called 'Berkeley' —in California. She wanted to go there to live."

Jude spoke with the ingratiating air of one child informing on another to a parent. Her lips quivered, she was so excited.

Still Leah was unable to respond. Trying to think what to say except her brain seemed to be partly shutting down as if she'd had a small stroke.

Jude said innocently, "I guess you didn't know this, Mrs. Bantry?" She bit at her thumbnail, squinting.

"Marissa told you that? She told you—those things?"

"Are you mad at me, Mrs. Bantry? You wanted me to tell."

"Marissa told you—she wanted to live with her 'dad'? Not with her mother but with her 'dad'?"

Leah's peripheral vision had narrowed. There was a shadowy funnel-shape at the center of which the girl with the chalky skin and frizzed hair squinted and grinned, in a show of repentance.

"I just thought you would want to know, see, Mrs. Bantry? Like, maybe Marissa ran away? Nobody is saying that, everybody thinks it's Mr. Zallman, like the cops are thinking it's got to be him. Sure, maybe it is. But—maybe!—Marissa called her dad, and asked him to come get her? Something weird like that? And it was a secret from you? See, a lot of times Marissa would talk that way, like a little kid. Like, not thinking about her mother's feelings. And I told her, 'Your mom, she's real nice, she'd be hurt real bad, Marissa, if you—'"

Leah couldn't hold back the tears any longer. It was as if she'd lost her daughter for the second time.

His first was to assume that, since he knew nothing of the disappearance of Marissa Bantry, he could not be "involved" in it.

His second was not to contact a lawyer immediately. As soon as he realized exactly why he'd been brought into police headquarters for questioning.

His third seemed to be to have lived the wrong life.

Pervert. Sex offender. Pedophile.
Kidnapper/rapist/murderer.
Mikal Zallman, thirty-one. Suspect.

"Mother, it's Mikal. I hope you haven't seen the news already, I have something very disturbing to tell you . . ."

Nothing! He knew nothing.

The name MARISSA BANTRY meant nothing to him.

Well, not initially. He couldn't be sure.

In his agitated state, not knowing what the hell they were getting at with their questions, he couldn't he sure.

"Why are you asking me? Has something happened to 'Marissa Bantry'?"

Next, they showed him photographs of the girl.

Yes: now he recognized her. The long blond hair, that was sometimes plaited. One of the quieter pupils. Nice girl. He recognized the picture but could not have said the girl's name because, look:

"I'm not these kids' teacher, exactly. I'm a 'consultant.' I don't have a homeroom. I don't have regular classes with them. In the high school, one of the math instructors teaches computer science. I don't get to know the kids by name, like their other instructors do."

He was speaking quickly, an edge to his voice. It was uncomfortably cold in the room, yet he was perspiring.

As in a cartoon of police interrogation. *They sweated it out of the suspect.*

Strictly speaking, it wasn't true that Zallman didn't know students' names. He knew the names of many students. Certainly, he knew their faces. Especially the older students, some of whom were extremely bright, and engaging. But he had not known Marissa Bantry's name, the shy little blond child had made so little an impression on him.

Nor had he spoken with her personally. He was certain.

"Why are you asking me about this girl? If she's missing from home what is the connection with *me*?"

That edge to Zallman's voice. Not yet angry, only just impatient.

He was willing to concede, yes: if a child has been missing for more than twenty-four hours that was serious. If eleven-year-old Marissa Bantry was missing, it was a terrible thing.

"But it has nothing to do with *me*."

They allowed him to speak. They were tape recording his precious words. They did not appear to be passing judgment on him, he was not receiving the impression that they believed him involved with the disappearance, only just a few questions to put to him, to aid in their investigation. They explained to him that it was in his best interests to cooperate fully with them, to straighten out the misunderstanding, or whatever it was, a misidentification perhaps, before he left police headquarters.

"Misidentification"? What was that?

He was becoming angry, defiant. Knowing he was God-damned innocent of any wrongdoing, no matter how trivial: traffic violations, parking tickets. *He was innocent!* So he insisted upon taking a lie-detector test.

Another mistake.

Seventeen hours later an aggressive stranger now retained as Mikal Zallman's criminal lawyer was urging him, "Go home, Mikal. If you can, sleep. You will need your sleep. Don't speak with anyone except people you know and trust and assume yourself under surveillance and whatever you do, man—don't try to contact the missing girl's mother."

Please understand I am not the one. Not the madman who has taken your beautiful child. There has been some terrible misunderstanding but I swear I am innocent, Mrs. Bantry, we've never met but please allow me to commiserate with you, this nightmare we seem to be sharing.

Driving home to North Tarrytown. Oncoming headlights blinding his eyes. Tears streaming from his eyes. Now the adrenaline rush was subsiding, leaking out like water in a clogged drain, he was beginning to feel a hammering in his head that was the worst headache pain he'd ever felt in his life.

Jesus! What if it was a cerebral hemorrhage . . .

He would die. His life would be over. It would be judged that his guilt had provoked the hemorrhage. His name would never be cleared.

He'd been so cocky and arrogant coming into police head-quarters, confident he'd be released within the hour, and now. A wounded animal limping for shelter. He could not keep up with traffic on route 9, he was so sick. Impatient drivers sounded their horns. A massive SUV pulled up to within inches of Zall-man's car bumper.

He knew! Ordinarily he was an impatient driver himself. Disgusted with overly cautious drivers on route 9 and now he'd become one of these, barely mobile at twenty miles an hour.

Whoever they were who hated him, who had entangled him in this nightmare, they had struck a first, powerful blow.

Zallman's bad luck, one of his fellow tenants was in the rear lobby of his building, waiting for the elevator, when Zallman staggered inside. He was unshaven, disheveled, smelling frankly of his body. He saw the other man staring at him, at first startled, recognizing him; then with undisguised repugnance.

But I didn't! I am not the one.

The police would not have released me if.

Zallman let his fellow tenant take the elevator up, alone.

Zallman lived on the fifth floor of the so-called condominium village. He had never thought of his three sparely furnished rooms as "home" nor did he think of his mother's Upper East Side brownstone as "home" any longer: it was fair to say that Zallman had no home.

It was near midnight of an unnamed day. He'd lost days of his life. He could not have stated with confidence the month, the year. His head throbbed with pain. Fumbling with the key to his darkened apartment he heard the telephone inside ringing with the manic air of a telephone that has been ringing repeatedly.

Released for the time being. Keep your cell phone with you at all times for you may be contacted by police. Do not REPEAT DO NOT leave the area. A bench warrant will be issued for your arrest in the event that you attempt to leave the area.

"It isn't that I am innocent, Mother. I know that I am innocent! The shock of it is, people seem to believe that I might not be. A lot of people."

It was a fact. A lot of people.

He would have to live with that fact, and what it meant of Mikal Zallman's place in the world, for a long time.

Keep your hands in sight, sir.

That had been the beginning. His wounded brain fixed obsessively upon that moment, at Bear Mountain.

The state troopers. Staring at him. As if.

(Would they have pulled their revolvers and shot him down, if he'd made a sudden ambiguous gesture? It made him sick to think so. It should have made him grateful that it had not happened but in fact it made him sick.)

Yet the troopers had asked him politely enough if they could search his vehicle. He'd hesitated only a moment before consenting. Sure it annoyed him as a private citizen who'd broken no laws and as a (lapsed) member of the ACLU but why not, he knew there was nothing in the minivan to catch the troopers' eyes. He didn't even smoke marijuana any longer. He'd never carried a concealed weapon, never even owned a gun. So the troopers looked through the van, and found nothing. No idea what the hell they were looking for but he'd felt a gloating sort of relief that they hadn't found it. Seeing the way they were staring at the covers of the paperback books in the backseat he'd tossed there weeks ago and had more or less forgotten.

Female nudes, and so what?

"Good thing it isn't kiddie porn, officers, eh? That stuff is illegal."

Even as a kid Zallman hadn't been able to resist wisecracking at inopportune moments.

Now, he had a lawyer. "His" lawyer.

A criminal lawyer whose retainer was fifteen thousand dollars.

They are the enemy.

Neuberger meant the Skatskill detectives, and beyond them the prosecutorial staff of the district, whose surface civility Zallman had been misinterpreting as a tacit sympathy with him, his predicament. It was a fact they'd sweated him, and he'd gone along with it naively, frankly. Telling him he was not *under arrest* only just *assisting in their investigation.*

His body had known, though. Increasingly anxious, restless, needing to urinate every twenty minutes. He'd been flooded with adrenaline like a cornered animal.

His blood pressure had risen, he could feel pulses pounding in his ears. Damned stupid to request a polygraph at such a time but—he was an innocent man, wasn't he?

Should have called a lawyer as soon as they'd begun asking him about the missing child. Once it became clear that this was a serious situation, not a mere misunderstanding or misidentification by an unnamed "eyewitness." (One of Zallman's own students? Deliberately lying to hurt him? For Christ's sake *why?*) So at last he'd called an older cousin, a corporation attorney, to whom he had not spoken since his father's funeral, and explained the situation to him, this ridiculous situation, this nightmare situation, but he had to take it seriously since obviously he was a suspect and so: would Joshua recommend a good criminal attorney who could get to Skatskill immediately, and intercede for him with the police?

His cousin had been so stunned by Zallman's news he'd barely been able to speak. "Y-You? Mikal? You're arrested—?"

"No. I am not arrested, Joshua."

He believes I might be guilty. My own cousin believes I might be a sexual predator.

Still, within ninety minutes, after a flurry of increasingly desperate phone calls, Zallman had retained a Manhattan criminal lawyer named Neuberger who didn't blithely assure him, as Zallman halfway expected he would, that there was nothing to worry about.

TARRYTOWN RESIDENT QUESTIONED

IN ABDUCTION OF 11-YEAR-OLD

SEARCH FOR MARISSA CONTINUES

SKATSKILL DAY INSTRUCTOR IN POLICE CUSTODY

6TH GRADER STILL MISSING

SKATSKILL DAY INSTRUCTOR QUESTIONED BY POLICE

TENTATIVE IDENTIFICATION OF MINIVAN

BELIEVED USED IN ABDUCTION

MIKAL ZALLMAN, 31, COMPUTER CONSULTANT

QUESTIONED BY POLICE IN CHILD ABDUCTION

ZALLMAN: "I AM INNOCENT"

TARRYTOWN RESIDENT QUESTIONED BY POLICE

IN CHILD ABDUCTION CASE

Luridly spread across the front pages of the newspapers were photographs of the missing girl, the missing girl's mother, and "alleged suspect Mikal Zallman."

It was a local TV news magazine. Neuberger had warned him not to watch TV, just as he should not REPEAT SHOULD NOT answer the telephone if he didn't have caller ID, and for sure he should not answer his door unless he knew exactly who was there. Still, Zallman was watching TV fortified by a half dozen double-strength Tylenols that left him just conscious enough to stare at the screen disbelieving what he saw and heard.

Skatskill Day students, their faces blurred to disguise their identities, voices eerily slurred, telling a sympathetic female broadcaster their opinions of Mikal Zallman.

Mr Zallman, he's cool. I liked him okay.

Mr Zallman is kind of sarcastic I guess. He's okay with the smart kids but the rest of us it's like he's trying real hard and wants us to know.

I was so surprised! Mr. Zallman never acted like that, you know— weird. Not in computer lab.

Mr. Zallman has, like, these laser eyes? I always knew he was scary.

Mr. Zallman looks at us sometimes! It makes you shiver.

Some kids are saying he had, like, a hairbrush? To brush the girls' hair? I never saw it.

This hairbrush Mr. Zallman had, it was so weird! He never used it on me, guess I'm not pretty-pretty enough for him.

He'd help you in the lab after school if you asked. He was real nice to me. All this stuff about Marissa, I don't know. It makes me want to cry.

And there was Dr. Adrienne Cory, principal of Skatskill Day, grimly explaining to a skeptical interviewer that Mikal Zallman whom she had hired two and a half years previously had excellent credentials, had come highly recommended, was a conscientious and reliable staff member of whom there had been no complaints.

No complaints! What of the students who'd just been on the program?

Dr. Cory said, twisting her mouth in a semblance of a placating smile, "Well. We never knew."

And would Zallman continue to teach at Skatskill Day?

"Mr. Zallman has been suspended with pay for the time being."

His first, furious thought was *I will sue*.

His second, more reasonable thought was *I must plead my case*.

He had friends at Skatskill Day, he believed. The young woman who thought herself less-than-happily married, and who'd several times invited Zallman to dinner; a male math teacher, whom he often met at the gym; the school psychologist, whose sense of humor dovetailed with his own; and Dr. Cory herself, who was quite an intelligent woman, and a kindly woman, who had always seemed to like Zallman.

He would appeal to them. They must believe him!

Zallman insisted upon a meeting with Dr. Cory, face-to-face. He insisted upon being allowed to present his side of the case. He was informed that his presence at the school was "out of the question" at the present time; a mere glimpse of Zallman, and faculty members as well as students would be "distracted."

If he tried to enter the school building on Monday morning, Zallman was warned, security guards would turn him away.

"But why? What have I done? What have I done that is anything more than rumor?"

Not what Zallman had done but what the public perceived he might have done, that was the issue. Surely Zallman understood?

He compromised, he would meet Dr. Cory on neutral territory, 8 A.M. Monday in the Trahern Square office of the school's legal counsel. He was told to bring his own legal counsel but Zallman declined.

Another mistake, probably. But he couldn't wait for Neuberger, this was an emergency.

"I need to work! I need to return to school as if nothing is wrong, in fact *nothing is wrong*. I insist upon returning."

Dr. Cory murmured something vaguely supportive, sympathetic. She was a kind person, Zallman wanted to believe. She was decent, well intentioned, she liked him. She'd always laughed at his jokes!

Though sometimes wincing, as if Zallman's humor was a little too abrasive for her. At least publicly.

Zallman was protesting the decision to suspend him from teaching without "due process." He demanded to be allowed to meet with the school board. How could he be suspended from teaching for no reason—wasn't that unethical, and illegal? Wouldn't Skatskill Day be liable, if he chose to sue?

"I swear I did not—*do it. I am not involved.* I scarcely know Marissa Bantry, I've had virtually no contact with the girl. Dr. Cory—Adrienne—these 'eyewitnesses' are lying. This 'barrette' that was allegedly found by police behind my building—someone must have placed it there. Someone who hates me, who wants to destroy me! This has been a nightmare for me but I'm confident it will turn out well. I mean, it can't be proven that I'm involved with—with—whatever has happened to the girl—because I am not involved! I need to come back to work, Adrienne, I need you to demonstrate that you have faith in me. I'm sure that my colleagues have faith in me. Please reconsider! I'm prepared to return to work this morning. I can explain to the students—something! Give me a chance, will you? Even if I'd been arrested—which I am not, Adrienne—under the law I am innocent until proven guilty and I can't possibly be proven guilty because I—I did not—*I did not do anything wrong.*"

He was struck by a sudden stab of pain, as if someone had driven an ice pick into his skull. He whimpered and slumped forward gripping his head in his hands.

A woman was asking him, in a frightened voice, "Mr. Zallman? Do you want us to call a doctor?—an ambulance?"

He needed to speak with her. He needed to console her.

On the fifth day of the vigil it became an overwhelming need.

For in his misery he'd begun to realize how much worse it was for the mother of Marissa Bantry, than for him who was merely the suspect.

It was Tuesday. Of course, he had not been allowed to return to teach. He had not slept for days except fitfully, in his clothes. He ate standing before the opened refrigerator, grabbing at whatever was inside. He lived on Tylenols. Obsessively he watched TV, switching from channel to channel in pursuit of the latest news of the missing girl and steeling himself for a glimpse of his own face, haggard and hollow-eyed and disfigured by guilt as by acne. *There he is! Zallman!* The only suspect in the case whom police had actually brought into custody, paraded before a phalanx of photographers and TV cameramen to arouse the excited loathing of hundreds of thousands of spectators who would not have the opportunity to see Zallman, and to revile him, in the flesh.

In fact, the Skatskill police had other suspects. They were following other "leads." Neuberger had told him he'd heard that they had sent men to California, to track down the elusive father of Marissa Bantry who had emerged as a "serious suspect" in the abduction.

Yet, in the Skatskill area, the search continued. In the Bear Mountain State Park, and in the Blue Mountain Reserve south of

Peekskill. Along the edge of the Hudson River between Peekskill and Skatskill. In parkland and wooded areas east of Skatskill in the Rockefeller State Park. These were search and rescue teams comprised of both professionals and volunteers. Zallman had wanted to volunteer to help with the search for he was desperate to do something but Neuberger had fixed him with a look of incredulity. "Mikal, that is not a good idea. Trust me."

There had been reports of men seen "dumping" mysterious objects from bridges into rivers and streams and there had been further "sightings" of the living girl in the company of her captor or captors at various points along the New York State Thruway and the New England Expressway. Very blond fair-skinned girls between the ages of eight and thirteen resembling Marissa Bantry were being seen everywhere.

Police had received more than one thousand calls and Web site messages and in the media it was announced that *all leads will be followed* but Zallman wondered at this. *All* leads?

He himself called the Skatskill detectives, often. He'd memorized their numbers. Often, they failed to return his calls. He was made to understand that Zallman was no longer their prime suspect—maybe. Neuberger had told him that the girl's barrette, so conspicuously dropped by Zallman's parking space, had been wiped clean of fingerprints: "An obvious plant."

Zallman had had his telephone number changed to an unlisted number yet still the unwanted calls—vicious, obscene, threatening, or merely inquisitive—continued and so he'd had the phone disconnected and relied now upon his cell phone exclusively, carrying it with him as he paced through the shrinking rooms of his condominium apartment. From the fifth floor, at a slant, Zallman could see the Hudson River on overcast days like molten lead but on clear days possessed of an astonishing slate-blue beauty. For long minutes he lost himself in contemplation of the view: beauty that was pure, unattached to any individual, destined to outlive the misery that had become his life.

Nothing to do with me. Nothing to do with human evil.

Desperately he wanted to share this insight with the mother of Leah Bantry. It was such a simple fact, it might be overlooked.

He went to Fifteenth Street where the woman lived, he'd seen the exterior of the apartment building on TV numerous times. He had not been able to telephone her. He wanted only to speak with her for a few minutes.

It was near dusk of Tuesday. A light chill mist-rain was falling. For a while he stood indecisively on the front walk of the barracks-like building, in khaki trousers, canvas jacket, jogging shoes. His damp hair straggled past his collar. He had not shaved for several days. A sickly radiance shone in his face, he knew he was doing the right thing now crossing the lawn at an angle, to circle to the rear of the building where he might have better luck discovering which of the apartments belonged to Leah Bantry.

Please I must see you.

We must share this nightmare.

Police came swiftly to intercept him, grabbing his arms and cuffing his wrists behind his back.

Is she breathing?

. . . Christ!

She isn't . . . is she? *Is* she?

She is. She's okay.

. . . like maybe she's being . . . poisoned?

We were getting so scared! Anita was crying a lot, then Anita was laughing like she couldn't stop. Denise had this eating-thing, she was hungry all the time, stuffing her mouth at meals and in the cafeteria at school then poking a finger down her throat to make herself vomit into a toilet flush-flush-flushing the toilet so if she was at home nobody in her family would hear or if she was at school other girls wouldn't hear and tell on her.

More and more we could see how they were watching us at school, like *somehow they knew.*

Since giving the white flowers to the Corn Maiden's mother nothing felt right. Denise knew, and Anita. Jude maybe knew but would not acknowledge it.

Mothers don't give a shit about their kids. See, it's all pretend.

Jude believed this. She hated the Corn Maiden's mother worse than she hated anybody, just about.

Anita was worried the Corn Maiden was being poisoned, all the strong drugs Jude was making her swallow. The Corn Maiden was hardly eating anything now, you had to mush it up like cottage cheese with vanilla ice cream, open her jaws and spoon it into her mouth then close her jaws and try to make her swallow but half the time the Corn Maiden began choking and gagging and the white mush just leaked out of her mouth like vomit.

We were begging, Jude maybe we better . . .

. . . we don't want her to die, like do we?

Jude? *Jude?*

The fun was gone now. Seeing TV news, and all the newspapers even *The New York Times,* and the posters HAVE YOU SEEN ME? and the fifteen-thousand-dollar reward, and all that, that made us laugh like hyenas just a few days ago but wasn't anything to laugh at now, or anyway not much. Jude still scorned the assholes, she called them, and laughed at how they ran around looking for the Corn Maiden practically under their noses out Highgate Avenue.

Jude was doing these weird things. On Monday she came to school with one of the Corn Maiden's butterfly barrettes she was going to wear in her hair but we told her Oh no better not! and she laughed at us but didn't wear it.

Jude talked a lot about fire, "immolation." On the Internet she looked up some things like Buddhists had done a long time ago.

The Sacrifice of the Corn Maiden called for the heart of the captive cut out, and her blood collected in sacred vessels, but you could burn the Corn Maiden, too, and mix her ashes with the soil Jude said.

Fire is a cleaner way, Jude said. It would only hurt at the beginning.

Jude was taking cell-phone pictures all the time now. By the end, Jude would have like fifty of these. We believed that Jude intended to post them on the Internet but that did not happen.

What was done with them, when the police took away Jude's cell phone, we did not know.

These were pictures to stare at! In some of them the Corn Maiden was lying on her back in the bier in the beautiful silky fabrics and brocades and she was *so little*. Jude posed her naked and with her hair fanned out and her legs spread wide so you could see the little pink slip between her legs Jude called her cut.

The Corn Maiden's cut was not like ours, it was a little-girl cut and nicer, Jude said. It would never grow *pubic hairs* Jude said, the Corn Maiden would be spared that.

Jude laughed saying she would send the TV stations these pictures they could not use.

Other poses, the Corn Maiden was sitting up or kneeling or on her feet if Jude could revive her, and slap-slap her face so her eyes were open, you would think she was awake, and smiling this wan little smile leaning against Jude, their heads leaning together and Jude grinning like Jude O and the Corn Maiden were floating somewhere above the earth in some Heaven where nobody could reach them, only just look up at them wondering how they'd got there!

Jude had us take these pictures. One of them was her favorite, she said she wished the Corn Maiden's mother could see it and maybe someday she would.

That night, we thought the Corn Maiden would die.

She was shivering and twitching in her sleep like she'd been mostly doing then suddenly she was having like an epileptic fit, her mouth sprang open *Uh-uh-uh* and her tongue protruded wet with spittle and really ugly like a freak and Anita was backing off and whimpering She's going to die! oh God she's going to die! Jude do something she's going to die! and Jude slapped Anita's face to shut her up, Jude was so disgusted. Fat ass, get away. What the fuck do you know. Jude held the Corn Maiden down, the Corn Maiden's skinny arms and legs were shaking so, it was like she was trying to dance laying down and her eyes came open unseeing like a doll's dead glass eyes and Jude was kind of scared now and excited and climbed up onto the bier to lay on her, for maybe the Corn Maiden was cold, so skinny the cold had gotten into her bones, Jude's arms were stretched out like the Corn Maiden's arms and her hands were gripping the Corn Maiden's hands, her legs quivering stretched out the Corn Maiden's legs, and the side of her face against the Corn Maiden's face like they were twin girls hatched from the same egg. I am here, I am Jude I will protect you, in the Valley of the Shadow of Death I will protect you forever AMEN. Till finally the Corn Maiden ceased convulsing and was only just breathing in this long shuddering way, but she was breathing, she would be okay.

Still, Anita was freaked. Anita was trying not to laugh this wild laugh you'd hear from her at school sometimes, like she was being tickled in a way she could not bear so Jude became disgusted and slapped Anita SMACK-SMACK on both checks calling her fat ass and stupid cunt and Anita ran out of the storage room like a kicked dog crying, we heard her on the stairs and Jude said, She's next.

On darkspeaklink.com where Jude O bonded with the Master of Eyes Jude showed us IF THERE IS A PERSON THERE IS A PROBLEM. IF THERE IS NO PERSON THERE IS NO PROBLEM. (STALIN)

Jude had never told the Master of Eyes that she was female or male and so the Master of Eyes believed her to be male. She had told him she had taken her captive, did he give her permission to Sacrifice? and the Master of Eyes shot back you are precocious/precious if 13 yrs old & where do you live Jude O? but the thought came to Jude suddenly the Master of Eyes was not her friend who dwelled in several places of the earth simultaneously but an FBI agent pretending to be her soul mate in order to capture her so Jude O disappeared from darkspeaklink.com forever.

Jude O knew, it was ending. Four days preceding the Sacrifice and this was the sixth day. No turning back.

Denise was breaking down. Dull/dazed like she'd been hit over the head and in morning homeroom the teacher asked, Denise are you ill and at first Denise did not hear then shaking her head almost you could not hear her *no*.

Anita had not come to school. Anita was hiding away at home, and would betray Jude. And there was no way to get to Anita now, Jude was unable to silence the traitor.

Jude's disciples, she had trusted. Yet she had not truly trusted them knowing they were inferiors.

Denise was begging, Jude I think we better . . .

. . . let the Corn Maiden go?

Because because if she, if . . .

The Corn Maiden becomes Taboo. The Corn Maiden can never be released. Except if somebody takes the Corn Maiden's place the Corn Maiden can never be released.

You want to take the Corn Maiden's place?

Jude, she isn't the Corn Maiden she's M-Marissa Ban—

A flame of righteous fury came over Jude O, SMACK-SMACK with the palm and back of her hand she slapped the offensive face.

When spotted hyenas are born they are usually twins. One twin is stronger than the other and at once attacks the other hoping to tear out its throat and why, because the other would try to kill it otherwise. There is no choice.

At the table at the very rear of the cafeteria where Jude O and her disciples perceived as pathetic misfit losers by their Skatskill Day classmates usually ate their lunches together except today only Jude O and Denise Ludwig, and it was observed how Denise was whimpering and pleading with Jude wiping at her nose in a way repellent to the more fastidious girl who said through clenched jaws I forbid you to cry, I forbid you to make a spectacle of yourself, but Denise continued, and Denise whimpered and begged, and at last a flame of indignation swept over Jude who slapped Denise and Denise stumbled from the table overturning her chair, ran blubbering from the cafeteria in full view of staring others, and in that same instant it seemed that wily Jude O fled through a rear exit running crouched over to the middle school bicycle rack, and fueled by that same passion of indignation Jude bicycled 2.7 miles home to the old Trahern house on Highgate Avenue several times nearly struck by vehicles that swerved to avoid the blind-seeming cyclist and she laughed for she was feeling absolutely no fear now like a hawk riding the crest of an updraft scarcely needing to move its wings to remain aloft, and lethal. A hawk! Jude O was a hawk! If her bicycle had been struck and crushed, if she'd died on Highgate Avenue the Corn Maiden would molder in her bier of silks and brocades, unseen. No one would find the Corn Maiden for a long time.

It is better this way, we will die together.

She would not have requested a jury trial, you had to utter such bullshit to sway a jury. She would have requested a judge merely.

A judge is an aristocrat. Jude O was an aristocrat.

She would have been tried as an adult! Would have insisted.

In the gardener's shed there was a rusted old lawnmower. A can of gasoline half full. You poured the gasoline through the funnel if you could get it open. Jude had experimented, she could get it open.

Her grandmother's old silver lighter engraved with the initials *G.L.T.* Click-click-click and a transparent little bluish-orange flame appeared pretty as a flicking tongue.

She would immolate the Corn Maiden first.

No! Better to die together.

Telling herself calmly *It will only hurt at first. Just for a few seconds and by then it will be too late.*

She laughed to think of it. Like already it was done.

Stealthily entering the house by the rear door. So the old woman watching afternoon TV would not hear.

She was very excited! She was determined to make no error. Already forgetting that perhaps she had erred, allowing both her disciples to escape when she'd known that they were weakening. And confiding in the Master of Eyes believing she could trust him as her twin not recalling the spotted hyena twin, of course you could not trust.

Well, she had learned!

Forced herself to compose the Suicide Note. In her thoughts for a long time (it seemed so, now!) Jude had been composing this with care knowing its importance. It was addressed to *you assholes* for there was no one else.

Smiling to think how *you assholes* would be amazed.

On TV and online and in all the papers including *The New York Times* front page.

Whywhy you're asking here's why her hair.

I mean *her hair*! I mean like I saw it in the sun . . .

So excited! Heart beating fast like she'd swallowed a dozen E's. Unlocking the padlock with trembling hands. If Denise had told, already! *Should have killed them both last night. When I had the chance.* Inside the storage room, the Corn Maiden had shifted from the lying-on-her-side position in which Jude had left her that morning after making her eat. This was proof, the Corn Maiden was shrewdly pretending to be weaker than she was. Even in her sickness there was deceit.

Jude left the storage room door open, to let in light. She would not trouble to light the scented candles, so many candles there was not time. And flame now would be for a different purpose.

Squatting breathless over the Corn Maiden, with both thumbs lifting the bruised eyelids.

Milky eyes. Pupils shrunken.

Wake up! It's time it's time.

Feebly the Corn Maiden pushed at Jude. She was frightened, whimpering. Her breath smelled of something rotted. She had not been allowed to brush her teeth since coming to Jude's house, she had not been allowed to bathe herself. Only as Jude and her disciples had bathed her with wetted soapy washcloths.

Know what time it is it's time it's time it's timetimetime!

Don't hurt me please let me go . . .

Jude was the Taboo Priest. Seizing the Corn Maiden's long silky hair in her fist and forcing her down onto the bier scolding No no no no *no* like you would scold a baby.

A baby that is flesh of your flesh but you must discipline.

The immolation would have to be done swiftly, Jude knew. For that traitor-cunt Denise had babbled by now. Fat ass Anita had babbled. Her disciples had betrayed her, they were unworthy of her. They would be so sorry! She would not forgive them, though. Like she would not forgive the Corn Maiden's mother for staring at her like she was a bug or something, loathsome. What she regretted was she would not have time to cut out the Corn Maiden's heart as the Sacrifice demanded.

Lay still, I said it's *time.*

A new thought was coming to her now. She had not hold of it yet, the way you have not yet hold of a dream until it is fully formed like a magnificent bubble inside your head.

Jude had dragged the gasoline can into the storage room, and was spilling gasoline in surges. This could be the priest blessing the Corn Maiden and her bier. The stink of gasoline was strong, that was why the Corn Maiden was revived, her senses sharpening.

No! no! Don't hurt me let me go! I want my mother.

Jude laughed to see the Corn Maiden so rebellious. Actually pushing free of Jude, so weak she could not stand but on hands and knees naked crawling desperately toward the door. Never had Jude left the door open until now and yet the Corn Maiden saw, and comprehended this was escape. Jude smiled seeing how desperate the Corn Maiden was, stark naked and her hair trailing the floor like an animal's mane. Oh so skin-and-bones! Her ribs, bony hips, even the ankle bones protruding. Skinny haunches no bigger than Jude's two hands fitted together. And her hinder. *Hinder* was a funny word, a word meant to make you smile. A long time ago a pretty curly-haired woman had been humming and singing daubing sweet-smelling white powder onto Jude's little *hinder* before drawing up her rubber underpants, pulling down Jude's smock embroidered with dancing kittens or maybe it had been a nightgown, and the underpants had been a diaper.

Jude watched, fascinated. She had never seen the Corn Maiden disobey her so openly! It was like a baby just learning to crawl. She had not known the Corn Maiden so desired to live. Thinking suddenly *Better for her to remain alive, to revere me. And I have made my mark on her she will never forget.*

The Priest was infused with the power. The power of life-and-death. She would confer life, it was her decision. Climbing onto the bier spilling gasoline in a sacred circle around her. The stink of gasoline made her sensitive nostrils constrict, her eyes were watering so she could barely see. But she had no need to see. All was within, that she wished to see. *It will only hurt at first. Then it will be too late.* Click-click-clicking the silver lighter with gasoline-slippery fingers until the bright little flame-tongue leapt out.

See what I can do assholes, you never could.

SEPTEMBER

The Little Family

It was their first outing together, at the Croton Falls Nature Preserve. The three of them, as a family.

Of course, Zallman was quick to concede, not an actual *family*.

For the man and woman were not married. Their status as friends/lovers was yet undefined. And the girl was the woman's child, alone.

Yet if you saw them, you would think *family*.

It was a bright warm day in mid-September. Zallman who now measured time in terms of before/after was thinking the date was exactly five months *after*. But this was a coincidence merely.

From Yonkers, where he now lived, Zallman drove north to Mahopac to pick up Leah Bantry and her daughter Marissa at their new home. Leah and Marissa had prepared a picnic lunch. The Croton Falls Nature Preserve, which Leah had only recently discovered, was just a few miles away.

A beautiful place, Leah had told Zallman. So quiet.

Zallman guessed this was a way of saying *Marissa feels safe here*.

Leah Bantry was working now as a medical technician at Woman/Space, a clinic in Mahopac, New York. Mikal Zallman was temporarily teaching middle school math at a large public school in Yonkers where he also assisted the soccer/basketball/baseball coach.

Marissa was enrolled in a small private school in Mahopac without grades or a formal curriculum in which students received special tutoring and counseling as needed.

Tuition at the Mahopac Day School was high. Mikal Zallman was helping with it.

No one can know what you and your daughter went through. I feel so drawn to you both, please let me be your friend!

Before Zallman had known Leah Bantry, he had loved her. Knowing her now he was confirmed in his love. He vowed to bear this secret lightly until Leah was prepared to receive it.

She wanted no more emotion in her life, Leah said. Not for a long time.

Zallman wondered: what did that mean? And did it mean what it meant, or was it simply a way of saying *Don't hurt me! Don't come near.*

He liked it that Leah encouraged Marissa to call him Uncle Mikal. This suggested he might be around for a while. So far, in Zallman's presence at least, Marissa did not call him anything at all.

Zallman saw the girl glance at him, sometimes. Quick covert shy glances he hesitated to acknowledge.

There was a tentative air about them. The three of them.

As if (after the media nightmare, this was quite natural) they were being observed, on camera.

Zallman felt like a tightrope walker. He was crossing a tightrope high above a gawking audience, and there was no safety net beneath. His arms were extended for balance. He was terrified of falling but he must go forward. If at this height your balance is not perfect, it will be lethal.

In the nature preserve in the bright warm autumnal sunshine the adults walked together at the edge of a pond. To circle the pond required approximately thirty minutes. There were other visitors to the preserve on this Sunday afternoon, families and couples.

The girl wandered ahead of the adults, though never far ahead. Her behavior was more that of a younger child than a child of eleven. Her movements were tentative, sometimes she paused as if she were out of breath. Her skin was pale and appeared translucent. Her eyes were deep-socketed, wary. Her pale blond hair shimmered in the sun. It had been cut short, feathery, falling to just below her delicate eggshell ears.

After her ordeal in April, Marissa had lost much of her beautiful long hair. She'd been hospitalized for several weeks. Slowly she had regained most of the weight she'd lost so abruptly. Still she was anemic, Leah was concerned that there had been lasting damage to Marissa's kidneys and liver. She suffered from occasional bouts of tachycardia, of varying degrees of severity. At such times, her mother held her tight, tight. At such times the child's runaway heartbeat and uncontrollable shivering seemed to the mother a demonic third presence, a being maddened by terror.

Both mother and daughter had difficulty sleeping. But Leah refused prescription drugs for either of them.

Each was seeing a therapist in Mahopac. And Marissa also saw Leah's therapist for a joint session with her mother, once a week.

Leah confided in Zallman, "It's a matter of time. Of healing. I have faith, Marissa will be all right."

Leah never used such terms as *normal, recovered.*

Mikal Zallman had been the one to write to Leah Bantry of course. He had felt the desperate need to communicate with her, even if she had not the slightest wish to communicate with him.

I feel that we have shared a nightmare. We will never understand it. I don't know what I can offer you other than sympathy, commiseration. During the worst of the nightmare I had almost come to think that I was responsible . . .

After Marissa was discharged from the hospital, Leah took her away from Skatskill. She could not bear living in that apartment another day, she could not bear all that reminded her of the nightmare. She was surrounded by well-intentioned neighbors, and through the ordeal she had made several friends; she had been offered work in the area. If she'd wished to return to work at the Nyack clinic, very likely Davitt Stoop would have allowed her to return. He had reconciled with his wife, he was in a forgiving mood. But Leah had no wish to see the man again, ever. She had no wish to drive across the Tappan Zee Bridge again, ever.

Out of the ordeal had come an unexpected alliance with her sister Avril. While Marissa was in the hospital, Avril had continued to stay in Skatskill; one or the other of the two sisters was always in Marissa's hospital room. Avril had taken an unpaid leave from her job in Washington, she helped Leah find another job and to relocate in Mahopac, fifty miles north in hilly Putnam County.

Enough of Westchester County! Leah would never return.

She was so grateful for Avril's devotion, she found herself at a loss for words.

"Leah, come on! It's what any sister would do."

"No. It is not what any sister would do. It's what my sister would do. God damn I love you, Avril."

Leah burst into tears. Avril laughed at her. The sisters laughed together, they'd become ridiculous in their emotions. Volatile and unpredictable as ten-year-olds.

Leah vowed to Avril, she would never take anyone for granted again. Never anything. Not a single breath! Never again.

When they'd called her with the news: *Marissa is alive.*

That moment. Never would she forget that moment.

In their family only Avril knew: police had tracked Marissa's elusive father to Coos Bay, Oregon. There, he had apparently died in 1999 in a boating mishap. The medical examiner had ruled the cause of death "inconclusive." There had been speculation that he'd been murdered . . .

Leah hadn't been prepared for the shock she'd felt, and the loss.

Now, he would never love her again. He would never love his beautiful daughter again. He would never make things right between them.

She had never spoken his name aloud to Marissa. She would never speak it aloud. As a younger child Marissa used to ask Where is Daddy? When will Daddy come back? But now, never.

The death of Marissa's father in Coos Bay, Oregon, was a mystery, but it was a mystery Leah Bantry would not pursue. She was sick of mystery. She wanted only clarity, truth. She would surround herself with good decent truthful individuals for the remainder of her life.

Mikal Zallman agreed. No more mysteries!

You become exhausted, you simply don't care. You care about surviving. You care about the banalities of life: *closure, moving on.* Before the nightmare he'd have laughed at such TV talk-show jargon but now, no.

Of Leah Bantry and Mikal Zallman, an unlikely couple, Zallman was the more verbal, the more edgy. He was from a tribe of talkers, he told Leah. Lawyers, financiers, high-powered salesmen. A rabbi or two. For Zallman, just to wake up in the morning in Yonkers, and not in Skatskill, was a relief. And not in April, during that siege of nightmare. To lift his head from the pillow and not wince with pain as if broken glass were shifting inside his skull. To be able to open a newspaper, switch on TV news, without seeing his own craven likeness. To breathe freely, not-in-police-custody. Not the object of a mad girl's vengeance.

Mad girl was the term Zallman and Leah used, jointly. Never would they utter the name *Jude Trahern.*

Why had the mad girl abducted Marissa? Why, of all the younger children she might have preyed upon, had she chosen Marissa? And why had she killed herself, why in such a gruesome way, self-immolation like a martyr? These questions would never be answered. The cowed girls who'd conspired with her in the abduction had not the slightest clue. Something about an Onigara Indian sacrifice! They could only repeat brainlessly that they hadn't thought the mad girl was serious. They had only just followed her direction, they had wanted to be her friend.

To say that the girl had been *mad* was only a word. But the word would suffice.

Zallman said in disgust, "To know all isn't to forgive all. To know all is to be sickened by what you know." He was thinking of the Holocaust, too: a cataclysm in history that defied all explanation.

Leah said, wiping at her eyes, "I would not forgive her, under any circumstances. She wasn't 'mad,' she was evil. She took pleasure in hurting others. She almost killed my daughter. I'm glad that she's dead, she's removed herself from us. But I don't want to talk about her, Mikal. Promise me."

Zallman was deeply moved. He kissed Leah Bantry then, for the first time. As if to seal an understanding.

Like Leah, Zallman could not bear to live in the Skatskill area any longer. Couldn't breathe!

Without exactly reinstating Zallman, the principal and board of trustees of Skatskill Day had invited him back to teach. Not immediately, but in the fall.

A substitute was taking his place at the school. It was believed to be most practical for the substitute to finish the spring term.

Zallman's presence, so soon after the ugly publicity, would be "distracting to students." Such young, impressionable students. And their anxious parents.

Zallman was offered a two-year renewable contract at his old salary. It was not a very tempting contract. His lawyer told him that the school feared a lawsuit, with justification. But Zallman said the hell with it. He'd lost interest in combat.

And he'd lost interest in computers, overnight.

Where he'd been fascinated by the technology, now he was bored. He craved something more substantial, of the earth and time. Computers were merely technique, like bodiless brains. He would take a temporary job teaching math in a public school, and he would apply to graduate schools to study history. A Ph.D. program in American studies. At Columbia, Yale, Princeton.

Zallman didn't tell Leah what revulsion he sometimes felt, waking before dawn and unable to return to sleep. Not for computers but for the Zallman who'd so adored them.

How arrogant he'd been, how self-absorbed! The lone wolf who had so prided himself on aloneness.

He'd had enough of that now. He yearned for companionship, someone to talk with, make love with. Someone to share certain memories that would otherwise fester in him like poison.

In late May, after Leah Bantry and her daughter Marissa had moved away from Skatskill—a departure excitedly noted in the local media—Zallman began to write to her. He'd learned that Leah had taken a position at a medical clinic in Mahopac. He knew the area, to a degree: an hour's drive away. He wrote single-page, thoughtfully composed letter to her not expecting her to reply, though hoping that she might. *I feel so close to you! This ordeal that has so changed our lives.* He'd studied her photographs in the papers, the grieving mother's drawn, exhausted face. He knew that Leah Bantry was a few years older than he, that she was no longer in contact with Marissa's father. He sent her postcards of works of art: van Gogh's sunflowers, Monet's water lilies, haunted landscapes of Caspar David Friedrich and gorgeous autumnal forests of Wolf Kahn. In this way Zallman courted Leah Bantry. He allowed this woman whom he had never met to know that he revered her. He would put no pressure on her to see him, not even to respond to him.

In time, Leah Bantry did respond.

They spoke on the phone. They made arrangements to meet. Zallman was nervously talkative, endearingly awkward. He seemed overwhelmed by Leah's physical presence. Leah was more wary, reticent. She was a beautiful woman who looked her age, she wore no makeup, no jewelry except a watch; her fair blond hair was threaded with silver. She smiled, but she did not speak much. She liked it that this man would do the talking, as men usually did not. Mikal Zallman was a personality of a type Leah knew, but at a distance. Very New York, very intense. Brainy, but naive. She guessed that his family had money, naturally Zallman scorned money. (But he'd been reconciled with his family, Zallman said, at the time of the ordeal. They had been outraged on his behalf and had insisted upon paying his lawyer's exorbitant fees.) During their conversation, Leah recalled how they'd first met at the Skatskill School, and how Zallman the computer expert had walked away from her. So arrogant! Leah would tease him about that, one day. When they became lovers perhaps.

Zallman's hair was thinning at the temples, there was a dented look to his cheeks. His eyes were those of a man older than thirty-one or -two. He'd begun to grow a beard, a goatee, to disguise his appearance, but you could see that it was a temporary experiment, it would not last. Yet Leah thought Mikal Zallman handsome, in his way rather romantic. A narrow hawkish face, brooding eyes. Quick to laugh at himself. She would allow him to adore her, possibly one day she would adore him. She was not prepared to be hurt by him.

Eventually she would tell him the not-quite-true *I never believed you were the one to take Marissa, Mikal. Never!*

The little family, as Zallman wished to think them, ate their picnic lunch, and what a lunch it was, on a wooden table on the bank of a pond, beneath a willow tree so exquisitely proportioned it looked like a work of art in a children's storybook. He noted that Marissa still had trouble with food, ate slowly and with an air of caution, as if, with each mouthful, she was expecting to encounter broken glass. But she ate most of a sandwich, and half an apple Leah peeled for her, since "skins" made her queasy. And afterward tramping about the pond admiring snowy egrets and great blue herons and wild swans. Everywhere lushly growing cattails, rushes, flaming sumac. There was a smell of moist damp earth and sunlight on water and in the underbrush red-winged blackbirds were flocking in a festive cacophony. Leah lamented, "But it's too soon! We're not ready for winter." She sounded genuinely hurt, aggrieved.

Zallman said, "But Leah, snow can be nice, too."

Marissa, who was walking ahead of her mother and Mr.

Zallman, wanted to think this was so: *snow, nice.* She could not clearly remember snow. Last winter. Before April, and after April. She knew that she had lived for eleven years and yet her memory was a windowpane covered in cobwebs. Her therapists were kindly soft-spoken women who asked repeatedly about what had happened to her in the cellar of the old house, what the bad girls had done to her, for it was healthy to remember, and to speak of what she remembered, like draining an abscess they said, and she should cry, too, and be angry; but it was difficult to have such emotions when she couldn't remember clearly. What are you feeling, Marissa, she was always being asked, and the answer was *I don't know* or *Nothing!* But that was not the right answer.

Sometimes in dreams she saw, but never with opened eyes.

With opened eyes, she felt blind. Sometimes.

The bad girl had fed her, she remembered. Spoon-fed. She'd been so hungry! So grateful.

All adults are gone. All our mothers.

Marissa knew: that was a lie. The bad girl had lied to her.

Still, the bad girl had fed her. Brushed her hair. Held her when she'd been so cold.

The sudden explosion, flames! The burning girl, terrific shrieks and screams—Marissa had thought at first it was herself, on fire and screaming. She was crawling upstairs but was too weak and she fainted and someone came noisy and shouting to lift her in his arms and it was three days later Mommy told her when she woke in the hospital, her head so heavy she could not lift it.

Mommy and Mr. Zallman. She was meant to call him "Uncle Mikal" but she could not.

Mr. Zallman had been her teacher in Skatskill. But he behaved as if he didn't remember any of that. Maybe Mr. Zallman had not remembered her, Marissa had not been one of the good students. He had only seemed to care for the good students, the others were invisible to him. He was not "Uncle Mikal" and it would be wrong to call him that.

At this new school everybody was very nice to her. The teachers knew who she was, and the therapists and doctors. Mommy said they had to know or they could not help her. One day, when she was older, she would move to a place where nobody knew Marissa Bantry. Away out in California.

Mommy would not wish her to leave. But Mommy would know why she had to leave.

At this new school, that was so much smaller than Skatskill Day, Marissa had a few friends. They were shy wary thin-faced girls like herself. They were girls who, if you only just glanced at them, you would think they were missing a limb; but then you would see, no they were not. They were *whole girls*.

Marissa liked her hair cut short. Her long silky hair the bad girls had brushed and fanned out about her head, it had fallen out in clumps in the hospital. Long hair made her nervous now. Through her fingers at school sometimes lost in a dream she watched girls with hair rippling down their backs like hers used to, she marveled they were oblivious to the danger.

They had never heard of the Corn Maiden! The words would mean nothing to them.

Marissa was a reader now. Marissa brought books everywhere with her, to hide inside. These were storybooks with illustrations. She read slowly, sometimes pushing her finger beneath the words. She was fearful of encountering words she didn't know, words she was supposed to know but did not know. Like a sudden fit of coughing. Like a spoon shoved into your mouth before you were ready. Mommy had said Marissa was safe now from the bad girls and from any bad people, Mommy would take care of her but Marissa knew from reading stories that this could not be so. You had only to turn the page, something would happen.

Today she had brought along two books from the school library: *Watching Birds!* and *The Family of Butterflies*. They were books for readers younger than eleven, Marissa knew. But they would not surprise her.

Marissa is carrying these books with her, wandering along the edge of the pond a short distance ahead of Mommy and Mr. Zallman. There are dragonflies in the cattails like floating glinting needles. There are tiny white moth-butterflies, and beautiful large orange monarchs with slow-pulsing wings. Behind Marissa, Mommy and Mr. Zallman are talking earnestly. Always they are talking, it seems. Maybe they will be married and talk all the time and Marissa will not need to listen to them, she will be invisible.

A red-winged blackbird swaying on a cattail calls sharply to her. *In the Valley of the Shadow of Death I will protect you AMEN.*

BEERSHEBA

Just injected the shot—the insulin—when the phone rang—as if whoever was calling was being courteous, or mock-courteous, and had waited until he'd retracted the needle—and he'd answered grunting "Yeh? Who's it?"—he wasn't expecting any calls, this time of evening. And the voice on the line was a female voice—a woman, or a girl—familiar—but hushed, breathless—"Brad Shiftke?—is that you?"

"Sure is. Who's this?"

A moment's hesitation—as if whoever it was had to consider this question seriously—then the voice turned coy, playful—"Guess!"

"Guess? I can't."

"Hey Brad c'mon—you're not even trying, man."

His heart gave a little kick. So quickly the voice had lurched into a teasing sort of reproach—sounding more familiar now—someone he'd known well? Someone—intimate?

Whoever it was wasn't from any recent time in his life, Brad was sure. Not one of the women he'd known these past five, six years—the women still speaking to him—would be addressing him like *this.*

Those years in his younger life—mid-twenties to thirty-eight, -nine—there'd been women who'd addressed Brad in such a tone. He'd married young, and separated; divorced, and married again; and in the interstices of domestic life in Florida and upstate New York, for which he'd been no more suited than a wild animal—raccoon, chimp—that can't be tamed, he'd seen women in secret. Overall he'd had a good time. He'd taken for granted that women liked him, and liked what he did with them and probably it could be said he'd had the whip hand in any relationship. First he'd been stationed at the Pensacola naval base where it was discovered he was good with computers then after his discharge moved north to Carthage, New York, which was close by his hometown but not too close he had to see his family often. But girls he'd known from high school and after—plenty of these. And this woman—girl—definitely, he knew her. The teasing way she was speaking like ghost-fingers stroking his hair, the nape of his neck which no woman had touched in a long time.

"C'mon try to guess, Brad—there was a time you'd know me right off."

"You going to give me some hint? Like—how long ago?"

"'How long ago'—you tell me."

"Or—you don't live around here, you're back visiting? That's it?"

"What about you, Brad?"

"Me? What's there about me?—you're the subject."

"Nooo Brad c'mon, man—you're the subject. That's why I called you, man."

What all this was about, Brad couldn't guess. All he knew he was becoming excited, aroused. The woman—or girl— had to be a mature woman he supposed—but sounded like a girl, breathy and giggly—was saying she'd called him hoping he'd remember her name at least and she'd been thinking if so, if Brad remembered her name, that would be a sign she should see him, and she'd been wanting to see him for a long time: she'd come to Carthage to look him up, or—maybe not entirely just for him—but she'd made a long drive and was staying at a motel out on Route 11 and for sure, Brad Shiftke was a primary reason she'd come but now—well now she didn't know what to think—"Seems like you don't have a clue who I am, Brad."

"Well—your voice is familiar. It's a voice—I know."

"But not my name, huh?"

"Well—almost. I can almost—"

"*Your* voice is a voice I know, Brad. Your voice is a voice in my dreams, I would not likely forget."

This stilted manner of speech was familiar, too—made him uneasy, recalling—not a recent memory but one that stirred him. He was wondering—was this woman taunting him? Some woman who'd had a disagreement with him, or a misunderstanding, he'd forgotten? He'd been accused of careless behavior, from women. Not mean or malicious—he'd never lay hands on any woman, no matter how provoked—but more like thoughtless, hurried in his manner—pushy, bossy—but good-hearted, protective—he'd had a drinking problem since high school—*that* was under control. Until he'd put on weight in his forties he'd been what you'd call fit—chiseled chest, biceps, and upper arms—wore his faded-carrot-color hair in a crew cut—good posture from his navy days and not bad-looking when he took time to shower and shave and wear clean clothes which, being chief computer techie at the community college, and pretty much his own boss, he could skip sometimes.

"How're you doing, Brad?" the woman was asking and Brad said, "Good. I'm doing good" and the woman said, "Really—I want to know, Brad. I heard some things," and with a quick laugh Brad said, "Heard some things from—who? Somebody stalking me?"

This annoyed him. Any thought of people discussing him. Worse yet feeling sorry for him.

Brad was on his feet now. He'd heaved himself up from the sofa sculpted to his heavy body, clicked the TV on MUTE. It was his mobile phone he had where the caller ID revealed WIRELESS CALLER NY—not much help. He was beginning to feel edgy, anxious—what had this woman been hearing about him?—couldn't be the drinking, that was five-six years back—the DWI and the other, a bullshit charge of second-degree assault—later dropped—had to be the diabetes—that was what the woman meant. He felt a flamey sensation of shame, fury—what right did she have, whoever it was, a stranger to him—alluding to *that*?

Brad didn't discuss his God-damn health with anyone even his family, friends. Zero interest he had in that.

Early last year, he'd been diagnosed—after he'd blacked out more than once, and the last time while driving his SUV on the thruway—what the doctor told him felt like the dull edge of an ax slammed against his head when he hadn't been prepared for such a blow but insulin injections kept it under control, insulin lispro was what the doctor prescribed for him, the fast-acting insulin so you don't have to plan too much about when you're eating. Hated injecting himself like some strung-out junkie but he'd learned to prepare the shot, sink the syringe needle into his midriff, fatty-flaccid flesh straining against his belt—even with shedding thirty pounds, he was still overweight—and after eighteen months still his fingers were clumsy as hell, it was easy to fuck up, drop the needle into his crotch or onto the floor cursing *Jesus! This is not me.* So ashamed, embarrassed he'd never told his closest friends or any woman about the diabetes but at his mother's house he didn't hesitate to lift his T-shirt and inject the needle in the living room watching TV or even at the dinner table with people looking on—"Uncle Brad that's *gross.*" He'd just laugh, what the hell—it was a vague simmering resentment of his, he'd inherited the condition from his mother's side of the family where all the years he'd been growing up he'd hear of older relatives—uncles, aunts—with some weird infirmity called *sugar diabetes.*

Now came a surprise. Just when he'd been worried the woman was going to hang up on him suddenly her voice dropped, drawled—"Well Brad my man—why I'm calling—how'd you like to get together tonight? Or—you tied up tonight?"

"Sure. I mean—no."

"There's nobody there?"

"No. There's nobody here."

"Heard you got married—more than once, was it?"

"That was a while back."

"No kids?"

"No."

"You sure?"

"Jesus yes—I'm sure."

"No kids you know of, you're saying."

Brad came to a full stop. Gripping the phone against his ear. Was this some kind of joke? Some girl calling him claiming she's his daughter?

"Hey Brad—you still there?"

"Sure . . ."

"Didn't mean to scare you, man. I'm not any kid of yours or anything nor am I aware of any kid of Brad Shiftke I'm just, like—y'know—making inquiries. What you know."

"What I know? About—what?"

"About whatever subject this is, Brad, we're talking about."

"You said—you wanted to get together?"

"Yes! That's what I said."

The plan was to meet at the Star Lake Inn which was about five miles from Brad's place in Carthage and a place where people

tended to know Brad Shiftke, or had known him when he'd
gone out drinking more, and Star Lake was one of his weekend
stops. In the bar he didn't see her—a solitary woman—figured
she'd be a good-looking woman but all of these he saw were
with guys or other people and out back on the veranda which
was where you could sit with drinks if you bought them inside
there was a woman smiling at him—hands on her hips as in a
pose, backs of her hands resting against her hips which were
fleshy, solid—and her head tilted to one side, where a thick
glossy braid fell over her shoulders. "Brad Shiftke—that's you?
Hi!" Before Brad could register any reaction except a startled
smile the woman stepped forward and thrust out her hand to
be shaken, her fingers were solid and strong, handshake firm as
a man's and the way she presented herself before him, bemused
and open-faced, feet apart, looking him in the eye, reminded him
of a man. He thought *Is this someone I know? It is not.* Trying not
to show the disappointment he was feeling the woman wasn't
very attractive—not like what her voice had hinted—though
she was young, in her twenties—large-boned girl with a head
that looked small, hair pulled back tight into the coarse braid,
plain darkish-tan face like an Indian-girl face, broad mouth and
heavy eyebrows, ironic eyes and skin roughened at the hairline as if with a rash or the remnants of acne. As they shook
hands—exchanged bantering greetings—Brad saw that the girl
had unusually large breasts—watermelon-breasts—straining at
the fabric of an ice blue satin T-shirt with a man's face on it—
Hispanic-looking, with a mustache—some kind of guerrilla cap,

uniform—a T-shirt face or tattoo-face familiar as Elvis but Brad couldn't place it—and the girl's jeans were designer jeans with brass studs. She had broad hips, thighs. On her large splayed bare feet were leather sandals durable enough for hiking but her toenails were painted frosted green—meant to be playful, Brad supposed. Her ears were intricately pierced, there was a curved glinting pin in her left eyebrow and another in her upper lip. Some kind of New Age hippie, the kind Brad and his friends sneered at, seeing on TV. In person you rarely saw them in this part of the Adirondacks.

"Still don't recognize me, Brad?—now I'm kind of hurt."

Brad stared at the girl. Those eyes—did he know them? Hazel-brown with thick lashes. She was laughing, her face was mottled with heat. It did seem to be so, Brad's confusion about who she was seemed to hurt her, unless she was pretending. Warmly Brad said, "Let me get us drinks, OK? Beers? You're not underage —are you?"

"Underage? Hell, no. I'm a big girl all growed up, Daddy."

At this—*Daddy*—Brad stopped dead in his tracks. Took a second look at the girl and saw—Jesus, was this Stacy Lynn? The daughter of Linda Gutshalk, who'd been Brad's second wife? Now it made some kind of sense—the mysterious girl resembled Linda, to a degree. It was coming back to Brad now—Linda had died in a car wreck, he'd been out of her life by that time. Stacy Lynn was just a little girl then. Linda's parents had taken her and had custody of her—she'd been theirs, and not Brad's. Brad had only been step-Daddy. And Brad hadn't been a very devoted step-Daddy during the four or five years he'd been married to Linda—the role had not come easily to him, no more than the husband-role had.

The girl was laughing, breathless. Wiping tears from her cheeks with both hands. Brad saw that her body wasn't fat so much as solid-packed like hard rubber. Sure she had to be someone worked out in a gym—he'd watched girls like this, half-repelled, fascinated by the way they inhabited bodies that, if a man woke up in, Jesus he'd blow off his head with a shotgun.

"Oh hey Brad. You didn't remember 'Stacy Lynn'—did you?"

"Hell yes. I did—I *do*. Just, you took me by surprise . . ."

Brad covered his embarrassment by hugging the girl. Her body was just as hard-rubbery as he'd thought but the big breasts were soft, like milk-filled sacs. Coming so close to her was disconcerting. Awkward. True that Brad hadn't remembered her—not exactly. But he'd been remembering her mother, hearing the girl's voice on the phone. Why he'd been feeling both excitement and anxious. Sexual excitement yet wariness, apprehension. Linda Gutshalk! Linda was one of the women he didn't care to think about especially when he was in a down mood like tonight. Like lots of nights recently. Most he had to do—most important thing—was to remember to take his insulin at the right time which was an indication of how things stood with Brad Shiftke these days, he didn't care to think about. Linda Gutshalk was the most beautiful girl he'd ever seen in actual life when he'd first met her, he had to concede that. Both of them drunk they'd gotten married in Niagara Falls one weekend shortly after he'd been discharged from the navy and moved back north—it hadn't exactly sunk in on him, Linda had been married before and had a little girl—meaning *responsibility*. Still less had Brad grasped that Linda was difficult to live with, to put it mildly—she hadn't liked being touched in any way she considered "over-familiar"—a problem in a marriage. And in the close quarters in which they'd had to live in Chautauqua Falls, in a mobile home.

Brad was taller than Stacy Lynn by only two or three inches. She'd grown considerably taller and larger than her mother—like some different species of female—but had her mother's tawny-brown hair he'd used to think was *fawn-colored* letting it ripple over his hand. Sobering to realize, Linda's shy little daughter was now a mature woman. She had none of her mother's delicate facial features and soft-seeming feminine manner but maybe this was a good thing.

The weight of those years was sweeping over him like a wave, a succession of waves where you couldn't get your breath, dark brackish water. Could be he was looking dazed, sick. In a throaty-flirty voice the girl was saying, cajoling—"Brad my man—you look like you need a drink. And *moi aussey*."

Had no idea what the hell she was talking about. Her hand on his forearm—large stubby fingers, nails chipped frosted green—went through him like an electric current.

Together they got beers at the bar inside—Brad had to insist, he was paying—returned to the veranda where they'd thought there was a table, but all the tables were taken—the kind of situation that made Brad self-conscious, irritable—God-damned people looking at him, guys he knew and him with the big-boned Indian-looking girl with the piercings in her face. Smiling like a man who's been kicked in the stomach and determined not to show it. On his way to Star Lake he'd been thinking that the woman who'd called him out of nowhere wanted to see him for some romantic purpose but no, turns out it's a stepdaughter of his he hadn't seen in possibly fifteen years and had not given a thought to in those years. His first beer went swiftly to his head—since the diabetes, he didn't drink like he used to. Stacy Lynn kept pushing close to him saying, "Oh Brad—Daddy-Brad—this is amazing isn't it? Never thought I would see Daddy-Brad again, my heart was broke when you and Mom split. Hey—I got my car here—let's go for a drive out Star Lake. Lots to catch up on. Too many people here."

Bold like some girl on TV Stacy Lynn grabbed his shoulders and aimed a kiss at his mouth—her hard-rubbery lips were wet, unexpectedly cool—her sizable arms around his neck—then she went slump-shouldered, as if weak, forehead pressed against his chest in an attitude of submission, female abnegation. Standing back from him smiling Stacy Lynn was looking better to Brad now, younger and more vulnerable.

Brad wanted to drive but Stacy Lynn insisted on driving. So adamant, Brad had to give in. Weird to be in a car—in a passenger seat—with a female driving—like he'd become some kind of disabled person and this strapping young woman with shining eyes and Indian braid halfway down her back like a horse's braided mane was in charge of him.

Star Lake was one of the larger lakes in the southern Adirondacks—twenty-seven miles north to south and six miles wide—only a small fraction of its shoreline was developed. The woods were dense pines, firs, and junipers with clumps of ghost-white birches glimmering here and there like patches of cloud. When he'd been a kid and in his twenties Brad had come out here a few times a year fishing, backpacking, and, in deer season, hunting with his buddies but no longer. Couldn't even say where some of those guys were, these days. Now the landmarks returned to him like slivers of dream elusive to memory. Through high vaporous clouds a three-quarter moon shone with unnatural brightness like phosphorescence. Stacy Lynn was drinking as she drove and talking nonstop, and some of this Brad was hearing, but mostly not, his thoughts scattered and the beer-buzz in his head like a hum of bees. "Like my car? Pretty cool, eh?"—some kind of upscale Toyota Brad doubted belonged to her. His own vehicle was a Grand Cherokee, second-hand, or maybe third-hand, he'd wished he had insisted upon driving.

Stacy Lynn turned off the lakeshore road and onto a gravel road—no houses or cottages out here—though Brad believed he'd been in this part of the lake, fishing—years ago—weird how bright the moon was, and the sky, and how inky-black the woods. "C'mon! Let's walk to the lake"—Stacy Lynn had a flashlight in hand, shining onto a faint path through the underbrush. Brad had finished his second can of beer—unless it was his third—and Brad was feeling a stir of—not sure what—some kind of arousal, yearning—not sexual exactly but the anticipation of sex—or of surprise—the kind of feeling that can turn on you, and plum-met, like a kite struck down by the wind. The girl was humming loudly, whistling between her teeth—drinking from a can of beer also—wielding the flashlight in her hand like a wand. "*Vite-vite*—c'mon Brad *mon ami*"—some foreign words, or mock-foreign words, teasing as you'd tease a clumsy child, fondly—for Brad was stumbling in the underbrush, cursing as brambles tore at his clothes and nicked his fingers. At the lakeshore—not a beach but rock-strewn, littered with storm debris and a faint stench of dead fish—Stacy Lynn surprised Brad by gripping the flashlight between her knees, grunting as she pulled off her satin T-shirt in a flourish, and beneath it she was wearing what looked like a sports bra in the same kind of shiny satin fabric except polka dots. Was she going to wade out into the water? How cold would the water be, in Star Lake? Her midriff spilled gently about the snug waistband of the designer jeans, soft female flesh Brad would've liked to squeeze, knead. His mouth had gone dry. Hairs stirred at the nape of his neck. The kiss aimed at his mouth was still damp and felt like a scar or a scab in his flesh. "See? 'Clair de lune'—light of the moon—just for us, Brad."

Her voice quavered. She'd been joking, or trying to joke—but her voice quavered and for an awkward moment Brad thought that she might start to cry.

Not that! Women's tears made him edgy, resentful. What did tears *mean*?

Star Lake—so named for its irregular star-shape, seen from the air—was both very dark and shimmering with broken moonlight.

The air had turned chilly but there was no wind, waves were flattened, only faintly agitated in areas of the lake as if stirred from beneath by mysterious and unnameable lake-creatures. Abruptly—playfully—Stacy Lynn turned to shine the flashlight in Brad's face—just for a moment, startling and blinding him—annoying him—then turned in another direction—"Brad! This way." Again her manner was girlish, provocative. No question of wading into the lake which was a damned good thing, Brad wasn't in a mood to follow her. Would've liked to bring this outing, or whatever it was, to an end—but had no choice except to trudge after the big-boned girl humming and whistling leading him—where?—the earth was both rocky and marshy— they were climbing an incline, away from the lake—"Wait, Stacy Lynn! Christ sake"—Brad pretended exhaustion, exasperation—in fact he was badly winded—there was a smell here of something rotted, an animal carcass—a quarter-mile from the lake still they were climbing uphill, Stacy Lynn in the lead, Brad hot-faced and panting behind—suddenly they were in what appeared to be a cemetery—a ravaged-looking old cemetery—behind an abandoned church. Once, there'd been a settlement here, oddly named—Beersheba—this had been the Beersheba Lutheran Church—some name out of the Bible, Brad supposed. The stone markers were mostly fallen, crumbled—covered with lichen— choked with vines and weeds—their inscriptions faint, flattened, unreadable by moonlight. Brad saw that some of the markers dated to 1790—so long ago, it was hard to believe anyone had ever lived here, in such a remote corner of Beechum County.

The girl was saying in a breathy voice like a girl in a TV movie, "Brad-Daddy—I mean *step*-Daddy—this is a secret place I used to come. When Mom stayed with some relatives at Star Lake, I'd bicycle out here. Haven't been here for—Jesus, how long?—ten years maybe. Mom isn't buried here but I came here, by myself. I have some good memories of this place."

" 'Mom isn't buried here'—why'd you say that? Nobody's been buried here for a hundred years."

"That's all you know, Brad my man."

This was the sort of pointless banter meant to arouse and excite or possibly tease, taunt; Brad wanted to think the girl was just in a party mood, joking, on the edge of being drunk. She was sitting—trying to sit—on one of the toppled-over grave markers —but her large haunches kept slipping off. She giggled, heaving herself into a more secure position, even as the flashlight slipped from her fingers into a patch of weeds. "Hey Brad, c'mon sit by me. See, it's romantic here"—as Brad stumbled toward her, not sure if he wanted to sit so close to Stacy Lynn, but aroused, excited by the prospect; somehow it happened that, as Brad approached her, the girl stooped, as if to snatch up the flashlight, but instead tugged Brad's pant leg upward—roughly, his left pant leg—so swiftly this bizarre action took place, Brad was too astonished to react, still less to shove the girl away or defend himself—even as something razor-sharp was being drawn—swiped, sawed—against the exposed skin of his left leg, above the ankle—there came a bolt of pain beyond measure—Ben screamed, lost all strength in his wounded leg and fell heavily into the rubble-strewn grass.

The girl leapt away from the stricken man. She was hooting with excitement, childish glee. What had she done?—what had she done to *him*? In her left hand she'd snatched up the flashlight and in her right hand she held something that gleamed in the moonlight—a knife-blade? Her eyes glowered. On her feet she was unexpectedly agile, like a young steer. "Know what, Brad?—that's your Achilles tendon that's been *severed*."

Helpless, Brad had fallen to the ground. Such pain, he could not bear. He was screaming, writhing and squirming like a hooked fish. Elated and exuberant the girl circled him stamping her feet and taunting. "Killed my mother you sorry prick, you God-damned wicked man—evil son of a bitch now you will pay. How d'you like it? That's your 'Achilles tendon' that's been severed, asshole. You can crawl like a worm, make your way home like a worm."

"Help me"—Brad was begging. He was delirious with pain, trying to drag himself—where, he couldn't have said—dragging his leg, that throbbed with pain as blood poured from the wound—as Stacy Lynn circled him gloating and furious. "You killed my mother! You treated my mother like shit! She was so hurt by you—so miserable—depressed—she'd drive her car half-drunk like nothing mattered to her—late at night she'd drive on the interstate—almost she took me with her that last time then changed her mind left me home watching TV—'If Mommy is late coming back, call Grandma.' *You* caused her death sure as if you'd shot her—stabbed her in the heart—didn't even come to her funeral! What're you going to do now, asshole?

Big-Daddy-Brad-asshole? How's it feel, you're the one in pain? You're the one made to crawl like a worm?" Stacy Lynn paused, breathing harshly. Her young solid-packed face glowed with an oily film of sweat and her eyes, that were nothing like her mother's eyes now, shone. "Know what, asshole?—I'm going to leave you here. This is a sacred place you don't deserve, to die in."

Brad was clutching at his bleeding leg as if trying to staunch the bleeding with his fingers. He was having difficulty comprehending what had happened—what had happened to *him*. Trying to reason with the girl—begging her not to leave him but to help him. With a part of his brain thinking, calculating—if his assailant understood how she'd hurt him already, if she understood the terrible pain he was feeling, how utterly broken he was, and no threat to her, she would have mercy on him—maybe—and not leave him. The old Lutheran cemetery was just a few miles from Star Lake but so remote a place, no one would discover him even if he shouted for help. Not for weeks, or months. The gravel road leading to the ruined church was a derelict road no longer maintained by the county.

The girl confronted him jeering—"Shit, that don't hurt like you're acting it does—you trying to manip'late me? Here, asshole. You're not gonna bleed to death."

In a gesture of disdain she tossed him something—a soiled rag. Desperately Brad pressed the rag against his bleeding leg.

The wound—a deep wound—was just above Brad's ankle, at the back of his leg. So far as he knew it was so—it was his Achilles tendon Stacy Lynn had slashed, and sawed-at—"severed." With unerring precision and astonishing boldness she'd yanked up his pant leg—the leg of his khakis—swiped and sawed at his flesh with what appeared to be a hunting knife—razor-sharp, less than eight inches long—a powerful stainless steel blade with a bluish cast—so quickly and with such skill she'd acted, the blade had pierced Brad's cotton sock and his skin—his flesh—in a matter of seconds. Disdainful of his agony Stacy Lynn jeered: "Make yourself a tourn'quit, asshole! Ain't you some hot-shit navy officer? Must be, you know how to take care of yourself. You're not gonna bleed to death if you make some God-damn *effort*."

Brad was pressing the rag against his wounded leg. Brad was pleading: "I didn't kill your mother, Stacy—I loved your mother. Please believe me, I loved your mother . . ."

"Like hell you loved my mother! That's a joke! Son of a bitch you never loved anyone."

Brad protested he did—he had—"I married your mother because I wanted to be her husband and I wanted to be a—father—to you. That was my hope, to be a good husband and a father . . ."

"This is such bullshit! You treated Mom like shit and you caused her to die—you wanted her to die, to get rid of her. So you wouldn't have to pay alimony, or give a shit about her. That was how it was."

"No—it wasn't that way."

"It wasn't? It wasn't that way? What other damn way was it, then?"

"I loved your mother—I loved you—"

Furious—laughing—the girl kicked at him. Brad shielded his face with his arms.

"Any damn desperate thing you'd say now, to save your miserable life. Not even you're lying, man, you don't know what the fucking truth *is*."

"Stacy—no. I loved your mother. I loved you . . ."

"Hell you did. Why'd you never even see me, then? Never once."

"Your grandparents wouldn't allow it . . ."

"This is such bullshit!"

More than the pain, and the bleeding, Brad was terrified that the girl would leave him here. He was shivering convulsively with cold, in terror of dying. The earth was icy-cold, he would expire of hypothermia. This prematurely balmy April day had turned cold when the sun set. In the southern Adirondacks, so near to Star Lake, the earth had rapidly darkened and the earth had rapidly cooled. Cold rose from the earth like departing spirits. The old cemetery was a place of broken stones, you'd think were the parts of human skeletons. Slabs of cracked granite, broken crockery like skulls, thick-snarled vines like pythons. The Beersheba Lutheran Church had been boarded up for at least ten years. The shingled roof had rotted through, the paint on the clapboards had mostly peeled off. At the front, saplings and wild rose grew in profusion, obscuring what remained of the church. From the road—should someone in a vehicle drive along the road—you could not see into the cemetery even by day. Frantically Brad was dragging himself toward the taunting girl—who kept a cautious distance between them—she'd drained her final can of beer and tossed it at him. She was laughing loudly, wiping at her mouth. She was drunk, or high on a drug, or intoxicated with her own adrenaline. Where tears had glistened on her fattish cheeks now beer glistened. In a voice of supreme disgust she said: "Also you did things to me, asshole. Like I had to beg for Cheez-bits, pizza—if Mommy was sleeping and I was hungry you'd make me beg—that turned you on, didn't it?—don't even remember do you? Got drunk and had me unzip your disgusting trousers. Had me 'scratch' you—ugh!"

Brad protested—he had not. He *had not* done such a thing.

Despite the pain in his leg and his terror of death he was genuinely shocked. He'd never done anything like that to Stacy Lynn—never . . .

"You did! You did! Not once but many times! I was just a little girl—nine, or eight—when it started. And Mommy knew—I know she did. I hated her—she pretended she didn't know but she *did*."

"Stacy, that isn't true. I swear—before God I swear—"

"'With God as my witness'—that's how you have to swear."

"'With God as my witness'—I did not harm you, and I did not harm your mother. If she claimed this—"

"She did not claim anything! She was a mentally ill woman you pushed over the edge. She was not a woman who wanted to die but when you were done with her, that is what she was, and that is what she *did*. And you walked away—you left us."

"Linda wasn't—mentally ill. She was sensitive, she was under stress—"

But it seemed to Brad that this was true. His young wife had been mentally ill. No one in the Gutshalk family had acknowledged this, even hinted this. And Brad hadn't realized. Too young, naïve, and stupid. Because Linda had been such a beautiful woman, he hadn't seemed to understand that she could be *sick*.

"Say you're sorry! Confess, murderer."

"But I—I didn't hurt her—"

"Say you're sorry, asshole—or I will cut your throat like the pig you are."

Knife in hand the girl lunged at Brad, feinted at him with whoops of glee and derision. Her manner was drunken, both playful and deadly serious. Her eyes shone with tears of indignation, cruelty. The sharp knife-tip caught him in the shoulder. He cried out like a rabbit stricken by an owl. Laughing she said: "Big baby! Asshole big baby! Crawl on your belly, you are wicked as Satan. Crawl—this way."

Blindly, Brad obeyed. At a distance of several feet Stacy Lynn whooped at him, kicked and feinted with the knife to drive him forward as you might drive a confused animal. Here the smell of organic rot, mold, and stone was overpowering. Surely it had to be, these were human bones, and broken fragments of bones, over which he was being made to crawl in abnegation like one before an idol-God. At the edge of the cemetery there was a sudden drop-off—a ravine—Stacy Lynn stood behind Brad and with her foot kicked, shoved, pushed him—forcing him over the edge—he fell, whimpering—the ravine was no more than twelve feet deep—a place of rocks, sharp stones, rubble and underbrush through which a shallow stream ran, icy water in glittering rivulets. In the clumsy fall Brad struck his head against a rock. Stunned he lay at the bottom of the ravine, his lips had gone numb with cold and he could hardly move like the stump of a person as the triumphant girl crouched above him. "You will be scourged of God—that's why you have been called to this place where there is nowhere to hide."

Brad pleaded he was a diabetic. He was a sick man, he had to have his insulin shot soon or he would go into a *diabetic coma* and die. At this the girl laughed cruelly. The girl laughed derisively. "You! 'Diabetic'! That's a joke. Crude pigs like you don't get sick—you make other, innocent people sick." She paused. She was panting, ecstatic in her triumph, peering down at him. "*I've* been sick. Since my mother died I've been plenty sick. They never let me see her again after the crash. I was not allowed to go to the funeral. I've been in rehab. More than once, in rehab. In different states. I moved away from here. I've been taught to come to terms. I let my mother down—I was eleven when she died. That is not a little child—eleven. I was the same person I am now, at eleven. In my heart I have not changed. In my soul. My mother was 'sick unto death' because of you—moving out the way you did, not even saying good-bye—she was wanting to die she was so unhappy and lying in bed all day like she was too weak to get up and dressed and I screamed at her I hated her—I said to her—you love him better than you love me, that nasty pig go live with him. You love him go live with *him*. Here—"

Stacy Lynn had been rummaging in her pockets. In the pockets of her jeans. She tossed down to Brad a notepad. And a pen. The pad—at first Brad had thought it was a pack of cigarettes—was a small spiral notebook with lined pages. By moonlight Brad could just discern this. In the rubble he was fumbling for the pen. He understood now—the girl was insane—he had no choice but to cooperate with her or he would die.

"Take this dictation, man! C'mon, man! Say—'I, Bradford Shiftke, resident of'—you can fill that in later, man—also the date—'am the cause of Linda Gutshalk's death in June 1985. I was a molester of her daughter Stacy Lynn when Stacy Lynn was a little girl between the ages of five and eleven. I molested that pathetic little girl sticking my fingers inside her and I made her touch my ugly nasty thing and hold it, and squeeze it—until white stuff came out of it like pus. I made her *beg for food* like her mother had to *beg for love.*'"

Like a figure in a silent film—contorted by pain, despair—yet the provocation of hilarity, in the observer—bizarrely Brad was trying to write, as the girl crouched above him dictating in a high-pitched urgent voice. His stiffened fingers could barely grasp the plastic ballpoint pen. He didn't know what he was writing—trying to write—yet he persevered, as if his life depended upon it. High overhead rubble-shaped clouds shuttered the moon briefly. Then, there came patches of moonlight like muffled cries. How long Brad wrote in the little notepad—how long, his legs twisted beneath him, he tried to write—he could not have said; yet though he persevered, suddenly his tormentor said, as if this were the punch line of a joke: "Hey asshole—desist! You'll retract any confession you make—think I don't know that? It's worthless. It's shit. Anything you touch is shit. You believed me did you—you pathetic old man. You're old now, you'd believe any shit to save your worthless life."

"Stacy—I won't retract it—I promise."

"My name is *Stacy Lynn* not *Stacy*! Fuck you have any right to utter my name or my mother's name—you're trash. Your soul is trash. Even Christ would spit upon you, you poison everyone you touch."

"No, please. I've never hurt anyone—not on purpose. I promise—"

"Bullshit! Tell it to some other female you betrayed and caused to die. I'm going now. I'm leaving you in just the right place. You can crawl back to Star Lake like a worm or you can die here like a worm, nobody will miss you. I'm not returning to Star Lake. I'm not returning to Carthage. At the motel I gave them a false name. It was my birthday last Friday—I am twenty-five years old. I had a health scare a few months ago, I had a biopsy at the county medical clinic and it turned out negative. I drove three thousand miles for this. For this moment, I drove three thousand miles and I lived three thousand years—ninety days in rehab. No one knows where I am. No one knows where you are. You are being punished, Brad-Daddy. You're shit, see? You don't even have a soul. My soul is stunted and deformed like a plant that has been growing beneath a rock or in a crack but my soul can prosper, if there's sun. If there's nourishment, and sun. But not you. Not you. A man like you." Stacy Lynn paused. Brad could hear her harsh, heavy breath. She laughed, striking the palms of her hands together in childish glee. "But know what?—I will let you live. God says forgive the worst enemies. Christ says forgive so I am letting you live, Brad."

He was alone. The girl had gone. The girl had heaved herself to her feet and departed. Half-conscious Brad could hear her making her way through the underbrush. Frantically he called after her to help him—not to leave him alone in this terrible place but to help him—but of course he was alone, his tormentor had left him alone in the ruins of the Beersheba Cemetery. In his fall into the ravine he'd struck his head, and his forehead—he was bleeding from a cut above his eye. He thought *I am not blinded. My eye has been spared.* His wounded leg was beginning to turn numb, as if it were the leg of another man. At a distance there was terrible pain but here Brad felt his body shake loose, float. He was very tired but the rocks were lifting him. The icy-glittering stream was related in some way to the coursing of his blood through his arteries and veins. His heart pounded like a fist against a locked door, he was breathing in shallow spurts like an old dog made to run by a cruel master. Yet she'd let him live. She'd had mercy on him, she'd given him back his life and he meant to take the gift of that life. When his strength returned he would crawl out of the ravine. When he was in the cemetery he would begin to call for help. He would drag himself to the road, he would call for help. His cries would be heard, eventually. He would not give up—he was not a crushed worm, to give up. Had the bleeding in his leg stopped? He thought possibly the bleeding had stopped. He thought *If the bleeding is stopped that is a good sign.*

NOBODY KNOWS
MY NAME

for Ellen Datlow

She was a precocious child, aged nine. She understood that there was danger even before she saw the cat with thistledown gray fur like breath, staring at her, eyes tawny-golden and unperturbed, out of the bed of crimson peonies.

It was summer. Baby's first summer they spoke of it. At Lake St. Cloud in the Adirondack Mountains in the summer house with the dark shingles and fieldstone fireplaces and the wide second-floor veranda that, when you stepped out on it, seemed to float in the air, unattached to anything. At Lake St. Cloud neighbors' houses were hardly visible through the trees, and she liked that. Ghost houses they were, and their inhabitants. Only voices carried sometimes, or radio music, from somewhere along the lakeshore a dog's barking in the early morning, but cats make no sound—that was one of the special things about them. The first time she'd seen the thistledown gray cat she'd been too surprised to call to it, the cat had stared at her and she had stared at the cat, and it seemed to her that the cat had recognized her, or in any case it had moved its mouth in a silent miming of speech—not a "meow" as in a silly cartoon but a human word. But in the next instant the cat had disappeared so she'd stood alone on the terrace feeling the sudden loss like breath sucked out of her and when Mommy came outside carrying the baby, the pretty candy cane towel flung over her shoulder to protect it from the baby's drool, she hadn't heard Mommy speaking to her at first because she was listening so hard to something else. Mommy repeated what she'd said, "Jessica—? Look who's here."

Jessica. That was the word, the name, the thistledown gray cat had mimed.

Back home, in the city, all the houses on Prospect Street which was their street were exposed, like in glossy advertisements. The houses were large and made of brick or stone and their lawns were large and carefully tended and never hidden from one another, never secret as at Lake St. Cloud. Their neighbors knew their names and were always calling out hello to Jessica even when they could tell she was looking away from them, thinking *I don't see anybody, they can't see me* but always there was the intrusion and backyards too ran together separated only by flower beds or hedges you could look over. Jessica loved the summer house that used to be Grandma's before she died and went away and left it to them though she was never certain it was *real* or only something she'd dreamt. She had trouble sometimes remembering what *real* was and what *dream* was and whether they could ever be the same or were always different. It was important to know because if she confused the two Mommy might notice, and question her, and once Daddy couldn't help laughing at her in front of company, she'd been chattering excitedly in that way of a shy child suddenly feverish to talk telling of how the roof of the house could be lifted and you could climb out using the clouds as stairs. Daddy interrupted to tell her no, no Jessie sweetheart that's just a dream, laughing at the stricken look in her eyes so she went mute as if he'd slapped her and backed away and ran out of the room to hide. And tore at her thumbnail with her teeth to punish herself.

Afterward Daddy came to her and squatted in front of her to look level in her eyes saying he was sorry he'd laughed at her and he hoped she wasn't mad at Daddy, it's just she's so *cute*, her eyes so *blue*, did she forgive Daddy? and she nodded yes her eyes filling with tears of hurt and rage and in her heart *No! no! no!* but Daddy didn't hear, and kissed her like always.

That was a long time ago. She'd only been in preschool then. A baby herself, so silly. No wonder they laughed at her.

The terrible worry was, for a while, they might not be driving up to Lake St. Cloud this summer.

It was like floating—just the name. Lake St. Cloud. And clouds reflected in the lake, moving across the ripply surface of the water. It was *up* to Lake St. Cloud in the Adirondacks when you looked at the map of New York State and it was *up* when Daddy drove, into the foothills and into the mountains on curving, sometimes twisting roads. She could feel the journey *up* and there was no sensation so strange and so wonderful.

Will we be going to the lake? Jessica did not dare ask Mommy or Daddy because to ask such a question was to articulate the very fear the question was meant to deny. And there was the terror, too, that the summer house was after all not *real* but only Jessica's *dream* because she wanted it so badly.

Back before Baby was born, in spring. Weighing only five pounds eleven ounces. Back before the "C-section" she heard them speak of so many times over the telephone, reporting to friends and relatives. "C-section"—she saw floating geometrical figures, octagons, hexagons, as in one of Daddy's architectural magazines, and Baby was in one of these, and had to be sawed out. The saw was a special one, Jessica knew, a surgeon's instrument. Mommy had wanted "natural labor" but it was to be "C-section" and Baby was to blame, but nobody spoke of it. There should have been resentment of Baby, and anger and disgust, for all these months Jessica was *good* and Baby-to-be *bad*. And nobody seemed to know, or to care. *Will we be going to the lake this year? Do you still love me?*—Jessica did not dare ask for fear of being told.

This was the year, the year of Mommy's swelling belly, when Jessica came to know many things without knowing how she knew. The more she was not told, the more she understood. She was a grave, small-boned child with pearly blue eyes and a delicate oval of a face like a ceramic doll's face and she had a habit of which all adults disapproved of biting her thumbnail until it bled or even sucking at her thumb if she believed she was unobserved but most of all she had the power to make herself invisible sometimes watching and listening and hearing more than was said. The times that Mommy was unwell that winter, and the dark circles beneath her eyes, and her beautiful chestnut hair brushed limp behind her ears, and her breath panting from the stairs, or just walking across a room. From the waist up Mommy was still Mommy but from the waist down, where Jessica did not like to look, the thing that was Baby-to-be, Baby-Sister-to-be, had swollen up grotesquely inside her so her belly was in danger of bursting. And Mommy might be reading to Jessica or helping with her bath when suddenly the pain would hit, Baby kicked hard, so hard Jessica could feel it too, and the warm color draining from Mommy's face, and the hot tears flooding her eyes. And Mommy would kiss Jessica hurriedly, and go away. And if Daddy was home she would call for him in that special voice meaning she was trying to keep calm. Daddy would say *Darling, you're all right, it's fine, I'm sure it's fine,* helping Mommy to sit somewhere comfortable, or lie down with her legs raised; or to make her way slow as an elderly woman down the hall to the bathroom. That was why Mommy laughed so much, and was so breathless, or began to cry suddenly. *These hormones!* she'd laugh. *Or, I'm too old! We waited too long! I'm almost forty! God help me, I want this baby so badly!* and Daddy would be comforting, mildly chiding, he was accustomed to handling Mommy in her moods, *Shhh! What kind of silly talk is that? Do you want to scare Jessie, do you want to scare* me? And though Jessica might be asleep in her room in her bed she would hear, and she would know, and in the morning she would remember as if what was *real* was also *dream,* with the secret power of *dream* to give you knowledge others did not know you possessed.

But Baby was born, and given a name: _____. Which Jessica whispered but, in her heart, did not *say.*

Baby was born in the hospital, sawed out of the C-section as planned. Jessica was brought to see Mommy and Baby _____ and the surprise of seeing them *the two of them so together* Mommy so tired-looking and so happy, and Baby that had been an *it,* that ugly swelling in Mommy's belly, was painful as an electric shock—swift-shooting through Jessica, even as Daddy held her perched on his knee beside Mommy's bed, it left no trace. *Jessie, darling—see who's here? Your baby sister_____ isn't she beautiful? Look at her tiny toes, her eyes, look at her hair that's the color of yours, isn't she beautiful?* and Jessica's eyes blinked only once or twice and with her parched lips she was able to speak, to respond as they wanted her to respond, like being called upon in school when her thoughts were in pieces like a shattered mirror but she gave no sign, she had the power, you must tell adults only what they want you to tell them so they will love you.

So Baby was born, and all the fears were groundless. And Baby was brought back in triumph to the house on Prospect Street flooded with flowers where there was a nursery repainted and decorated specially for her. And eight weeks later Baby was taken in the car up to Lake St. Cloud, for Mommy was strong enough now, and Baby was gaining weight so even the pediatrician was impressed, already able to focus her eyes, and smile, or seem to smile, and gape her toothless little mouth in wonderment hearing her name ____! ____! ____! so tirelessly uttered by adults. For everybody adored Baby, whose very poop was delightful to them. For everybody was astonished at Baby, who had only to blink and drool and gurgle and squawk red-faced moving her bowels inside her diaper or, in her battery-operated baby swing, fall abruptly asleep as if hypnotized—*isn't she beautiful! isn't she a love!* And to Jessica was put the question again, again, again *Aren't you lucky to have a baby sister?* and Jessica knew the answer that must be given, and given with a smile, a quick shy smile and a nod. For everybody brought presents for Baby, where once they had brought presents for another baby. (Except, as Jessica learned, overhearing Mommy talking with a woman friend, there were many more presents for Baby than there had been for Jessica. Mommy admitted to her friend there were really *too* many, she felt guilty, now they were well-to-do and not scrimping and saving as when Jessica was born, *now* they were deluged with baby things, almost three hundred presents!—she'd be writing thank-you notes for a solid year.)

At Lake St. Cloud, Jessica thought, it will be different.

At Lake St. Cloud, Baby won't matter so much.

But she was wrong: immediately she knew she was wrong, and wanting to come here was maybe a mistake. For never before had the big old summer house been so *busy*. And so *noisy*. Baby was colicky sometimes, and cried and cried and cried through the night, and certain special rooms like the first-floor sunroom that was so beautiful, all latticed windows overlooking the lake, were given over to Baby and soon took on Baby's smell. And sometimes the upstairs veranda where pine siskins, tame little birds, fluttered about the trees, making their sweet questioning cries—given over to Baby. The white wicker bassinet that was a family heirloom, pink and white satin ribbons threaded through the wicker, the gauzy lace veil drawn across sometimes to shield Baby's delicate face from the sun; the changing table heaped with disposable diapers; the baby blankets, baby booties, baby panties, baby pajamas, baby bibs, baby sweaters, baby rattles, mobiles, stuffed toys—everywhere. Because of Baby, more visitors, including distant aunts and uncles and cousins Jessica did not know, came to Lake St. Cloud than ever before; and always the question put to Jessica was *Aren't you lucky to have a baby sister? a beautiful baby sister?* These visitors Jessica dreaded more than she'd dreaded visitors in the city for they were intruding now in this special house, this house Jessica had thought would be as it had always been, before Baby, or any thought of Baby. Yet even here Baby was the center of all happiness, and the center of all attention. As if a radiant light shone out of Baby's round blue eyes which everybody *except Jessica* could see.

(Or were they just pretending?—with adults, so much was phony and outright lying, but you dared not ask. For then they would *know* that you *know*. And they would cease to love you.)

• • •

This secret, Jessica meant to tell the thistledown gray cat with the fur like breath but she saw in the cat's calm measuring unperturbed gaze that the cat already knew. He knew more than Jessica for he was older than Jessica, and had been here, at Lake St. Cloud, long before she was born. She'd thought him a neighbor's cat but really he was a wild cat belonging to nobody—*I am who I am, nobody knows my name.* Yet he was well fed, for he was a hunter. His eyes tawny-gold capable of seeing in the dark as no human being's eyes could. Beautiful with his filmy gray fur threaded just perceptibly with white, and his clean white bib, white paws and tail tip. He was a long-hair, part Persian, fur thicker and fuller than the fur of any cat Jessica had ever seen before. You could see he was strong-muscled in his shoulders and thighs, and of course he was unpredictable in his movements—one moment it seemed he was about to trot to Jessica's outstretched hand to take a piece of breakfast bacon from her, and allow her to pet him, as she pleaded, "Kitty-kitty-kitty! Oh kitty—" and the next moment he'd vanished into the shrubbery behind the peony bushes, as if he'd never been there at all. A faint thrashing in his wake, and then nothing.

Tearing at her thumbnail with her teeth to draw blood, to punish herself. For she was such a silly child, such an ugly stupid left-behind child, even the thistledown gray cat despised her.

• • •

Daddy was in the city one week from Monday till Thursday and when he telephoned to speak to Mommy, and to speak babytalk to Baby, Jessica ran away to hide. Later Mommy scolded her, "Where were you?—Daddy wanted to say hello," and Jessica said, eyes widened in disappointment, "Mommy, I was here all along." And burst into tears.

The thistledown gray cat, leaping to catch a dragonfly and swallowing it in midair.

The thistledown gray cat, leaping to catch a pine siskin, tearing at its feathers with his teeth, devouring it at the edge of the clearing.

The thistledown gray cat, leaping from a pine bough to the railing of the veranda, walking tail erect along the railing in the direction of Baby sleeping in her bassinet. And where is Mommy?

I am who am, nobody knows my name.

Jessica was wakened from sleep in the cool pine-smelling dark in this room she didn't recognize at first by something brushing against her face, a ticklish sensation in her lips and nostrils, and her heart pounding in fear—but fear for what, for what had been threatening to suck her breath away and smother her, what was it, who was it, she did not know.

It had crouched on her chest, too. Heavy, furry-warm. Its calm gold-glowing eyes. Kiss? Kiss-kiss? Kissy-kiss, Baby?—except *she was not Baby*. Never Baby!

• • •

It was July, and the crimson peonies were gone, and there were fewer visitors now. Baby had had a fever for a day and a night, and Baby had somehow (how? during the night?) scratched herself beneath the left eye with her own tiny fingernail, and Mommy was terribly upset, and had to be restrained from driving Baby ninety miles to a special baby doctor in Lake Placid. Daddy kissed Mommy and Baby both and chided Mommy for being too excitable, for God's sake honey get hold of yourself, this is nothing, you know this is nothing, we've been through this once already, haven't we?—and Mommy tried to keep her voice calm saying, Yes but every baby is different, and I'm different now, I'm more in love with _____ than ever with Jessie, God help me I think that's so. And Daddy sighed and said, Well I guess I am, too, it's maybe that we're more mature now and we know how precarious life is and we know we're not going to live forever the way it used to seem, only ten years ago we *were* young, and through several thicknesses of walls—at night, in the summer house above the lake, voices carried as they did not in the city—Jessica sucked on her thumb, and listened; and what she did not hear, she dreamt.

For that was the power of the night, where the thistledown gray cat stalked his prey, that you could dream what was real— and it *was* real, because you dreamt it.

Always, since Mommy was first unwell last winter, and Baby-to-be was making her belly swell, Jessica had understood that there was danger. That was why Mommy walked so carefully, and that was why Mommy stopped drinking even white wine which she loved with dinner, and that was why no visitors to the house, not even Uncle Albie who was everybody's favorite, and a chain-smoker, were allowed to smoke on the premises. Never again! And there was a danger of cold drafts even in the summer—Baby was susceptible to respiratory infections, even now she'd more than doubled her weight. And there was a danger of somebody, a friend or relative, eager to hold Baby, but not knowing to steady Baby's head and neck, which were weak. (After twelve weeks, Jessica had yet to hold her baby sister in her arms. She was shy, she was fearful. *No thank you, Mommy,* she'd said quietly. Not even seated close beside Mommy so the three of them could cuddle on a cozy, rainy day, in front of the fireplace, not even with Mommy guiding Jessica's hands—*No thank you, Mommy.*) And if Mommy ate even a little of a food wrong for Baby, for instance lettuce, Baby became querulous and twitchy after nursing from gas sucked with Mommy's milk and cried through the night. *Yet nobody was angry with Baby.*

And everybody was angry with Jessica when, one night at dinner, Baby in her bassinet beside Mommy, gasping and kicking and crying, Jessica suddenly spat out her food on her plate and clamped her hands over her ears and ran out of the dining room as Mommy and Daddy and the weekend house guests stared after her.

And there came Daddy's voice, "Jessie?—come back here—"

And there came Mommy's voice, choked with hurt, "Jessica!—that's *rude*—"

• • •

That night the thistledown gray cat climbed onto her window-sill, eyes gleaming out of the shadows. She lay very still in bed frightened *Don't suck my breath away! don't!* and after a long pause she heard a low hoarse-vibrating sound, a comforting sound like sleep, and it was the thistledown gray cat purring. So she knew she was safe, and she knew she would sleep. And she did.

Waking in the morning to Mommy's screams. Screaming and scream-ing her voice rising like something scrambling up the side of a wall. Screaming except now awake Jessica was hearing jays' cries close outside her window in the pines where there was a colony of jays and where if something disturbed them they shrieked and flew in quick darting swoops flapping their wings to protect themselves and their young.

The thistledown gray cat trotting behind the house, tail stiffly erect, head high, a struggling blue-feathered bird gripped be-tween his strong jaws.

All this time there was one thing Jessica did not think about, ever. It made her stomach tilt and lurch and brought a taste of bright hot bile into her mouth so *she did not think about it ever*.

Nor did she look at Mommy's breasts inside her loose-fitting shirts and tunics. Breasts filled with warm milk bulging like balloons. *Nursing* it was called, but Jessica did not think of it. It was the reason Mommy could never be away from Baby for

more than an hour—in fact, Mommy loved Baby so, she could
never be away from Baby for more than a few minutes. When
it was time, when Baby began to fret and cry, Mommy excused
herself a pride and elation showing in her face and tenderly she
carried Baby away, to Baby's room where she shut the door behind them. Jessica ran out of the house, grinding her fists into
her tight-closed eyes even as she ran stumbling, sick with shame.
I did not do that, ever. I was not a baby, ever.

And there was another thing Jessica learned. She believed it was
a trick of the thistledown gray cat, a secret wisdom imparted
to her. Suddenly one day she realized that, in the midst of witnesses, even Mommy who was so sharp-eyed, she could "look
at" Baby with wide-open eyes yet not "see" Baby—where Baby
was, in her bassinet, or in her perambulator or swing, or cradled
in Mommy's or Daddy's arms, *there was an emptiness.*

Just as she was able calmly to hear Baby's name _____ and
even speak that name _____ if required yet not acknowledge it
in her innermost heart.

She understood then that Baby would be going away soon.
For, when Grandma took sick and was hospitalized, Grandma
who was Daddy's mother and who had once owned the summer
place at Lake St. Cloud, though Jessica had loved the old woman
she'd been nervous and shy around her once she'd begun to smell
that orangish-sweet smell lifting from Grandma's shrunken body.
And sometimes looking at Grandma she would narrow her eyes
so where Grandma was there was a figure blurred as in a dream

and after a while an emptiness. She'd been a little girl then, four years old. She'd whispered in Mommy's ear, "Where is Grandma going?" and Mommy told her to hush, just hush, Mommy had seemed upset at the question so Jessica knew not to ask it again, nor to ask it of Daddy. She hadn't known if she was scared of the emptiness where Grandma was or whether she was restless having to pretend there was anything there in the hospital bed, anything that had to do with *her*.

Now the thistledown gray cat leapt nightly to her windowsill where the window was open. With a swipe of his white paw he'd knocked the screen inward so now he pushed his way inside, his tawny eyes glowing like coins and his guttural mew like a human query, teasing—*Who? You?* And the deep vibrating purr out of his throat that sounded like laughter as he leapt silently to the foot of Jessica's bed and trotted forward as she stared in astonishment to press his muzzle—his muzzle that was warm and sticky with the blood of prey only just killed and devoured in the woods—against her face! *I am who I am, nobody knows my name.* The thistledown gray cat held her down, heavy on her chest. She tried to throw him off, but could not. She was trying to scream, no she was laughing helplessly—the stiff whiskers tickled so. "Mommy! Daddy—" she tried to draw breath to scream but could not, for the giant cat, his muzzle pressed against her mouth, sucked her breath from her.

I am who I am, nobody knows my name, nobody can stop me.

• • •

It was a cool sky-blue morning in the mountains. At this hour, seven-twenty, Lake St. Cloud was clear and empty, no sailboats and no swimmers and the child was barefoot in shorts and T-shirt at the edge of the dock when they called to her from the kitchen door and at first she didn't seem to hear then turned slowly and came back to the house and seeing the queer, pinched look in her face they asked her was she feeling unwell?—was something wrong? Her eyes were a translucent pearly blue that did not seem like the eyes of a child. There were faint, bruised indentations in the skin beneath the eyes. Mommy who was holding Baby in the crook of an arm stooped awkwardly to brush Jessica's uncombed hair from her forehead which felt cool, waxy. Daddy who was brewing coffee asked her with a smiling frown if she'd been having bad dreams again?—she'd had upsetting dreams as a small child and she'd been brought in to sleep with Mommy and Daddy then, between them in the big bed where she'd been safe. But carefully she told them no, no she wasn't sick, she was fine. She just woke up early, that was all. Daddy asked her if Baby's crying in the middle of the night had disturbed her and she said no she didn't hear any crying and again Daddy said if she had bad dreams she should tell them and she said, in her grave, careful voice, "If I had some dreams, I don't remember them." She smiled then, not at Daddy, or at Mommy, a look of quick contempt. "I'm too old for *that*."

Mommy said, "No one's too old for nightmares, honey." Mommy laughed sadly and leaned to kiss Jessica's cheek but already Baby was stirring and fretting and Jessica drew away.

She wasn't going to be trapped by Mommy's tricks, or Daddy's. Ever again.

This is how it happened, when it happened.

On the upstairs veranda in gusts of sunshine amid the smell of pine needles and the quick sweet cries of pine siskins Mommy was talking with a woman friend on the cellular phone, and Baby who had just nursed was asleep in her heirloom bassinet with the fluttering satin ribbons, and Jessica who was restless this afternoon leaned over the railing with Daddy's binoculars staring at the glassy lake—the farther shore, where what appeared to the naked eye as mere dots of light were transformed into tiny human figures—a flock of mallards in an inlet at the edge of their property—the tangled grasses and underbrush beyond the peony bed where she'd seen something move. Mommy murmured, "Oh, damn!—this connection!" and told Jessica she was going to continue her conversation downstairs, on another phone, she'd be gone only a few minutes, would Jessica look after Baby? And Jessica shrugged and said yes of course. Mommy who was barefoot in a loose summer shift with a dipping neckline that made Jessica's eyes pinch peered into Baby's bassinet checking to see Baby *was* deeply asleep, and Mommy hurried downstairs, and Jessica turned back to the binoculars, which were heavy in her hands, and made her wrists ache unless she rested them on the railing. She was dreamy counting the sailboats on the lake, there were five of them within her range of vision, it made her feel bad because it was after Fourth of July now and Daddy kept promising he'd get the sailboat fixed up and take her out, always in previous summers Daddy had sailed by now though as he said he wasn't much of a sailor, he required perfect weather and today had been perfect all day—balmy, fragrant, gusts of wind but not too much wind—but Daddy was in the city at his office today, wouldn't be back till tomorrow evening—and Jessica was brooding, gnawing at her lower lip recalling now there was Baby, Mommy probably wouldn't go with them in the boat anyway, all that was changed. And would never be the same again. And Jessica saw the movements of quick-flitting birds in the pine boughs, and a blurred shape gray like vapor leaping past her field of vision, was it a bird? an owl? she was trying to locate it in the pine boughs which were so eerily magnified, every twig, every needle, every insect enlarged and seemingly only an inch from her eyes, when she realized she'd been hearing a strange, unnerving noise, a gurgling, gasping noise, and a rhythmic creaking of wood, and in astonishment she turned to see, less than three yards behind her, the thistledown gray cat hunched inside the bassinet, on Baby's tiny chest, pressing its muzzle against Baby's mouth . . .

The bassinet rocked with the cat's weight and the rough kneading motions of his paws. Jessica whispered, "No!—oh, no—" and the binoculars slipped from her fingers. As if this were a dream, her legs and arms were paralyzed. The giant cat, fierce-eyed, its filmy gray fur lifting light as milkweed silk, its white-tipped plume of a tail erect, paid her not the slightest heed as he sucked vigorously at the baby's mouth, kneading and clawing at his small prey who was thrashing for life, you would not think an infant of only three months could so struggle, tiny arms and legs flailing, face mottled red, but the thistledown cat was stronger, much stronger, and could not be deflected from his purpose—*to suck away Baby's breath, to suffocate, to smother with his muzzle.*

For the longest time Jessica could not move—this is what she would say, confess, afterward. And by the time she ran to the bassinet, clapping her hands to scare the cat away, Baby had ceased struggling, her face still flushed but rapidly draining of color, like a wax doll's face, and her round blue eyes were livid with tears, unfocused, staring sightless past Jessica's head.

Jessica screamed, "Mommy!"

Taking hold of her baby sister's small shoulders to shake her back into life, the first time Jessica had ever really touched her baby sister she loved so, but there was no life in the baby—it was too late. Crying, screaming, "Mommy! Mommy! Mommy!"

And that was how Mommy found Jessica—leaning over the bassinet, shaking the dead infant like a rag doll. Her father's binoculars, both lenses shattered, lay on the veranda floor at her feet.

FOSSIL-FIGURES

1.

Inside the great belly where the *beat beat beat* of the great heart pumped life blindly. Where there should have been one, there were two: the demon brother, the larger, ravenous with hunger, and the other, the smaller brother, and in the liquidy darkness a pulse between them, a beat that quivered and shuddered, now strong, now lapsing, now strong again, as the demon brother grew ever larger, took the nourishment as it pulsed into the womb, the heat, the blood, the mineral strength, kicked and shuddered with life so the mother, whose face was not known, whose existence could only be surmised, winced in pain, tried to laugh but went deathly pale, trying to smile gripping a railing *Ah! My baby. Must be a boy.* For in her ignorance the mother did not yet know that inside her belly there was not one but two. Flesh of my flesh and blood of my blood and yet not one but two. And yet not two equally, for the demon brother was the larger of the two, with but a single wish to suck suck suck into his being the life of the other, the smaller brother, all of the nourishment of the liquidy-dark womb, to suck into himself the smaller brother about whom he was hunched as if embracing him, belly to curving spine and the forehead of the demon brother pressed against the soft bone of the back of the head of the smaller brother. The demon brother had no speech but was purely appetite *Why there be this other here—this thing! Why this, when there is me! There is me, me, me there is only me.* The demon brother did not yet feed by mouth, had not yet sharp teeth to tear, chew, devour and so could not swallow up the smaller brother into his gut, and so the smaller brother survived inside the swollen belly where the *beat beat beat* of the great heart pumped life blindly and in ignorance until the very hour of the birth, when the demon brother forced his way out of the womb headfirst, a diver, a plunger, eager for oxygen, thrusting, squawling, struggling to declare himself, drew his first breath in a shudder of astonishment and began to bawl loudly, hungrily, kicking his small legs, flailing his small arms, a furious purple-flushed face, half-shut glaring eyes, strands of startlingly dark and coarse hair on the flushed infant-scalp *A Boy! Nine-pound boy! A beautiful—perfect—boy!* Swathed in the mother's oily blood, glistening like pent-up fire, a sharp scream and frenzied kicking as the umbilical cord attached to his navel was deftly severed. And what shock then—was it possible?—there was yet another baby inside the mother, but this not a perfect baby, a runt, cloaked in oily blood, a tiny aged man with a wizened face expelled from the mother after fourteen grunting minutes in a final spasm of waning contractions *Another! There is another boy* yet so tiny, malnourished, five pounds nine ounces, most of this weight in the head, bulbous blue-veined head, purple-flushed skin, the skull forceps-dented at the left temple, eyelids stuck together with bloody pus, tiny fists weakly flailing, tiny legs weakly kicking, tiny lungs weakly drawing breath inside the tiny rib cage *Oh but the poor thing won't live—will he?* Tiny caved-in chest, something twisted about the tiny spine and only faintly, as if at a distance, came the choked bleating cries. In contempt the demon brother laughed. From his place at the mother's breast suck suck sucking the mother's rich milk yet the demon brother laughed in contempt and anger for *Why there be this other here, why this, why "brother," why "twin," when there is me. Only be one of me.*

Yet not one: two.

At a fever pitch childhood passed for the demon brother who was first in all things. At a glacial pace childhood passed for the smaller brother who trailed behind his twin in all things. The demon brother was joyous to behold, pure infant fire, radiant thrumming energy, every molecule of his being quivering with life, appetite, *me me me.* The smaller brother was often sick, lungs filled with fluids, a tiny valve in his heart fluttered, soft bones of his curving spine, soft bones of his bowed legs, anemia, weak appetite, and the skull subtly misshapen from the forceps delivery, his cries were breathy, bleating, nearly inaudible *me? me?* For the demon brother was first in all things. In the twins' crib the first to roll onto his stomach, and the first to roll onto his back. The first to crawl. The first to rise on shaky baby-legs. The first to toddle about wide-eyed in triumph at being vertical. The first to speak: Ma*ma*. The first to drink in, to swallow up, to suck nourishment from all that he encountered, eyes widened in wonder, in greed, his first word Ma*ma* not an appeal or a plea but a command: Ma*ma*! Belatedly the smaller brother followed the demon brother, uncertain in his movements, poorly coordinated his legs, his arms, the very tilt of his head questionable, and his head quivering on frail shoulders, the eyes rapidly blinking, watery, seemingly weak as the facial features were less defined than those of the demon brother of whom it was claimed proudly *He's all boy!* while of the smaller brother it was murmured *Poor thing! But he is growing.* Or it was murmured *Poor thing! But what a sweet sad smile.* In these early years the smaller brother was often sickly and several times had to be hospitalized (anemia, asthma, lung congestion, heart-valve flutter, sprained bones) and in these interims the demon brother did not seem to miss the smaller brother but basked in the full attention of their parents and grew yet taller and stronger and soon it could scarcely be claimed that the brothers were twins—even "fraternal" twins—for observers would react with baffled smiles *Twins? How can that be possible!* For by the age of four, the demon brother was several inches taller than the smaller brother whose spine curved, and whose chest caved in upon itself, and whose eyes blinked teary and vaguely focused, and it came to seem that the brothers were not twins but, simply, brothers: the one older than the other by two or three years, and much healthier. *We love the boys equally. Of course.* At bedtime the demon brother sank into sleep with the abruptness of a rock sinking into dark water, come to rest in the soft dark mud below. At bedtime the smaller brother lay with opened eyes and stem-thin limbs twitching for he feared sleep as one might fear sinking into infinity *Even as a young child I understood that infinity is a vast fathomless chasm inside the brain into which we fall and fall through our lives, fall and fall unnamed, faceless and unknown where even, in time, the love of our parents is lost. Even the love of our mothers is lost. And all memory* waking from a thin tormented sleep like frothy water spilled across his face and he's struggling to breathe, choking and coughing, for the demon brother has sucked up most of the oxygen in the room, how can the demon brother help it, his lungs are so strong, his breath so deep and his metabolism so heated, naturally the demon brother will suck up the oxygen in the brothers' room where each night at bedtime their parents tuck the boys in, in twin beds, kissing each, declaring their love for each, and in the night the smaller brother is wakened from a nightmare of suffocation, his weak lungs unable to breathe panicked and whimpering in a plea for help managing to crawl from his bed and out of the room and into the hall, collapsed partway between the brothers' room and their parents' room where in the early morning the parents will discover him.

Such meager life, yet such life struggles to save itself!—so the demon brother would recall, in contempt.

Of course we love Edgar and Edward equally. They are both our sons.

This declaration the demon brother knew to be a lie. Yet was angered by the thought that, when the parents uttered the lie, as they did frequently, those who heard it might believe. And the smaller brother, the sickly brother, with his caved-in chest, crooked spine, wheezy asthmatic breath, yearning teary eyes and sweet smile wished to believe. To rebuke him, the demon brother had a way of turning on him when they were alone, for no (evident) reason pushing him, shoving him, wrestling him to the floor, as the smaller brother drew breath to protest straddling him with his knees, gripping the breakable rib cage like a vise, thump-thump-thumping the little freak's head against the floor, the moist hard palm of a hand camped over the little freak's mouth to prevent him from crying for help *Mama mama mama* faint as a dying lamb's bleating and so unheard by the mother in another part of the house downstairs in her bliss of ignorance not hearing the thump-thump-thump of the smaller brother's head against the carpeted floor of the boys' room until at last the smaller brother goes limp, ceases to struggle, ceases to struggle for breath, his pinched little face has turned blue, and the demon brother relents, releases him panting and triumphant.

Could've killed you, freak. And I will, if you tell.

For why were there two, and not one? As in the womb, the demon brother felt the injustice, and the illogic.

School! So many years. Here the demon brother, who was called Eddie, was first in all things. As the smaller brother, who was called Edward, lagged behind. Immediately in elementary school the brothers were not perceived to be twins but only just brothers, or relatives sharing a last name.

Edgar Waldman. Edward Waldman. But you never saw them together.

At school, Eddie was one of the popular boys. Adored by girls, emulated and admired by boys. He was a big boy. A husky boy. He was a natural leader, an athlete. Waved his hand, and teachers called upon him. His grades were never less than B. His smile was a dimpled smile, sly-sincere. He had a way of looking you frankly in the eye. By the age of ten Eddie had learned to shake hands with adults and to introduce himself *Hi! I'm Eddie* provoking smiles of admiration *What a bright precocious child!* and, to the demon brother's parents *How proud you must be of your son* as if in fact there were but one son, and not two. In sixth grade, Eddie ran for president of his class and was elected by a wide margin.

I am your brother, remember me!

You are nothing of mine. Go away!

But I am in you. Where can I go?

Already in elementary school the smaller brother Edward had dropped behind his twin. The problem wasn't his schoolwork—for Edward was a bright, intelligent, inquisitive boy—his grades were often As, when he was able to complete his work—but his health. So frequently absent from his fifth grade classes, he'd had to repeat the year. His lungs were weak, he caught respiratory infections easily. His heart was weak, in eighth grade he was hospitalized for weeks following surgery to repair the faulty heart valve. In tenth grade he suffered a "freak accident"—observed only by his brother Eddie, in their home—falling down a flight of stairs, breaking his right leg and kneecap and his right arm and several ribs and injuring his spine and thereafter he had to hobble about stricken with shyness, wincing in pain, on crutches. His teachers were aware of him, the "younger" Waldman boy. His teachers regarded him with sympathy, pity. In high school, his grades became ever more erratic: sometimes As but more often Cs, Ds, Incompletes. The smaller brother seemed to have difficulty concentrating in his classes, he fidgeted with pain, or stared open-eyed in a haze of painkillers, scarcely aware of his surroundings. When he was fully awake, he had a habit of hunching over his notebooks, that were unusually large, spiral notebooks with unlined pages, like sketchbooks, and in these notebooks he appeared to be constantly drawing, or writing; he frowned and bit his lower lip, lost in concentration, ignoring the teacher and the rest of the class *Slipping into infinity, a pleat in time and a twist of the pen and there's freedom!* The pen had to be black felt-tip with a fine point. The notebooks had to have marbled black-and-white covers. The teacher had to call upon "Edward" several times to get the boy's full attention and in his eyes then, a quick flaring-up, like a match lighted, shyness supplanted by something like resentment, fury. *Leave me alone can't you, I am not one of you.*

By the time the brothers were eighteen, Eddie was a senior bound for college, president of his class and captain of the football team and in the school yearbook "most likely to succeed" and Edward was trailing behind by a year, with poor grades. He'd begun to arrive at school with a wheelchair, brought by his mother, now in the throes of spinal pain from a slipped disk, and in this wheelchair he was positioned at the front, right-hand corner of his classes, near the teacher's desk, a broken, freaky figure with a small pinched boy's face, waxy skin and slack lips, drowsy from painkillers, or absorbed in his spiral notebooks in which he only pretended to take notes while in fact drawing bizarre figures—geometrical, humanoid—that seemed to spring from the end of his black felt-tip pen.

In the spring of his junior year, stricken with bronchitis, Edward didn't complete his courses and never returned to school: his formal education had ended. In that year, Eddie Waldman was recruited by a dozen universities offering sports scholarships and, shrewdly, he chose the most academically prestigious of the universities, for his goal beyond the university was law school.

Resembling each other as a shadow can be said to resemble its object. Edward was the shadow.

By this time the brothers no longer shared a room. The brothers no longer shared—even!—the old, cruel, childish custom of the demon brother's wish to harm his smaller twin; the demon brother's wish to suck all the oxygen out of the air, to swallow up his smaller twin entirely. *Why be this other here—this thing! Why this, when there is me!*

Here was the strange thing: the smaller brother was the one to miss the bond between them. For he had no other so deeply imprinted in his soul as his brother, no bond so fierce and intimate. *I am in you, I am your brother, you must love me.*

But Eddie laughed, backing away. Shook hands with his sickly brother for whom he felt only a mild repugnance, the mildest pang of guilt, and he said good-bye to his parents, allowed himself to be embraced and kissed and went away, smiling in anticipation of his life he went away with no plan to return to his hometown and to his boyhood house except for expediency's sake as a temporary visitor who would be, within hours of his return, restless, bored, eager to escape again to his "real" life elsewhere.

2.

Now in their twenties the brothers rarely saw each other. Never spoke on the phone.

Eddie Waldman graduated from law school. Edward Waldman continued to live at home.

Eddie excelled, recruited by a prominent New York City law firm. Edward suffered a succession of "health crises."

The father divorced the mother, abruptly and mysteriously it seemed, for the father, too, had a "real" life elsewhere.

Eddie entered politics, under the tutelage of a prominent conservative politician. Edward, suffering spinal pain, spent most days in a wheelchair. Inside his head calculating numbers, imagining equations in which the numerical, the symbolic, and the organic were combined, inventing music, rapidly filling large sheets of construction paper with bizarre yet meticulously detailed geometrical and humanoid figures in settings resembling those of the surrealist painter de Chirico and the visionary artist M. C. Escher. *Our lives are Möbius strips, misery and wonder simultaneously. Our destinies are infinite, and infinitely recurring.*

In the affluent suburb of the great American city, on a residential street of large, expensive house, the Waldman house, a clapboard Colonial on a two-acre lot, began by degrees to fall into disrepair, decline. The front lawn was unmowed and spiky, moss grew on the rotting shingle boards of the roof and newspapers and flyers accumulated on the front walk. The mother, once a sociable woman, began to be embittered, suspicious of neighbors. The mother began to complain of ill health, mysterious "hexes." The mother understood that the father had divorced her as a way of divorcing himself from the misshapen broke-backed son with the teary, yearning eyes who would never grow up, would never marry, would spend the rest of his life in the fevered execution of eccentric and worthless "art."

Frequently the mother called the other son, the son of whom she was so proud, whom she adored. But Eddie seemed always to be traveling and rarely responded to his mother's messages.

In time, within a decade, the mother would die. In the now derelict house (visited, infrequently, by a few concerned relatives) Edward would live as a recluse in two or three downstairs rooms, one of which he'd converted into a makeshift studio. The embittered mother had left him enough money to enable him to continue to live alone and to devote himself to his work; he hired help to come to the house from time to time to clean it, or to attempt to clean it; to shop for him, and to prepare meals. *Freedom! Misery and wonder!* On large canvases Edward transcribed his bizarre dream-images, among galaxies of hieroglyphic shapes in a sequence titled *Fossil-Figures.* For it was Edward's belief, that had come to him in a paroxysm of spinal pain, that misery and wonder are interchangeable and that one must not predominate. In this way time passed in a fever-heat for the afflicted brother, who was not afflicted but blessed. Time was a Möbius strip that looped back upon itself, weeks, months, and years passed and yet the artist grew no older, in his art. (In his physical being, perhaps. But Edward had turned all mirrors to the wall and had not the slightest curiosity what Edward now "looked like.")

The father, too, died. Or disappeared, which is the same thing. Relatives ceased to visit, and may have died.

Into infinity, which is oblivion. But it is out of that infinity we have sprung: why?

It began to be, as if overnight, the era of the Internet. No man need be a recluse now. However alone and cast off by the world.

Via the Internet *E.W.* communicated with companions—soul mates—scattered in cyberspace of whom, at any given time, there were invariably a few—but E.W.'s needs were so minimal, his ambition for his art so modest, he required only a few—fascinated by the *Fossil-Figures* he displayed on the Web, who negotiated to buy them. (Sometimes, bidding against one another, for unexpectedly high sums.) And there were galleries interested in exhibiting the works of *E.W.*—as the artist called himself—and small presses interested in publishing them. In this way, in the waning years of the twentieth century, *E.W.* became something of an underground cult figure, rumored to be impoverished, or very wealthy; a crippled recluse living alone in a deteriorating old house, in a deteriorating body, or, perversely, a renowned public figure who guarded his privacy as an artist.

Alone yet never lonely. For is a twin lonely?

Not so long as his twin-self continues to exist.

The brothers were never in contact now yet, on TV, by chance as sometimes Edward flicked through channels like one propelling himself through the chill of intergalactic space, he came upon images of his lost brother: giving impassioned speeches ("sanctity of life"—"pro-life"—"family values"—"patriotic Americans") to adoring crowds, being interviewed, smiling into the camera with the fiery confidence of one ordained by God. There was the demon brother elected to the U.S. Congress from a district in a neighboring state, the smaller brother hadn't known he was living in; there, the demon brother beside an attractive young woman, gripping the young woman's hand, a wife, a Mrs. Edgar Waldman, the smaller brother hadn't known he had married. The demon brother had been taken up by rich, influential elders. In a political party, such elders look to youth to further their political heritage, their "tradition." In this political party the "tradition" was identical with economic interests. No values, no morals, no goals other than economic interests. This was the triumphant politics of the era. This was the era of the self. *Me, me, me! There is me, me, me there is only me.* Cameras panned rapturous audiences, fervently applauding audiences. For in *me*, there is the blind wish to perceive *we*. As in the most primitive, wrathful, and soulless of gods, humankind will perceive *we*. In the most distant galaxies, infinities of mere emptiness, the ancient yearning *we*.

So Edward, the left-behind brother, hunched in his wheel-chair, regarded the demon brother glimpsed on TV with no bitterness nor even a sense of estrangement as one might feel for a being of another species but with the old, perverse yearning *I am your brother, I am in you. Where else can there be, that I am?*

Here was the inescapable fact: the brothers shared a single birth-day. Even beyond their deaths, that fact would never change.

January 26. The dead of winter. Each year on that day the brothers thought of each other with such vividness, each might have imagined that the other was close beside him, or behind him, a breath on his cheek, a phantom embrace. *He is alive, I can feel him* Edward thought with a shiver of anticipation. *He is alive, I can feel him* Edgar thought with a shiver of revulsion.

3.

There came a January 26 that marked the brothers' fortieth birthday. And a few days later there came to an exhibit of E.W.'s new exhibit *Fossil-Figures* in a storefront gallery in the warehouse district near the Hudson River at West and Canal streets, New York City, U.S. Congressman Edgar Waldman who'd given a political speech that afternoon in Midtown, alone now, a limousine with U.S. federal plates waiting at the curb. Noting with satisfaction that the exhibit rooms were nearly deserted. Noting with disgust how the old, cracked linoleum stuck against the bottoms of his expensive shoes. The handsome congressman wore very dark glasses, he looked at no one, in dread of being recognized in this sordid place. Especially he was in dread of seeing the crippled brother—"E. W."—whom he had not seen in nearly twenty years but believed that he would recognize immediately though by this time the twins—"fraternal" twins—looked nothing alike. Edgar anticipated the stunted broken figure in a wheelchair, yearning teary eyes and wistful smile that maddened, made you want to strike with your fists, that offer of forgiveness where forgiveness was not wanted. I *am your brother, I am in you. Love me!* But there was no one.

Only just E. W.'s work, pretentiously called by the gallery "collage paintings." These *Fossil-Figures* lacked all beauty, even the canvases upon which they were painted looked soiled and battered and the walls upon which they were (unevenly) hung were streaked as if the hammered-tin ceiling leaked rust. What were these artworks covered in dream/nightmare shapes, geometrical, yet humanoid, shifting into and out of one another like translucent guts, deeply offensive to the congressman who sensed "subterfuge"—"perversion"—"subversion" in such obscure art, and what was obscure was certain to be "soulless"—even "traitorous." Most upsetting, the *Fossil-Figures* seemed to be taunting the viewer, anyway this viewer, like riddles, and he had no time for God-damned riddles, the rich man's daughter he'd married to advance his career was awaiting him at the St. Regis, this visit to West and Canal streets was an (unmarked) stop in Congressman Waldman's itinerary for the day. Wiping his eyes to better see an artwork depicting the night sky, distant galaxies and constellations, almost there was beauty here, suns like bursting egg yolks swallowing up smaller suns, comets shaped like—was it male sperm?—blazing male sperm?—colliding with luminous bluish-watery planets; and, protruding from the rough surface of the canvas, a thing so unexpected, so ugly, the congressman stepped back in astonishment: was it a nestlike growth of some kind? a tumor? comprised of plasticine flesh and dark crinkly hairs and—could it be baby teeth? arranged in a smile?—and a scattering of baby bones?

A fossil, it was. A thing removed from the human body. Something very ugly discovered in a cavity of a surviving twin's body. The fossil-soul of the other, that had never breathed life.

Stunned, quivering with disgust, the congressman turned away.

Walked on, in a haze of denunciations, denials. Seeing that some of the canvases were beautiful—were they?—or were they all ugly, obscene, if you knew how to decode them?—he was made to think that he was endangered, something was going to happen to him, there was the blunt statistical fact that in the last election he'd been reelected to his seat in Congress by a smaller majority than in any of the preceding elections, in such victory there is the presentiment of defeat. Through the maze of rooms circling back to the start of the exhibit and at a glass-topped counter there was a bored-looking girl with dead-white skin and a face glittering with piercings who seemed to be working for the gallery and he asked of her in a voice that quavered with indignation if these ridiculous "fossil-figures" were considered "art" and she told him politely yes of course, everything the gallery exhibited was art and he asked if the exhibit was supported by public funds and seemed but partly mollified to learn that it was not. He asked who the "so-called artist" E.W. was and the girl spoke vaguely saying nobody knew E.W. personally, only the proprietor of the gallery had ever seen him, he lived by himself outside the city and never came into the city, not even to oversee the exhibit, didn't seem to care if his artworks sold, or what prices they were sold for.

"He's got some 'wasting-away' disease, like muscular dystrophy, or Parkinson's, but last we knew, E.W. is alive. He's alive."

And I won't go away. You will come to me instead.

Each year: January 26. One year, one insomniac night, Edward is flicking restlessly through TV channels and is surprised to see a sudden close-up of—is it Edgar? The demon brother Edgar? TV news footage from earlier in the day, rerun now in the early hours of the morning, suddenly this magnification of a man's head, thick-jawed face, an aging face obscured by dark glasses, skin gleaming with oily sweat, an arm lifted to shield the disgraced congressman from a pack of pursuing reporters, photographers and TV camera crews, there's Congressman Edgar Waldman being briskly walked into a building by plainsclothes police officers. *Indicted on multiple charges of bribe taking, violations of federal campaign laws, perjury before a federal grand jury.* Already the rich man's daughter has filed for divorce, there's the quick smile, a suggestion of bared teeth. In the brothers' childhood house in which Edward lives in a few downstairs rooms Edward stares at the TV screen from which the lost brother has faded uncertain if the thumping sensation in his head is a profound shock, a pang of hurt that must beat within the brother, or his own excitement, eagerness. *He will come to me now. He will not deny me, now.*

EPILOGUE

It was so. The demon brother would return home, to his twin who awaited him.

For he knew himself now *Not one but two.* In the larger world he'd gambled his life and lost his life and would retreat now, to the other. In retreat a man sets aside pride, disgraced, divorced, bankrupt and a glisten of madness in the washed-out blue eyes. His heavy jaws were silvery-dark with stubble, a tremor in his right hand that had been lifted in a federal court to swear that Edgar Waldman would tell the truth the whole truth and nothing but the truth *Yes I swear* and in that heartbeat it was all over for him, a taste like bile rising at the back of his mouth.

Still the wonder. Disbelief. The corroded ruin of a face like clay that has been worn down by rivulets of water, wind. And that glisten of madness in the eyes: *Me?*

In retreat now returning to his childhood home, he had shunned for years. The left-behind, broke-backed younger brother who'd been living alone since their mother's death, now many years ago. As a young man he'd never considered time as anything other than a current to bear him aloft, propel him into his future, now he understood that time is a rising tide, implacable inexorable unstoppable rising tide, now at the ankles, now the knees, rising to the thighs, to the groin and the torso and to the chin, ever rising, a dark water of utter mystery propelling us forward not into the future but into infinity which is oblivion.

Returning to the suburban town of his birth and to the house he'd shunned for decades seeing now with a pang of loss how the residential neighborhood had changed, many of the large houses converted to apartment buildings and commercial sites, and most of the plane trees lining the street severely trimmed or removed altogether. And there was the old Waldman home, that had once been their mother's pride, once so splendidly white, now a weatherworn gray with sagging shutters and a rotting roof and a lush junglelike front lawn awash in litter as if no one had lived there for a long time. Edgar had been unable to contact Edward by phone, there was no directorial listing for a phone under the name Edward Waldman, now his heart pounded in his chest, he felt a wave of dread *He has died, it is too late.* Hesitantly knocking at the front door and listening for a response from within and knocking again, more loudly, hurting his knuckles, and at last there came from within a faint bleating sound, a voice asking who it was and he called out *It's me.*

Slowly as if with effort the door opened. And there, in his wheelchair, as Edgar had imagined him, but not so ravaged as Edgar had imagined him, was his brother Edward whom he hadn't seen in more than two decades: a shrunken individual of no obvious age with a narrow, pale, pinched yet unlined face, a boy's face, and his hair threaded with gray like Edgar's, and one bony shoulder higher than the other. Pale blue eyes filling with moisture he swiped at with the edges of both hands and in a scratchy voice that sounded as if it hadn't been used in some time he said *Eddie. Come in.*

. . . when it happened could never be determined precisely since the bodies were frozen and preserved from decay found together on a leather sofa made as a bed pulled to within a foot of a fireplace heaped with ashes in a downstairs room of the old clapboard Colonial crowded with furniture and what appeared to be the accumulated debris of decades but which may have been materials for artworks or the very artworks themselves of the eccentric artist known as E.W., the elderly Waldman brothers in layers of bulky clothing must have fallen asleep in front of a fire in the otherwise unheated house, the fire must have burnt out in the night and the brothers died in their

sleep in a protracted January cold spell: the brother to be identified as Edgar Waldman, eighty-seven, embracing his brother Edward Waldman, also eighty-seven, from behind, protectively fitting his body to his brother's crippled body, forehead tenderly pressed to the back of the other's head, the two figures coiled together like a gnarled organic material that has petrified to stone.

DEATH-CUP

Amanita phalloides he began to hear in no voice he could recognize.

Murmurous, only just audible—*Amanita phalloides*.

More distinctly that morning, a rain-chilled Saturday morning in June, at his uncle's funeral. In the austere old Congregationalist church he only entered, as an adult, for such ceremonies as weddings and funerals. As, seated beside his brother Alastor of whom he disapproved strongly, he leaned far forward in the cramped hardwood pew, framing his face with his fingers so that he was spared seeing his brother's profile in the corner of his eye. Feeling an almost physical repugnance for the man who was his brother. He tried to concentrate on the white-haired minister's solemn words yet was nervously distracted by *Amanita phalloides*. As if, beneath the man's familiar words of Christian forbearance and uplift another voice, a contrary voice, strange, incantatory, was struggling to emerge. And during the interlude of organ music. The Bach Toccata and Fugue in D-minor which his uncle, an amateur musician and philanthropist, had requested be played at his funeral. Lyle was one who, though he claimed to love music, was often distracted during it; his mind drifting; his thoughts like flotsam, or froth; now hearing the whispered words, only just audible in his ears *Amanita phalloides, Amanita phalloides.* He realized he'd first heard these mysterious words the night before, in a dream. A sort of fever-dream. Brought on by his brother's sudden, unexpected return.

He did not hate his brother Alastor. Not here, in this sacred place.

Amanita phalloides. Amanita phalloides . . .

How beautiful, the Bach organ music! Filling the spartan-plain, dazzlingly-white interior of the church with fierce cascades of sound pure and flashing as a waterfall. Such music argued for the essential dignity of the human spirit. The transcendence of physical pain, suffering, loss. All that's petty, ignoble. *The world is a beautiful place if you have the eyes to see it and the ears to hear it* Lyle's uncle had often said, and had seemed to believe through his long life, apparently never dissuaded from the early idealism of his youth; yet how was such idealism possible, Lyle couldn't help but wonder, Lyle who wished to believe well of others yet had no wish to be a fool, how was such idealism possible after the evidence of catastrophic world wars, the unspeakable evil of the holocaust, equally mad, barbaric mass-slaughters in Stalin's Russia, Mao's China? Somehow, his uncle Gardner King had remained a vigorous, good-natured and generous man despite such facts of history; there'd been in him, well into his seven-ties, a childlike simplicity which Lyle, his nephew, younger than he by decades, seemed never to have had. Lyle had loved his uncle, who'd been his father's eldest brother; fatherless himself since the age of eleven, he'd been saddened by his uncle's gradual descent into death from cancer of the larynx, and had not wanted to think that he would probably be remembered, to some degree, in his uncle's will. The bulk of the King estate, many millions of dollars, would go into the King Foundation, which was nominally directed by his wife, now widow, Alida King; the rest of it would be divided among numerous relatives. Lyle was troubled by the anticipation of any bequest, however modest. The mere thought filled him with anxiety, almost a kind of dread. *I would not wish to benefit in any way from Uncle Gardner's death, I could not bear it.*

To which his brother Alastor would have replied in his glib, jocular way, as, when they were boys, he'd laughed at Lyle's overscrupulous conscience *What good's that attitude? Our uncle is dead and he isn't coming back, is he?*

Unfortunate that Alastor had returned home to Contracoeur on the very eve of their uncle's death, after an absence of six years. Still, it could only have been coincidence. So Alastor claimed. He'd been in communication with none of the relatives, including his twin brother Lyle.

How murmurous, teasing in Lyle's ears—*Amanita phalloides.*

Intimate as a lover's caressing whisper, and mysterious—*Amanita phalloides.*

Lyle was baffled at the meaning of these words. Why, at such a time, his thoughts distracted by grief, they should assail him.

In the hardwood pew, unpleasantly crowded by Alastor on his left, not wanting to crowd, himself, against an elderly aunt on his right, Lyle felt his lean, angular body quiver with tension. His neck was beginning to ache from the strain of leaning forward. It annoyed him to realize that, in his unstylish matte-black gabardine suit that fitted him too tightly across the shoulders and too loosely elsewhere, with his ash-colored hair straggling past his collar, his face furrowed as if with pain, and the peculiar way he held his outstretched fingers against his face, he was making himself conspicuous among the rows of mourners in the King family pews. Staring at the gleaming ebony casket so prominently placed in the center aisle in front of the communion rail, that looked so forbidding; so gigantic; far larger than his uncle Gardner's earthly remains, diminutive at the end, would seem to require. *But of course death is larger than life. Death envelops life: the emptiness that precedes our brief span of time, the emptiness that follows.*

A shudder ran through him. Tears stung his cheeks like acid. How shaky, how emotional he'd become!

A nudge in his side—his brother Alastor pressed a handkerchief, white, cotton, freshly laundered, into his hand, which Lyle blindly took.

Managing, even then, not to glance at his brother. Not to upset himself seeing yet again his brother's mock-pious mockgrieving face. *His* watery eyes, in mimicry of Lyle's.

Now the organ interlude was over. The funeral service was ending—so soon! Lyle felt a childish stab of dismay, that his uncle would be hurried out of the sanctuary of the church, out of the circle of the community, into the impersonal, final earth. Yet the white-haired minister was leading the congregation in a familar litany of words beginning, "Our heavenly father . . ." Lyle wiped tears from his eyelashes, shut his eyes tightly in prayer. He hadn't been a practicing Christian since adolescence, he was impatient with unquestioned piety and superstition, yet there was solace in such a ritual, seemingly shared by an entire community. Beside him, his aunt Agnes prayed with timid urgency as if God were in this church and needed only to be beseeched by the right formula of words, and in the right tone of voice. On his other side, his brother Alastor intoned the prayer, not ostentatiously but distinctly enough to be heard for several pews; Alastor's voice was a deep, rich baritone, the voice of a trained singer you might think, or an actor. A roaring in Lyle's ears like a waterfall—*Amanita phalloides! Amanita phalloides!* and suddenly he remembered what *Amanita phalloides* was: the death-cup mushroom. He'd been reading a pictorial article on edible and inedible fungi in one of his science magazines and the death-cup mushroom, more accurately a "toadstool," had been imprinted on his memory.

His mouth had gone dry, his heart was hammering against his ribs. With the congregation, he murmured, "Amen." All volition seemed to have drained from him. Calmly he thought *I will kill my brother Alastor after all. After all these years.*

Of course, this would never happen. Alastor King was a hateful person who surely deserved to die, but Lyle, his twin brother, was not one to commit any act of violence; not even one to fantasize any act of violence. *Not me! Not me! Never.*

In the cemetery behind the First Congregationalist Church of Contracoeur the remainder of the melancholy funeral rite was enacted. There stood Lyle King, the dead man's nephew, in a daze in wet grass beneath a glaring opalescent sky, awakened by strong fingers gripping his elbow. "All right if I ride with you to Aunt Alida's, Lyle?" Alastor asked. There was an edge of impatience to his lowered voice as if he'd had to repeat his question. And Lyle's twin brother had not been one, since the age of eighteen months, to wish to repeat questions. He was leaning close to Lyle as if hoping to read his thoughts; his eyes were steely-blue, narrowed. His breath smelled of something sweetly chemical, mouthwash probably, to disguise the alcohol on his breath; Lyle knew he was carrying a pocket flask in an inside pocket. His handsome ruddy face showed near-invisible broken capillaries like exposed nerves. Lyle murmured, "Of course, Alastor. Come with me." His thoughts flew ahead swiftly—there was Cemetery Hill that was treacherously steep, and the High Street Bridge—opportunities for accidents? Somehow Lyle's car might swerve out of control, skid on the wet pavement, Alastor who scorned to wear a seat belt might be thrown against the windshield, might be injured, might die, while he, Lyle, buckled in safely, might escape with but minor injuries. And blameless. Was that possible? Would God watch over him?

Not possible. For Lyle would have to drive other relatives in his car, too. He couldn't risk their lives. And there was no vigilant God.

A simple self-evident fact, though a secret to most of the credulous world: Alastor King, attractive, intelligent and deathly "charming" as he surely was, was as purely hateful, vicious and worthless an individual as ever lived. His brother Lyle had grown to contemplate him with horror the way a martyr of ancient times might have contemplated the engine of pain and destruction rushing at him. *How can so evil a person deserve to live?* Lyle had wondered, sick with loathing of him. (This was years ago when the brothers were twenty. Alastor had secretly seduced their seventeen-year-old cousin Susan, and within a week or two lost interest in her, causing the girl to attempt suicide and to suffer a breakdown from which she would never fully recover.) Yet, maddening, Alastor had continued to live, and live. Nothing in the normal course of events would stop him.

Except Lyle. His twin. Who alone of the earth's billions of inhabitants understood Alastor's heart.

And so how shocked Lyle had been, how sickened, having hurried to the hospital when word came that his uncle Gardner was dying, only to discover, like the materialization of one of his nightmares, his brother Alastor already there! Strikingly dressed as usual, with an expression of care, concern, solicitude, clasping their aunt Alida's frail hand and speaking softly and reassuringly to her, and to the others, most of them female relatives, in the visitors' waiting room outside the intensive care unit. As if Alastor hadn't been mysteriously absent from Contracoeur for six years, not having returned even for their mother's funeral; as if he hadn't disappeared abruptly when he'd left, having been involved in a dubious business venture and owing certain of the relatives money, including Uncle Gardner (an undisclosed sum—Lyle didn't doubt it was many thousands of dollars) and Lyle himself (three thousand five hundred dollars).

Lyle had stood in the doorway, staring in disbelief. He had not seen his twin brother in so long, he'd come to imagine that Alastor no longer existed in any way hurtful to him.

Alastor cried, "Lyle, brother, hello! Good to see you!—except this is such a tragic occasion."

Swiftly Alastor came to Lyle, seizing his forearm, shaking his hand vigorously as if to disarm him. He was smiling broadly, with his old bad-boyish air, staring Lyle boldly in the face and daring him to wrench away. Lyle stammered a greeting, feeling his face burn. *He has come back like a bird of prey, now Uncle Gardner is dying.* Alastor nudged Lyle in the ribs, saying in a chiding voice that he'd returned to Contracoeur just by chance, to learn the sad news about their uncle—"I'd have thought, Lyle, that you might have kept your own brother better informed. As when Mother died, too, so suddenly, and I didn't learn about it for months."

Lyle protested, "But you were traveling—in Europe, you said—out of communication with everyone. You—"

But Alastor was performing for Aunt Alida and the others, and so interrupted Lyle to cry, with a pretense of great affection, "How unchanged you are, Lyle! How happy I am to see you." It wasn't enough for Alastor to have gripped Lyle's hand so hard he'd nearly broken the fingers, now he had to embrace him; a rough bearlike hug that nearly cracked Lyle's ribs, calculated to suggest to those who looked on *See how natural I am, how spontaneous and loving, and how stiff and unnatural my brother is, and has always been, though we're supposed to be twins.* Lyle had endured this performance in the past and had no stomach for it now, pushing Alastor away and saying in an angry undertone, "You! What are you doing here! I'd think you'd be damned ashamed, coming back like this." Not missing a beat, Alastor laughed and said, winking, one actor to another in a play performed for a credulous, foolish audience, "But why, brother? When you can be ashamed for both of us?" And he squeezed Lyle's arm with deliberate force, making him wince, as he'd done repeatedly when they were boys, daring Lyle to protest to their parents. *Daring me to respond with equal violence.* Then slinging a heavy arm around Lyle's shoulders, and walking him back to the women, as if Lyle were the reluctant visitor, and he, Alastor, the self-appointed host. Lyle quickly grasped, to his disgust, that Alastor had already overcome their aunt Alida's distrust of him and had made an excellent impression on everyone, brilliantly playing the role of the misunderstood prodigal son, tender-hearted, grieved by his uncle's imminent death and eager—so eager!—to give comfort to his well-to-do aunt.

How desperately Lyle wanted to take Aunt Alida aside, for she was an intelligent woman, and warn her *Take care! My brother is after Uncle Gardner's fortune!* But of course he didn't dare; it wasn't in Lyle King's nature to be manipulative.

In this way, Alastor King returned to Contracoeur.

And within a few days, to Lyle's disgust, he'd reestablished himself with most of the relatives and certain of his old friends and acquaintances; probably, Lyle didn't doubt, with former women friends. He'd overcome Alida King's distrust and this had set the tone for the others. Though invited to stay with relatives, he'd graciously declined and had taken up residence at the Black River Inn; Lyle knew that his brother wanted privacy, no one spying on him, but others interpreted this gesture as a wish not to intrude, or impinge upon family generosity. How thoughtful Alastor had become, how kind, how *mature*. So Lyle was hearing on all sides. It was put to him repeatedly, maddeningly: "You must be so happy, Lyle, that your brother has returned. You must have missed him terribly."

And Lyle would smile wanly, politely, and say, "Yes. Terribly."

The worst of it was, apart from the threat Alastor posed to Alida King, that Lyle, who'd succeeded in pushing his brother out of his thoughts for years, was forced to think of him again; to think obsessively of him again; to recall the myriad hurts, insults, outrages he'd suffered from Alastor; and the numerous cruel and even criminal acts Alastor had perpetrated, with seeming impunity. And of course he was always being thrown into Alastor's company: always the fraudulent, happy cry, "Lyle! Brother!"—always the exuberant, rib-crushing embrace, a mockery of brotherly affection. On one occasion, when he'd gone to pick up Alastor at the hotel, Lyle had staved Alastor off with an elbow, grimacing. "Damn you, Alastor, *stop*. We're not onstage, no one's watching." Alastor said, laughing, with a contemptuous glance around, "What do you mean, brother? Someone is always watching."

It was true. Even on neutral ground, in the foyer of the Black River Inn, for instance, people often glanced at Alastor King. In particular, women were drawn to his energetic, boyish good looks and bearing.

As if they saw not the man himself but the incandescent, seductive image of the man's desire: his wish to deceive.

While, seeing Lyle, they saw merely—Lyle.

What particularly disgusted Lyle was that his brother's hypocrisy was so transparent. Yet so convincing. And he, the less demonstrative brother, was made to appear hesitant, shy, anemic by comparison. Lacking, somehow, manliness itself. Alastor was such a dazzling sight: his hair that should have been Lyle's identical shade of faded ashy-brown was a brassy russet-brown, lifting from his forehead in waves that appeared crimped, while Lyle's thinning hair was limp, straight. Alastor's sharply blue eyes were alert and watchful and flirtatious while Lyle's duller blue eyes were gently myopic and vague behind glasses that were invariably finger-smudged. Apart from a genial flush to his skin, from an excess of food and drink, Alastor radiated an exuberant

sort of masculine health; if you didn't look closely, his face appeared youthful, animated, while Lyle's was beginning to show
the inroads of time, small worried dents and creases, particularly
at the corners of his eyes. Alastor was at least twenty pounds
heavier than Lyle, thick in the torso as if he'd been building up
muscles, while Lyle, lean, rangy, with an unconscious tendency
to slouch, looked by comparison wan and uncoordinated. (In
fact, Lyle was a capable swimmer and an enthusiastic tennis
player.) Since early adolescence Alastor had dressed with verve:
at the hospital, he'd worn what appeared to be a suit of suede,
honey-colored, with an elegantly cut jacket and a black silk shirt
worn without a tie; after their uncle's death, he'd switched to
theatrical mourning, in muted-gray fashionable clothes, a linen
coat with exaggerated padded shoulders, trousers with prominent
creases, shirts so pale a blue they appeared a grieving white and
a midnight blue necktie of some beautiful glossy fabric. And he
wore expensive black leather shoes with soles that gave him an
extra inch of height—so that Lyle, who had always been Alastor's height exactly, was vexed by being forced *to look at him*.
Lyle, who had no vanity, and some might say not enough pride,
wore the identical matte-black gabardine suit in an outdated
style he'd worn for years on special occasions; often he shaved
without really looking at himself in the mirror, his mind turned
inward; sometimes he rushed out of the house without comb-
ing his hair. He was a sweet-natured, vague-minded young-old
man with the look of a perennial bachelor, held in affectionate

if bemused regard by those who knew him well, largely ignored by others. After graduating summa cum laude from Williams College—while Alastor had dropped out, under suspicious circumstances, from Amherst—Lyle had returned to Contracoeur to lead a quiet, civilized life: he lived in an attractively converted carriage house on what had been his parents' property, gave private music lessons, and designed books for a small New England press specializing in limited editions distinguished within the trade, but little known elsewhere. He'd had several moderately serious romances that had come to nothing yet he harbored, still, a vague hope of marriage; friends were always trying to match him with eligible young women, as in a stubborn parlor game no one wished to give up. (In fact, Lyle had secretly adored his cousin Susan, whom Alastor had seduced; after that sorry episode, and Susan's subsequent marriage and move to Boston, Lyle seemed to himself to have lost heart for the game.) It amused Lyle to think that Alastor was considered a "world traveler"—an "explorer"—for he was certain that his brother had spent time in prison, in the United States; in Europe, in his late twenties, he'd traveled with a rich older woman who'd conveniently died and left him some money.

It wasn't possible to ask Alastor a direct question, and Lyle had long since given up trying. He'd given up, in fact, making much effort to communicate with Alastor at all. For Alastor only lied to him, with a maddening habit of smiling and winking and sometimes nudging him in the ribs, as if to say *I know you despise me, brother. And so what? You're too cowardly to do anything about it.*

At the funeral luncheon, Lyle noted glumly that Alastor was seated beside their aunt Alida and that the poor woman, her mind clearly weakened from the strain of her husband's death, was gazing up at Alastor as once she'd gazed at her husband Gardner: with infinite trust. Aunt Alida was one of those women who'd taken a special interest in Lyle from time to time, hoping to match him with a potential bride, and now, it seemed, she'd forgotten Lyle entirely. But then she was paying little attention to anyone except Alastor. Through the buzz and murmur of voices—Lyle winced to hear how frequently Alastor was spoken of, in the most laudatory way—he could make out fragments of their conversation; primarily Alastor's grave, unctuous voice. "And were Uncle Gardner's last days peaceful?—did he look back upon his life with joy?—that's all that matters." Seeing Lyle's glare of indignation, Alastor raised his glass of wine in a subtly mocking toast, smiling, just perceptibly winking, so that no one among the relatives could guess the message he was sending to his twin, as frequently he'd done when they were boys, in the company of their parents. *See? How clever I am? And what gullible fools these others are, to take me seriously?*

Lyle flushed angrily, so distracted he nearly overturned his water goblet.

Afterward, questioned about his travels, Alastor was intriguingly vague. Yet all his tales revolved around himself; always,

Alastor King was the hero. Saving a young girl from drowning
when a Greek steamer struck another boat, in the Mediterra-
nean; establishing a medical trust fund for beggars, in Cairo;
giving aid to a young black heroin addict adrift in Amsterdam
. . . Lyle listened with mounting disgust as the relatives plied
Alastor with more questions, believing everything he said no
matter how absurd; having forgotten, or wishing to forget, how
he'd disappeared from Contracoeur owing some of them money.
Alastor was, it seemed, now involved in the importing into the
United States of "masterworks of European culture"; ellipti-
cally he suggested that his business would flourish, and pay off
investors handsomely, if only it might be infused with a little
more capital. He was in partnership with a distinguished Italian
artist of an "impoverished noble family" . . . As Alastor sipped
wine, it seemed to Lyle that his features grew more vivid, as if
he were an actor in a film, magnified many times. His artfully
dyed brassy-brown hair framed his thuggish fox-face in crimped
waves so that he looked like an animated doll. Lyle would have
asked him skeptically who the distinguished artist was, what was
the name of their business, but he knew that Alastor would give
glib, convincing answers. Except for Lyle, everyone at the table
was gazing at Alastor with interest, admiration and, among the
older women, yearning; you could imagine these aging women,
shaken by the death of one of their contemporaries, looking
upon Alastor as if he were a fairy prince, promising them their
youth again, their lost innocence. They had only to believe in
him unstintingly, to "invest" in his latest business scheme. "Life

is a ceaseless pilgrimage up a mountain," Alastor was saying. "As long as you're in motion, your perspective is obscured. Only when you reach the summit and turn to look back, can you be at peace."

There was a hushed moment at the table, as if Alastor had uttered holy words. Aunt Alida had begun to weep, quietly. Yet there was a strange sort of elation in her weeping. Lyle, who rarely drank, and never during the day, found himself draining his second glass of white wine. *Amanita phalloides. Amanita . . .* He recalled how, years ago, when they were young children, Alastor had so tormented him that he'd lost control suddenly and screamed, flailing at his brother with his fists, knocking Alastor backward, astonished. Their mother had quickly intervened. But Lyle remembered vividly. *I wasn't a coward, once.*

Lyle drove Alastor back to the Black River Inn in silence. And Alastor himself was subdued, as if his performance had exhausted him. He said, musing aloud, "Aunt Alida has aged so, I was shocked. They all have. I don't see why you hadn't kept in closer touch with me, Lyle; you could have reached me care of American Express any time you'd wanted in Rome, in Paris, in Amsterdam . . . Who will be overseeing the King Foundation now? Aunt Alida will need help. And that enormous English Tudor house. And all that property: thirty acres. Uncle Gardner refused even to consider selling to a developer, but it's futile to hold out much longer. All of the north section of Contracoeur is being developed; if Aunt Alida doesn't sell, she'll be surrounded

by tract homes in a few years. It's the way of the future, obviously." Alastor paused, sighing with satisfaction. It seemed clear
that the future was a warm beneficent breeze blowing in his
direction. He gave Lyle, who was hunched behind the steering
wheel of his nondescript automobile, a sly sidelong glance. "And
that magnificent Rolls-Royce. I suppose, brother, you have your
eye on *that*?" Alastor laughed, as if nothing was more amusing
than the association of Lyle with a Rolls-Royce. He was dabbing
at his flushed face, overheated from numerous glasses of wine.

Quietly Lyle said, "I think you should leave the family alone,
Alastor. You've already done enough damage to innocent people
in your life."

"But—by what measure is 'enough'?" Alastor said, with mock
seriousness. "By your measure, brother, or mine?"

"There is only one measure—that of common decency."

"Oh well, then, if you're going to lapse into 'common' decency," Alastor said genially, "it's hopeless to try to talk to you."

At the Black River Inn, Alastor invited Lyle inside so that they
could discuss "family matters" in more detail. Lyle, trembling
with indignation, coolly declined. He had work to do, he said;
he was in the midst of designing a book, a new limited edition
with hand-sewn pages and letterpress printing, of Edgar Allan
Poe's short story "William Wilson." Alastor shrugged, as if he
thought little of this; not once had he shown the slightest interest
in his brother's beautifully designed books, any more than he'd
shown interest in his brother's life. "You'd be better off meeting
a woman," he said. "I could introduce you to one."

Lyle said, startled, "But you've only just arrived back in Contracoeur."

Alastor laughed, laying a heavy hand on Lyle's arm, and squeezing him with what seemed like affection. "God, Lyle! Are you serious? Women are everywhere. And any time."

Lyle said disdainfully, "A certain kind of woman, you mean."

Alastor said, with equal disdain, "No. There is only one kind of woman."

Lyle turned his car into the drive of the Black River Inn, his heart pounding with loathing of his brother. He knew that Alastor spoke carelessly, meaning only to provoke; it was pointless to try to speak seriously with him, let alone reason with him. He had no conscience in small matters as in large. *What of our cousin Susan? Do you ever think of her, do feel remorse for what you did to her?*—Lyle didn't dare ask. He would only be answered by a crude, flippant remark which would upset him further.

The Black River Inn was a handsome "historic" hotel recently renovated, at considerable cost, now rather more a resort motel than an inn, with landscaped grounds, a luxurious swimming pool, tennis courts. It seemed appropriate that Alastor would be staying in such a place; though surely deep in debt, he was accustomed to first-rate accommodations. Lyle sat in his car watching his brother stride purposefully away without a backward glance. Already he'd forgotten his chauffeur.

Two attractive young women were emerging from the front entrance of the inn as Alastor approached. Their expressions when they saw him—alert, enlivened—the swift exchange of smiles, as if in a secret code—cut Lyle to the quick. *Don't you know that man is evil? How can you be so easily deceived by looks?* Lyle opened his car door, jumped from the car, stood breathless and staring at the young women as they continued on the walk in his direction; they were laughing together, one of them glanced over her shoulder after Alastor (who was glancing over his shoulder at her, as he pushed into the hotel's revolving door) but their smiles faded when they saw Lyle. He wanted to stammer—what? Words of warning, or apology? Apology for his own odd behavior? But without slowing their stride the women were past, their glances sliding over Lyle; taking him in, assessing him, and sliding over him. They seemed not to register that Alastor, who'd so caught their eye, and Lyle were twins; they seemed not to have seen Lyle at all.

Recalling how years ago in circumstances long since forgotten he'd had the opportunity to observe his brother flirting with a cocktail waitress, a heavily made-up woman in her late thirties, still a glamorous woman yet no longer young, and Alastor had drawn her out, asking her name, teasing her, shamelessly flattering her, making her blush with pleasure; then drawing back with a look of offended surprise when the waitress asked him his name, saying, "Excuse me? I don't believe that's any of your business, miss." The hurt, baffled look on the woman's face! Lyle saw how, for a beat, she continued to smile, if only with her mouth; wanting to believe that this was part of Alastor's sophisticated banter. Alastor said, witheringly, "You don't seem to take your job seriously. I think I must have a conversation with the manager." Alastor was on his feet, incensed; the waitress immediately apologized, "Oh, no, sir, please—I'm so sorry— I misunderstood—" Like an actor secure in his role since he has played it numberless times, Alastor walked away without a backward glance. It was left to Lyle (afterward, Lyle would realize how deliberately it had been left to him) to pay for his brother's drinks, and to apologize to the stunned waitress, who was still staring after Alastor. "My brother is only joking, he has a cruel sense of humor. Don't be upset, please!" But the woman seemed scarcely to hear Lyle, her eyes swimming with tears; nor did she do more than glance at him. There she stood, clutching her hands at her breasts as if she'd been stabbed, staring after Alastor, waiting for him to return.

It would be cream of *Amanita phalloides* soup that Lyle served to his brother Alastor when, at last, Alastor found time to come to lunch.

An unpracticed cook, Lyle spent much of the morning preparing the elaborate meal. The soft, rather slimy, strangely cool pale-gray-pulpy fungi chopped with onions and moderately ground in a blender. Cooked slowly in a double boiler in chicken stock, seasoned with salt and pepper and grated nutmeg; just before Alastor was scheduled to arrive, laced with heavy cream and two egg yolks slightly beaten, and the heat on the stove turned down. How delicious the soup smelled! Lyle's mouth watered, even as a vein pounded dangerously in his forehead.

When Alastor arrived in a taxi, a half hour late, swaggering into Lyle's house without knocking, he drew a deep startled breath, savoring the rich cooking aroma, and rubbed his hands together in anticipation. "Lyle, wonderful! I didn't know you were a serious cook. I'm famished."

Nervously Lyle said, "But you'll have a drink first, Alastor? And—relax?"

Of course Alastor would have a drink. Or two. Already he'd discovered, chilling in Lyle's refrigerator, the two bottles of good Italian chardonnay Lyle had purchased for this occasion. "May I help myself? You're busy."

Lyle had found the recipe for cream of mushroom soup in a battered Fanny Farmer cookbook in a secondhand bookshop in town. In the same shop he'd found an amateur's guide to fungi, edible and inedible, with pages of illustrations. Shabby mane, chanterelles, beefsteak mushrooms—these were famously edible. But there amid the inedible, the sinister look-alike toadstools, was *Amanita phalloides*. The death-cup. A white-spored fungi, as the caption explained, with the volva separate from the cap. Highly poisonous. And strangely beautiful, like a vision from the deepest recesses of one's dreams brought suddenly into the light.

The "phallic" nature of the fungi was painfully self-evident. How ironic, Lyle thought, and appropriate. For a man like Alastor who sexually misused women.

It had taken Lyle several days of frantic searching in the woods back beyond his house before he located what appeared to be *Amanita phalloides*. He'd drawn in his breath at the sight—a malevolent little crop of toadstools luminous in the mist, amid the snaky gnarled roots of a gigantic beech tree. Almost, as Lyle quickly gathered them with his gloved hands, dropping them into a bag, the fungi exuded an air of sentient life. Lyle imagined he could hear faint cries of anguish at he plucked at them, in haste; he had an unreasonable fear of someone discovering him. *But those aren't edible mushrooms, those are death-cups, why are you gathering those?*

Alastor was seated at the plain wooden table in Lyle's spartan dining room. Lyle brought his soup bowl in from the kitchen and set it, steaming, before him. At once Alastor picked up his soup spoon and began noisily to eat. He said he hadn't eaten yet that day; he'd had an arduous night—"well into the morning." He laughed, mysteriously. He sighed. "Brother, this *is* good. I think I can discern—chanterelles? My favorites."

Lyle served crusty French bread, butter, a chunk of goat's cheese, and set a second bottle of chardonnay close by Alastor's place. He watched, mesmerized, as Alastor lifted spoonfuls of soup to his mouth and sipped and swallowed hungrily, making sounds of satisfaction. How flattered Lyle felt, who could not recall ever having been praised by his twin brother before in his life. Lyle sat tentatively at his place, fumbling with icy fingers to pick up his soup spoon. He'd prepared for himself soup that closely resembled Alastor's but was in fact Campbell's cream of mushroom slightly altered. This had never been a favorite of Lyle's and he ate it now slowly, his eyes on his brother; he would have wished to match Alastor spoon for spoon, but

Alastor as always ate too swiftly. The tiny, near-invisible capillaries in his cheeks glowed like incandescent wires; his steely-blue eyes shone with pleasure. *A man who enjoys life, where's the harm in that?*

Within minutes Alastor finished his large deep bowl of steaming hot creamy soup, licking his lips. Lyle promptly served him another. "You have more talent, brother, than you know," Alastor said with a wink. "We might open a restaurant together: I, the keeper of the books; you, the master of the kitchen." Lyle almost spilled a spoonful of soup as he lifted it tremulously to his lips. He was waiting for *Amanita phalloides* to take effect. He'd had the idea that the poison was nearly instantaneous, like cyanide. Evidently not. Or had—the possibility filled him with horror—boiling the chopped-up toadstool diluted its toxin? He was eating sloppily, continually wiping at his chin with a napkin. Fortunately Alastor didn't notice. Alastor was absorbed in recounting, as he sipped soup, swallowed large mouthfuls of bread, butter and cheese, and the tart white wine, a lengthy lewd tale of the woman, or women, with whom he'd spent his arduous night at the Black River Inn. He'd considered calling Lyle to insist that Lyle come join him—"As you'd done that other time, eh? To celebrate our twenty-first birthday?" Lyle blinked at him as if not comprehending his words, let alone his meaning. Alastor went on to speak of women generally. "They'll devour you alive if you allow it. They're vampires." Lyle said, fumblingly, "Yes, Alastor, I suppose so. If you say so." "Like Mother, who sucked life out of poor Father. To give birth to *us*—imagine!" Alastor shook his head, laughing. Lyle nodded gravely, numbly; yes, he would try to imagine. Alastor said, with an air almost of bitterness, though he was eating and drinking with as much appetite as before, "Yes, brother, a man has to be vigilant. Has to make the first strike." He brooded, as if recalling more than one sorry episode. Lyle had a sudden unexpected sense of his brother with a history of true feeling, regret. Remorse? It was mildly astonishing, like seeing a figure on a playing card stir into life.

Lyle said, "But what of—Susan?"

"Susan?—who?" The steely-blue eyes, lightly threaded with red, were fixed innocently upon Lyle.

"Our cousin Susan."

"Her? But I thought—" Alastor broke off in midsentence. His words simply ended. He was busying himself swiping at the inside of his soup bowl with a piece of crusty bread. A tinge of apparent pain made his jowls quiver and he pressed the heel of a hand against his midriff. A gas pain, perhaps.

Lyle said ironically, "Did you think Susan was dead, Alastor? Is that how you remember her?"

"I don't in fact remember her at all." Alastor spoke blithely, indifferently. A mottled flush had risen from his throat into his cheeks. "The girl was your friend, brother. Not mine."

"No. Susan was never my friend again," Lyle said bitterly. "She never spoke to me, or answered any call or letter of mine, again. After . . . what happened."

Alastor snorted in derision. "Typical!"

"'Typical'—?"

"Female fickleness. It's congenital."

"Our cousin Susan was not a fickle woman. You must know that, Alastor, damn you!"

"Why damn *me*? What have I to do with it? I was a boy then, hardly more than a boy, and you—so were *you*." Alastor spoke with his usual rapid ease, smiling, gesturing, as if what he said made perfect sense; he was accustomed to the company of uncritical admirers. Yet he'd begun to breathe audibly; perspiration had broken out on his unlined forehead in an oily glisten. His artfully dyed and crimped hair that looked so striking in other settings looked here, to Lyle's eye, like a wig set upon a mannequin's head. And there was an undertone of impatience, even anger, in Alastor's speech. "Look, she did get married and move away—didn't she? She did—I mean didn't—have a baby?"

Lyle stared at Alastor for a long somber moment.

"So far as I know, she did not. Have a baby."

"Well, then!" Alastor made an airy gesture of dismissal, and dabbed at his forehead with a napkin.

Seeing that Alastor's soup bowl was again empty, Lyle rose silently and carried it back into the kitchen and a third time ladled soup into it, nearly to the brim: this was the end of the cream of *Amanita phalloides* soup. Surely, now, within the next few minutes, the powerful poison would begin to act! When Lyle returned to the dining room with the bowl, he saw Alastor draining his second or third glass of the tart white wine and replenishing it without waiting for his host's invitation. His expression had turned mean, grim; as soon as Lyle reappeared, however, Alastor smiled up at him, and winked. "Thanks, brother!" Yet there was an air of absolute complacency in Alastor as in one accustomed to being served by others.

Incredibly, considering all he'd already eaten, Alastor again picked up his spoon and enthusiastically ate.

So the luncheon, planned so obsessively by Lyle, passed in a blur, a confused dream. Lyle stared at his handsome ruddy-faced twin who spoke with patronizing affection of their aunt Alida—"A befuddled old woman who clearly needs guidance"; and of the King Foundation—"An anachronism that needs total restructuring, top to bottom"; and of the thirty acres of prime real estate—"The strategy must be to pit developers against one another, I've tried to explain"; and of the vagaries of the international art market—"All that's required for a thousand percent profits is a strong capital base to withstand dips in the economy." Lyle could scarcely hear for the roaring in his ears. What had gone wrong? He had mistaken an ordinary, harmless, edible mushroom for *Amanita phalloides* the death-cup? He'd been so eager and agitated out there in the woods, he hadn't been absolutely certain of the identification.

Numbed, in a trance, Lyle drove Alastor back to the Black River Inn. It was a brilliant summer day. A sky of blank blue, the scales of the dark river glittering. Alastor invited Lyle to visit him at the Inn sometime soon, they could go swimming in the pool—"You meet extremely interesting people, sometimes, in such places." Lyle asked Alastor how long he intended to stay there and Alastor smiled enigmatically and said, "As long as required, brother. You know me!"

At the Inn, Alastor shook Lyle's hand vigorously, and, on an impulse, or with the pretense of acting on impulse, leaned over to kiss his cheek! Lyle was startled as if he'd been slapped.

Driving away he felt mortified, yet in a way relieved. *It hasn't happened yet. I am not a fratricide, yet.*

Gardner King's will was read. It was a massive document enumerating over one hundred beneficiaries, individuals and organizations. Lyle, who hadn't wished to be present at the reading, heard of the bequest made to him from his brother Alastor, who had apparently escorted Aunt Alida to the attorney's office. Lyle was to receive several thousand dollars, plus a number of his uncle's rare first-edition books. With forced ebullience Alastor said, "Congratulations, brother! You must have played your cards right, for once." Lyle wiped at his eyes; he'd genuinely loved their uncle Gardner, and was touched to be remembered by him in his will; even as he'd expected to be remembered, to about that degree. *Yes and there's greater pleasure in the news, if Alastor has received nothing.* At the other end of the line Alastor waited, breathing into the receiver. Waiting for—what? For Lyle to ask him how he'd fared? For Lyle to offer to share the bequest with him? Alastor was saying dryly, "Uncle Gardner left me just a legal form, 'forgiving' me my debts." He went on to complain that he hadn't even remembered he owed their uncle money; you would think, wouldn't you, with his staff of financial advisors,

Gardner King could have reminded him; it should have been his responsibility, to remind him; Alastor swore he'd never been reminded—not once in six years. Vividly Lyle could imagine his brother's blue-glaring eyes, his coarse, flushed face and the clenched self-righteous set of his jaws. Alastor said, hurt, "I suppose I should be grateful for being 'forgiven,' Lyle, eh? It's so wonderfully Christian." Lyle said coolly, "Yes. It is Christian. I would be grateful, in your place."

"In my place, brother, how would you know what you would be? You're 'Lyle' not 'Alastor.' Don't give yourself airs."

Rudely, Alastor hung up. Lyle winced, as if his brother had poked him in the chest as so frequently he'd done when they were growing up together, as a kind of exclamation mark to a belligerent statement of his.

Only afterward did Lyle realize, with a sick stab of resentment, that, in erasing Alastor's debt to him, which was surely beyond $10,000, their uncle had in fact given Alastor the money; and it was roughly the equivalent of the amount he'd left Lyle in his will. *As if, in his uncle's mind, Alastor and he were of equal merit after all.*

She came to him when he summoned her. Knocking stealthily at his door in the still, private hour beyond midnight. And hearing him murmur *Come in!* and inside in the shadows he stood watching. How she trembled, how excited and flattered she was. Her girlish face, her rather too large hands and feet, a braid of golden-red hair wrapped around her head. In her uniform that fitted her young shapely body so becomingly. In a patch of caressing moonlight. Noiselessly he came behind her to secure the door, lock and double-lock it. He made her shiver kissing her hand, and the soft flesh at the inside of her elbow. So she laughed, startled. He was European, she'd been led to believe. A European gentleman. Accepting the first drink from him, a toast to mutual happiness. Accepting the second drink, her head giddy. How flattered by his praise *Beautiful girl! Lovely girl!* And: *Remove your clothes please*. Fumbling with the tiny buttons of the violet rayon uniform. Wide lace collar, lace cuffs. He kissed her throat, a vein in her throat. Kissed the warm cleft between her breasts. *Lee Ann is it? Lynette?* In their loveplay on the king-size bed he twisted her wrist just slightly. Just enough for her to laugh, startled; to register discomfort; yet not so emphatically she would realize he meant anything by it. *Here, Lynette. Give me a real kiss.* Boldly pressing her fleshy mouth against his and her heavy breasts against his chest and he bit her lips, hard; she recoiled from him, and still his teeth were clamped over her lips that were livid now with pain. When at last he released her she was sobbing and her lips were bleeding and he, the European gentleman, with genuine regret crying *Oh what did I do!—forgive me, I was carried away by passion, my darling*. She cringed before him on her hands and knees her breasts swinging. Her enormous eyes. Shining like a beast's. And wanting still to believe, how desperate to believe so within a few minutes she allowed herself to be persuaded it had been an accident, an accident of passion, an accident for which she was herself to blame being so lovely so desirable she'd made him crazed. Kissing her hands pleading for forgiveness and at last forgiven and tenderly he arranged her arms and legs, her head at the edge of the bed, her long wavy somewhat coarse golden-red hair undone from its braid hanging over onto the carpet. She would have screamed except he provided a rag to shove into her mouth, one in fact used for previous visitors in suite 181 of the Black River Inn.

"How can you be so cruel, Alastor!"

Laughing, Alastor had recounted this lurid story for his brother Lyle as the two sat beside the hotel pool in the balmy dusk of an evening in late June. Lyle had listened with mounting dismay and disgust and at last cried out; Alastor said carelessly, "'Cruel'?—why am I 'cruel'? The women love it, brother. Believe me."

Lyle felt ill. Not knowing whether to believe Alastor or not—wondering if perhaps the entire story had been fabricated, to shock. Yet there was something matter-of-fact in Alastor's tone that made Lyle think, yes, it's true. He wished he'd never dropped by the Black River Inn to visit with Alastor, as Alastor had insisted. And he would not have wished to acknowledge even to himself that Alastor's crude story had stirred him sexually.

I am falling into pieces, shreds. Like something brittle that has been cracked.

The day after the luncheon, Lyle had returned to the woods behind his house to look for the mysterious fungi; but he had no luck retracing his steps, and failed even to locate the gigantic beech tree with the snaky exposed roots. In a rage he'd thrown away *The Amateur's Guide to Fungi Edible & Inedible.* He'd thrown away *The Fanny Farmer Cookbook.*

Since the failure of the *Amanita phalloides* soup, Lyle found himself thinking obsessively of his brother. As soon as he woke in the morning he began to think of Alastor, and through the long day he thought of Alastor; at night his dreams were mocking, jeering, turbulent with emotion that left him enervated and depressed. It was no longer possible for him to work even on projects, like the book design for Poe's "William Wilson," that challenged his imagination. Though he loved his hometown, and his life here, he wondered despairingly if perhaps he should move away from Contracoeur for hadn't Contracoeur been poisoned for him, by Alastor's presence? Living here, with Alastor less than ten minutes away by car, Lyle had no freedom from thinking of his evil brother. For rumors circulated that Alastor was meeting with local real estate developers though Gardner King's widow was still insisting that her property would remain intact as her husband had wished; that Alastor was to be the next director of the King Foundation, though the present director was a highly capable man who'd had his position for years and was universally respected; that Alastor and his aunt Alida were to travel to Europe in the fall on an art-purchasing expedition, though Alida King had always expressed a nervous dislike, even a terror, of travel and had grown frail since her husband's death. It had been recounted to Lyle by a cousin that poor Alida had said, wringing her hands, "Oh, I do hope I won't be traveling to

Europe this fall, I know I won't survive away from Contracoeur!"
and when the cousin asked why on earth she might be traveling
to Europe if she didn't wish to, Alida had said, starting to cry,
"But I may decide that I do want to travel, that's what frightens
me. I know I will never return alive."

Cocktail service at poolside had ended at 9 P.M.; the pool was
officially closed, though its glimmering synthetic-aqua water was
still illuminated from below; only boastful Alastor and his somber brother Lyle remained in deck chairs, as an eroded-looking
but glaring bright moon rose in the night sky. Alastor in swim
trunks and a terry cloth shirt trotted off barefoot for another
drink and Lyle, looking after him, felt a childish impulse to flee
while his brother was in the cocktail lounge. He was sickened by
the story he'd been told; knowing himself sullied as if he'd been
present in Alastor's suite the previous night. As if, merely hearing
such obscenities, he was an accomplice of Alastor's. *And perhaps
somehow in fact he'd been there, helping to hold the struggling girl
down, helping to thrust the gag into her mouth.*

Alastor returned with a fresh drink. He was eyeing Lyle with a
look of bemusement as he'd done so often when they were boys,
gauging to what extent he'd shocked Lyle or embarrassed him.
After their father's death, for instance, when the brothers were
eight years old, Lyle had wept for days; Alastor had ridiculed
his grief, saying that if you believed in God (and weren't they all
supposed to believe in God?) you believed that everything was
ordained; if you were a good Christian, you believed that their
father was safe and happy in heaven—"So why bawl like a baby?"

Why, indeed?

Alastor was drunker than Lyle had known. He said commandingly, his voice slurred, "Midnight swim. Brother, c'mon!"

Lyle merely laughed uneasily. He was fully dressed; hadn't brought swim trunks; couldn't imagine swimming companionably with his brother, even as adults; he who'd been so tormented by Alastor when they were children, tugged and pummeled in the water, his head held under until he gasped and sputtered in panic. *Your brother's only playing, Lyle. Don't cry. Alastor, be good!*

Enlivened by drink, Alastor threw off his shirt and announced that he was going swimming, and no one could stop him. Lyle said, "But the pool is closed, Alastor"—as if that would make any difference. Alastor laughed, swaggering to the edge of the pool to dive. Lyle saw with reluctant admiration and a tinge of jealousy that his brother's body, unlike his own, was solid, hardpacked; though there was a loose bunch of flesh at his waist, and his stomach had begun to protrude, his shoulders and thighs were taut with muscle. A pelt of fine glistening hairs covered much of his body and curled across his chest; the nipples of his breasts were purply-dark, distinct as small staring eyes. Alastor's head, held high with exaggerated bravado as he flexed his knees, positioning himself to dive, was an undeniably handsome head; Alastor looked like a film star of another era, a man accustomed to the uncritical adoration of women and the envy of men. The thought flashed through Lyle like a knife blade *It's my moral obligation to destroy this man, because he is evil; and because there is no one else to destroy him but me.*

With the showy ebullience of a twelve-year-old boy, Alastor dived into the pool at the deep end; a less-than-perfect dive that must have embarrassed him, with Lyle as a witness; Lyle who winced feeling the harsh slap of the water, like a retributive hand, against his own chest and stomach. Like a deranged seal, Alastor surfaced noisily, blowing water out of his nose, snorting; as he began to swim in short, choppy, angry-looking strokes, not nearly so coordinated as Lyle would have expected, Lyle felt his own arm and leg muscles strain in involuntary sympathy. How alone they were, Lyle and his twin brother Alastor! Overhead the marred moon glared like a light in an examination room.

Lyle thought *I could strike him on the head with—what?* One of the deck chairs, a small wrought-iron table caught his eye. And even as this thought struck Lyle, Alastor in the pool began to flail about; began coughing, choking; he must have inhaled water and swallowed it; drunker than he knew, in no condition to be swimming in water over his head. As Lyle stood at the edge of the pool staring he saw his brother begin to sink. And there was no one near! No witness save Lyle himself! Inside the Inn, at a distance of perhaps one hundred feet, there was a murmur and buzz of voices, laughter, music; every hotel window facing the open courtyard and the pool area was veiled by a drape or a blind; most of the windows were probably shut tight, and the room air conditioners on. No one would hear Alastor cry for help even if Alastor could cry for help. Excited, clenching his fists, Lyle ran to the other side of the pool to more closely observe his brother, now a helpless, thrashing body sunk beneath the surface of the water like a weighted sack. A trail of bubbles lifted from his distorted mouth; his dyed hair too lifted, like seaweed. How silent was Alastor's deathly struggle, and how lurid the bright aqua water with its theatrical lights from beneath. Lyle was panting like a dog, crouched at the edge of the pool, muttering, "Die! Drown! Damn your soul to hell! You don't deserve to live!"

The next moment, Lyle had kicked off his shoes, torn his shirt off over his head, and dived into the water to save Alastor. With no time to think, he grabbed at the struggling man, overpowered him, hauled him to the surface; he managed to get Alastor's head in a hammerlock and swim with him into the shallow end of the pool; managed to lift him, a near-dead weight, a dense body streaming water, onto the tile. Alastor thrashed about like a beached seal, gasping for breath; he vomited, coughed and choked, spitting up water and clots of food. Lyle crouched over him, panting, as Alastor rolled onto his back, his hair in absurd strings about his face and his face now bloated and puffy, no longer a handsome face, as if in fact he'd drowned. His breath was erratic, heaving. His eyes rolled in his head. Yet he saw Lyle, and must have recognized him. "Oh God, Lyle, w-what happened?" he managed to say.

"You were drunk, drowning. I pulled you out."

Lyle spoke bitterly. He, too, was streaming water; his clothes were soaked; he felt like a fool, a dupe. Never, never would he comprehend what he'd done. Alastor, deathly pale, weak and stricken still with the terror of death, not hearing the tone of Lyle's voice or seeing the expression of impotent fury on Lyle's face, reached out with childlike pleading to clutch at Lyle's hand.

"Brother, thank you!"

The world is a beautiful place if you have the eyes to see it and the ears to hear it.

Was this so? Could it be so? Lyle would have to live as if it were, for his brother Alastor could not be killed. Evidently. Or in any case, Lyle was not the man to kill him.

A week after he'd saved Alastor from drowning, on a radiantly sunny July morning when Lyle was seated disconsolately at his work bench, a dozen rejected drawings for "William Wilson" scattered and crumpled before him, the telephone rang and it was Alastor announcing that he'd decided to move after all to Aunt Alida's house—"She insists. Poor woman, she's frightened of 'ghosts'—needs a man's presence in that enormous house. Brother, will you help me move? I have only a few things." Alastor's voice was buoyant and easy; the voice of a man perfectly at peace with himself. Lyle seemed to understand that his brother had forgotten about the near-drowning. His pride would not allow him to recall it, nor would Lyle ever bring up the subject. Lyle drew breath to say sharply, "No! Move yourself, damn you," but instead he said, "Oh, I suppose so. When?" Alastor said, "Within the hour, if possible. And, by the way, I have a surprise for you—it's for both of us, actually. A memento from our late beloved uncle Gardner." Lyle was too demoralized to ask what the memento was.

When he arrived at the Black River Inn, there was Alastor proudly awaiting him at the front entrance, drawing a good deal of admiring attention. A tanned, good-looking youthful man with a beaming smile, in a pale-pink-striped seersucker suit, collarless white shirt and straw hat, a dozen or more suitcases and valises on the sidewalk; and, in the drive beneath the canopy, a gleaming-black chrome-glittering Rolls-Royce. Alastor laughed heartily at the look on Lyle's face. "Some memento, eh, brother? Aunt Alida was so sweet, she told me, 'Your uncle would want both you boys to have it. He loved you so—his favorite nephews.'"

Lyle stared at the Rolls-Royce. The elegant car, vintage 1971, was as much a work of art, and culture, as a motor vehicle. Lyle had ridden in it numerous times, in his uncle's company, but he'd never driven it. Nor even fantasized driving it. "How— did it get here? How is this possible?" Lyle stammered. Alastor explained that their aunt's driver had brought the car over that morning and that Lyle should simply leave his car (so ordinary, dull and plebeian a car—a compact American model Alastor merely glanced at, with a disdainful look) in the parking lot, for the time being. "Unfortunately, I lack a valid driving license in the United States at the present time," Alastor said, "or I would drive myself. But you know how scrupulous I am about obeying the law—technically." He laughed, rubbing his hands briskly together. Still Lyle was staring at the Rolls-Royce. How like the hearse that had borne his uncle's body from the funeral home to the church it was; how magnificently black, and the flawless chrome and windows so glittering, polished to perfection. Alastor poked Lyle in the ribs to wake him from his trance, and passed to him, with a wink, a silver pocket flask. Pure scotch whiskey at 11 A.M. of a weekday morning? Lyle raised his hand to shove the flask aside but instead took it from his brother's fingers, lifted it to his lips and drank.

And a second time, drank. Flames darted in his throat and mouth, his eyes stung with tears.

"Oh! God."

"Good, eh? Just the cure for your ridiculous anemia, brother," Alastor said teasingly.

While Alastor settled accounts in the Black River Inn, using their aunt's credit, Lyle and an awed, smiling doorman loaded the trunk and plush rear seat of the Rolls with Alastor's belongings. The sun was vertiginously warm and the scotch whiskey had gone to Lyle's head and he was perspiring inside his clothes, murmuring to himself and laughing. *The world is a beautiful place. Is a beautiful place. A beautiful place.* Among Alastor's belongings were several handsome new garment bags crammed, apparently, with clothing. There were suitcases of unusual heaviness that might have been crammed with—what? Statuary? There were several small canvases (oil paintings?) wrapped hastily in canvas and secured with adhesive tape; there was a heavy sports valise with a broken lock, inside which Lyle discovered, carelessly wrapped in what appeared to be women's silk underwear, loose jewelry of all kinds—gold chains, strings of pearls jumbled together, a silver pendant with a sparkling-red ruby, bracelets and earrings and a single brass candlestick holder and even a woman's high-heeled slipper, stained (bloodstained?) white satin with a carved mother-of-pearl ornament. Lyle stared, breathless. What a treasure trove! Once, he would have been morbidly suspicious of his brother, suspecting him of theft—and worse. Now he merely smiled, and shrugged.

By the time Lyle and the doorman had loaded the Rolls, Alastor emerged from the Inn, slipping on a pair of dark glasses. By chance—it must have been chance—a striking blond woman was walking with him, smiling, chatting, clearly quite impressed by him—a beautiful woman of about forty with a lynx face, a bold red mouth and diamond earrings who paused to scribble something (telephone number? address?) on a card and slip it into a pocket of Alastor's seersucker jacket.

Exuberantly Alastor cried, "Brother, let's go! Across the river and to Aunt Alida's—to our destiny."

Like a man in a dream Lyle took his place behind the wheel of the Rolls; Alastor climbed in beside him. Lyle's heart was beating painfully, with an almost erotic excitement. Neither brother troubled to fasten his seat belt; Lyle, who'd perhaps never once driven any vehicle without fastening his seat belt first, seemed not to think of doing so now as if, simply by sliding into this magnificent car, he'd entered a dimension in which old, tedious rules no longer applied. Lyle was grateful for Alastors passing him the silver flask, for he needed a spurt of strength and courage.

He drank thirstily, in small choking swallows: how the whiskey burned, warmly glowed, going down! Lyle switched on the ignition, startled at how readily, how quietly, the engine turned over. Yes, this was magic. He was driving his uncle Gardner King's Rolls-Royce as if it were his own; as he turned out of the hotel drive, he saw the driver of an incoming vehicle staring at the car, and at him, with frank envy.

And now on the road. In brilliant sunshine, and not much traffic. The Rolls resembled a small, perfect yacht; a yacht moving without evident exertion along a smooth, swiftly running stream. What a thrill, to be entrusted with this remarkable car; what sensuous delight in the sight, touch, smell of the Rolls! Why had he, Lyle King, been a puritan all of his life? What a blind, smug fool to be living in a world of luxury items and taking no interest in them; as if there were virtue in asceticism; in mere ignorance. Driving the Rolls on the highway in the direction of the High Street Bridge, where they would cross the Black River into the northern, affluent area of Contracoeur in which their aunt lived, Lyle felt intoxicated as one singled out for a special destiny. He wanted to shout out the car window *Look! Look at me! This is the first morning of the first day of my new life.*

Not once since Alastor's call that morning had Lyle thought of—what? What had it been? The death-cup mushroom, what was its Latin name? At last, to Lyle's relief, he'd forgotten.

Alastor sipped from the pocket flask as he reminisced, tenderly, about the old Contracoeur world of their childhood. That world, that had seemed so stable, so permanent, was rapidly passing now, vanishing into a newer America. Soon, all of the older gen-eration of Kings would be deceased. "Remember when we were boys, Lyle? What happy times we had? I admit, I was a bit of a bastard, sometimes—I apologize. Truly. It's just that I resented you, you know. My twin brother." His voice was caressing yet lightly ironic.

"Resented *me*? Why?" Lyle laughed, the possibility seemed so far-fetched.

"Because you were born on my birthday, of course. Obviously, I was cheated of presents."

Driving the daunting, unfamiliar car, that seemed to him higher built than he'd recalled, Lyle was sitting stiffly forward, gripping the elegant mahogany steering wheel and squinting through the windshield as if he was having difficulty seeing. The car's powerful engine vibrated almost imperceptibly like the coursing of his own heated blood. Laughing, though slightly anxious, he said, "But, Alastor, you wouldn't have wished me not to have been born, would you? For the sake of some presents?"

An awkward silence ensued. Alastor was contemplating how to reply when the accident occurred.

Approaching the steep ramp of the High Street Bridge, Lyle seemed for a moment to lose the focus of his vision, and jammed down hard on the brake pedal; except it wasn't the brake pedal but the accelerator. A diesel truck crossing the bridge, belching smoke, seemed then to emerge out of nowhere as out of a tun-nel. Lyle hadn't seen the truck until, with terrifying speed, the Rolls careened up the ramp and into the truck's oncoming grille.

There was a sound of brakes, shouts, a scream, and as truck and car collided, a sickening wrenching of metal and a shattering of glass. Together the vehicles tumbled from the ramp, through a low guardrail and onto an embankment; there was an explosion, flames; the last thing Lyle knew, he and his shrieking brother were being flung forward into a fiery-black oblivion.

Though badly injured, the driver of the diesel truck managed to crawl free of the flaming wreckage; the occupants of the Rolls-Royce were trapped inside their smashed vehicle, and may have been killed on impact. After the fire was extinguished, emergency medical workers would discover in the wreckage the charred remains of two Caucasian males of approximately the same height and age; so badly mangled, crushed, burned, they were never to be precisely identified. As if the bodies had been flung together from a great height, or at a great speed, they seemed to be but a single body, hideously conjoined. It was known that the remains were those of the King brothers, Alastor and Lyle, fraternal twins who would have been thirty-eight years old on the following Sunday. But which body was which, whose charred organs, bones, blood had belonged to which brother, no forensic specalist would ever determine.

HELPING HANDS

1.

He came into her life when it had seemed to her that her life
was finished.

He was not a volunteer at the charity thrift shop but an employee. You could see that he had no choice but to be working
in this dismal place on this dismal November afternoon.

DISABLED VETERANS OF NEW JERSEY HELPING HANDS—from
the street the shop appeared to be little more than a storefront.
She'd had a difficult time locating the weatherworn brown-brick
building on South Falls Street, Trenton, amid a neighborhood
that resembled a broken and part-disarticulated spine—small
shuttered stores, pawnshops and taverns and rib shacks, vast
rubble-strewn vacant lots as in the aftermath of a cataclysm.

This was Trenton, the capital city of New Jersey! Only a few
blocks from the Mercer County Courthouse and the New Jersey
State Courthouse and the gold-domed New Jersey State House
overlooking the Delaware River.

The storefront window was layered in grime. On display were mismatched items of furniture, men's clothing and boots. A faded poster depicting a pair of clasped hands beneath the words HELPING HANDS and a smiling crinkly-blue-eyed young soldier in a U.S. Army uniform regarding the onlooker with a look of disconcerting frankness—THANK YOU FOR ALL YOU CAN GIVE! WE WHO HAVE SERVED YOU ARE GRATEFUL.

"Grateful!"—Helene felt the sting of irony. For the smiling soldier was disabled, presumably.

Or—was she imagining the scorpion-sting of irony, where none was intended?

Hesitantly she pushed open the heavy door half-expecting it to be locked, as the twilit interior seemed to suggest that Helping Hands wasn't open.

In her arms she was carrying several plastic bags neatly tied shut and containing *gently used clothing*—(socks, underwear, T-shirts formerly her husband's)—awkwardly managing to open the door and to wedge her way inside in the hopeful way of one who expects someone to witness her struggle, and the goodwill behind the struggle, and to hurry to help her.

He took no notice of her, it seemed: the single figure at the rear of the shop, behind a counter and barely visible to her.

"Hello? Are you—open?"

With difficulty—for one of the several bundles had begun to slip from her embrace, and the strap of her heavy handbag was looped around her weakening wrist—Helene made her way into the cluttered interior of the shop where at the rear, behind a waist-high counter, the clerk still hadn't noticed her.

Helping Hands at 821 South Falls Street, Trenton, was both a thrift shop and a drop-off location for donations to the disabled veterans' charity. It was a drafty, inhospitable place—more a storage warehouse than a shop. Overhead was a high ceiling of hammered tin, an ancient ceiling from which paint had peeled and flaked like leprous skin. The floor appeared to be bare floorboards covered haphazardly with rug- and linoleum-remnants like jigsaw puzzle pieces that had worked their way apart. And the smell—dust, grime, something acidulous, gingery-medicinal mixed with the outer, gritty smoky-chemical air of Trenton—that stung her nostrils. What chagrin she felt to be bringing her husband's intimate articles of clothing to this place that was a graveyard of unwanted things: sofas that looked as if, if beaten with a broom, they would explode in a fury of dust; lamps with stained and drunk-tilted shades; rolled-up carpets stacked against the wall like cast-aside bodies; bins of heaped shoes and boots as in those horrific photographs taken after the liberation of the Nazi death camps; a small platoon of (men's) clothes sagging on wire hangers on gurney-like racks, like hunched figures in a soup kitchen line.

Behind the counter a radio was playing, turned low. Here was a comfortable if slovenly space someone had fashioned for himself, like an animal's den. Here was a warm nimbus of light from a floor lamp, and in a sagging leather chair a man with a dark-stubbled jaw and straggling dark hair was sprawled reading a book—Euripides' *Plays*.

Belatedly—with a just-perceptible tinge of apology, unless it was annoyance—the stubble-jawed man glanced up.

"Ma'am! Let me help you."

With a show of deferential haste he set the book down—facedown, not minding if the spine cracked—untwined himself from the leather chair without quite straightening up and scrambled around to the front of the counter. He moved—limped, lurched—as one with an artificial leg might move, pumping himself forward.

"Sorry! Didn't see you come in, way back here."

His smile was a quick flash baring small slightly uneven teeth and one dark space where a lower incisor was missing.

From the widow's arms he took the neatly tied plastic bags. For surely his work at Helping Hands had made him practiced at identifying *widow, bereft woman. Alone.*

With care the stubble-jawed man positioned her bags on a table as if their contents were likely to be novel, precious. Helene wanted to explain that she'd brought just small articles of clothing—she hadn't yet confronted the task of going through her husband's larger things—but her voice faltered and failed and at last she stood staring at the bags in a kind of abashed silence. Before the catastrophe in her life she'd been a woman who spoke easily to strangers, as to friends—now, her voice unaccountably faltered, often she seemed to lose the thread of what she was saying. And now she was fearful suddenly that her husband's

things didn't qualify as *gently used,* as the Helping Hands advertisement in the Mercer County yellow pages had requested—or
weren't clean; she was fearful that the stubble-jawed clerk would
examine her donation and reject it.

But he spoke kindly, as if sensing her distress: "You can
call Helping Hands, y'know. To arrange for a pickup at your
residence."

Residence. Why did he not say *home.*

Probably just quoting from the Helping Hands brochure yet
it seemed to Helene significant, he'd avoided saying *home.*

She had no *home* now—only just a house she'd shared for
more than twenty years with a man who had died.

"I—I wanted to save someone a drive. All the way out to . . ."

Her voice trailed off. Better not to say where she lived. For
the suburban village contiguous with Princeton was so very
different from Trenton, New Jersey, the very articulation of its
name might strike an ironic note in this dreary place.

"That's our job, ma'am. My job, mostly."

Though his voice was grittily hoarse the clerk spoke cheerfully.
The smile flashed, and vanished.

Helene wondered: was the man a veteran? *Disabled?*

He was older than he'd appeared at first glance. Probably he
was thirty-five, at least. His right cheek was riddled and ridged
with scar tissue and there were soft discolored indentations in
his skin. His eyes were small, stone-colored, alert and alight. His
hair was dark threaded with silver filaments and looked as if it
had been roughly finger-combed, straggling over his collar like

a pelt. The stubbled jaws gave him a look of boyish aggression, playful swagger. You could see that he thought well of himself, in secret. Yet always he was deferential to the woman, eager to please as the light, restless eyes played over her.

He wore a rust-colored *faux*-suede sport coat too large for his narrow shoulders, a beige crewneck sweater with a stretched neck, "dress" gabardine trousers with cuffs that spilled onto the floor—mismatched articles of clothing surely appropriated from the Helping Hands rack a few yards away. And on his feet salt-stained hiking boots that reminded Helene of the hiking boots—better quality, in better condition—her husband had often worn when she'd first met him, nearly twenty-five years ago at the University of Minnesota.

"And it's a nasty day. Especially in Trenton."

Very lightly the word *Trenton* was accentuated, in irony.

He'd cast a sidelong glance at the widow's face and sensed the precariousness of her emotions which resembled unstable rocks on a hillside—the slightest nudge, an avalanche.

"I—I wanted to see your headquarters. I was reading about Helping Hands and I thought . . ."

Thought? What had she *thought*? In the pain-wracked haze following an insomniac night leafing through the phone directory looking under CHARITABLE ORGANIZATIONS—struck by the drawing of tight-clasped hands that had roused in her a sensation of envy, yearning, conviction.

Her husband would want his things given away, she knew. At his death he'd become a donor of body organs, eyes.

She would recall his laughter at her unease, when years before he'd signed the organ-donor form, in their lawyers' office. Where they'd gone to make out their wills.

Helene had not wished to sign the form—just yet. And her husband had laughed at her, though not cruelly.

What will you do with your beautiful brown eyes, your kidneys, liver, heart in the afterlife?

She'd shuddered. He'd kissed her.

Laughter, in the innocence—ignorance?—of those long-ago days.

In fact she'd driven to Trenton because she'd been desperate to escape the house that she and her husband had so loved, and had lived in happily for so long—for not one room was safe for her, to glance into: when she did she saw the ghostly afterimage of her husband, seated in his chair in the living room, or at his desk in his study; it was terrible to enter their bedroom, and see—almost see—-his figure in their bed, motionless beneath the covers as he'd been motionless in the hospital bed, when they'd summoned her to the hospital. . . .

And there was the sound of his footfall on the stairs, and his murmuring voice now indistinct and no longer playful as so often it had been playful, for all jokes cease with death.

Where am I, what has happened to me. . . . Helene!

She shuddered. So clearly she heard the terror in her husband's voice.

"This isn't our 'headquarters,' ma'am. There's an office in Newark." The stubble-jawed clerk was observing her closely.

"Yes? What? Oh yes. Newark."

Her mind had gone blank. *Newark?*

"Can I trouble you to please fill out this form? For our files."

She was given a form, and a ballpoint pen. The stubble-jawed man cleared a space for her so that she could write.

Strange it seemed to her, the widow. To be in this place. But all places were strange to her now.

A faint rising wind, driving rain. That sensation of acute and indescribable unreality rising like dark water, to drown her.

She felt like an amputee uncertain which of her limbs has been severed.

"Ma'am? Sorry."

The ballpoint pen—cheap, black plastic—stamped with a pair of tinselly clasped hands—had slipped from her fingers and clattered to the floor. With a muffled grunt—as if his back hurt him, or a stiff leg—the stubble-jawed man stooped to retrieve it for her.

"Thank you."

She spoke softly. She felt tears sting her eyes. The slightest gesture of kindness was touching to her now. Lately it was happening, others were not so kind to her, or so patient—tapping their horns on the turnpike entrance ramp when she ventured too cautiously out into traffic, staring rudely at her in the post office when she blundered into the midst of a queue unaware of others who'd been waiting before her. At the Mercer County Courthouse where she'd held up the security checkpoint queue when a bag in which she'd been carrying her husband's *Last Will & Testament*, her husband's death certificate and other documents had spilled onto the grimy floor.

Ma'am! Move along please!

Ma'am you maybe need some assistance? Somebody from home, to help you?

It was so, she could have used assistance. But she had not wanted assistance. She'd been stubborn, insisting she would go alone to Trenton. She was capable of executing the exhausting *death-duties* herself.

She dreaded pity! Even sympathy is a form of pity.

She dreaded the terrible intimacy of grief. She was a wounded creature preferring to crawl away, to nurse her pain, and not to share it with others.

No one can help me in what is essential. No one can come near.

At last she'd begun to sort through her husband's things and to discard and to "donate"—to make available, to others in need, those things which her husband, deceased, would never again require. This was a ritual that needed to be done—(did it?)—and there was no one to do it except the widow.

How many had died, and their clothing brought to Helping Hands! There were racks of crammed-together clothes, bins of carelessly folded shirts, sweaters, pajamas. . . . Hard to believe that anyone, let alone *disabled veterans*, would be helped much by this graveyard of cast-off things.

At least, her husband's clothing was in good condition. Some of the articles of clothing were new, or nearly new; most was of high quality. Some, little-worn. Some, still in dry cleaner's bags. Helene had not brought those, that were too precious to be given away just yet.

After she'd emptied her husband's bureau drawers of socks (neatly bunched together, in pairs), underwear, T-shirts, she'd stared into the empty drawers with a strange fixed smile like one about to plunge into an abyss. Thinking *But why? Why have I done this?* It seemed madness to her, to have emptied her husband's things onto their bed, so that she would have to place them in bags, for the veterans' charity; madness, to empty drawers that had not needed to be emptied.

She could not shake the conviction that, having signed the contract for her husband's remains to be cremated, she had violated the deep, intimate bond between them: she had destroyed her husband's body, for the sake of convenience.

Of course her husband had wanted to be *cremated*. Matter-of-fact and seemingly without sentiment like all of their friends, this had been his clearly stated wish.

"Ma'am? I can take that."

It had taken Helene several minutes to complete the form. In the *afterlife* of the widow, time itself moves haltingly.

The stubble-jawed man glanced through the form. Helene had been aware of him watching her, overseeing her effort as if he knew how difficult this small task was for her.

He was breathing through his mouth, like an asthmatic. She wondered if this was a result of his being wounded—*disabled*. And his sloping shoulders, and slightly curved back—a certain wariness in the way he held himself, physically—suggested pain, or the anxious expectation of pain.

Still he was taller than Helene by several inches, and seemed protective of her.

The thought came to her *He, too, has been wounded. Of course, he understands.*

And, with a sensation of relief *Maybe it was meant—I would meet a friend today in this melancholy place.*

All of Helene's friends—relatives, neighbors—had known her husband: and she could not bear seeing them, and seeing her grief reflected in their faces, as in a cruel fun house mirror.

The stubble-jawed man stood close to her. This might have been accidental but Helene did not think so. She could smell his clothes, his hair—that needed to be washed. A salty-sweaty smell of his body—the man inside the secondhand, rumpled clothes—that was comforting to her, and not unpleasant.

Her own skin was rubbed raw, and had become painful to the touch, by her frequent showers, which had begun during the hospital vigil when she'd showered twice a day, to rid herself of the strong hospital odor. And her hair, to which the hospital-smell still clung, in Helene's imagination—her poor hair, that had been so thick and glossy, a rich mahogany color, less than two months ago, now falling out, thinning. . . .

She saw the clerk's practiced eyes move quickly down the page. She felt a small frisson of satisfaction, or of apprehension—now he would see that in fact she'd driven a considerable distance, and that she lived in Quaker Heights.

"Ma'am—is it 'Mrs. Haidt'? Thank you!"

She hesitated. Was it accurate, or logical, that there could be a *Mrs. Haidt,* if there was no *Mr. Haidt?*

"'Mrs. Haidt'—yes. But please call me 'Helene.'"

"'Helene.' That's a beautiful name."

A warm sensation rose in her throat, into her face. She smiled in confusion like one who has been pushed too close to a mirror, who cannot see.

"Good to meet you—'Helene.'"

The stubble-jawed man surprised her by reaching for her hand and shaking it vigorously. His fingers were strong and decisive and she had to resist the instinct to pull away. She didn't quite hear his name—Nicolas? Jelinski? *Zelinski?*

"Just—'Nicolas' is fine."

"'Nicolas.'"

This seemed to her a beautiful name, too. She was certain that she'd never heard it before, in quite this way.

"Next time call us, Helene. There are Helping Hand pickups every three weeks in Quaker Heights."

It was so, she'd seen such pickup vans in her neighborhood— Rescue Mission of Trenton, Salvation Army, Goodwill Industries —possibly even Disabled Veterans of New Jersey Helping Hands. In this terrible recession there was much poverty, homelessness.

In the ninth year of a folly of a war in which few American citizens believed any longer, yet which continued like a great grinding wheel crushing the innocent in its mechanical turning, there were many *disabled*.

"Yes. Yes. I will. . . ."

"You can ask for me, will you? 'Nicolas.'"

"Yes. 'Nicolas.'"

There was a precarious intimacy between them. Helene felt that if the stubble-jawed man were to touch her again, she would become faint.

Now I must leave. Exactly now.

But hearing herself say instead, in a bright curious voice: "I see that you're reading Euripides. . . ."

"Trying to."

He was embarrassed, was he?—self-conscious suddenly.

"'Eur-rip-id-des'—that's how you pronounce it?"

"Yes. 'Eu-rip-id-dees.'"

She thought of telling Nicolas that she'd once taught Greek tragedies in an introductory literature course in a small liberal arts college in Minneapolis—she'd taught Euripides' *Bacchae* and *Medea*. A wave of vertigo came over her, a sense of her old, lost life.

But she didn't want to sound boastful. "Are you a—student?"

"Not now."

"But you were—where? When?"

"Before I went in the service, at Rutgers. And, for a few months, after I was discharged."

"You were in the army?"

"I was in the army."

His smile was pained, his eyes were veiled, evasive. His words were uttered as if to echo Helene's—she hoped not in mockery.

Yet she persisted: "And was it—a war?"

"Yes, ma'am. 'It was a war.'"

More clearly the man's remark echoed Helene's awkward words, in mockery.

War might mean—what? Afghanistan? Iraq? And before these—the first Gulf War?

Beyond that was the Vietnam War—but Nicolas was too young for the Vietnam War. Helene tried to calculate dates, years. . . . She wondered: had the intimacy between them been rent, so quickly? Or was it deepening, in the intensity of their awareness of each other?

She felt her face beat with blood, this was the first emotion she'd experienced since her husband's death that was not raw pitiless grief but something finer and more hopeful.

"I—I'm sorry, Nicolas. I didn't mean to . . ."

She spoke so softly, he had to relent.

"No, ma'am. Just that—there's things I'd rather not talk about, right now."

"I understand. Of course."

Of course: he has been wounded. Disabled.

His eyes!

She'd offended him, unwittingly. She saw the stiffness in his mouth, the pained half-smile.

She knew, she must leave. She'd been lingering too long in this place. (Fortunately, no one had come in since she'd arrived. Just once the phone had rung, but Nicolas had made no effort to answer it, which was flattering to her.)

Since her husband's death—seven weeks, five days before this bleak November afternoon—Helene found herself in a kind of *afterlife* in which she often misspoke, miscalculated and mis-stepped. Often she wasn't sure if she had spoken aloud since most of her speech had become interior, accusing and despairing, warning—*Why am I here, what has brought me here? This desolate place—why?*

Even before her husband had died, during the hospital vigil of nine days in which his doctors had assured her he'd been steadily "improving," these words had begun to assail her.

And now since his death the answer came bluntly, cruelly—*Why not here? Here is as good as anywhere.*

It was so: there could be no reason why the widow should be in one place and not another since all places were identical now: equidistant from her lost home.

"Would you like a receipt, ma'am? For tax purposes?"

Ma'am. Why did he not say *Helene.*

"Thank you, no. That isn't necessary. . . ."

She'd been fumbling with the belt of her Burberry coat, that had loosened at her waist. All of her clothes fit her loosely now, even this coat.

In the *afterlife* of the widow there is the fear, like the fear of stepping too close to the edge of a high building, or an abyss, of stumbling, falling—making a mistake that will be irrevocable. The warning came to her *Say good-bye to him now. You must not embarrass yourself further.*

"You sure, ma'am? It's my job, I'm happy to do."

She was sure! That this man would assume she would want to claim a tax deduction for so modest a donation—forty dollars' worth, she'd estimated on the form—was insulting to her.

Coolly she said good-bye to him, and turned to leave. Now that the magical intimacy between them was shattered, like a torn cobweb, Helene wanted to escape quickly. She hoped Nicolas would understand that she too had been offended.

How to get out of this place! Almost, Helene couldn't find her way, though she'd managed to make her way in. No choice but to pass through a gauntlet of mirrors: a half-dozen mirrors, leaning against furniture and against a wall: reflecting the widow's blurred and disjointed figure in a sequence of jerky images like a poorly sliced film.

At the front door she heard the gravelly-voiced clerk call after her a belated *Good-bye.* And again *Thanks, ma'am.*

This was hateful to her—*ma'am.*

Quasi-respectful, yet cruel.

She was not so very old—was she? Forty-six is not *old.*

Too young for widow. Too young to lose your husband.

Oh, but he died too young! What a tragedy.

She was tugging at the damned door, for at first it would

not open. She'd given no sign of hearing the man's words for they were perfunctory and impersonal and she'd had enough of Helping Hands.

For a moment, outside, Helene couldn't recall where she was—this unfamiliar neighborhood of run-down buildings, cracked and littered pavement—where had she parked her car?—compulsively a widow searches her handbag, in craven terror of losing her *keys*.

If the widow loses her *keys*, the widow will be doubly, trebly bereft—homeless, afoot.

Across the street was a weatherworn stone church Helene hadn't noticed before. Once a church of some distinction, judging by its size and the impressive masonry of its facade, but now its front door had been painted a jarringly bright yellow and there was a matching yellow sign with fire-engine red letters EMMANUEL BRETHREN CARING & SHARING—this too was a charitable organization of some kind, a soup kitchen, or a homeless shelter. A half-dozen individuals—men, dark-skinned, judging by their appearance homeless and derelict—had assembled on the steps, awaiting entry.

The *walking wounded* of America. Helene felt a stab both of guilt and of dread, that they would see her.

A sudden revulsion came over her, for such places—*caring & sharing, helping hands. Disabled.*

Quickly she walked to her car. After the stifling interior of Helping Hands even the tainted air of Trenton smelled fresh to her. Overhead the November sky mottled with storm clouds like soiled upholstery drew her eyes upward, in relief and exaltation.

"Never again! But this once, it was right."

She could not have said why she was so happy. Like one who'd narrowly escaped a terrible danger.

By dusk, in a crawl of traffic on northbound route 1, she'd returned to Quaker Heights.

2.

Not the next day, nor the next, but on the third day.

For some mysterious *turn* had happened in the previous night, in sleep—and when the widow awakened, at first dazed, confused, not knowing where she was—(and why alone)—a new resolve came to her, fully formed, incontestable.

"Yes. Of course!"

Morning and into early afternoon she spent feverishly sorting through her husband's clothing to bring a selection to South Falls Street, Trenton: several shirts, a handful of neckties, an Icelandic cableknit sweater, the beige cashmere blazer that was so beautiful, she could barely bring herself to remove it from the closet.

Her heart felt torn, when she touched the blazer. Pressed her face against it. Then thinking *But it will make someone else happy. He would want this.*

"Hello?"—boldly this time Helene entered the dim-lit thrift shop, knowing beforehand that the door was heavy and required

266

being pushed-against with the weight of her slender body. And with breathless laughter for she gripped unwieldy garment bags in both arms, so long they trailed on the ground.

He was taken by surprise. *He* stared at her with a look of startled recognition—"Ma'am? Is it—Mrs. Haidt?"

It was a pleasure to Helene, to see how surprised Nicolas Zelinski was, that she'd returned.

And so flattering, he remembered her.

Quickly he came to her, in his loose limping stride, to take the heavy garment bags from her and lay them on a table.

"You're back! Is it—'Helen'?"

" 'Helene.' "

Nicolas was staring at her. She saw not the quick-flashing smile that had verged upon insolence but another sort of smile, of recognition.

And the intimacy of recognition: for each was revealed to the other, in the cluttered and twilit interior of Helping Hands.

"Yes—I thought—I would bring a few more things. I . . ."

Helene's heart beat rapidly with relief, that Nicolas Zelinski had not forgotten her. For she'd been thinking of him a good deal, since the other afternoon.

She'd driven from Quaker Heights on route 1 south into Trenton in thunderous traffic, eighteen-rig trucks and massive SUVs careening past her in the left lane, and throwing up skeins of spray onto her windshield, yet she hadn't been intimidated; at the Market Street exit she hadn't hesitated. A wild sort of elation, or recklessness, had guided her. The maze of one-way streets through derelict neighborhoods had not fazed her.

To her disappointment Helene saw that Nicolas wasn't alone this afternoon—he'd been setting up a display of small rugs, with the help of a coworker, a burly black man. The two had been struggling with odd-sized rugs that were intended to be spread out in a fan-like, imbricated fashion on the floor and on a wall to a height of about three feet; their faces shone with perspiration. Not one of the rugs was even reasonably attractive and Helene had the impression that the men hadn't been working well together and that her interruption was welcome to both.

Nicolas introduced Helene to his coworker Gideon—(Gideon's surname was African-polysyllabic, passing by Helene like a floridly-feathered parrot)—telling him that Helene had brought a clothes contribution to Helping Hands just the day before.

"Not yesterday—Monday. I was here on Monday."

But Helene only faintly protested, the point was so trivial.

Nicolas was looking better-groomed than the other day. His lean jaws were clean-shaven, or nearly; his hair looked as if it had been recently shampooed and combed, flaring back from his forehead like a blue jay's crest. The ridged and rippled scar tissue on his cheek seemed less inflamed. The stony-pale eyes were alert and alight and Helene felt weak, as they glided over her.

"Mrs. Haidt—Helene—lives way up in Quaker Heights. You been up there in the van, Gid?—haven't you?"

Nicolas spoke almost boastfully. In his hoarse gravelly voice the name "Helene" was startling.

Gideon shrugged but seemed to be saying *yes*. He was staring just a little too frankly at Helene, as if he didn't think so very much of Quaker Heights. Helene saw his gaze drop to her feet— her Italian leather shoe-boots, that were not new, but clearly expensive—and lift to her face, the taut-skinned white-woman face, a small faint smile fixed like a prosthesis. Gideon was older than Nicolas Zelinski by several years, thick-set, short-legged, in a stained gray sweatshirt imprinted with red lettering—N.J. VETS HELPING HANDS—above the clasped-hands symbol that Helene thought so striking.

Helene was touched that Nicolas seemed pleased to see her again. She'd hoped that he would react in this way and yet—she hadn't been certain.

But don't ever doubt me. I am your friend, Helene.

There followed then a magical interlude, after Nicolas told Gideon he could leave for the day: Helene removed her husband's clothing from the garment bags, item by item, to display for Nicolas. She hoped that her hands weren't trembling. She heard in her voice a strange eager buoyancy.

"I thought I might as well bring a few more things for Helping Hands. Since no one will be wearing them any longer . . ."

She paused. She hadn't meant to say these words, exactly.

No one. Any longer.

Tactful Nicolas heard, but did not comment.

Tactful Nicolas had surely seen the engagement and wedding

rings on Helene's finger, that had grown loose in recent weeks.
But he was too sensitive of her feelings to comment.

". . . these are Brooks Brothers shirts, in quite good condition
as you can see. This one is still in the dry cleaner's bag, it was
never removed. And this . . ."

It was the Icelandic wool sweater, she'd given to her husband
for a birthday, years ago. A beautiful thick-knit sweater, warm as
a coat, of the hue of heather, with tortoiseshell buttons.

"You might like this for yourself, Nicolas? 'Icelandic
wool' . . ."

Her eyes blurred with tears. Her voice quavered. Nicolas stood
near. When Helene fumbled removing the heavy sweater from
the garment bag Nicolas took it from her.

Eagerly Helene asked if Nicolas would like to try it on?

Nicolas glanced about, as if uneasy. But the shop was empty
except for Helene and him: Gideon had left by a rear door.

"Ma'am, I don't know. It's maybe kind of—expensive."

"Yes, but—it's very warm. And it would suit you, I think."

"Would it!"

"It has barely been worn, in fact. He—the previous owner—
had so many lovely sweaters. . . ."

"We're not supposed to just take things for ourselves, ma'am.
There's records we're supposed to keep for our files."

Helene took back the sweater from Nicolas and held it up
against his chest. It was an impulsive gesture—an intimate
gesture—but it seemed appropriate under the circumstances.

"It looks as if it would fit you. And the color is so—subtle. Let me put it aside for right now, over here."

Next, Helene removed the beige cashmere blazer from the garment bag, on its special wooden hanger.

"And this too, I think you should try on, Nicolas."

"Ma'am, thanks! But—"

"Please call me 'Helene.' You know my name."

"'Helene'—yes."

In the days and now weeks following her husband's death, often Helene had found herself at opened closets, staring inside. Slowly and deliberately she moved at such times, as if her limbs were attached to her body in some rudimentary way, by sheer force of will. The mere act of *seeing* required such effort! Touching her husband's beautiful clothes, leaning her face against them, to inhale their special, faint smell, she felt a sense of utter loss, grief, and then lassitude overcame her; her brain was struck dumb as if from lack of oxygen, for long dazed minutes she could not move.

But no longer. Not since she'd discovered Helping Hands.

She would explain to anyone who questioned her *Now I will live for others. I have had enough of the old, self-enclosed life.*

For what is grief but self-pity. She must push herself beyond that, now.

Feeling this almost girlish anticipation, excitement. And a kind of residual pride, that her husband's clothes were of such high quality, and so tastefully chosen.

Nicolas took up the cashmere blazer. An expression of something like pain came into his ravaged face. He was wearing a plaid flannel shirt and corduroy trousers and on his feet the battered hiking boots of the other day.

With Helene's encouragement and assistance, Nicolas pushed his arms into the blazer's sleeves. Helene tugged at the sleeves which were slightly too short for Nicolas's long arms, even as the shoulders appeared to be slightly too large for his narrow shoulders.

"Here's a mirror. Come look!"

Almost shyly Nicolas came to stand before one of the mirrors. The contrast between his worn corduroy trousers and the dazzling blazer was such, he had to laugh.

"Oh but the blazer looks wonderful on you, Nicolas! Maybe the sleeves could be adjusted by a tailor."

Nicolas gazed at his mirror-reflection, with an expression both abashed and pleased. Helene saw in the glass that his eyes were deep-socketed, and thin-lashed; the bony ridge above his eyes seemed to curve in a permanent scowl. His gaze locked with Helene's.

"Sure it's nice. But maybe not for me. I could get in serious trouble, taking these things."

"You aren't 'taking,' Nicolas—I am 'giving.' They are mine to give."

Helene spoke quickly, concerned that Nicolas would remove the blazer and lay it down beside the Icelandic sweater.

Her husband's beautiful things, rejected by *him*.

With a kind of ritual precision Helene removed other articles of clothing from the garment bags—short-sleeved shirts, sport shirts, a cardigan sweater with leather-patch elbows, neckties. Her heart was lacerated—each of the neckties was so *beautiful,* and each contained its own small story, now known only to Helene, and of no interest to anyone else. These items she didn't offer directly to Nicolas though she hoped that he would see how very special they were, how precious.

It was not the widow's vanity, to see that the clothing she'd brought to this thrift shop was of a much, much higher quality than anything in sight.

Nonetheless Nicolas removed the cashmere blazer. Thoughtfully he returned it to its hanger and set it aside, with the Icelandic sweater and not with the other articles of clothing Helene had brought.

Which seemed to mean—he would keep them for himself?

Did it seem strange to Helene, that Nicolas hadn't asked about her husband, or anything about the circumstances of her life that had brought her to Helping Hands?

She thought *Of course he knows. By instinct he knows.*

She thought *This man knows my heart.*

It wasn't clear that anything had been decided but Helene supposed it was time for her to leave. The November afternoon had quickly waned, what she could see of South Falls Street through the murky front window of the shop was near-twilight. A vehicle with lighted headlights lumbered by.

Very rarely, Helene had spoken to her husband in this voice

of subtle coercion, for in their relationship her husband had been the stronger-willed, as he'd been older. But now with this stranger Helene heard herself persist, with uncharacteristic ardor: "Nicolas, I hope that you'll keep the blazer and the sweater, at least—they're for *you*. I wouldn't have brought them otherwise."

Nicolas held himself stiffly. In the mirror, stubbornly his face was averted from the woman.

Half pleading she said: "You're deserving of so much, Nicolas. You are a veteran—aren't you? You've been wounded, I think— haven't you?"

Nicolas shrugged. "Have I!"

"I mean—you've served in the army. You've served your country."

Served your country—what flat banal language—yet Helene had no other words.

"You've had that experience, that few of your fellow citizens have had."

Not one person Helene knew, in fact. Not one person in her or her husband's extended families, nor certainly in the family of any friend, acquaintance or neighbor in affluent Quaker Heights.

At least, not enlisted soldiers. Perhaps there were officers in these families, of high rank. But even these, Helene had never heard of. It was common in these circles to talk of the war—the war in Iraq and the war in Afghanistan—but only as politics: not as actions involving individuals like Nicolas Zelinski.

No one knew a veteran! Still less, a *disabled veteran*.

Helene felt a flush of shame, indignation. Badly she wanted to make up this injustice to this stoic man.

"Yes. You could say so." Nicolas spoke slowly, in a voice of careful neutrality. "I have 'had that experience.'"

Behind the counter, the phone began to ring. Slowly Nicolas moved to answer it, just perceptibly dragging his left leg.

Of course he is wounded. He is too proud to speak of it.

He doesn't want pity any more than I do.

Helene saw, behind the counter, on a shelf crowded with books of which most were ragged paperbacks, the old stained leather-bound *Euripides: Plays*.

The titles of the other books, which Nicolas seemed to have been reading, or had purloined from a bin of donated books with the intention of reading, were not visible to Helene.

The telephone call was perfunctory, not personal. Helene tried not to overhear.

A caller requesting a pickup. Giving directions, which Nicolas took down.

Helene had turned off her cell phone, leaving Quaker Heights for Trenton. Or was it that Helene's cell phone didn't seem to work in Trenton. There were friends in Quaker Heights and relatives scattered in the Midwest who called her frequently since her husband's death, concerned for her; worried that she was no longer answering their calls, as she once had; but Helene had no wish to speak to these people. All they could tell her was that they too missed her husband, and grieved for him, and felt so very sorry—so very sorry—for her; beyond this, they had nothing to tell her of value to her, for her survival. With a defiant sort of gaiety she thought *No more! I am not to be pitied any longer.*

"Do many people come into the shop, on an average day?"

Nicolas laughed. "*Many?* No. But those who do are very —special."

"Are we!"

"Some of the donations that come into the shop, like those you brought yesterday, that are classified as 'necessities,' aren't usually sold here but distributed to veterans and their families in the area. We work with Mercer County services—'welfare.'"

"And is that—do you feel that that is—fulfilling? Rewarding?"

Nicolas looked at Helene as if she'd said something witty. But Nicolas did not laugh.

Fulfilling, rewarding—these were not the right words. Helene was in a panic not knowing the right words.

"How—how long have you been here?"

"Too God-damned long. It's—like—a tear in my actual life— the life I was supposed to live—some kind of 'black hole' that sucked me in—now I can't climb out."

Helene wanted to ask *And what is your actual life?*

Badly Helene wanted to ask *Would you accept help, to reenter your actual life?*

He'd been given a job at Helping Hands after he'd been discharged from rehab, he said. This was at the VA hospital in New Brunswick—the rehab clinic. A year, eighteen months . . .

Helene thought of her husband who'd died shortly before his fifty-second birthday. He had been a kindly, courteous, thoughtful man—a reticent man, highly intelligent and brilliant in his field of highly specialized estate law—yet in essential ways he'd been an immature man; for they'd never had children, to force maturity upon them. Nor had Helene's husband experienced much risk, physical hardship or danger—the adventures of his life, mountain hiking, sailing, backpacking in eastern Europe as a college student, had all been elective, volitional. And here was Nicolas Zelinski—his young life torn from him.

Helene wanted to ask Nicolas if he'd been married, or was married now. If he'd had children.

Badly she wanted to ask! But she dared not.

Instead she asked, as if it were a casual question: "Where will you go, Nicolas, when the shop closes?"

"You mean—goes out of business?"

The sardonic quick-flash of a smile, that seemed to be teasing her.

"No—when you lock up, tonight."

"When I 'lock up'—tonight—I will go—where d'you think I will go?"

Helene smiled, uncertainly. Was the man being sarcastic, or was this a playful sort of banter? An affectionate sort of banter?

"Well—I don't know: home?"

Home was not an easy word to utter. With a cruel sort of childlike naïveté Helene hoped that Nicolas had not a *home*.

"Half-right, ma'am."

Half-right? Helene didn't understand.

Some sort of *half-home*?

"And—where is this?"

"East Trenton."

"Do you—drive?"

"I take a bus."

"A bus! I see."

"I walk over to Broad Street and get the bus there, out to Liberty. I live just off Liberty."

Nicolas was speaking more congenially now. As if the circumstances of his life were absurd, comical—or not his own, exactly.

"And do you have a—family?"

"Not anymore."

Helene wanted to lay her hand on Nicolas's wrist, in commiseration. But maybe the man didn't want commiseration from a stranger? Maybe having no family was his choice?

"If you—you'd like—a ride home—I'll be driving in that direction, I think."

Her heart beat rapidly. It was as if—she'd run up a flight of stairs!

In fact Helene had no idea in what direction she would be driving, to return to route 1. She knew only that Broad Street was a major thoroughfare in Trenton and that very likely Broad intersected with route 1.

Helene believed that Nicolas would tell her—stiffly—that the shop wouldn't be closing for a while, or that he didn't need a ride anywhere. Instead he said, "OK."

Outside, it had grown dark. Helene peered at her watch seeing with surprise that the time was late—nearly 6 P.M.

Nicolas told her he had only a few things to do before he locked up for the night.

"Don't hurry!" Helene said. "I can wait."

Why here, this place. This terrible place.

But where, otherwise? For all places are equidistant from home now.

In Helene's car as she drove toward the center city Nicolas said, "Just take me to the bus stop, that's far enough, thanks"—but Helene insisted upon driving him home. Following his directions along Broad Street in early-evening traffic for a mile or two— surprising to Helene, so many people in Trenton seemed to be taking buses; there were so many buses!—and how rare it was to see a bus in Quaker Heights where everyone, even teenaged children, owned their own vehicles. Nicolas said, shifting his long legs uncomfortably, "I have a car, actually. I don't drive it much, it needs work." You could see that Nicolas admired Helene's car which had been her husband's car, a new-model silvery Acura sedan, but—out of masculine pride?—he said nothing.

Helene's thoughts raced. So much to ask this man! . . . so much to tell him. She could ask him about the veterans' charity, and how she might become more personally involved; she could ask him about college, why he'd dropped out; and about his wartime experience, in the Middle East. . . . So badly she wanted to tell him *I am so very lonely. I think that I will die, I am so very lonely.*

Already they were at Liberty Street, intersecting with Broad. So quickly!

Helene had an impression of a street of row houses. Like South Falls the street was lined with parked vehicles—some of them abandoned and denuded, flattened tires on metal wheel rims.

"Guess you won't mind, ma'am, if I don't invite you inside."

Before Helene could reply, Nicolas snatched her hand and pressed his mouth—hungry, wet—against her startled skin. And in the next instant he'd slammed out of the car, and was limping away without a backward glance.

Came into her life when it seemed her life was finished.

3.

"Jesus! Ridiculous."

Waking in the morning with a jolt—that terrible sinking sensation when the brain, stunned by sedation, clicks *on*—and will not click *off* for many hours—she understood with devastating clarity that she must never, she must never *never* return to Trenton again, to the veterans' thrift shop on South Falls Street.

"Not ever."

That graveyard of cast-off things, soiled and battered furniture and ugly machine-made rugs, not one of which Helene would have placed even at the rear entrance of her house, that led into the garage; not one of which Helene would have placed in the garage. Her nostrils contracted with the recalled odors of Helping Hands, and the contaminated air of Trenton; she gave a shudder recalling *his* smell—the intimate smell of the ravaged man's body, his clothes and his hair.

The sensation of his mouth against the back of her hand: not a kiss, you would not call it a kiss, just the abrupt press of his lips, teeth, tongue onto her skin, that felt afterward as if it had been burnt.

"Ridiculous! No more."

The Savile Row suit, the handsome black wool overcoat, many pairs of shoes—"dress" shoes—these, the widow had kept back. The widow had not yet "donated."

Reasoning *Too much, too soon* is not a good idea.

In the days following, her life resumed.

This was the widow's truncated life: the remnants of the life she'd lived with her husband, now deceased. For a widow remains the wife of the deceased. So many *death-duties* were required, and all involving the *death certificate* which is the document a widow comes to fear most.

For the *death certificate* is an absolute and inviolable fact.

And the *death certificate* is a starkly impersonal document suggesting how impersonal, how ordinary, how unimaginative, how banal the terrible death is, that the bereaved mourns with such emotion.

Helene was thinking of *him*—the man with the stubbled jaws, whom she'd first seen oblivious of her, essentially indifferent to her: uncaring whether she lived, died or had ever existed. But then she was thinking of Nicolas Zelinski who'd smiled at her with genuine emotion; she was sure, it had been genuine emotion. Embarrassed when she'd held the Icelandic sweater up against him, in an intimate and even wifely gesture but yes, he'd been moved as well.

He'd looked at her with desire, of a kind: she was sure.

The pale eyes fixed upon her, the rich man's widow, a woman past the first bloom of her beauty and yet not much older than he, now rather gaunt-faced, stark-eyed, with a nervous bright hopeful smile that transformed her face so that you could see— you could almost see—the vibrant young woman she'd been, once; and in her innermost heart, she remained.

We had not met at the right time. But now—it can be the right time.

• • •

Where in her previous life Helene had had little concern for money, now in the *afterlife* of the widow she became sick with anxiety. Waking in the night panicked that she'd forgotten to pay bills—that she knew which bills were to be paid, and when—(the Quaker Heights property tax bill, for instance, which was near nine thousand dollars quarterly); panicked that services might be shut off without warning—gas, heat, water, electricity. Her husband's computer was a blank, black screen, she could not access his e-mail accounts. She'd heard of women so paralyzed with depression they neglected to open mail, failed to pay mortgages, taxes, and lost their houses. She discovered that she wasn't any longer opening letters but letting them accumulate on a kitchen counter. Her stomach cramped as if it were being devoured from within by a rapacious parasite. She wept easily, she had little control of her emotions that fluttered and whipped like small flags in the wind. Frantically she searched for her husband's financial records, at the insistence of their accountant. For income taxes had to be paid, both federal and New Jersey. She could make little sense of what she discovered—investment reports, printouts from Merrill Lynch, thick brochures of hundreds of pages. It was a nightmare from which there could be no waking except the most stuporous sleep. The accountant came to the house, met with Helene in her husband's study, a middle-aged man of no singular distinction at whom Helene had never really looked before: seeing now in his close-set eyes a look of sinister intent, though addressing Helene he seemed innocent, concerned for her—"professional."

Checks made out to the U.S. Treasury and the New Jersey Department of Taxation—checks for large sums of money—the widow numbly signed at his bequest.

I must have someone I can trust.

Only in love is there trust—even the possibility of trust.

The accountant did not love *her*—how then could she trust *him*?

She thought *Someone who would love me.*

Who?

In her handbag she discovered a little card—New Jersey Disabled Veterans Helping Hands Trenton. She must have picked it up at the thrift shop, but could not remember.

She called the number. She asked for "Nicolas."

A heavily accented voice informed her: "Not in today."

She felt a pang of disappointment. Her hand shook, gripping the receiver. Yet wryly she thought, *It's a good thing. No more.*

Later, looking for the little card, she couldn't find it. Even in the recycled-paper container, she could not find it. And so, she looked up Helping Hands in the yellow pages another time.

Seeing that she'd circled the quarter-page advertisement in red, like an exclamation. The line drawing of a pair of clasped hands had snatched at her eye, irresistibly.

Listed in the yellow pages were numerous "charitable organizations." She might have chosen Rescue Ministry of Trenton,

Children's Home Society of New Jersey, Goodwill Industries, Big Brothers & Big Sisters of Mercer Co., Gateway Foundation, Salvation Army, Military Order of the Purple Heart which resembled Helping Hands but lacked the magical clasped-hands that so stirred the heart.

He had seized her hand, unexpectedly. Her right hand, gripping the steering wheel of her car.

As he'd prepared to climb out of the car, at the intersection of Broad and Liberty streets, he had seized her hand and kissed it, suddenly. Almost faint, she recalled the brush of his lips against her skin, and not the hungry wet pressure like an animal's mouth; she remembered her astonishment, and afterward the sensation of warmth that suffused her heart.

And all the way back home to Quaker Heights, to the five-bedroom wood, fieldstone and stucco Colonial on three acres shaded with oak trees, white pines and red maples, the kiss had burned in her heart.

4.

In a lowered voice he spoke.

In a lowered voice confiding in *her.*

In the candlelit dining room of the old inn on the Delaware River. In a corner table, near a fireplace in which romantic flames—gas-jet, simulated—rippled sinuously without heat.

"... died when I was at Rutgers ... my first year ... I had a scholarship ... wanted to study history, and law ... maybe classics ... I liked to write poetry ... what I called 'poetry' ... died of a 'fast-acting pancreatic' cancer ... I had to drop out of school ... my head was messed up ... had to work ... got into some trouble with drugs ... more messed up ... the world rushes past you if you drop out ... if you are 'wounded' ... 'disabled' ... can't get back to the life that was meant for you ... rushes past and never returns."

He was speaking quietly. He was not speaking bitterly. As he spoke his pale eyes drifted over her, Helene's hands, Helene's beautiful hands, clasped together on the tabletop, on the white linen cloth, in candlelight. *Is this a dream? I am so happy, I am frightened.*

That this man would confide in her, so intimately. What a triumph it was for the widow, in her aloneness!

He'd been speaking of his mother. The loss of his mother. It was clear—(Helene thought it was clear)—that Nicolas had loved his mother very much but also blamed her for dying and leaving him.

There was great sorrow in the man, and also great anger. Heat wafted from his body as he spoke to Helene in a halting yet forward-plunging voice like one unaccustomed to speech.

The physical presence, physical *closeness* of the man. Helene was transfixed as if she had not ever—not ever, yet in her life—experienced such *closeness,* that threatened to overwhelm her.

Please let me take you to dinner she'd said. It's the least I can do for you she'd said.

It was an impersonal gesture of gratitude. She hoped he would understand that. *You who have served your country. You who have been "disabled" in the line of duty.*

On this evening in late November in the dining room of the historic old General Washington Inn, just across the Delaware River from Trenton, in Pennsylvania. On the walls were myriad reproductions of the Battle of Trenton of December 1776: Revolutionaries firing upon Hessian soldiers in their red British uniforms. And above the fireplace a reproduction of the iconic *General George Washington Crossing the Delaware.* Helene had wanted to take her newfound friend to a special place, not an ordinary Trenton restaurant, and so she'd brought him to this locally celebrated inn where other diners observed them with a flattering sort of covert interest.

Their waiter, too. Courteously attentive while at the same time frankly staring.

For they were a mysterious couple, Nicolas Zelinski and Helene. It wasn't likely that they were married: not only were their ages not quite right but the man with the scarred face was speaking much too intensely to the woman, leaning close to her and scarcely ever looking away from her; as the woman, listening intently, scarcely ever looked away from him.

Nor was it likely that they were related: for they were so clearly from very different backgrounds and social classes.

Though Nicolas was wearing, just slightly uncomfortably, the beige cashmere blazer, a long-sleeved white shirt and an Italian silk necktie that Helene had given him.

When they'd first been seated, Nicolas had caught sight of his reflection in a mirror and recoiled with a pained smile. Helene, laying a hand on his wrist, assured him—"But you look very handsome, Nicolas! Please don't frown."

A glass of red wine, and a second glass, and Nicolas's creased face began to relax.

During dinner the subject of Euripides arose. *The Bacchae,* which Nicolas had been reading. Helene recalled the vivid, catastrophic ending—the ritual sacrifice of the (mortal) King Pentheus to the (god) Dionysus.

A band of crazed women, followers of Dionysus, had torn the man's body to pieces in an erotic ecstasy, beheading him. His own mother is seen carrying the severed head under the illusion that it is the head of a wild beast.

Weird! Nicolas marveled.

"Not like anything you could do today on a stage—people would laugh—but in a movie, maybe: a woman with some guy's severed head. And the woman his *mother.*"

Near as he could figure, Nicolas said, the ancient Greeks were nothing like Americans today. Terrible fantastic things happened to them that were caused by "gods"—the blame was always some "god"—which they didn't question.

Helene said yes, the Greeks were religious but not in the way that Americans are religious: their sense of life was tragic, and the only response was to accept suffering. "The Greeks didn't believe in a transcendent God who loved them, or in a savior who died for them. They didn't believe in 'good works' or even in 'faith' like Christians. Whatever would happen, would happen. You deserved your fate—like Pentheus—even if you didn't 'deserve' it."

Nicolas shifted and squirmed in his chair. A pained grimace rippled over his face. Helene wondered if the discussion of Greek "fate" hit too close to home for him. Unconsciously he'd been rubbing the wasted thigh muscles of his left leg.

Nicolas drank, and ate; within minutes he'd devoured a twelve-ounce plank steak, scalloped potatoes and hunks of bread; and took up a third glass of wine. His face flushed red, his eyes shone with a kind of aggrieved resentment: "My mother died and my life fell apart. Getting sick when she did. It happened at the wrong time like my asshole drunk-father walking out when I was starting ninth grade in a new school . . . you could count on him to fuck things up for his kids when he could. And *her* . . ." In this account it seemed that Nicolas had been enrolled at the Newark campus of Rutgers University, not New Brunswick; then it seemed that he'd taken courses at the local community college, in business and computer science; it wasn't clear that Nicolas had ever finished any course—always he'd dropped out even when his grades were high.

Why was this, Helene wondered.

Jinxed by *fate* all his life.

Worst mistake then, Nicolas said vehemently, he'd enlisted in the U.S. Army. Twenty-six years old, desperate for some fucking purpose to his life. Wound up in Operation Desert Storm— 1991—U.N. troops led by the U.S. and the U.K. Sandstorms, sand fleas, terrible heat and nobody knowing what the fuck they were doing there, in someplace nobody knew—"Middle East." He'd seen some of the guys in his platoon get hit bad and one he'd seen die. He'd been shot up—taken for dead—half his face blown off—some kind of shrapnel in his skull. Worst thing was, he was fucking sure it'd been the U.N. "coalition" that was responsible—"friendly fire"—like a bad joke. Couldn't prove it, but he'd known. Anyway it happened fast. He woke in some shitty hospital. Kept waking in some shitty hospital someplace and finally it was told to him, you are back home in New Jersey —in the VA hospital in New Brunswick, New Jersey. Weird how he'd been shipped back home without knowing it. Kind of in pieces like some broken thing, the pieces jiggle around and break more, he'd been shipped home in pieces not knowing it. And a worse joke yet was rehab where it was a long time before he could walk like even a cripple walks, eat food with his actual mouth not through a funnel, shit in the way you're supposed to shit, or keep his eyes from jumping all around like an actual screw was loose inside his head. Half the muscle was missing from his left-leg thigh and what was left looked like string dark-meat chicken.

Helene was deeply moved. Wanting to promise *I will be different, Nicolas. I will not abandon you.*

"You get shipped out to die. When you are shipped back you are dead not knowing it."

Harshly Nicolas laughed, then began to cough. His flushed face grew redder still and angry tears leaked in the corners of his eyes.

Helene was thinking: she could pay Nicolas's tuition, if he wanted to return to school. Clearly he was very intelligent. He could take the SAT exam and be readmitted. Surely there were special provisions for veterans and particularly disabled veterans. . . .

". . . see, they lied to me. They lie to every asshole enlists in the U.S. fucking Army. This-here you see ain't *me*. It's what's left of *me*. Fuck I'm gonna complain to them, that just fucks you up more, nobody wants to hear some banged-up asshole saying he's in pain, his head is in pain, every thirty days I got to have a 'blood infusion' to keep my blood from rotting. They're saying my 'T-count' is too high, or too low—my 'immune system' is fucked. See, I am a dead man, but I am not *dead*."

Helene laid her hand on Nicolas's wrist. "Of course you are not *dead*. I will help you—all that I can—to retrieve your life for you."

Now diners at nearby tables were openly staring at them. How rawly aggrieved Nicolas's voice, and how hoarse and labored his breath had become! Helene made a gesture as if to brush the man's damp hair back off his forehead and he stiffened suddenly, as if recoiling; then said, in a tremulous voice, "You are a beautiful woman, Helen—*Helene*. Must be, God sent you."

He was drunk. His mouth twisted strangely. Tears welled in his eyes. Helene saw that a cuff of the beige cashmere blazer was stained with watery steak-blood. When Nicolas tried to stand, his left leg buckled beneath him. Blindly he grabbed at the tablecloth, the table almost overturned, their waiter came hurrying with a look of acute alarm. "*Fuck fuck fuck you all*"—the widow would be certain, afterward, she had not heard.

Stricken with guilt, and with something more intimate than guilt, the widow could not sleep.

She would hire the disabled veteran Nicolas: she would pay him generously.

Nicolas could be her driver, perhaps. When she needed to travel to New York City or to Philadelphia, she would hire *him*.

He would be loyal, trustworthy. He would be devoted to *her*.

Whatever his duties were at Helping Hands, Helene was certain he could replicate them in her household. Helping to maintain the five-bedroom house in which she now lived alone; in which, as she recalled, a caretaker had once lived in a basement apartment, to oversee the household for the elderly couple who'd owned the house previously.

Of course, forty-six is far from elderly. But the maintenance of the expensive house and grounds was more than Helene could do by herself.

She was a widow with money, Nicolas was a just slightly younger man, intelligent, sensitive, respectful of her. Nicolas was cultured, in his way—or could become so.

They would attend the Metropolitan Opera in New York City. They would visit museums, travel to Europe. They would visit Rome, Florence, Sienna, Venice. They would stay in five-star hotels and their rooms would be next to each other and with (maybe) a door between.

It was not difficult to imagine: Nicolas Zelinski would be her companion.

He was the age of a younger cousin, or brother. In the clothes she would give him, he would not look so desperate. She would see that he received the very best medical care—not the VA hospital in New Brunswick but specialists in New York City.

Surgery at the New York Hospital for Special Surgery. His damaged leg, back.

Dental work to replace the missing incisor that gave him, even when he smiled, a look of animal rapacity.

As her escort he would accompany her to events to which she could not otherwise bear to go alone. He would drop her off at the entrances of buildings, in bad weather. He would hold an umbrella over her head. He would be her younger, devoted brother. He would be an old dear college friend. A bachelor friend of her late husband's who had stepped forward to protect the widow, in her bereavement.

In time, this trusted companion could handle Helene's

business affairs perhaps. The complicated finances, the many investments, the exacting tedium of bookkeeping.

Helene? We need to speak with you. Please.
    Helene—can we come to see you? Please.
    Or—would you like to come here?
    Come visit! Stay with us! Please.
    It has been too long.
    We miss him too, you know. We are mourning him too.

These messages Helene deleted.

"You have the wrong person. That woman doesn't live here anymore."

But this was a shock. She called Helping Hands and asked for "Nicolas" and was informed, in a drawling/nasal New Jersey voice: "Not here today."

A second call, and she was told: "'N'c'las?' Nobody here by that name."

Calmly she said: "I'm calling for 'Nicolas Zelinski'—Helping Hands. I have his card."

"Nah, ma'am. No 'Zoo-lin-ski' here."

"The name is 'Nicolas Ze-lin-ski.' He is certainly there."

"Nobody here by that name, ma'am."

She was very upset. She was agitated, sleepless. She was a starving woman and yet she could not eat. Her heart had atrophied, like the wounded man's thigh muscles. You could reach your fingers into such a wound, as into the wounded side of Christ.

Another time, nearing the darkest day of the year, the accountant came to the house on Birnam Wood Circle, Quaker Heights. The accountant with the close-set sinister eyes arriving midmorning following one of the widow's sleepless nights. She'd served him coffee—(Helene was an unfailingly gracious woman, she'd been bred to serve others)—but could not concentrate on his words. When he passed to her checks prepared for her signature she could not sign, her hand shook too badly.

"Can I trust you? How can I trust *you*? And what is the point of this? Oh God—what will I do with so much money?"

She wondered: had Nicolas been dismissed from Helping Hands?

He'd been so angry, the last time she'd seen him. After the dinner at the General Washington Inn had come to an abrupt end. After she'd enlisted their waiter to help her walk Nicolas out to her car—she'd given the man a twenty-dollar tip. Collapsing into the passenger's seat flailing his fists, mumbling and laughing mirthlessly and he'd lapsed into an open-mouthed sleep smelling of red wine which he'd spilled onto his shirt front and at Liberty Street she'd tried to help him from the car and part-waking with a laughing grunt he'd grabbed at her, pawed and struck at her, seizing her head, lowering her head to him, pressing his hot wet mouth against her mouth, and as Helene shook her head he gripped her harder, prodding her lips with his tongue, now penetrating her mouth with his tongue, and Helene had pushed him away—-"Nicolas! Oh please—please *stop*."

The fury in the man's eyes, the savage twist of his mouth— she'd felt a stir of dread, and yet of excitement knowing *He is my friend. He would not hurt me really. God has sent me to him.*

At last she called Helping Hands and left a message on the voice mail.

Calmly as if reciting a poem.

> *This message is for Nicolas.*
> *Please come to 28 Birnam Wood Circle, Quaker Heights. I have things for Helping Hands—men's clothing in very good condition. And also appliances, furniture.*
> *Please come soon!*
> *My name is Helene.*
> *This message is for Nicolas.*

5.

He had come to her house, at last.

On a bright December morning the front doorbell rang. Quickly Helene came downstairs to answer, seeing the van in the driveway—metallic gray with DISABLED VETERANS OF NEW JERSEY HELPING HANDS in red letters on the side and the clasped-hands insignia beneath—and there on the doorway stood Nicolas Zelinski and his coworker Gideon.

"Why, hello! I wasn't expecting . . ."

It was a shock to Helene, to see Nicolas on her doorstep—so suddenly. Smiling at her and calling her "Mrs. Haidt"—tactfully, since Gideon was present—explaining that Helping Hands was behind in pickups but they hoped she still had her donations for them.

". . . I mean yes of course. Please come inside."

"Thanks, ma'am! OK we keep our boots on?"

"Your boots? Oh yes of course . . ."

The stony-pale eyes lit upon Helene, and past Helene into the dazzling interior of the house, in a way that was both intimate and yet discreet, impersonal. You could not have known— (grim-faced Gideon could not have known)—that there was any connection between the Helping Hands staff worker and Mrs. Haidt of 28 Birnam Wood Circle, let alone an emotional bond; you could not have guessed that Helene's heart was beating so rapidly, she felt for a moment that she might faint.

Several times she'd called Helping Hands and left her plaintive message. Nearly two weeks had passed and she'd reconciled herself to the possibility of not seeing Nicolas again, unless— again!—she drove back to South Falls Street, Trenton, with more of her husband's clothes which she could not quite bring herself to do, just yet.

Must not abase myself. Must take care!

Telling herself that she would hear from Nicolas again. Unless something had happened to him, he would reenter her life.

The men had been gazing upward at the house which was

large—a Colonial-contemporary of fieldstone, brick, wood and stucco with numerous latticed windows, several chimneys and a massive slate roof—though not so large as other custom-designed houses in the residential neighborhood Birnam Wood.

The driveway was long—uphill—designed to loop about a stand of Scotch pines, in front of the house, while continuing to the side, to the three-car garage not visible from the front door.

Inside, from the foyer and front hall you could look through the beautifully furnished living room to a floor-to-ceiling latticed glass door and through this door to a long sloping lawn lightly stippled with frost and abutting a lake upon which white swans paddled in decorous idleness like figures in a pastoral painting.

Both men glanced about with veiled gazes as Helene led them to the rear of the house, into the kitchen.

She was pained to see that Nicolas was walking stiffly, dragging his left foot. He wore a soiled windbreaker, work trousers and on his head a woolen cap that looked like something purloined from a bin at Helping Hands. His jaws had not been recently shaved and the ridged and rippled scar tissue on his cheek glared red. His graying-dark hair had been tied back into a short pigtail at the nape of his neck—Helene had never seen Nicolas's hair in a pigtail, that gave the man a swaggering piratical look. On his feet were the heavy hiking boots, trailing bits of damp leaves onto the floor.

"Beautiful house, Mrs. Haidt. Big!"

There came the quick-flash of Nicolas's smile, and a glimpse of the empty socket in his lower jaw, where the incisor was missing.

And how dazzling-bright the kitchen, with Mexican tiles on the floor, a center-island work area of gleaming hardwood, eight-burner Luxor stove and copper pans overhead hanging from hooks; the counter space was considerable, in flawless white. The room included a breakfast space with a mounted TV and a latticed bay window overlooking the sloping back lawn and the lake.

"What d'ya think, Gid? You seen anything like Mrs. Haidt's house before?"

Nicolas spoke admiringly, and not ironically—Helene was sure. But the burly black man in a Helping Hands denim jacket thrust out his lower lip saying what sounded like *Yah sure, been in Bir'm Woods before.*

Helene was explaining that she had both clothes donations and some appliances and furniture, which were downstairs in the basement; there was a basement door they could use, to bring things outside without taking the stairs up to the kitchen, but one of them would have to move the van around to the garage.

Nicolas sent Gideon off on this errand. Alone in the kitchen with Helene he moved about self-consciously, shifting his shoulders as if he were uncomfortable. His gaze was restless, evasive. His mouth worked and twitched. He was pretending an interest in framed photographs on the walls—travel photographs of Greece and Italy, taken long ago by Helene's husband. Helene wanted to draw near him and touch his arm but sensed that Nicolas would ease away with a frown. In a bright hostess-voice she asked, "How are you, Nicolas? Have you been—busy?"

Nicolas shrugged, yes.

"I left messages for you, I'd hoped that you might call back. I was worried—just a little. You'd said something about a 'blood infusion'. . . ."

But this was a mistake: Nicolas did not want Helene to speak of his health, or of anything personal, intimate. She supposed, not with Gideon near.

They waited for Gideon to return. Helene's heart was still beating painfully and her mouth had gone dry. If only Nicolas had come to her house alone . . .

But then? What then?

It was a weekday, 9:20 A.M. Helene hadn't expected any delivery or tradesman that morning; she'd assumed that Helping Hands would call to arrange for a pickup date and time. She hadn't had time to prepare for a visit from Nicolas—though she was wearing dove-gray wool flannel trousers, a black Shetland sweater, low-heeled canvas shoes in anticipation of going out later in the day on errands.

If she'd known that Helping Hands was in the neighborhood, she'd have done more with her hair that morning than run a brush through it hurriedly; she'd have applied makeup to her thin, sallow face, darkened her eyebrows, reddened her mouth.

She'd have tied a silk scarf around her throat. A touch of color, to gladden the heart.

Still, in the reflective bottoms of the copper pans, Helene had a glimpse of an attractive and even composed female face; the face of a gracious woman, welcoming visitors into her house though they'd taken her by surprise. Helene had to check herself from offering the Helping Hands men something to drink—coffee?—fruit juice?—the instinct in her to be hospitable, as an American woman of her class, was so strong.

Gideon returned, and Helene led the men into the basement, by a staircase adjacent to the kitchen. Here was a back corridor that led to another wing of the house, overlooking an expanse of wooded land.

Switching on a light, descending into the basement, Helene had the terrible—unbidden and baseless—thought that these strangers could shove her down the stairs, cause her to fall and crack her skull, rob her. . . .

Who would know? And when?

This was absurd of course. Helene would have been deeply ashamed, if either of the men knew what she'd been thinking.

Particularly, Helene was not a *racist*.

Neither she nor her husband had ever been, in any of their sympathies, *racists*.

Nor was Birnam Wood, still less Quaker Heights, *segregated by race*.

At the foot of the stairs were two doors: one to the left, that led into the finished part of the basement, which contained the family room with its large flat-screen TV and attractive furnishings, an exercise room and her husband's wine cellar; the other, that led into the large, unheated and unfinished part of the basement containing the furnace, hot water heater, electrical boxes and switches and the door and steps to the outside of the house. This was not a part of the basement in which Helene felt comfortable for it was chilly and smelled faintly of backed-up drains; the things it contained—furnace, switches—she did not understand and dreaded that they might break down. The majority of the space was used for storage and contained items long ago exiled from the upstairs—furniture, lamps, cartons of clothing, books. None of these things was shabby or useless and yet none had been seen upstairs for years. An upholstered cobbler's bench with a frayed wicker back, a coffee table in Scandinavian blond wood with a just slightly cracked glass top, orphaned dining room chairs, box springs and headboards, Venetian blinds, folded curtains layered in dust . . . Helene did not want to look too closely at a white leather sofa that had once been the pride of their living room, or at boxes of college textbooks her husband had been reluctant to part with though acknowledging that probably he would never read the books again.

Annually the subject had come up: they should call one of the charity organizations, Goodwill perhaps, to come and haul away the things accumulating in the basement, for much here was in good condition, usable and even valuable. But neither had ever gotten around to doing it and now the task fell to the smiling widow.

"Nicolas, Gideon—here we are! Please take all these things away. Just in this room, not in the other part of the basement—not in the 'family room.' All this furniture, these boxes, clothing . . ." Helene's voice faltered. She saw both men looking at her with—sympathy? pity? She supposed it was routine in their lives, Helping Hands summoned to take away clothes and household possessions after a death in the family.

She was routine in Nicolas's eyes. Yet she could not believe that, so much had passed between them.

"The door to the outside is here, I can open it for you."

Helene tugged at the door, and managed to open it. Mossy stone steps led up, outside. There was a smell of wintry damp, earth. Helene hadn't used these steps for years though furnace repairmen, plumbers and electricians used them routinely.

Immediately, without hesitation, like a practiced team, Nicolas and his frowning dark-skinned coworker hoisted up tables, chairs. Helene stepped out of the way as they headed for the opened door. It was striking to her, how efficient and capable both men were, at a task that would have defeated her both physically and emotionally.

She'd thought that she might oversee the pickup, to speak with Nicolas perhaps, but felt a touch of vertigo, as of inexpressible sorrow, and went back upstairs.

Through a back window she observed the men carrying furniture across a stretch of lawn and to the van, for just a few minutes. The *impersonality* of what she saw made her feel weak, debilitated. She wondered if she'd made a terrible and irremediable mistake—what urgent need was there to clear out stored things in the basement, now that her husband had departed?

His college textbooks! Helene felt a stab of something like anguish, that these books would be hauled into the dim-lit interior of Helping Hands, dumped into a bin with other unwanted books, to be sold for pennies.

Of course: she'd hoped that Nicolas would come to the house, and she'd hoped he would come alone.

She had several precious things to give to him—one of her husband's Savile Row suits, his black wool overcoat, a floral-print shirt from Liberty of London.

"Will you have something to drink? Coffee, fruit juice . . ."

By the time the men had finished hauling her things out to the van, and brought the printed form for Helene to sign, she'd recovered from her spell of melancholy; she'd hurried upstairs to put on makeup, lipstick; she'd knotted a pink-striped silk scarf around her neck. In the mirror she'd looked surprisingly young, even radiant.

". . . you've worked so hard! Please let me give you something before you leave. . . ."

Despite the cold air, the men were warm from their exertions. Hesitating at first, Nicolas unzipped his windbreaker and allowed Helene to take it from him, to drape over the back of a kitchen chair; Gideon unfolded a handkerchief and wiped his dark, oily face.

At first the men asked for ice water. Then, Nicolas asked if Helene had any beer.

"If you got any, ma'am. Otherwise, no matter."

Beer! It wasn't yet noon.

Helene laughed, and brought two bottles of German lager from the refrigerator. For weeks—now, months—these bottles had been at the back of the refrigerator. Helene had been reluctant to remove them—she hadn't wanted to remove any of her husband's things—his special fig jam, his favorite black olives, even a chunk of hardened Gorgonzola cheese. These bottles of beer Helene was delighted to serve to the Helping Hands men who'd worked so hard.

They were self-conscious at first, sitting at the breakfast table. Helene gave them glasses to pour the beer into but they preferred to drink from the bottles. She set out a plate of multigrain bread, sliced cheddar cheese, black olives. She went away, and returned with the Savile Row suit, the black wool overcoat, the floral-print shirt from Liberty, all on hangers. Both men were eating hungrily when she returned.

She saw in Nicolas's eyes an understanding that yes, he knew these beautiful articles of clothing were for him personally; but no, he did not want Helene to say anything, in Gideon's presence.

"I'd forgotten these. I'd meant to bring them downstairs with the other things, but . . ."

On a hook in the kitchen Helene hung the suit, the overcoat, the floral-print shirt.

The men mumbled thanks ma'am! As quickly they downed their beers.

Gideon asked to use a bathroom and Helene directed him to the guest bathroom in the back hall, with its William Morris–style wallpaper, rose-marble sink and brass faucets, a glistening spotless pale-rose ceramic toilet; in a marble soap dish, fragrant hand-soap stamped Dior. When Gideon returned to the kitchen, Nicolas asked to use the bathroom.

Without asking if they wanted a second beer—(for Helene could see that they were restless, wanting to leave)—Helene brought out two more bottles of lager from the refrigerator. By this time the plate of bread and cheese had been emptied and Helene sliced more bread, more cheese, set out more black olives and a little bowl of cashews.

It was painful to her—she did not want the men to leave! Desperately she wanted them to stay a while longer, to talk with her—not as Mrs. Haidt, not as a well-to-do donor to their organization, but as an equal, and a friend. But when she asked the men about their lives—particularly, what had brought them to Helping Hands, what their experiences in the army had been—Gideon frowned and shrugged, and would not meet Helene's eye; Nicolas was silent at first, staring at his feet, then, abruptly, he began telling Helene that the worst mistake he'd ever made had been to enlist in the U.S. Army but—at the same time—what the army brought him to in the Middle East was a "revelation" to him, he wouldn't have had at home.

"See, the way the world *is*. Seeing it in movies and TV isn't the real thing, the war-thing, you have got to be *in it*."

Gideon grunted, and grinned. These harsh words of Nicolas's, he agreed with.

Helene asked uneasily what did Nicolas mean? She was sitting across from the men at the breakfast table, her arms folded tightly beneath her breasts as if she were cold, and trying not to shiver. Sitting only just eighteen inches from Nicolas, and from Gideon, she felt that she herself was on the brink of a profound revelation, no neighbor of hers in Birnam Wood would ever know.

Nor could her poor, deceased husband have known. His widow had gone so far beyond him, now.

"What do I *mean*? What'd you think I mean, ma'am? Getting shipped over to Iraq, trained to be a soldier 'defending democracy'—with a rifle—for a while, inside a tank—firing at whatever was out there, from a tank—sure we killed people, why not? That's what we were sent there for."

Helene was disconcerted, Nicolas smiled so frankly at her. Yet his voice was jeering, derisive.

"But you—you were a soldier, Nicolas. You hadn't any choice. . . ."

"Civilians, too. 'Iraqis'"—contemptuously the word sounded from Nicolas's lips: *Eeer rak eees*—"some of them women, old people shrieking like pigs being slaughtered—kids . . . First I thought, Jesus! This ain't right, we're Americans!—then, seeing what the other guys did, I thought, Why the fuck not? Prob'ly I won't be coming back anyway, who gives a shit."

Helene shrank from Nicolas, shocked and offended. His eyes on her were disdainful. Noisily he drained his bottle of German lager, laughed and wiped his mouth on his sleeve.

"So? You don't want to hear, Mrs. Haidt? Why'd you ask, then? All of you—'civilians'—always ask, and always regret it. Why'd you call me, to come here?"

"I—I—called Helping Hands—to make a donation. . . ."

"Like hell. Ma'am, you called *me*."

Helene had stumbled to her feet, drawing away. Confusedly she thought that—if something happened—she could run into another part of the house: her husband's downstairs study.

There, she could lock the door. She could dial 911.

Gideon said he was out of here, and left the house; Nicolas lingered to finish the remainder of the food. He ate with his fingers hungrily, insolently. Within minutes he'd seemed to become drunk, an elated and violent sort of drunk, repulsive to Helene. Boastfully he was telling her about what a feeling it is, outside the "U.S. territory of law"—"like, free to do any God-damn thing you want to, your buddies will look the other way that's why they are called *buddies*." Seeing the look in Helene's face he leaned close to her, telling her that the rehab hospital he'd been in, in New Brunswick, wasn't just for "physical trauma" but "psy-chi-at-tic" too: "See, thing is, ma'am—Gid and me, we're both *dead*. You'd thought it was some *live vets* coming out in the van but thing is, we are *dead*."

Laughing, Nicolas lurched to his feet. "Good-bye, ma'am! Thanks for these! 'Bye!" Carelessly he seized her husband's beautiful suit, overcoat, floral-print shirt as if they were ordinary articles of cast-off clothing, slung them across his arms, and left the house.

His companion, who had trotted around the corner of the house to get the van, drove now to the circle driveway where Nicolas climbed inside and both men drove away.

In a state of shock, Helene stood unmoving for several minutes. Then, she went to check the guest bathroom: the toilet had not been flushed. The towel on the rack had been used roughly, soiled and wet and twisted. Was something missing from the sink counter?—the marble soap dish? The expensive Dior soap was in the sink as if it had been flung there.

Not Nicolas but Gideon must have done this. Helene could not believe that her friend who'd admired her so, could have done this.

Flushing the toilet, turning away.

Then, she hurried downstairs to check the unfinished basement—all of the furniture, all of the clothes and other items were gone. Though this had been Helene's directive, now she felt a further shock for how bare, how vast the basement was, how grubby the concrete floor! You could see the outlines of objects that had been stored here for years; silhouettes in the floor, only just slightly less dirty than the rest of the floor.

The door to the outside had been left carelessly ajar. Helene went to close and lock it.

Helene left the unfinished basement and would have returned upstairs except, impulsively, she opened the door to the finished basement, the "family room"—and saw in disbelief that this room, too, had been emptied.

The men had taken away the sofa, the chairs—the coffee table—even the carpet; they'd managed to detach and haul away the fifty-two-inch flat-screen TV. They'd taken away the exercise machines—treadmill, StairMaster—that had not been used for years. The door to the wine cellar was ajar; Helene had no need to look inside to know that Helping Hands had emptied the shelves of wine bottles.

In the vacated room Helene stood trembling. On the floor of this room as in the wake of a whirlwind were left-behind, broken things—pottery, a small lamp, vases containing dried grasses and wildflowers. She was too numb to know what to do. Thinking *But it has to be a mistake—doesn't it? This could not be deliberate.*

She saw again the derision in the man's eyes—*That's what I was sent there for. Why'd you ask!*

6.

She began to see the van in the neighborhood.

From an upstairs window she saw the metallic-colored van with red lettering on its side—Helping Hands—passing her driveway to turn into a neighbor's house.

And elsewhere in Birnam Wood, and in Quaker Heights— there was the bullet-shaped vehicle making its slow determined

way along tree-lined circuitous streets. Among the elegant Co-
lonials, French Normandy, quasi-Edwardian, quasi-Georgian
houses set back from curving lanes with names like Eucalyptus
Way, Pheasant Hill, Deer Hill Drive, Pilgrim Lane, Old Mill and
Birnam Wood Pass—the red letters HELPING HANDS. Daily in
the rolling hills of Quaker Heights were vehicles bearing lawn
crews, carpenters, roofers, painters, Guatemalan housemaids—
a continuous stream of service vehicles—and among these the
Helping Hands van was not so very different from the rest.

Helene saw, and felt a jolt of emotion—alarm, dread—but
also something like envy. For *he* might be coming to another
woman's house, and not to her.

She had not called 911, to report theft. She could not have
sworn—the Helping Hands men might testify to this—that
she'd made it absolutely clear, she had not wanted them to enter
the finished part of the basement. *A misunderstanding—maybe.*

One night she saw an ambulance pull into the driveway of
the neighbor's house, which the Helping Hands van had visited
that morning. The wailing siren had wakened her from a sedative
sleep. At the corner of Birnam Wood Circle and Foxcroft Lane
was a fieldstone manor with a remarkable slate roof, larger than
Helene's house. She recalled—a widow lived in that house. An
older woman, in her sixties, whose husband had died before Helene's husband, the previous spring. How remote it had seemed
to Helene, the death of a man in his sixties! A widow in her
sixties! Helene had not known the couple well but she'd walked
over to the house, after a few days, to bring potted flowers to

the bereaved woman; the woman had been gracious to Helene but distracted, clearly she'd preferred to be alone.

Helene dreaded now to learn what might have happened to Mrs. Windriff.

7.

Why'd you ask me. Why'd you send for me.

In the twilight of her bedroom he came to her. His face was shadowed, the quick-flashing bared teeth and the glisten of his eyes were all she could see of his face. She knew his smell: unmistakable. Her body tensed against him. Her heart was beating close to bursting. Her shoulders, her back, her hips and buttocks, her straining head, were pinned against the bed by the weight of his body. His hands on her throat, fingers tightening. *You called me, you wanted me here. This is what you wanted.* Through the house there was a heavy pulsing silence. The grandfather clock in the downstairs hall had ceased its solemn chiming weeks before. For in the Haidt household it had been Helene's husband who oversaw the Stickley clock, inherited from his family. Helene had begun to realize that she hadn't been hearing the clock for—how long? The tolling of time had simply ceased.

For this is death—the tolling of time has ceased.

Yet the man did not strangle her. His fingers relaxed—then again tightened, and again relaxed—tightened, relaxed: this was mercy, that he would allow her to breathe. For the gift of breath was the man's to give her, it was not for her to take.

Weakly she pushed at the man, whose coarse skin scraped against her skin, the scarred and pitted face, the stubbled jaws, a mouth like a sucking predator-fish. One of his legs was atrophied, the thigh-muscles badly wasted, yet still he was strong, pinning her against the bed, paying no heed to her cries, her pleas and her desperation, she had not wanted this, she had wanted the man as a friend, as a companion, as a lover who would love *her*—she had not wanted this. His hand slapped over her mouth, to silence her. His gritty hand that tasted of salt and dirt, to silence her. Her head struck against the headboard like the rapping of knuckles on a door until—at last—something gave, something broke, the door opened and she fell through.

8.

Now in the wintry morning in the circle drive outside the widow's front door, the metallic-colored van with HELPING HANDS in red letters on the side.

Just inside the door she crouched, panting. Barefoot and her hair in her face. She could not see who was driving the van—sunshine reflected from the windshield, blinding.

She would not! Not ever.

A Hole in the Head

Strange!—though Dr. Brede wore latex gloves when treating patients and never came into direct contact with their skin, when he peeled off the thin rubber gloves to toss them into the sanitary waste disposal in his examination room his hands were faintly stained with rust-red streaks—*blood*?

He lifted his hands, spread his fingers to examine them. His hands were those of an average man of his height and weight though his fingers were slightly longer than average and the tips were discernibly tapered. His nails were clipped short and kept scrupulously clean and yet—how was this possible?—inside the latex gloves, they'd become ridged with the dried rust-red substance he had to suppose was blood. He thought, *There must be a flaw in the gloves. A tear.*

It wasn't the first time this had happened—this curiosity. In recent months it seemed to be happening with disconcerting frequency. Lucas considered retrieving the used gloves from the trash to inspect them, to see if he could detect minuscule tears in the rubber—but the prospect was distasteful to him.

In the lavatory attached to his office Lucas Brede washed his hands vigorously. A swirl of rust-red water disappeared down the drain. This was a mystery! Few of his patients ever "bled" in his office. Dr. Brede was a cosmetic surgeon and the procedures he performed on the premises—collagen and Botox injection, microdermabrasion, sclerotherapy, laser (wrinkle removal), chemical peeling, therma therapy—involved virtually no blood loss. More complicated surgical procedures—face-lift, rhinoplasty, vein removal, liposuction—were performed at a local hospital with an anesthesiologist and at least one assistant.

On the operating table Dr. Brede's patients bled considerably —the face-lift in particular was bloody, as it involved deep lacerations in both the face and the scalp—but nothing out of the ordinary—nothing that Dr. Brede couldn't staunch with routine medical intervention. But *this*!—this mysterious evidence of bloodstains, inside the latex gloves!—he couldn't comprehend. There had to be a defect in the rubber gloves.

He would ask his nurse-receptionist Chloe to complain to the supplier—to demand that the entire box of defective gloves be replaced. It wouldn't be the first time that medical suppliers had tried to foist defective merchandise on Lucas Brede in recent years, with the worsening of the U.S. economy there'd been a discernible decrease in quality and in business ethics. Lucas hadn't wanted to credit rumors he'd been hearing recently about malpractice settlements that certain of his cosmetic surgeon-colleagues had been forced to make, suggesting that medical ethics, too, in some quarters, had become compromised.

In desperate times, desperate measures. Whoever had said that, it had not been Hippocrates.

In the mirror above the sink the familiar face confronted him—a hesitant smile dimpling the left cheek, a narrowing of the eyes, as if seeing Lucas Brede at such close quarters he couldn't somehow believe what he was seeing.

Is this me? Or who I've become?

He was Lucas Brede, M.D. He was forty-six years old. He was a "plastic" surgeon—his specialty was rhinoplasty. He took pride in his work—in some aspects of his work—and, rare in his profession, he hadn't yet been sued for malpractice. For the past eight years he'd rented an office suite on the first-floor, rear level of Weirlands, a sprawling glass, granite and stucco medical center set back from a private road on an elegantly landscaped hillside on the outskirts of Hazelton-on-Hudson, Dutchess County, New York. In this late-winter season of dark pelting rains—the worsening economic crisis, foreclosures of properties across the nation, "domestic ruin"—and thousands of miles away beyond the U.S. border a spurious and interminable "war to protect freedom" was in its sixth year—Lucas Brede and the other physicians-residents at Weirlands were but marginally affected. Most of their patients were affluent, and if the ship of state was sinking, they were of the class destined to float free.

In addition, Dr. Brede's patients were almost exclusively female, and vitally, one might say passionately, devoted to their own well-being: faces, bodies, "lifestyles." They were the wives, ex-wives or widows of rich men; some were the daughters of rich men; a significant fraction were professional women in high-paying jobs—determined to retain their youthfulness and air of confidence in a ruthlessly competitive marketplace. Occasionally Lucas happened to see photographs of his patients in the local Hazelton paper, or in *The New York Times* society pages—glamorous clothes, dazzling smiles, invariably looking much younger than their ages—and felt a stir of pride. *That face is one of mine.*

He liked them, on the whole. And they liked him—they were devoted to him. For all were attractive women, or had been: their well-being depended upon such attractiveness, maintained *in perpetuity.*

Already in their early forties, the blond, fair-skinned women were past the bloom of their beauty, and wore dark glasses indoors, expensive moisturizers and thick creams at night. No cosmetic procedure could quite assuage their anxiety, that they were *looking their age.* Lucas couldn't imagine any husband—any man—embracing one of these women, in the night; they must insist upon sleeping alone, as they'd slept alone as girls. (Lucas's wife now slept apart from him. But not because she wanted to preserve her beauty.) His patients were nervous women who laughed eagerly. Or they were edgy women who rarely laughed, fearing laugh lines in their faces. Their eyes watered—they'd had Lasik eye surgery, their tear ducts had been destroyed. Botox injections and face-lifts had left their faces tautly smooth, in some cases flawless as masks. But their necks!—their necks were far more difficult to "lift." And their hands, and the flaccid flesh of their upper arms. In their wish to appear younger than their ages, as beautiful as they'd once been, or more beautiful—*what they were not*—they were childlike, desperate. The more Dr. Brede injected gelatinous liquids into their skin—collagen, Botox, Restylane, Formula X—the more eager they were for more drastic treatments: chemical peels, dermabrasion, cosmetic surgery. They feared hair-fine wrinkles as one might fear melanomas. They feared soft crepey flesh beneath their eyes, they feared the slackening of jowls, jawlines, as in another part of the world one might fear leprosy.

To assuage their skittishness, for they were hypersensitive to pain, Dr. Brede provided them with small hard rubber balls to grip when he injected their faces with his long transparent needles; he gave them mildly narcotizing creams to rub into their skin, before arriving at his office; he gave them tranquilizers, or, occasionally, placebos; it amused him, and sometimes annoyed him, that his patients reacted to pain so disproportionately—sometimes, before he'd actually pushed the needle into their faces. The most delicate procedure was the injection of Botox, Restylane or Formula X into the patient's forehead where, if Dr. Brede was not exceedingly careful, the needle struck bone, and gave every evidence of being genuinely painful. (Dr. Brede had never injected himself with any of these solutions and so had no idea what they felt like, nor did he have any inclination to experiment.) His patients were devoted to him, but they were uneasy and emotional, like children—who could be angry with children?

He wanted to assure them *My touch is magic! I bring you mercy.*

He liked—loved—his work—his practice at Weirlands—but there were times when the prospect of doing what he was doing forever filled him with sick terror.

Leave then. Quit. Do another kind of medicine. Can't you?

His wife hadn't understood. There'd been a willful opacity in her pose of righteousness. He'd tried to explain to her—to a degree—but she hadn't understood. He needed to take on more patients—he needed to convince his patients to upscale their treatment—in the aftermath of this fiscal year that had been so devastating for all. Lucas wanted only to keep his finances—his investments—as they were, without losing more money; he'd had to deceive his wife about certain of these investments, of which she knew virtually nothing. Audrey's signature was easy to come by—trustingly she signed legal and financial documents without reading them closely, or at all; so trustingly, Lucas sometimes skirted the nuisance of involving her, and signed her signature—her large schoolgirl hand—himself. Certain of his financial problems he'd confided in no one, for there was no one in whom he could confide. Nor could he share his more exciting, hopeful news—that he'd been experimenting with an original gelatinous substance that resembled Botox chemically but was much cheaper. There was a marginal risk of allergic reactions and chemical "burning"—he knew, and was hypercautious. This magical substance, to which he'd given the name Formula X, Dr. Brede could prepare in his own lab in his office suite and be spared the prohibitively high prices the Botox manufacturers demanded.

One day, maybe, Lucas Brede would perfect and patent Formula X, and enter into a lucrative deal with a pharmaceutical company—though making money in itself wasn't his intention.

"I'm going *in*."

So matter-of-factly the neurosurgeon spoke, you would not have thought him boastful.

Lucas Brede had entered medical school intending to be a neurosurgeon. Except the training was too arduous, expensive. Except his fellow students—90 percent of them Jews from the Metropolitan New York region—were too ambitious, too ruthless and too smart. Except his instructors showed shockingly little interest in Lucas Brede—as if he were but one of many hundreds of med students, indistinguishable from the rest. As in the Darwinian nightmare-struggle for existence, Lucas Brede hadn't quite survived, he'd been devoured by his fierce competitors, he'd been the runt of the litter.

How fascinated he'd been as a medical student, and then an intern, and finally a resident at the Hudson Neurosurgical Institute in Riverdale, New York—how envious—observing with what confidence the most revered neurosurgeons dared to open up the human skull and touch the brain—the *living brain*. He was eager to emulate them—eager to be accepted by this elite tribe of elders—even as in his more realistic moments he knew he couldn't bear it, the very thought of it left him faint, dazed—an incision into the skull, a drilling-open of a hole into the skull to expose the *living brain.*

Vividly he remembered certain episodes in his two-year residency at the Institute. Memories he'd never shared with anyone, still less with the woman he married whose high opinion of Lucas Brede he could not risk sullying.

Ten-, twelve-hour days. Days indistinguishable from nights. He'd assisted at operations—from one to three operations a day, six days a week. He'd interviewed patients, he'd prepped patients. He'd examined CAT scans. Once confronted with a CAT scan he'd stared and stared at the dense-knotted tangle of wormy arteries and veins amid the spongelike substance that was the *brain* and all that he'd learned of the brain seemed to dissolve like vapor. Here was a malevolent life-form—a *thing* of unfathomable strangeness. He'd tasted panic like black bile in his mouth. For more than twenty-four hours he'd gone without sleeping, and in his state of exhaustion laced with caffeine and amphetamines he'd been both overexcited and lethargic—his thoughts careened like pinballs, or drifted and floated beyond his comprehension. Somehow he was confusing the brain-picture illuminated before him with a picture of his own brain. . . . What he was failing to see was a brain stem glioma, a sinister malignancy like a serpent twined about the patient's brain stem and all but invisible to inexpert eyes. "Ordinarily these tumors are inoperable," the neurosurgeon said, "—but I'm going *in.*" Lucas shivered. Never would he have the courage to utter such words. Never would he have such faith in himself. *Going in.*

Not that he dreaded the possibility of irrevocably maiming or killing a patient so much as he dreaded the public nature of such failure, the terrible judgment of others.

He hadn't failed his residency, explicitly. In some ways he'd performed very well. But he'd known, and everyone around him had known, that he would never be a neurosurgeon. A shameful thing had happened when he assisted in his first trepanation, or craniectomy—he'd been the one to drill open the skull—this was the skull of a living person, a middle-aged man being prepped for surgery—handed a heavy power drill and bluntly told, "Go to it." By this time in his residency he'd observed numerous craniectomies—he'd observed numerous brain surgeries. He knew that the human skull is one of the most durable of all natural substances, a bone hard as mineral; to penetrate it you need serious drills, saws, brute force. In the dissection lab in medical school he'd experimented with such drilling, but in this case the head was a living head, the brain encased in the skull was a *living brain* and this fact filled him with horror as well as the fact that he knew the patient, he'd interviewed the patient and had gotten along very well with the anxious man. Now, as in a ghoulish comic-book torture this man had been placed in a sitting position, clamped into position; mercifully, for the resident obliged to drill a hole in his head, he'd been rolled beneath the instrument table and was virtually invisible beneath a sterile covering and towels. All that Lucas was confronted with was the back of the man's head, upon which, in an orange marking pen, the neurosurgeon had drawn the pattern of the opening Lucas was to drill. "Go to it"—the older man repeated. The patient's scalp had been cut, blood had flowed freely and was wiped away, now a flap of the scalp was retracted and the skull—the bone—exposed. Calmly—he was sure he exuded calm—Lucas pressed the power drill against the bone—but couldn't seem to squeeze the trigger until urged impatiently, "Go *on*." Blindly then he squeezed—jerked at—the trigger; there was a high-pitched whining noise; slowly the point of the drill turned, horribly cutting into the skull. Lucas's eyes so flooded with tears, he couldn't see clearly. Blindly he held the drill in place, the instrument was heavy and clumsy in his icy hands, and seemed to be pulsing with its own, interior life. How hard the human skull was, and adamant—but the stainless-steel drill was more powerful—a mixture of bone-shavings and blood flew from the skull—a flurry of bloodied shavings—the drill ceased abruptly when the point penetrated the skull, to prevent it from piercing the dura mater just beyond, a dark-pink rubbery membrane threaded with blood vessels and nerves. Lucas smelled burnt bone and flesh—he'd been breathing bone dust—he began to gag, light-headed with nausea. But there was no time to pause for recovery—he had to drill three more holes into the skull, in a trapezoid pattern, first with the large drill and then with a smaller more precise drill. The smell of burnt bone and flesh was overwhelming, hideous—he held his breath not wanting to breathe it in—now with a plierlike instrument pulling and prying at the skull—panting, desperate—turning the holes into a single opening. He thought *This isn't real. None of this is real* yet how ingenious, the "skull" oozed blood, now the single hideous hole in the skull was stuffed with surgical sponges immediately soaked with blood. Then he was speaking to someone—he was speaking calmly and matter-of-factly—the procedure was completed and the next stage of the surgery was now to begin—he was certain that this was so, he'd done all that was required of him and he'd done it without making a single error yet somehow the tile floor tilted upward, rose to meet him—as all stared the young resident's knees buckled—the nerve-skeleton that bore him aloft and prevented him from dissolving into a puddle of helpless flesh on the floor collapsed, shriveled and was gone.

It was fatigue. Caffeine, speed. The pressure of his work. The eyes of the others. Dazed and not seeming to know where he was at first—in the corridor outside the OR—not wanting to ask what had happened, only if the patient was all right, if he'd completed the craniectomy satisfactorily and he had been assured yes, he had.

Nineteen years he'd been a cosmetic surgeon in Hazelton-on-Hudson, New York. Eight years since he'd moved his practice to prestigious Weirlands at the outskirts of town. As a suburban physician Dr. Brede avoided all surgeries involving pathologies and all surgeries except the most familiar and routine, and high paying—face-lifts were the most lucrative and the most reliable. The procedure was ghastly as a sadist's fantasy and horribly bloody when the facial skin-mask was "lifted" and "stretched"—"stapled" to the scalp—but no one had ever died of a face-lift—at least not one of Dr. Brede's patients. One of these operations was very like another, as most human faces, attractive or otherwise, beneath the skin-mask, are very like one another.

Of course he knew—and he resented—that in the pantheon of physicians and surgeons Dr. Lucas Brede's life's-work was considered trivial, contemptible. And he himself trivial, contemptible. He knew, and tried not to know. He tried not to be bitter. Thinking *I would feel this way myself, about myself. If my life had gone otherwise.*

In this season of dark-pelting rains. Snow swirling like sticky clumps of mucus out of a sheet-metal sky. His 4:15 patient Mrs. Druidd in whose sallow sagging face he'd been injecting Formula X—slowly, carefully—wiping away blood with sterile gauze-pads—an itchy film of perspiration on his face—began to be restless, skittish. On her previous visit to Dr. Brede, just before Christmas, Mrs. Druidd had had a chemical peeling; now, follow-up injections to plump out lines and wrinkles in her face, much of this was routine except Dr. Brede was substituting his own Formula X for Restylane—a substitution that was entirely ethical, he believed, in the way that substituting generic drugs for pricey brand-name drugs was ethical—but the mild tranquilizer he'd given her didn't seem to be effective, and with each injection she seemed to be feeling more pain. "Squeeze the balls. Both balls"—Dr. Brede advised. His manner was calm, kindly. If he was deeply annoyed you would never have guessed so from his affable smile.

"Oh! That *hurts*."

Mrs. Druidd had never spoken so petulantly to Dr. Brede— this was a surprise. Lucas saw to his alarm that there were deep bruises in the woman's face, where he'd been injecting Formula X; collagen and Restylane caused bruising too, but nothing like this. And that weltlike mark on one side of the woman's mouth, he knew wouldn't fade readily.

Three to five days was the usual estimate, for bruising following injections. Very likely it might be more than a week, this time.

Mrs. Druidd asked if this was something new he was injecting into her face—"It feels different. It stings and *burns*."

Lucas hesitated just a moment before assuring her, this was the identical treatment she'd had numerous times in his office.

"I don't remember it stinging so and *burning*. I'm afraid to see what I look like. . . ."

The woman was fifty-seven years old, what did she expect? A miracle? Even with the lurid bruising, the effect of Dr. Brede's treatments over the past several years gave Mrs. Druidd the appearance of a woman of thirty-five, perhaps—if you didn't look too closely at the small damp fanatic eyes.

Here was a rich man's wife, or ex-wife. Dr. Brede had seen Mrs. Druidd's photograph in the Hazelton paper, he was sure. Chairwoman of the Friends of the Hazelton Public Library. Chairwoman of the Hazelton Medical Clinic's annual Spring

Fling. With her dramatic dark hair and flawless-seeming face Mrs. Druidd managed to hold her own with women of her daughter's generation. Her sessions with Dr. Brede, that had more often the air of custom and ritual, usually went more smoothly.

Dr. Brede had no choice but to bring the hand mirror to Mrs. Druidd's face. This was a part of the ritual; he could hardly avoid it. At first Mrs. Druidd drew in her breath sharply, as if she'd been slapped—then she touched her tender, wounded skin—unexpectedly she laughed—"Well! It felt worse than this! I suppose I deserve it—after all." She paused, with a rueful sort of flirtatiousness. "How long will this awful bruising last, Doctor?"

Even now, the woman yearned to trust Dr. Brede. For women yearn to trust men—all women, all men. And Dr. Brede wanted to believe that certainly yes, he was a man worthy of a woman's trust.

"The usual—three to five days. Unless you become anxious and stressed—stress will exacerbate the bruising, as you know."

"Yes—yes!—'stress.'" Mrs. Druidd spoke as if repentant. Chloe had brought in an ice pack for Mrs. Druidd to take away with her, for a minimum extra charge—standard procedure in Dr. Brede's office and much appreciated by his patients.

Badly he wanted this pathetic woman to depart. He was tugging off his latex gloves impatiently—"Be sure to keep the ice pack on your face as much as possible. If you do—as you know—your face will heal much more quickly." The latex gloves seemed to be sticking to his fingers, he tore them off in haste, as if suffocating. As Mrs. Druidd left his office pressing the ice bag to her reddened and swollen face, walking as a dazed or drunken woman might walk, the sobering thought came to Dr. Brede *I will never see her again. She will never call.*

His 5:15 P.M. patient, his last of the day, Mrs. Drake, another of his long-term patients, proved even more difficult. There was an edgy querulousness about Mrs. Drake as she climbed up onto the examination table, lay back stiffly and allowed Chloe to position her; she failed to relax as Dr. Brede indicated, on her face, in Magic Marker ink, where the injections would be; instead of squeezing the rubber balls Dr. Brede gave her, to deflect pain, as Dr. Brede began the injections she sat up abruptly, touching her face—"That hurts! That *burns*! It doesn't feel like last time."

Calmly Lucas assured her that certainly it was the same solution—the identical solution—Botox—he'd given her in the past—"You must be more tense today. Tension heightens sensitivity to even mild discomfort." He was holding the syringe with the two-inch needle in his hand, that trembled slightly—though Mrs. Drake was too distracted to notice.

"Doctor, are you blaming *me*?"

The woman spoke so aggressively, Lucas was taken by surprise. He'd been accustomed to the tractability of his female patients; it was like them to murmur apologetically for wincing with pain. But Irena Drake was the wife of a Dutchess County supreme court judge, a woman with a strident voice and accusing eyes. Her chestnut-colored hair was synthetically lightened and her skin that had once been luminous and creamy seemed to be now drying out though she was only in her late forties. Lucas "lifted" Mrs. Drake's face several years before and attended to it at three-month intervals; between patient and doctor there had arisen a quasi-flirtatious rapport, not so much sexual as social, or so Dr. Brede had imagined. Now Mrs. Drake was wincing with pain though he had hardly touched her.

It was Formula X he was using, having decided to dilute it just slightly after his experience with Mrs. Druidd. Lucas was certain that this liquid solution couldn't possibly be causing a "burning" sensation—the hypersensitive woman had to be imagining it. But when he began to inject her forehead—where fine white wrinkles had formed unmistakably since Mrs. Drake's last injection six months before—Lucas felt the needle slip, and strike bone—the hard bone just above the eye. Mrs. Drake screamed and shoved him away. "Dr. Brede! You did that on purpose!"

"I—I certainly did not."

"You did! You did that to hurt me—to punish me!"

"Mrs. Drake—Irena!— why would I want to hurt you?—punish you? Please try to be calm—take a deep breath and release slowly. . . ."

"Have you been drinking, Dr. Brede?"

"Drinking? Of course not."

He'd had only a twenty-minute break between patients, at 2 P.M. Eating a late lunch at his desk, on the phone with his accountant who was preparing his New York State tax documents, he'd had just a double shot of Johnnie Walker he kept in a cabinet in his office and he'd rinsed his mouth with Listerine afterward. He was certainly not drunk. Nowhere near drunk. This hysterical woman could not smell alcohol on his breath.

"Then you're—drugged. You're taking something. I've seen TV documentaries—doctors like you. You've hurt me—look at me."

On Mrs. Drake's furrowed forehead was a bright blotch like a birthmark. Where he'd been injecting, with enormous care, minuscule quantities of Formula X to plump out the wrinkles and to "freeze" the nerves, to prevent such unattractive furrowing. All this was routine procedure, or nearly—still it was troubling, the patient's face was hot and swollen to the touch after only a few injections.

"Dr. Brede! I will report you to the county medical board—I will tell my husband. *He* will know what to do. I am leaving now, and *I am not paying for this treatment.*"

"But, Irena—I haven't completed the injections. I haven't half-completed the treatment. Chloe can put ice on your face and wait a few minutes before proceeding—"

"No. I'm finished. Let me out."

"You can't possibly want to leave without—"

"Yes. I do. I want to leave now."

Like a child in a tantrum Mrs. Drake tore off the sheet of white paper covering her to the chin and threw it onto the floor. On this paper was a fine lacy pattern of blood-specks like overlapping cobwebs, of a kind Lucas had not noticed before.

"You signed a waiver, Mrs. Drake. Before coming into treatment, you signed a waiver with me."

"'Signed a waiver'! Of course I 'signed a waiver'—doctors like you won't treat patients otherwise. But would such a waiver stand up in court, if I can prove negligence? Malpractice? If I have photos taken of my injured face? I doubt it."

"Your face—is not 'injured.' Swelling and bruising is perfectly normal as you must know. . . ."

Dr. Brede was stunned by the woman's unprecedented hostility. In his nineteen years of practice no patient had ever spoken to him like this. Some change had occurred, almost overnight; he couldn't think that it had exclusively to do with him but with the era itself—the plummeting economy, the ongoing wars, the malaise of a protracted winter. He thought *I will have to stop this madwoman. Someone must stop this madwoman* but the prospect of touching Mrs. Drake, trying to restrain her, was distasteful. If he tried to prevent her leaving—in order to speak to her reasonably—she would react by screaming, and Chloe would hear.

"Good-bye! I'm never coming back! And—*I am not paying.*"

Indignant Mrs. Drake left the examination room, kicking at the sheet of paper she'd thrown to the floor. Her harridan-face was luridly bruised as if she'd been tattooed by a whimsical and erratic tattooist.

"Dr. Brede?"—there was Chloe gazing at him with concerned eyes.

"It's all right, Chloe. Mrs. Drake had to leave suddenly."

"But—"

"I said it's *all right*."

"But—shall I send her a bill? Or—"

"No. Don't send her a bill, please. Expunge her."

It was both flattering to Lucas, and discomforting, that his nurse-receptionist behaved at times as if she were in love with him; Lucas was too gentlemanly to take advantage of her, though since his separation from his wife Chloe's tender solicitude toward him was more marked. Now he would have turned away impatiently except Chloe dared to restrain him, as an older sister might—"Dr. Brede? Let me get this"—stooping to swipe at something on his trouser cuff with a tissue—a dark, damp stain? Blood? Then, as she straightened, Chloe noticed a similar, smaller stain on a cuff of Dr. Brede's white shirt and this too she hurriedly swiped at with the tissue.

"A drop of something," she murmured, frowning as if embarrassed, not quite meeting her employer's eye, "—wet."

To his wife he'd pleaded *Have faith in me!*

"'Trepanning'—you know what that is, Doctor?"

"Yes. Of course."

"It's a—controversial medical procedure, I think?"

"Not controversial. Not a 'medical' procedure."

Ms. Steene was a stranger who'd called to make an "emergency appointment" with Dr. Brede for a consultation. He'd assumed that the woman wanted to discuss possible cosmetic treatments to restore a look of youthfulness to her creased face, that appeared to be prematurely weathered; she was slender, if not markedly underweight, and wore sweatpants and a sweatshirt embossed with shiny green letters—*HARMONY ACRES FOR A BETTER WORLD*. On the form she'd filled out for Dr. Brede's files she gave her age as fifty-six. Emphatically she'd crossed out the little boxes meant to designate sex and marital state as if in objection to such queries into her personal life.

With an air of correcting the uninformed physician Ms. Steene said reprovingly, "Not a *medical* procedure, Doctor. A *spiritual* procedure."

How unexpected this was, and annoying. One of Dr. Brede's long-term patients had also asked him about trepanning the other day, and Chloe reported calls to the office with similar inquiries. There must have been something about trepanning on television recently, on one of the morning or afternoon in-terview shows aimed at women viewers. Politely Dr. Brede said, "Trepanning is not a 'spiritual' procedure, any more than it's a medical procedure, Ms. Steene. It's medieval pseudoscience in which holes are drilled into the skull to reduce pressure or to allow 'disease' or evil spirits to escape. It's a thoroughly discred-ited procedure that's very dangerous—like exorcism."

Stubbornly Ms. Steene said, "It isn't 'medieval,' doctor. You can say that it predates the history of Homo sapiens—there is evidence that Neanderthal man practiced trepanning. Through-out the ancient world—in the East, in Egypt—trepanning has been practiced. In 1999 it was revived, in several parts of the world simultaneously. There are no practitioners in this part of the country, however. I was wondering if—"

"Ms. Steene, no reputable doctor would 'trepan' a patient. That is just not possible. There's no medical purpose to it, and as I said it's very dangerous, as you can surmise. I don't quite see why you came to me. . . ."

Ms. Steene wasn't an unattractive woman but her voice set Lucas's nerves on edge, like sandpaper rubbed against sandpaper. She seemed to be peering at him with an unusual avidity, as if indeed there was a reason why she'd made an appointment to see him which he wasn't willing to acknowledge. "I came to inquire whether you might administer this treatment to me, Doctor. It's very simple—a single hole to start with. The recommended size is three-quarters inch in diameter in this area of the skull"—with bizarre matter-of-factness the woman indicated a portion of her scalp several inches above her right eye.

Brusquely Dr. Brede said, "I'm sorry. No."

"Just—'no'? But why not? If you do 'face-lifts'—'liposuction'— procedures for mere vanity's sake—why won't you do this, for the sake of the *spirit*?"

Because there is no such entity as "spirit." Because you are a madwoman.

"I'm afraid not, Ms. Steene. And I don't recommend that you look around for another 'surgeon' to do this ridiculous 'proce-dure' for you."

On this note the consultation ended abruptly. With a forced courteous smile Dr. Brede showed Ms. Steene to the door. How his face ached, like a mask clamped too tightly in place! Though he was incensed and indignant from the insult to his professional integrity, yet he managed to behave courteously to Ms. Steene; even now the woman left his office reluctantly as if, despite the doctor's unambiguous words, he might change his mind and summon her back.

Chloe complained that Ms. Steene hadn't paid the consultation fee but had simply walked out of the office, rudely. Dr. Brede assured her it was all right, the consultation hadn't taken long—"Just expunge Ms. Steene from our records. As if she'd never been."

This season of dark-pelting rains! That seemed never to be ending except in patches of ferocious sunshine so blinding, Dr. Brede had to wear dark glasses when he stepped outside, and was forced to drive his car—a silver Jaguar SL—with unusual concentration, for fear of having an accident. He was disturbed by frequent FOR SALE signs in the more affluent areas of Hazelton-on-Hudson; even at Weirlands, where once there'd been a waiting list for tenants, there were beginning to be vacated offices. It was a shock to see that the Hazelton Neck & Spine Clinic had departed with rude abruptness from its large suite in an adjoining building.

Yet more troubling, Dr. Brede's patients were canceling appointments, often failing to make new appointments, and failing to pay their bills. One of these patients had moved to Arizona—"No forwarding address!" Chloe lamented—and one was reputedly hospitalized after what might have been a suicide attempt.

It wasn't likely that Dr. Brede would be paid what he was owed by these women—more than $19,000 had accumulated in the past six months in unpaid patients' bills. Turning such delinquent accounts over to a collection agency was a desperate move Dr. Brede hesitated to make: even if the agency collected, he'd receive only a fraction of the money owed him.

Civilization is faces, "appearances": when these collapse, civilization collapses as well.

His last patient of the day. In fact, late Friday afternoon, Dr. Brede's last patient of the week.

"'Trepanning'—you've heard of it, Dr. Brede?"

The woman spoke in a thrilled, lowered voice. Her bright fanatic eyes were fixed on Lucas's face.

"Doctor, I realize—it's a controversial procedure. It's—unorthodox."

Lucas stared at the woman, dismayed. Was this some sort of cruel joke? The image came to him of carrion birds circling a fallen creature not yet dead.

Irma Siegfried, the divorced wife of a rich Hazelton business-man, was a long-term patient of Lucas Brede's. For the past decade she'd seen him faithfully—collagen injections, Botox, and Restylane—face-lift, "eyelid lift"—liposuction; and now, unexpectedly, to Dr. Brede's chagrin, it was a very different sort of procedure—*trepanning*— about which she'd come to consult with him.

Lucas knew that Irma Siegfried was devoted to him; yet he had reason to suspect that from time to time, especially when Irma spent part of the winter in Palm Beach or in the Caribbean, she'd had work done on her face by other cosmetic surgeons. The woman's fair, thin, dry skin—the skin of a natural, if now faded blonde—was the sort of skin that aged prematurely despite the most diligent cosmetic precautions, and so now Irma's naive-girlish manner, a childlike sort of seductiveness, that had been so effective only a few years before, was increasingly at odds with her appearance. In her eyes a hurt, wounded, reproachful glisten that touched Lucas Brede to the heart—*Help me Doctor! You alone have the power.*

Initially Irma Siegfried pleaded the case for trepanning in a reasonable tone. She wasn't the sort of patient—like the contentious Ms. Steene—to bluntly confound her doctor's professional wisdom, still less his integrity. Irma told him that she'd reached a "spiritual impasse" in her life—she'd had "serious doubts" whether the Christian God existed during this seemingly endless winter, in the last months of the Bush administration—"And Mr. Bush was a man I voted for, Doctor—my family has always been Republican, but now"—in a tremulous voice telling Lucas that she'd come to the conclusion that only a "radical"—"revolutionary"—alteration of her spirit-consciousness could save her: *trepanning.*

Lucas asked what on earth she knew of *trepanning*. He did his best to disguise the astonishment and disapproval he felt.

Irma said that she'd learned through books and the

Internet—"The New World Trepanation Order"—and had only just the previous week realized how essentially it was for her to have the procedure. "It isn't for everyone, of course. But I know it's for *me*. I need to relieve the terrible stress of my nerves and certain 'noxious memories'—as *trepanning* has done for so many others."

"Really? What others?"

"On the Internet—they've given testimony. I've been corresponding with some of them—women like myself—'pilgrims.' I signed a pledge to establish an 'endowment'—at the New World Order—which is based in Geneva, Switzerland. The director is 'medically trained'— his teaching is that we are living in a debased 'Age of Lead' and radical measures are required for our salvation. And *trepanning* is very simple: a hole bored in the skull."

Lucas listened with disdain, disbelief. How casually the woman uttered these words—*a hole bored in the skull.*

"Doctor, I know it's 'dangerous'—of course! All that is courageous in our lives is 'dangerous'—even 'reckless.' I've come to you because I know you, and I trust you. All that you've done for me—which has been considerable, Dr. Brede—won't begin to compare with what I am asking you to do for me now, if you will find it in your heart to help me! If you can't, I will have to turn to a nonmedical practitioner of some sort—unless I fly to Geneva—there are *trepannists* who advertise on the Internet. The procedure is painless, it's said—or almost—but there is a risk of infection if amateurs perform it. And if the dura mater is penetrated in some way to cause hemorrhaging, that could be serious. But in recent dreams . . ."

Yet more bizarre, the matter-of-fact way in which the woman alluded to dura mater, as if she had the slightest idea what she was talking about, and how disabling, if not fatal, such a wound, carelessly executed, might be.

Bizarre too, that Lucas was listening courteously to her, and not bringing their conference to an abrupt close. If he insulted Irma Siegfried he might never hear from her again, this was a risk he must take. His professional integrity! His common sense! Yet it was difficult to interrupt Irma, who spoke with such naive hope of having a hole drilled in her head to release "toxic" thoughts, emotions and memories that had been accumulating since her childhood—"Like a well that has been slowly poisoned."

It was touching that for her visit to Dr. Brede, Irma Siegfried was wearing elegant clothing—cream-colored cashmere, a strand of pearls around her neck, glittering but tasteful rings. Yet disconcerting when she began to speak more forcefully, like a balked child, charging that physicians like Dr. Brede made careers out of concentrating on the "physical" and neglecting the "spiritual"—the procedures she'd had on her face had been "stopgaps" with no power to satisfy "spiritual yearnings."

And how did she know this?—she'd had "numinous dreams" since the New Year.

"Doctor, I'm not happy—not any longer—with just 'appearances.' The face-lifts, the injections—have created a 'false face'—what is necessary for us, to transcend our 'fallen' selves, is to return to the 'original face'—the 'original soul'—that is the child-soul, unblemished by the world. *Trepanation* has been a sacred ritual in many cultures, you know—as ancient as the Egyptians long before Christ—in prehistory, practiced by Neanderthals. There are 'trepanned' skulls to prove this—I've seen evidence on the Internet. It's believed that this is what poets mean by 'trailing wisps of glory'—'memory'—this return to the pure child-self. I remember my 'child-self,' Doctor—I was so happy then! Yet it hardly seems that that child was *me,* so many years have passed."

"That may be true, Irma—to a degree"—but what was Lucas saying, did he believe this nonsense?—"but *trepanation* is not the solution. No reputable doctor would perform this 'sacred ritual' for you—I'm sure."

He felt a tug of emotion for the agitated woman, as for himself. It was so—so many years! His childhood in Camden, Maine, belonged now to a boy he no longer recalled, on the far side of an abyss.

"Doctor, if you, with your surgical skill, refuse me—I will have to turn to a stranger, on the Internet. I may have to fly to Geneva, alone—in secret, since my family disapproves. Please say that you will help me, Dr. Brede!"

"I can't 'help' you! The procedure is dangerous, and useless—it can't possibly be of 'help.' It's true, radical and once-discredited procedures like lobotomies and electroshock treatment have been reexamined lately—but in very rare instances, and when other methods have failed. There is no medical justification for 'trepanning'—drilling holes into a healthy human head."

Whenever Lucas spoke, Irme Siegfried listened, or gave that impression; but in the way of a pilgrim whose fanatic faith can't be dampened by another's logic. "Dr. Brede, I would pay you, of course—twice the fee for a face-lift. This would be a 'spirit-lift'—it would save my life."

"Irma, I don't think we should discuss this any longer. . . ."

Yet there was irresolution in Dr. Brede's voice—the faintest note, near-imperceptible. Like a dog sensing fear in a human voice, however it's disguised, Irma Siegfried leaned forward, baring her small porcelain-white teeth in a ghastly seductive smile. "Doctor, I would tell no one—of course! This would be our utter secret! I will pay you in advance of the procedure—you would not even need to bill me. Here, I've brought—a drawing—the 'sacred triangle'—"

Irma was smoothing out a sheet of paper. Here was a drawing of a triangle as a child might have drawn it with a ruler. "Three very small holes, just above the hairline—here." Irma drew back her hair, to suggest the positioning of the holes, in the area of what was called the frontal lobe—though she wouldn't have known this, still less what crucial functions the frontal lobe controlled. Sensing Lucas's reluctant interest, determined not to lose it, Irma was recounting how she'd dreamt the "sacred triangle"—which was in fact an ancient symbol predating even

Egyptian history—out of the vast reservoir of the "collective unconscious"; she'd dreamt this design which was fated for *her*.

Somberly, Dr. Brede listened. The tight affable smile had clamped the lower part of his face.

This is madness. You know the woman is mad.

Yes, but she has money. She will pay you.

Do I need money? How badly?

Such yearning in the woman's eyes! Lucas had seen that look of yearning in the eyes of countless others, that filled him with both repugnance and something like exhilaration, pride—so a priest might feel presiding over sacred rites, ritual confession, absolution and blessing.

Or an execution, a sacrifice.

Lucas was thinking—would it matter? If he drilled, or pretended to drill, a few very small holes in this woman's scalp, barely penetrating the hard bone of the skull? It would be a kind of cosmetic treatment, above the hairline; he would take care not to penetrate the dura mater. The smile clamped tighter about his jaws.

"Dr. Brede? Will you—?"

Lucas hesitated. His heart clanged like a metronome. Yet hearing himself say, with infinite relief: "Irma, no. I think—no. I'm sorry."

Tears welled in the woman's eyes. Abruptly then the consultation ended.

Lucas stumbled into the adjoining lavatory. He ran cold water and splashed it on his burning face. How close he'd come to a terrible danger!—but he'd drawn back in time.

No. We can't. It would be a tragic mistake we could never undo.

In the photos—you can see the child is brain damaged. Some sort of birth-injury. The eyes aren't in focus. There's a look of cretinism. . . .

We can't risk it. We can't get involved. We've been forewarned—these Russian "orphans" . . .

No. No. No. Absolutely no.

How was it his fault?—for years his wife had taken fertility drugs. A specialist had encouraged her, at enormous expense. Lucas had not been optimistic, though he'd wanted a child as badly as she did—of course. Soon he'd come to see that the powerful hormone supplements were adversely affecting her—her fixation upon a child, her emotional instability, mood swings. Her resentment of him, as a *man*. And when finally—almost unbelievably—she did become pregnant, at the age of thirty-nine, the sonogram had revealed serious defects in both the heart and brain.

Audrey please understand—there is no choice.

It is not infanticide! It is an act to prevent suffering. To put the fetus out of its misery before it is born.

Then, the desperation. Internet adoption agencies to which without Lucas's knowledge Audrey gave their credit card number. In a weak moment he'd promised her *Yes we can adopt we can try to adopt* but afterward he'd realized his error. Never had the woman forgiven him his error.

I.S.—these initials he penciled lightly on his personal appointment calendar. For Chloe wasn't to know.

The procedure was so simple, he wouldn't need an assistant.

She would be an outpatient, in his office. He would prep for the procedure himself.

The plan was: the patient would arrive at Dr. Brede's office soon after 7 P.M.—when it was certain that Chloe would have left for the day. She would have taken a tranquilizer at 6 P.M. and when she arrived Lucas would give her a more powerful sedative; if needed, he could administer chloroform in very small doses.

Trepanation—so primitive a procedure, one would not have to practice beforehand.

Very carefully Dr. Brede would drill into the woman's scalp— very shallowly, into her skull. He believed he could do this. The diagram called for three minuscule holes to be opened into an equilateral triangle measuring a quarter inch on each side. Irma had been adamant about paying Lucas beforehand, a check for twelve thousand, six hundred dollars.

Doctor, thank you I am so grateful. Doctor, I will owe you my life—my new life.

Irma's teeth chattered slightly, she was so excited. Lying back on the table in Dr. Brede's examining room. Her eyelids that were blue-tinged as if with cold were shut tight and her thin hands were tight-clasped below her small soft bosom. Though her skin was sallow beneath the harsh fluorescent lighting, and fine white lines puckered at the corners of her eyes, yet Irma was an attractive woman and it was touching to see that she'd shampooed her hair just recently and had creamed and powdered her face. Coral lipstick darkened her lips. On a thin gold chain around her neck she wore a small gold cross, that slipped behind her neck when she lay back.

Doctor thank you. I will adore you forever.

Soon then the patient was asleep. Her mouth drooped open, like an infant's. Determined to be cautious—Lucas didn't want the patient to wake up suddenly—he soaked a cloth in chloroform and held it beneath her nostrils for a count of three.

Lucas tugged on latex gloves. He was eager to begin. A sensation of elation, almost a kind of giddiness gripped him. *New life! Owe you my life my new life!* He parted the woman's fine, soft, sparrow-colored hair, clamped it aside. He dabbed her scalp with Betadine. The stinging sensation caused her to murmur faintly, querulously. With a small scalpel he made an incision in the skin—retracted the skin, less smoothly than he'd have wished—for his hands were shaky; he would have scraped the damp exposed bone clean but felt a wave of something like nausea sweep over him—he had to pause, to recover. Already the tiny wound was bleeding—this was distracting. And now—the drill!

If he'd have had time to prepare more thoroughly for this unorthodox office procedure, Lucas would have purchased a small dental drill from a dental supply store; but he'd been rushed, he'd made his decision overnight, and so the drill he'd acquired—at a hardware store at the North Hills Mall—was an eight-inch stainless-steel PowerLuxe. A handyman's tool, there was no disguising the fact. The sharp whirring of the motor, the eerie spin of the drill, the gleam of the stainless steel—Lucas's icy fingers trembled.

"Irma? Are you—asleep?" The woman's blue-tinged eyelids fluttered though it was evident that she was soundly unconscious. Her breathing was slow, deep. Her breath smelled of something sweet—mouthwash, mint—and beneath a more acrid, slightly sour smell of animal apprehension, fear. *She knows!—her sleeping self knows. There is danger.*

Lightly he touched the drill against the woman's scalp—bright blood appeared at once, in a swift stream—this was more than he'd have expected, for such wounds don't commonly bleed quite so freely—he was prepared to sponge it away—yet, so rapidly the blood flowed, as the unconscious woman twitched and whimpered, immediately Lucas lifted the drill from her head. His heart was beating rapidly, the panic-chill rose into his throat. He waited until the woman quieted and resumed her deep breathing; he touched the drill to her scalp another time—again the bright blood startled him—and a smell of burning bone— distasteful, repugnant. This time the patient seemed on the verge of waking—her eyelids fluttered—her lips trembled—he could see the white of her eyeball, a glimpse of unfocused eyes that made him think of a zombie's eyes, or the eyes of one in a coma. *Tape her eyes shut. Her mouth. Secure her. To prevent hysteria.*

This advice seemed to come to Lucas from a source outside himself. He tried to identify the voice—one of the supervisors at the Institute—but could not.

These prudent steps he took. These precautions. This was not an emergency situation but you never knew—in an instant, in the OR, emergencies can erupt. This situation—the *trepanning*—seemed to be within control. The latex gloves were slippery with blood and the adhesive tape was slippery with blood but he had no trouble taping the woman's eyes and her mouth and Lucas had no trouble strapping the patient to the table except the paper was badly torn already, and bloodstained—so quickly. And blood on the tile floor—the doctor's crepe-soled shoes would leave distinct footprints.

Lucas lifted the drill. Now!—he drew a deep breath. His blood-slick rubber gloves caused the drill to slip, just slightly. It was a heavy crude instrument, that belonged in a handyman's workshop, not in a surgeon's hands.

The *trepanation* would have gone far more smoothly except the doctor was nervous. He'd poured a shot glass of whiskey for himself after his nurse-receptionist left for the evening and he'd swallowed two thirty-milligram tranquilizers of the kind he kept in his office for his skittish patients' short-term use. Immediately he'd felt better. Now in the stress of the moment he was considering a third tranquilizer but *No. Clarity is required. Clearheadedness. Courage.*

Like one leaning over a steep drop Lucas leaned over the woman who lay limply on the examination table, unconscious, or comatose—the torn scalp bleeding profusely and the faded-girl's face now deathly white, contorted by the adhesive tape he'd wrapped tightly around her head. He'd covered her eyes and her mouth—but remembered to leave her nostrils free for breathing. And quickly, shallowly and erratically the woman was breathing. Lucas lifted the drill, positioning the razor-sharp spiral borer against the bloody scalp. He saw that bloody clumps of hair and skin were stuck to the borer, that would shake off, or fly off, when he began drilling. The revelation came to him as if from a great distance *This is not Lucas Brede, M.D. This is another person, who does trepanning.*

After several false starts he managed to finish the first of the tiny holes—*trepanation* was not so easy, as it was not quite so primitive, as the medical profession might think. Skill was involved here, in not penetrating the dura mater. The drill seemed steadier now in his hands—though still a clumsy, crude instrument—Lucas began the second hole, a quarter inch from the first, as the whirring sound of the drill filled the room like an amplified scream. Still, the blood was a distraction—in the familiar quarters of his office he wasn't accustomed to such an excess—if a patient's face bled, Dr. Brede or Chloe wiped it away easily with a sponge. Now there was so much blood from the patient's head wounds that he couldn't sponge it away quickly enough. He was having difficulty seeing where the sharp point of the drill pierced the scalp—a fine mist of blood coated the lenses of his glasses—how to clean his glasses, in the midst of this procedure?—no choice but to remove them. Now too Lucas regretted not having taken time to mark the patient's scalp with orange ink—he'd reasoned that after all *trepanation* wasn't neurosurgery and didn't have to be so specifically directed. He wasn't "opening" the skull for brain surgery but only just perforating it, aerating it.

Like a well that has been slowly poisoned.

A new life.

The skeptics in his profession—the notoriously conservative "medical community"—would have little sympathy for Lucas Brede if he suggested to them that *trepanation* might not be so bizarre after all, as a kind of alternative medical procedure; since childhood Lucas himself had felt the slow leakage of his "soul"—his personality trapped and disfigured by the confinement of the bone-armor of the skull.

Of course Lucas had been skeptical also, and initially jeering —yet open-minded enough, after having sent Irma Seigfried away, to reconsider her request, and to summon her back.

He'd spent much of a night—one of his insomniac nights, which lately he'd come to welcome as a respite from heavy stuporous sedative-sleep—researching *trepanation* on the Internet. To his surprise he'd come to concede that the ancient custom was either beneficial or harmless if executed by a skilled practitioner. Through the centuries holes had been drilled in the skulls of myriad individuals and these holes showed evidence of having healed; there were skulls with several holes suggesting that among some primitive people *trepanation* may have been a routine procedure, like removing infected teeth.

There was an ethical issue here, Lucas thought. As licensed surgeons are best equipped to perform abortions, so licensed surgeons are best equipped to perform *trepanations*. Refusing to serve desperate individuals for purely selfish reasons was as unconscionable in the one case as in the other.

You could argue that tattoos were much more dangerous than a skilled *trepanation* since needles are easily infected, and "tattoo-artists" were hardly licensed surgeons.

Maybe there was, as Internet testimonies suggested, a parallel world in counterpoise to Western medicine. It was just prejudice that valued Western medicine above all others.

The whirring of the drill was fierce in his ears, the weight of the drill increasingly heavy as he was obliged to hold it at an awkward angle, uplifted. Lucas was beginning to feel light-headed, dazed. The smell of singed hair and flesh, and the excessive blood, was making him ill.

He was stuffing strips of gauze into the bleeding wounds but these soaked with blood immediately and were of no use. How tired he felt, required to maintain such a high degree of concentration, with no one to assist him or even to offer to wipe his face, or polish the lenses of his glasses; a surgeon isn't accustomed to working alone. Lucas was thinking he might pause for a few minutes—he should pause—to examine the patient's pulse—her heartbeat—for the patient no longer seemed to be breathing through her frantic widened nostrils—but a reckless sensation came over him, a sense of defiance—he would not turn back, now that he'd come so far.

Not many minutes had passed since Lucas had switched on the power tool but these minutes had flown by swiftly as in an accelerated film.

He would clean out the wounds carefully, and dress them. He would caution the woman not to show anyone and not to speak of the *trepanning*. For this was a sacred ritual, meant to remain private. When she woke the woman would feel some discomfort, he supposed—some pain—the brain didn't register pain but the scalp, the skull and the dura mater registered pain—he would give her a prescription for Percodan—primarily she would feel an airiness, a strangeness—a floating sensation; almost, Lucas envied her; for it was enviable, to be so naive, and trusting; it was enviable to be a child once again; as he, Lucas Brede, never entirely had been a child, but always confined, held captive by his elders' expectations of him. Thinking these resentful thoughts and holding the drill at a precarious angle Lucas felt it begin to slip—the rubber fingers of his latex gloves were slippery with blood—or, what was more likely, Lucas may have blacked out for a moment. And what happened, happened so fast he would have no clear comprehension of what it was—his hand slipped, the spinning borer must have penetrated the skull too deeply, and down, into the dura mater—in an instant this mishap had happened—the woman's body jerked, convulsed—her knees buckled, her legs flailed against the restraining straps—Lucas was grateful that her eyes were taped shut, he was spared locking his gaze with the gaze of the stricken woman—he heard a scream—a muffled scream—inside the adhesive gag.

But no, this wasn't possible. The woman had not regained consciousness. This was not possible, the scream had to be Lucas's feverish imagination.

Soon then the convulsing body lay limp. The struggle had ceased, the muffled screams had ceased. Dr. Brede staggered with exhaustion. He could not have been more drained if he'd performed an eight-hour surgery before witnesses. His eyeglasses he groped for, couldn't remember where he'd dropped them, still the lenses were misted with blood and nearly opaque. The thought came to him as a consolation *You have put this one out of her mercy. That is—misery.*

The patient's remains, the sprawled and befouled female body, Dr. Brede would have to dispose of.

For he had no assistant. He was alone. It had always been so, Lucas Brede's soul.

The shrewdest stratagem was to begin cleaning up the premises as he waited for Weirlands to darken. A few scattered lights remained, at 8:28 P.M.

Forty minutes he'd labored to revive the patient.

Forty minutes he'd tried to breathe air into the patient's collapsed lungs, he'd thumped her chest and shouted at her pleading and furious. His excellent medical training was of little use to him now for a dead body will remain *dead*.

Awkwardly—impatiently—for he was unaccustomed to such a task—Lucas tore black trash bags into halves and wrapped the body in them, as best he could. The patient was partly dressed in the growing chill of death and on parts of the exposed body the torn and bloodied paper stuck. Lucas observed himself removing from the body's fingers the expensive glittering rings for, *They would steal from her, whoever did this to her.*

His nostrils pinched. A pungent odor of singed flesh, singed hair, rank animal panic and terror. In her death throes the woman had soiled herself.

Chloe would know what to do. Chloe would cry *Oh Doctor —what has happened? I will help you.*

Relief swept over Lucas, that Chloe wasn't at the scene. That Chloe hadn't returned to the office wanting to check on him. *Oh Doctor—I saw the light still on here. I thought—I saw your car—*

His heart like a metronome. If he'd had to kill her, too. Poor Chloe who was in love with him.

Thinking *That, I have been spared. Thank God!*

He was a good man, a generous man. Chloe would testify on his behalf. Every female employee he'd ever had.

This was good to know—this was important to keep in mind— but he was beginning to feel anxious seeing how much there was yet to be swabbed clean in this befouled room with paper towels, hot water and disinfectant.

No time now. He had to be practical. These mundane tasks he would perform *after.*

The urgent task was the disposal of the body. He envisioned a remote wooded area, or a river—the deep rushing Hudson River, by night—if the rain-clouds cleared, by moonlight—and then he would return to his office. And then he would clean what had to be cleaned.

Not a trace would remain. He would use several pairs of latex gloves if necessary. He would dump disinfectant, bleach on the floor.

There was the question—how exactly had the patient died?

Things are not always so evident as they seem.

Small holes drilled into the skull above the forehead could not explain death for these were trivial wounds. Such wounds to the frontal lobe many an individual has sustained, and survived.

Violent blows to the head, bullets and shrapnel lodged in the very brain, fractured skulls causing the brain to swell like a maddened balloon—*These wounds are curious. But insufficient to explain death* the medical examiner would note.

Lucas Brede knew the medical examiner of Dutchess County. Not well but the men knew and respected each other.

Only an autopsy can determine. This is common knowledge.

Cardiac arrest probable. Suddenly plummeting *blood pressure, the consequence of shock.*

For it was not reasonable to think that Lucas had caused the patient's death by a sole act of *his*. When the dura mater had scarcely been penetrated.

He'd been careful. Obsessively so. The demanding woman

355

had wanted "holes" drilled into her skull but he would not drill "holes" of course only small wounds.

The drill had failed him.

The drill was defective, was it?—surgical drills are set to shut off automatically when the skull is penetrated. But this drill purchased at a hardware store at the mall had failed to shut off.

He'd paid in cash. Hadn't given the salesclerk his credit card.

Calm in this terrible hour, like one whose professional behavior—posture, even—"dignity"—was being preserved on tape. Lucas stooped to wrap the body in black plastic trash bags, kept in a storage closet in the corridor.

"Irma? Are you . . ."

Inside the mummy-wrapping of several trash bags he'd scissored to make a single large bag the body had twitched. The body was heavier than you would expect, in its sprawling limbs a female slovenliness that suggested defiance, derision. Still around the ravaged head were strips of soiled adhesive tape covering the eyes that would be, Lucas knew, accusing eyes, and the mouth, that would accuse as well.

"Irma. My God—I am so sorry."

Was he?—this wasn't clear. His lips moved numbly in resentment but by nature Dr. Brede was courteous.

His women patients adored him. His nurse-receptionist adored him. His wife had ceased to adore him and the thought of Audrey filled him with such rage, he began to tremble anew.

How bizarre the body would appear, when the slatternly

trash bags were unwrapped! Around the head of graying matted bloodied hair the strips of soiled adhesive tape he'd wrapped carefully (he recalled) but the look of it was frantic, random. As if the deceased were a madwoman who had wrapped her own head for what crazed notion, whim or expectation, who could say?

Recalling too: the latex gloves, that were surely torn; the blood-splattered surgeon-clothes, shoes and even socks, that must be disposed of also. Thinking *It can all go in the same bag. And in the Dumpster. If they find one they may as well find the other.*

This logic he could not fully comprehend. Instinctively he felt this was a practical/sensible step.

He'd located the woman's purse also which was an expensive purse of soft dark leather. He would take bills from the wallet, credit cards, keys—for whoever had done such a cruel thing to this woman would certainly take these items.

Drive some distance. Away from Weirlands. A far corner of Dutchess County deep in the country in the night.

If not a Dumpster, a rural dump. A landfill. Lucas would drag other trash bags over his, to hide it. The vision came to him, of a vast open pit in the earth out of which steam lifted, a pit that opened into Hell. But if he kept well back from the rim of the pit, he would be safe.

Thinking of this place somewhere in Dutchess County he felt relief as if thinking were doing and in an instant the arduous task was *done.*

Fortunately he had a change of clothes at the office, khaki pants and a flannel shirt, running shoes. Underwear, and socks.

After he would return to the condomium overlooking the Hudson River. Possibly by then he'd be hungry, he would eat. In the refrigerator was a reserve of emergency meals, takeout from previous evenings, an excellent Brie from the Hazelton Bon Appetit and those crisp Danish crackers.

No: this was wrong. This was not right. *After* he would return to Weirlands. Hours of clean-up awaited him, he must not lose track of these crucial plans.

It was 9:19 P.M. Those lighted windows at Weirlands he'd been nervously eyeing were still lighted and so he thought *No one is there. Just lights on.* This was a relief. This meant freedom. Stooping he pulled the body along the floor—along the corridor to the door at the rear—this, the delivery door and not the door that patients used. He was perspiring badly, though he was also shivering. Impulsively he left the body on the floor wedged partly against a doorjamb, went to his office and dialed the number of his former home and with the stoic resignation of one who knows beforehand that he will be disappointed he waited for the phone to ring and was thus badly surprised, shaken by the failure of the phone even to ring and the smug recorded female voice *You have dialed a number no longer in service. This number has been disconnected.*

He would never forgive Audrey for abandoning him. For betraying him. He would never forgive any of them.

At last—Weirlands appeared to be deserted. Only three

vehicles remained in the parking lot—Lucas's car, a car presumably belonging to his patient and, at the far end of the lot, a commercial van. Out of his darkened doorway Lucas dragged the lifeless body in the trash bags, now heavy as a slab of concrete. His shoulders and upper spine were shot with pain.

Belatedly he thought of the woman's coat—for surely this well-to-do woman would have worn a coat to his office—which was very likely hanging in the waiting room to be discovered by Chloe in the morning. This crucial thought too he filed *After*.

How chill the night air, how fresh and invigorating! Lucas felt a surge of hope. Too much was expected of cosmetic surgeons; he hadn't trained to be a holy priest after all. . . . The wisest stratagem would be to remove the woman's body from the premises as quickly as possible—he would drag it uphill through the parking lot and into the uncultivated area beyond the Weirlands property line, where no one ever went. A half mile to the east was the Hazelton Pike, a half mile to the north was the New York Thruway; in the interstices of smaller roads, a prestigious new residential development called Foxcroft Hills, and the new, artificial Foxcroft Lake, were pockets of uncultivated land, less likely to be explored than the open countryside of previous decades.

No one will ever find it. Her.

Lucas had in mind a faint trail he'd noticed from the parking lot, through tall grasses—a shady area where someone had placed a single picnic table for Weirlands office workers—therapists, secretaries. Not once had Lucas ever seen anyone eating lunch at this table overlooking the asphalt parking lot nor could he have said exactly where the table was, or had once been, but it was in this direction he dragged the body, sweating now heavily inside his clothes. How annoying it was, the parking lot was littered at its periphery with fallen and shattered tree limbs; it was an effort to drag the body here, colliding with storm debris, making his task so much more arduous. . . .

Suddenly the thought came to him *Her car!*

Of course—*the woman's car.* Lucas would have to get rid of *her car.*

If he failed to remove the woman's car from the Weirlands lot, it would be discovered in the morning; the woman would be traced to Weirlands Medical Center, and to Dr. Lucas Brede. Rapidly his brain worked—of course, he would have to dispose not only of the woman's body but of her car as well.

Logically then, to save steps he might place the body *inside the car.*

In the trunk! He would place the body in the trunk—of course—and he would drive the woman's car some distance from Weirlands—twenty miles, thirty—across the George Washington Bridge and into New Jersey.

Once in a remote area of New Jersey off the turnpike he would abandon both the car and the body in the trunk of the car. He would drive the car to the edge of a steep precipice, above the Hudson River, or another body of water, or some sort of quarry, or gravel pit. He seemed to know that New Jersey would be a safe territory, if he could but get there. He would jump out of the car at the last possible moment and the car would plummet down into oblivion as into a pit of Hell. . . . Lucas Brede would be safe then, for he would leave nothing of his own in the woman's car. And the car, and the body, would never be discovered.

Except: he would have no way of returning then to Weirlands. No way of returning to his expensive but mud-splattered Jaguar SL parked at the rear of Weirlands.

He hadn't thought of this. The thought was an obvious one like a tree root he'd just tripped over, nearly causing him to fall atop the tattered trash bags.

Quickly modifying his plan. For his brain worked swiftly, like the brain of a machine. As it wasn't practical to drag the woman's body into the woods above Weirlands, so it wasn't practical to drag the woman's body to her car and haul it to New Jersey: instead, he would have to drag the body to his own car and lift it into the trunk—panting and cursing as he struggled to lift the cumbersome thing, that seemed to taunt him with its heaviness, and its smells that made him gag. And his arms ached, his body was faint with exhaustion. At last he managed to get the damned body into the trunk, to force its odd-angled limbs into the confining space beneath a spare tire and a tire iron. Horrible it seemed to him, that he had to stoop, to lift this so physical and obdurate *thing*; he had to grip it in his embrace, lift it into the trunk and slam the trunk lid down but hastily and carelessly so that a torn part of a trash bag was visible, fluttering outside the trunk like a woman's black silk slip.

Doctor I am so grateful. My new life.

361

He worried that some sort of inevitable moisture—blood, urine, liquid feces—was leaking through the plastic material, into the trunk of his car, that had been until now pristine-clean. The thought came to him *The trunk can be cleaned. At the car wash. Inside and out.*

If the car wash couldn't disinfect the trunk totally, he would dump disinfectant and bleach inside. The most virulent bacteria teeming in the bowels of the dead can be fatal to the touch of the living.

Next, he climbed into his car. This was strange! Because so ordinary, commonplace. He turned the key in the ignition—the Jaguar was sometimes slow to start—this time the motor came to life at once and the windshield wipers came on and the radio which was tuned to WQRS. Nor did he have difficulty driving out of the Weirlands parking lot and along the private Weirlands Road to a busier street. He would follow this street until the intersection with route 11 and he would turn south and continue for miles out of Hazelton-on-Hudson and through the suburban villages of Drummond, Sleepy Hollow, Riverdale; he would pass the exit for Fort Tryon Park; he would exit for the George Washington Bridge and he would bring the body in the trunk into New Jersey as it was planned for him and there he would discard the body, he would know where when the exit loomed in his headlights. Again this thought was so vivid it was as if he'd already executed it, in the instant of thinking it. Then, he would turn the Jaguar around and return across the George Washington Bridge—he would take the lower level returning, if he took the higher level going—details like that were crucial. By midnight if he hadn't any delays he would return to Weirlands and he would then drive the woman's car no more than two or three miles to the small Hazelton train depot where he'd park it unobtrusively and where often vehicles were parked overnight. This would attract no attention! This was a very practical idea. Once he left the woman's car in a safe unobtrusive place he could wait on the train platform for a train to arrive; he would mingle with passengers, and hail a taxi at the foot of the stairs.

Where're you going sir?

D'you know that new condominium complex on the river? There.

Just beyond the exit ramp for the George Washington Bridge traffic was being rerouted into a detour. Here were police cars, medical emergency vehicles, blinding lights. Traffic was backing up for miles.

Lucas leaned out his window, sick with apprehension. He lowered his window and called out to a police officer directing traffic in the rain—what was wrong? Why were they being held up? how long?—but the officer, a young man, rudely ignored him. In the roadway were fiery flares, sawhorses blocking the lanes. Farther he leaned out the window of his car calling out to another police officer, but smiling—remembering to smile—his strained affable doctor-smile—for Dr. Brede would want these law enforcement officers to see, if it came to giving testimony, or evidence, that he'd behaved calmly; Lucas Brede had been in a genial, rational, reasonable mood at this crucial time; somewhat edgy of course, and impatient, as any driver would be in such circumstances.

Evidently there'd been an accident. Two vehicles—three vehicles. Giddily lights spun atop emergency vehicles. Sirens pierced his eardrums. Quickly Lucas lowered his car window. "Officer? Do you need any help? I'm an M.D."

Politely Lucas was told no, told to remain in his car. Told no, his services as a doctor weren't needed, or weren't wanted, there was an ambulance at the scene. *Please remain in your car, sir. Do not leave your car.* Seeing the wrecked vehicles on the roadway like broken bodies, piteous female bodies and glass glittering on pavement, confused by the piercing sirens, Lucas opened the Jaguar door and began to climb out into the roadway but another time was told, sternly this time he was being shouted at, instructed *No.* Trying to remain pleasant, reasonable—"I don't think you heard me—I'm a doctor—a neurosurgeon. I can examine the victims—I can determine if there's dangerous hemorrhaging in the brain." An older police officer came to Lucas and asked for his driver's license. Lucas fumbled to comply. He was clearly not drunk nor even agitated. His hands shook badly—this might be palsy. This might be the onset of Parkinson's. There was blood on his khaki cuffs but the flashing red lights did not detect blood. Smears of blood on the front of his coat, mysteriously—for he'd been careful with the trash bags which he'd tied with the unwieldy body inside, he was sure he hadn't brushed against them. Yet there it was, a smear of blood like a bird's wing. And on his hands. Unless this was older, long-dried blood from earlier in the day, that had been a very long day beginning with dark pelting rain before dawn.

"But I want to be of help, officer. Please let me help. I'm a doctor—this is my mission."

They had no time for him. His offer was rebuked. Rudely he was made to climb back into his Jaguar, and to wait like the other drivers. Eventually traffic bound for the bridge was rerouted. Eventually the stream of vehicles began to move. The terrible dark rain had lessened, now columns of mist lifted from the river far below like ectoplasm. Which river was this Lucas could not have immediately said though he knew its name as he knew his own. He accelerated his vehicle onto the bridge. It was the upper level he chose. In the mist, the farther shore and the length of the great bridge were obscured. Lights shimmered uncertainly along the vast river, evidence of lives within. He started out, he would cross to that farther shore.